Dear Reader,

Okay, I'll admit it—authors have favorite books. I know, I know, books are like children and we don't always want to admit to liking one better than another, but it's true. The Goddess Summoning books are my favorite children.

As with my bestselling young adult series, the House of Night, my Goddess Summoning books celebrate the independence, intelligence, and unique beauty of modern women. My heroes all have one thing in common: they appreciate powerful women and are wise enough to value brains as well as beauty. Isn't respect and appreciation an excellent aphrodisiac?

Delving into mythology and reworking ancient myths is fun! In Goddess of the Sea *I retell the story of the mermaid Undine—who switches places with a female U.S. Air Force sergeant who needs to do some escaping of her own. In* Goddess of Spring, *I turn my attention to the Persephone/Hades myth, and send a modern woman to Hell! Who knew Hell and its brooding god could be hot in so many wonderful, seductive ways?*

From there we take a lovely vacation in Las Vegas with the divine twins, Apollo and Artemis, in Goddess of Light. *Finally we come to what is my favorite of all fairy tales, "Beauty and the Beast." In* Goddess of the Rose *I created my own version of this beloved tale, building a magical realm from whence dreams originate—good and bad—and bringing to life a beast who absolutely took my breath away.*

I hope you enjoy my worlds, and my wish for you is that you discover a spark of goddess magic of your own!

P. C. Cast

Praise for *Goddess of Spring*

"One of the top romantic fantasy mythologists today."

—*Midwest Book Review*

"As always, there's a dash of humor and lots of meltingly hot sex."

—*Affaire de Coeur*

"Enchanting . . . Lovely." —*The Romance Readers Connection*

"A veritable feast for readers who just can't get enough fantasy dished up with their romance. Mythology has never been so fun!"

—*Romance Reviews Today*

Goddess of the Sea

"Suspense, fantasy, time travel, all topped off with a very healthy dollop of romance . . . The good news is that this is just the beginning."

—*Romance Reviews Today*

"Captivating—poignant, funny, erotic! Lovely characters, wonderful romance, constant action, and a truly whimsical fantasy . . . Delightful. A great read." —*The Best Reviews*

"A fun combination of myth, girl power, and sweet romance [with] a bit of suspense. A must-read . . . A romance that celebrates the magic of being a woman." —*Affaire de Coeur*

"[An] adult fairy tale . . . the audience will cherish."

—*Midwest Book Review*

"Vivid and colorful . . . splendid blend of fantasy, history, intrigue, and passion . . . outstanding. Watch out for this author." —*Rendezvous*

"Most innovative . . . From beginning to end, the surprises in P. C. Cast's new page-turner never stopped. Its poignancy resonates with both whimsy and fantasy . . . I loved it!" —*New York Times* bestselling author Sharon Sala

"Sweet and funny." —*Huntress Reviews*

Goddess of Light

"A charmer . . . Cast continues her unique brand of delightfully mixing a modern-day romance with a mythological legend . . . Creative."

—*Midwest Book Review*

"Pure enjoyment . . . Anything can [happen] when gods and mortals mix."

—*Rendezvous*

"A fanciful mix of mythology and romance with a dash of humor for good measure . . . Engages and entertains . . . Lovely." —*Romance Reviews Today*

Goddess of the Rose

"P. C. Cast [is] well-known for her blending of mythological tales and romance . . . [A] beautiful adult fairy tale . . . Readers will be enchanted."

—*The Best Reviews*

"Outstanding . . . magic, myth, and romance with a decidedly modern twist. Her imagination and storytelling abilities are true gifts to the genre."

—*Romantic Times*

Goddess of Love

"Sexy, charming, and fun, *Goddess of Love* is the fantasy romance of the year! You will fall in love with this book. (I did!)"

—*New York Times* **bestselling author Susan Grant**

"Touching, clever, and an excellent heiress to the Goddess Summoning series. Cast's ability to subvert misogynistic mythology . . . and reaffirm what makes women wonderful is always worth celebrating . . . I bestow my snarky blessings on this book." —*Smart Bitches Trashy Books*

"Scorchingly sensual, utterly delicious! P. C. Cast is a true master of her craft." —*New York Times* **bestselling author Gena Showalter**

Sensation Titles by P. C. Cast

The Goddess Summoning Series

GODDESS OF THE SEA
GODDESS OF SPRING
GODDESS OF LIGHT
GODDESS OF THE ROSE
GODDESS OF LOVE
WARRIOR RISING

Anthologies

MYSTERIA
(with MaryJanice Davidson, Susan Grant, and Gena Showalter)
MYSTERIA LANE
(with MaryJanice Davidson, Susan Grant, and Gena Showalter)

Goddess OF *Spring*

P. C. Cast

THE BERKLEY PUBLISHING GROUP
Published by the Penguin Group
Penguin Group (USA) Inc.
375 Hudson Street, New York, New York 10014, USA
Penguin Group (Canada), 90 Eglinton Avenue East, Suite 700, Toronto, Ontario M4P 2Y3, Canada
(a division of Pearson Penguin Canada Inc.)
Penguin Books Ltd., 80 Strand, London WC2R 0RL, England
Penguin Group Ireland, 25 St. Stephen's Green, Dublin 2, Ireland
(a division of Penguin Books Ltd.)
Penguin Group (Australia), 250 Camberwell Road, Camberwell, Victoria 3124, Australia
(a division of Pearson Australia Group Pty. Ltd.)
Penguin Books India Pvt. Ltd., 11 Community Centre, Panchsheel Park, New Delhi—110 017, India
Penguin Group (NZ), 67 Apollo Drive, Rosedale, North Shore 0632, New Zealand
(a division of Pearson New Zealand Ltd.)
Penguin Books (South Africa) (Pty.) Ltd., 24 Sturdee Avenue, Rosebank, Johannesburg 2196, South Africa

Penguin Books Ltd., Registered Offices: 80 Strand, London WC2R 0RL, England

Cover art by Don Sipley.
Cover design by Diana Kolsky.
Interior text design by Tiffany Estreicher.

Berkley Sensation trade paperback ISBN: 978-0-425-22708-4

PRINTING HISTORY
Berkley Sensation mass-market edition / August 2004
Berkley Sensation trade paperback edition / November 2008

The Library of Congress has cataloged a prior edition under LCCN: 2004718976.

PRINTED IN THE UNITED STATES OF AMERICA

10 9 8 7 6 5 4 3 2 1

To the other three parts of the Core Four—
Kim, Robin and Teresa.
I cherish the blessing of our friendship.

Acknowledgments

I am thankful for the continued magic of my editor, Christine Zika, and for the brilliance of my agent, Meredith Bernstein. What a fabulous team we make!

I am profoundly grateful to my friend Lola Palazzo for her expertise. Thank you for helping me to create a dream bakery and for educating me about baking in general. Lola—you would be doing Tulsa (and your friends) a great service if you opened another restaurant!

Thank you, Sean Georges, for your research help. Once again, we work very well together.

I appreciate Pamela Chew for taking the time to answer my questions about the Italian language. Any inaccuracies in translation are my own.

Prologue

"EVEN amidst the lovely Dryads your daughter shines, my Lady," Eirene said. She wasn't looking at me as she spoke. Instead she was smiling at Persephone in a proud, motherly fashion, and she did not notice that my lips tightened into a thin line at her words.

"She is Spring personified and even the beauty of the nymphs cannot begin to compete with her splendor."

At the sound of my words, Eirene's sharp gaze immediately shifted to my face. My faithful nursemaid had known me too long not to recognize my tone.

"The child troubles you, Demeter?" she asked gently.

"How could she not!" I snapped.

Only Eirene's silence betrayed her hurt. I shifted my golden scepter from my right hand to my left, and leaned forward so that I could touch her arm in a wordless apology. As usual, she stood near my throne, always ready to serve me. But she was, of course, much more to me than a simple nursemaid or servant. She was my confidant and one of my most loyal advisors. As such she deserved to be treated with respect, and my harsh tone toward her was a sign of how distracted I had become.

Her distinctive gray eyes softened with understanding at my touch.

"Would you like wine, Great Goddess?" she asked.

"For us both." I did not smile; it was not my way. But she understood me and my moods so completely that often only a look or a word was needed between us.

I studied my daughter as Eirene called for wine. The little Nysaian meadow had been the perfect choice in which to spend the unseasonably warm afternoon. Persephone and her wood nymph companions complemented the beauty that surrounded us. Though the day was pleasant, the trees that ringed the meadow were already beginning to shed their summer clothes. I watched Persephone twirl gracefully under one ancient oak, making a game of trying to catch the brilliantly colored falling leaves. The nymphs aided the young goddess by dancing on the limbs to assure a steady waterfall of orange and scarlet and rust.

As usual, Eirene was correct. The woodland Dryads were ethereal and delicate. Each of them was a breathing masterpiece. It was easy to understand why mortals found them irresistible. But when compared to Persephone, their beauty turned mundane. In her presence they became common house slaves.

My daughter's hair shone with a rich mahogany luster, the color of which never ceased to amaze me because I am so fair. It does not curl, either, as do my grain-colored tresses. Instead her hair was a ripple of thick, brilliant waves that lapped around the soft curve of her waist.

Obviously feeling my scrutiny, she waved joyously at me before capturing another watercolored leaf. Her face tilted in my direction. It was a perfect heart. Enormous violet-colored eyes were framed by arched brows and thick, ebony lashes. Her lips were lush and inviting. Her body was lithe. I felt my own lips turn down.

"Your wine, my Lady." Eirene offered me a golden goblet filled with chilled wine the color of sunlight.

I sipped thoughtfully, speaking my thoughts aloud, secure in the knowledge that they were safe with Eirene. "Of course Persephone is supple and lovely. Why would she not be? She spends all her time frolicking with nymphs and picking flowers."

"She also creates glorious feasts."

I made a very ungoddess-like noise through my nose. "I am quite aware that she produces culinary masterpieces, and then lolls about feasting to all hours with"—I wafted my hand in the direction of the Dryads—"semi-deities."

"She is much beloved." Eirene reminded me patiently.

"She is frivolous." I countered.

Suddenly, I closed my eyes and cringed as another voice rose from the multitudes and rang with the insistence of a clarion bell throughout my mind. *Lover, somber Goddess of the Fields and Fruits and Flowers, strong and just, please aid our mother's spirit as she roams restless through the Darkened Realm without the comfort of a goddess . . .*

"Demeter, are you well?" Eirene's concern broke through the supplication, effectively causing the voice to dissipate like windblown dust.

Opening my eyes I met her gaze. "It has become never-ending." Even as I spoke more voices crowded my mind. *O Demeter, we do call upon thee, that our sister who has passed Beyond be accorded the comfort of a goddess . . . and . . . O gracious goddess who gives life through the harvest, I do ask your indulgence for my beloved wife who has passed through the Gates of the Underworld and dwells evermore beyond the comfort of a goddess . . .*

With a mighty effort I blocked the teeming throng from my mind.

"Something must be done about Hades." My voice was stone. "I understand the mortals. Their entreaties are valid. It is fact that there is no Goddess of the Underworld." I leapt up and began to pace back and forth in frustration. "But what am I to do? The Goddess of the Riches of the Field cannot abandon her realm and descend into the Land of the Dead."

"But the dead do require the touch of a goddess," Eirene agreed firmly.

"They need more than just the touch of a goddess. They need light and care and . . ." My words faded away as Persephone's bright laughter filled the meadow. "They need the breath of Spring."

Eirene's eyes widened. "You cannot mean your daughter!"

"And why can I not! Light and life follow the child. She is exactly what is needed within that shadowy realm."

"But she is so young."

I felt my gaze soften as I watched Persephone leap over a narrow stream, allowing her hand to trail over the dried remains of the season's last wildflowers. Instantly the stalks filled and straightened and burst into brilliant bloom. Despite her faults, she was so precious, so filled with the joy of life. There was no doubt that I loved her dearly. I often wondered if my fierce devotion had kept her from growing into a goddess of her own realm. I straightened my shoulders. It was past time that I taught my daughter how to fly.

"She is a goddess."

"She will not like it."

I set my already firm jaw. "Persephone will obey my command."

Eirene opened her mouth as if she wished to speak, then seemed to change her mind and instead drank deeply of her wine.

I sighed. "You know you may speak your mind to me."

"I was just thinking that it would not be a matter of Persephone obeying your command, but rather . . ." She hesitated.

"Oh, come! Tell me your thoughts."

Eirene looked decidedly uncomfortable. "Demeter, you know that I love Persephone as if she were my own child."

I nodded impatiently. "Yes, yes. Of course."

"She is delightful and full of life, but she has little depth. I do not think she has enough maturity to be Goddess of the Underworld."

A hot retort came to my mind, but wisdom held my tongue. Eirene was correct. Persephone was a lovely young goddess, but her life had been too easy, too filled with cosseted pleasures. And I was at fault. My frivolous daughter was proof that even a goddess could make mistakes as a parent.

"I agree, my old friend. Before Persephone can become Goddess of the Underworld, she must mature."

"Perhaps she should spend some time with Athena," Eirene said.

"No, that would only teach her to pry into the affairs of others."

"Diana?" Eirene offered.

I scowled. "I think not. I would someday like to be blessed with grandchildren." I narrowed my eyes. "No, my daughter must grow up and see that life is not always filled with Olympian pleasures and luxury. She needs to learn responsibility, but as long as she can draw upon the power of a goddess, as long as she can be recognized as my daughter, she will never learn—" Suddenly I knew what I must do.

"My Lady?"

"There is only one place where Persephone will truly learn to be a goddess. It is a place where she must first learn to be a woman."

Eirene drew back, her face taking on a horrified expression as she began to understand.

"You will not send her there!"

"Oh, yes. *There* is exactly where I shall send her."

"But they will not know her; they do not even know you." Eirene's deeply lined brow furrowed in agitation.

I felt my lips turning up in one of my rare smiles. "Exactly, my friend. Exactly."

Chapter One

Oklahoma, Present Day

"No, it's not that I don't 'get it,' it's that I don't understand how you could have let it happen." Lina spoke slowly and distinctly through clenched teeth.

"Ms. Santoro, I have already explained that we had no idea until the IRS contacted us yesterday that there had been any error at all."

"Did you not have any checks and balances? The reason I pay you to manage the taxes for my business is because I need an expert." She glanced down at the obscene number typed in neat, no-nonsense black and white across the bottom of the government form. "I understand accidents and mistakes, but I don't understand how something this *large* could have escaped your notice."

Frank Rayburn cleared his throat before answering. Lina had always thought he looked a little like a gangster-wannabe. Today his black pinstriped suit and his slippery demeanor did nothing to dispel the image.

"Your bakery did very well last year, Ms. Santoro. Actually, you more than doubled your income from the previous year. When we're talking about a major increase in figures, it is easy for mistakes to happen. I think that what would be more productive for us now is to focus on how you can pay what you owe the government instead of casting blame." Before she could speak he hurried on, "I have drawn up several suggestions." He pulled out another sheet of paper filled with bulleted columns and numbers and handed it to her. "Suggestion number one is to borrow the money. Interest rates are very reasonable right now."

Lina felt her jaw clench. She hated the idea of borrowing money, especially that much money. She knew it would make her feel exposed and vulnerable until the loan was repaid. *If* the loan could be repaid. Yes, she had been doing well, but a bakery wasn't exactly a necessity to a community, and times were hard.

"What are your other suggestions?"

"Well, you could introduce a newer, more glitzy line of foods. Maybe add a little something for the lunch crowd, more than those . . ." He hesitated, making little circles in the air with one thick forefinger. "Baby pizza things."

"Pizette Fiorentine." She bit the words at him. "They are mini-pizzas that originated in Florence, and they are not meant to be a meal, they are meant to be a mid-afternoon snack served with cheese and wine."

He shrugged. "Whatever. All I'm saying is that it doesn't draw you a very big lunch crowd."

"You mean like a fried chicken buffet would? Or maybe I could even crank up the grill and churn out some burgers and fries?"

"Now there's an idea," he said, totally missing the sarcasm in her tone. "Suggestion number three would be to cut your staff."

Lina drummed her fingers on the top of the conference table. "Go on," she said, keeping her voice deceptively pleasant.

"Number four would be to consider bankruptcy." He held up a hand to stop her from speaking, even though she hadn't uttered a sound. "I know it sounds drastic, but after those expensive renovations you just completed, you really don't have any reserves left to fall back on."

"I only commissioned those expensive renovations because you assured me that Pani Del Goddess could afford them." Lina's hands twitched with the desire to wrap themselves around his neck.

"Be that as it may, your reserves are gone." He said condescendingly. "But bankruptcy is only one option, and not the one I would recommend.

Actually, I would recommend option number five—sell to that big chain that offered to buy you out a couple months ago. They just want your name and your location. Give it to 'em. You'll have enough money to pay your debt and start over with a new name and place."

"But I've spent twenty years building up the Pani Del Goddess name, and I have no desire to move." If Frank Rayburn had been the least bit intuitive, he would have recognized the storm that brewed in Lina's expressive eyes, even though it had not yet reached her mouth.

Frank Rayburn was not intuitive.

"Well, I just tell ya the options." Frank leaned back in the plush chair and crossed his arms while he gave Lina what he liked to think of as his stern, fatherly look. "You're the boss. It's your job to decide from there."

"No, you're wrong." Lina's voice was still calm and soft, but it was edged with steel. "You see, I am not your boss anymore. You are fired. You have proven yourself to be as incompetent with my business as you are with your choice of attire. My lawyer will be in contact with you. I'll make sure that she has several *options* drawn up for you to consider. Maybe one of them will keep you out of court. Now, good day, Mr. Rayburn, and as my dear, sainted grandmother would say, '*Tu sei un pezzo di merda. Fongule e tuo capra!*'" Lina stood, smoothed her skirt and snapped shut her leather briefcase. "Oh, how rude of me. You don't speak Italian. Allow me to translate my grandmother's sage words: 'You are a piece of shit. Fuck you and your goat!' Arrivederci."

Lina turned and strode through the professionally decorated office grinning wickedly at the well-rouged receptionist.

Chapter Two

GUT instinct, she reminded herself as she gunned her BMW and almost flew over the Highway 51 overpass, heading away from Tulsa's downtown business area to the trendy Cherry Street location of her bakery. Next time she was going to listen to her gut, and when it told her to run screaming in the opposite direction she wouldn't be stupid enough to hire another jerk. What in the hell had she been thinking?

Lina sighed. She knew what she'd been thinking. She'd needed help. The money management end of her business had never been one of her strengths. Her father had always taken care of that for her, but three years ago he and her mother had joined her grandmother in a Florida retirement community. Dad had been so sure she could handle her business finances herself that she hadn't wanted to admit it to him last year when she had finally given up and hired an accountant. So instead of asking for his advice in who she should hire, she'd bumbled ahead and, in a stressed-out rush, chosen Frank Rayburn, Mr. Sleazy Non-Personality.

"It's what you deserve for allowing your pride to get the best of you," Lina muttered to herself as she turned east onto 15th Street—the street that would, within a couple of blocks, morph into the area known as Cherry Street, and lead her to the door of her wonderful, incredible, beautiful, and now completely broke, bakery.

The pit of her stomach ached. There must be a way to pay her debt and keep her two long-time employees as well as her name and location. She gripped the steering wheel with one hand and twirled a short strand of hair around and around her finger. She would not sell her name. She couldn't.

Pani Del Goddess, or Breads of the Goddess—the name sang like magic. It was indelibly tied to all the most wonderful memories of her childhood. *Pani del goddess* is what she and her beloved grandmother used to create on long winter afternoons as they watched old black-and-white movies and drank fragrant, honey-sweetened tea.

"Carolina Francesca, you bake like a little goddess!"

Lina could still hear the echo of her grandmother's voice from her childhood, encouraging her to experiment with classic recipes from the Old Country, her beloved Italia.

"Si, *bambina,* first learn the recipe as it was written, test it and try it, then begin to add *un poco*—a little here, and a little there. That is how to make the breads your own."

And Lina had made them her own, with a talent and a flare that had even impressed her grandmother, who was renowned as an exceptional cook. It had been her grandmother who had bragged so much to her friends that they began asking Lina to bake "something special" for them on the occasion of birthdays or anniversaries. By the time Lina graduated from high school, she had a steady stream of customers, mostly retired widows and widowers who appreciated the taste of quality homemade breads.

When her grandmother had offered to send her to Florence to study at the famous school of baking, Apicius, she had begun shaping the design of her dream—the dream of owning her own bakery. When she was a child, her grandmother had whispered to her that Italy and baking were in her blood. After she graduated from Apicius, Lina followed the whispers of her childhood back to Tulsa. With her she brought a little piece of Italy, its style and its romance—as well as its amazingly rich assortment of breads and pastries. Again her grandmother helped her. Together they discovered a worn-down old building smack in the middle of the artsy area of Tulsa known as Cherry Street. They'd bought it and slowly turned it into a shining sliver of Florence.

Lina shook her head and flipped off the radio. She couldn't let Pani Del Goddess fail. It wouldn't just break her own heart; it would cut her grandmother to the bone. And what about her customers? Her bakery was the meeting place for a delightfully eclectic group of regulars, made up mostly of local eccentrics, celebrities and retirees. It was more than a bakery. It was a unique social hub.

And what would Anton and Dolores do? The two had been working for her for ten and fifteen years. She knew it was a cliché, but they were more than employees; they were family to her, especially since she had no children of her own.

Lina sighed again, and then she inhaled deeply. Despite the horrors of the day, her lips curved up. Pinyon smoke drifted through the BMW's partially rolled down windows. She was passing Grumpy's Garden, the little shop that signaled the beginning of the Cherry Street District, and, as usual, "Grumpy," who was actually a very nice lady named Shaun and not grumpy at all, had several of her huge chimeneas perpetually burning, perfuming the neighborhood with the distinctive smell of southwest pine.

She felt the knot in her stomach loosen as she downshifted and slowed her car, careful of the pedestrians crossing the streets while they moved back and forth from antique shops, to new-age bookstores, to posh interior design studios and unique restaurants. And finally, in the heart of the street, nestled between a trendy little spa and a vintage jewelry store, sat Pani Del Goddess.

As usual, there were few parking spaces available on the street, and Lina turned into the alley to park in one of the reserved spaces behind her building. She had barely stepped out of her car when she felt an all too familiar tug at her mind. The feeling was always the same, though it varied in degree and intensity. Today it was like someone far away had spoken her name, and the wind had carried the echo of the sound to her mind without having to reach her ears first. She closed her eyes. She really didn't have time for this . . . not today.

Almost instantly Lina regretted the thought. Mentally she shook herself. No, she wouldn't let financial troubles change who she was—and part of who she was, was this. It was her gift.

Glancing around her, Lina peered into the shadows at the edges of the building.

"Where are you, little one?" she coaxed. Then she focused her mind and a vague image came to her. Lina smiled. "Come on, kitty, kitty, kitty," she called. "I know you're there. You don't have to be afraid."

With a pathetic mew, a skinny orange tabby stepped hesitantly from behind the garbage receptacle.

"Well, look at you. You're nothing more than a delicate flower. Come here, baby girl. Everything will be fine now."

Mesmerized, the small orange cat walked straight into Lina's outstretched arms. Ignoring what the cat's matted, dirty fur could do to her very clean, very expensive silk suit, Lina cuddled the mangy animal. Staring up at her rescuer, eyes filled with adoration, the cat rewarded Lina with thunderous purring.

Lina could not remember a time when she hadn't felt a special affinity for animals. As a small child, she had only to sit quietly in her backyard and soon she would be visited by rabbits and squirrels and even nervous little field mice. Dogs and cats loved her. Horses followed her like giant puppies. Even cows, who Lina knew had big, mushy brains, lowed lovingly at her if she got too close to where they pastured. Animals had always adored her, but it hadn't been until Lina had become a teenager that she had really realized the extent of her gift.

She could understand animals. Sort of. She wasn't Dr. Doolittle or anything ridiculous like that; she couldn't carry on conversations with animals. She liked to think of herself as if she were a horse whisperer, only her abilities weren't limited to horses. And she had an extra "thing" that most people didn't have. Sometimes the "thing" told her that there was a cat that needed her help. The "thing" was something that went off in her mind, like a connection she could plug into.

She knew it was weird.

For a brief time in high school she had considered becoming a veterinarian. She'd even volunteered at a veterinary clinic during the summer between her sophomore and junior years—a summer that had taught her that while blood and parasites were definitely not a part of her special animal "thing," they certainly were two things that were a consistent part of veterinarian work. Just remembering it made Lina shudder in revulsion and want to scratch her scalp.

"In a bakery, you never, ever have to deal with blood *or* parasites," she told the little orange cat as she stepped out of the alley, turned left and inhaled deeply.

"Magnifico," she murmured in her grandmother's voice.

The enticing aroma of freshly baked bread soothed her senses. She sniffed appreciatively, expertly identifying the subtle differences in the fragrance of olives, rosemary and cheese, wedded to the sweet smells of the butter, cinnamon, nuts, raisins and the liqueurs that went into the creation of the bakery's specialty bread, gubana, which was the sweetbread of Friuli, a small region east of Venice.

Lina paused in front of the large glass window that fronted her bakery. She nodded appreciatively at the beautifully arranged crystal platters that were displayed on tiers and filled with a fresh assortment of Italian pastries and cookies. Pride filled Lina. As always, everything was perfect.

She glanced beyond the window display to see that about half of the dozen little mosaic-topped café tables were occupied. Not bad, she thought, for late Friday afternoon. She shifted the cat in her arms and checked her watch. It was almost 4:00 P.M. and they closed at 5:00 P.M.; usually the hour or so before closing was a quiet, winding-down time.

Maybe that was one answer. Maybe she should extend her hours. But wouldn't she have to hire more help then? Anton and Dolores already worked full-time shifts, and Lina herself was rarely absent from the bakery. Wouldn't the additional cost of another employee cancel out any revenue generated by staying open longer?

Lina could feel the beginnings of a serious tension headache.

Forcing herself to relax, Lina squinted past the glare of the highly polished picture window. She could see the newly painted frescoes that decorated the walls—part of the expensive renovation that had just been completed. But the price had been worth it. Lina had commissioned Kimberlei Doner, a well-known local artist and illustrator, to fill the walls of Pani Del Goddess with authentic scenes from ancient Florence. The paintings, coupled with the vintage light fixtures and café tables, created an atmosphere that made her patrons feel like they had stepped off the streets of Tulsa and had been temporarily transported to magical, earthy Italy.

"Let's go in and see what we can do about you," she told the cat, who was still purring contentedly in her arms. "First I'll take care of you, then I'll figure out what to do about the money," she said, wishing desperately that money was as easy to come by as cats.

The wind chime over the door tinkled happily as Lina entered Pani Del Goddess. She stood there for a moment, basking in the familiar scene. Anton was fiddling with the cappuccino machine and humming the chorus of the song "All That Jazz" from *Chicago*. Dolores was explaining the difference between panettones and colombe to a middle-aged couple Lina didn't recognize. They were the only people in the shop that she didn't recognize.

Anton glanced up as several customers called hellos to her. His full lips began a grin when he saw Lina, but then they pursed into a resigned pout when he noticed the cat in her arms.

"Oh, look, it's our fearless leader—the Cat Savior." Anton fluttered his fingers in Lina's direction.

"Don't start with me, Anton, or I'll take back the DVD of *Chicago* that I got you for your birthday," Lina said with mock severity.

Anton's pout turned into a gasp, and he clasped his hands over his heart as if she had just stabbed him. "You're wounding me!"

Dolores giggled as she rang up the couple's order. "He's been tapping to 'All That Jazz' all day. It's worse than his *Moulin Rouge* phase."

"Musicals are not a phase with me; they're my passion," Anton said.

"Then you should understand me perfectly. Helping animals is my passion," Lina said.

Anton rolled his eyes and sighed dramatically. "I think it's more than slightly disturbing that I have the number to the Street Cats Rescue Line memorized."

"Just make the call," Lina told him, but Anton was already dialing the number. She winked her thanks to him.

"Well, Lina! I was hoping to see you today."

Lina smiled and walked over to the table closest to the picture window. But instead of speaking to the dark-haired woman who had waved her over, first she greeted the miniature schnauzer who sat ramrod stiff on a scarlet-colored cushion at his mistress's feet.

"Dash, you are certainly looking handsome today." The cat stirred in her arms, but Lina soothed it with an absentminded caress.

"He should. He just came from the groomers."

Lina grinned at the well-mannered little dog. "A day of beauty, huh? Honey, it's what we all need." She turned her attention to Dash's mistress. "How is the olive bread today, Tess?"

"Excellent. Simply excellent as usual." Tess's distinctive Tahlequah drawl was lazy and melodic. "And this San Angelo Pinot Grigio that Anton recommended is absolutely perfect with it."

"I'm glad you think so. We aim to please."

"Which is why I wanted to talk with you. The Poets and Writers Association has chosen their Oklahoma Author of the Year, and we'll be having several functions to honor her next week. I want to make sure we have a selection of your excellent breads for the dinner."

Lina's mind raced ahead. Tess Miller was director of Oklahoma's Poets and Writers Association, as well as the host of a very popular regional talk show—and one of Pani Del Goddess's most loyal customers. For years she and Dash had been stopping in the bakery during their daily walks, Lina had even had a doggie cushion made for the little schnauzer, which she kept in a special cubby underneath the cash register. There would certainly be no one better with which to begin her expansion. Even if she wasn't sure exactly what that expansion was yet.

"Uh, Tess," Lina cleared her throat. "Of course I would be happy to provide any breads you might need, but I would also like to talk with you about our new expanded menu. Perhaps we could cater the whole meal for you."

"Well, that would be just splendid! I'm sure anything you come up with will be perfect. Why don't I call you Monday? You can give me my menu choices and I'll fill you in on the details?"

Lina felt herself nodding and smiling as she turned away from the table. She kept the tight smile plastered on her face while she made her way to the counter, speaking to each of her patrons as she passed them. It was only when she reached the counter and ran into the blank expressions of shock that had taken up residence on Anton's and Dolores's faces that she faltered.

"Did I hear you say the word *cater*?" Anton whispered.

"And *whole meal*?" Dolores squeaked.

Lina jerked her head toward the back of the bakery before stepping through the cream-colored swinging doors that divided the kitchen, the storeroom and her office from the rest of the bakery. Her two employees scurried after her. Lina spoke quickly as she pushed the startled orange cat into the carrier she retrieved from the coat closet.

"You know the appointment I had with my accountant today? It wasn't good news. I owe money. Big money. To the IRS."

Anton blanched and sucked in air.

"Oh, Lina. Is it really bad?" Dolores sounded twelve years old.

"Yes." She looked carefully at each of them. "It is really bad. We're going to have to make some changes." Lina registered the twin looks of horror on their faces. Instantly Anton's eyes began to fill with tears. Dolores's already pale face drained of even the pretense of color. "No, no, no! Not that! There will be none of that—you'll be keeping your jobs. We'll all be keeping our jobs."

"Oh, God. I need to sit down." Anton fanned himself with his fingers.

"My office. Quickly. And there will be absolutely no fainting." She picked up the cat carrier and clucked at the ruffled tabby as she headed to her office. Over her shoulder she said, "And no crying either. Remember—"

Anton finished the sentence for her. "—There's no crying in baking."

Dolores nodded vigorous agreement.

Lina set the cat carrier next to her desk before taking a seat behind it. Anton and Dolores sank into the two plushly upholstered antique chairs that faced her. No one spoke.

Hesitating, Anton made a vague gesture in the direction of the cat. "Patricia from Street Cats said that she'd stay a little past closing today, so if you want me to, I can drop off that little orange thing on my way home. It's really not out of my way." He finished with a weak smile.

"Thank you, Anton, even though you called her a little orange thing, I'll take you up on your kind offer."

"Well, I meant little orange beast, but I was trying to be nice," Anton said, sounding more like himself and looking less likely to hyperventilate.

"What are we going to do?" Dolores asked.

True to form, Dolores was ready for the bottom line. Though only twenty-eight, she had been working for Lina for ten years. The reason Lina had hired her was not just because she had a flair for baking pastries and a way with old people, but Lina appreciated her no-nonsense personality. And she was the perfect balance for Anton, who was—Lina glanced at her other employee who sat with his legs crossed delicately, the sheen of almost-tears still pooled in his eyes—decidedly more dramatic. They fit together well, the three of them, and Lina intended that they stay that way.

"We expand our menu," Lina said firmly.

Dolores nodded her head thoughtfully. "Okay, we can do that."

Anton gnawed on the side of his thumb. "Do you mean, like, add sandwiches or something?"

"I'm not exactly sure yet," Lina said slowly. "I haven't had time to think it through. I just know that we have to make more money, which means we need to bring in more customers. It only makes sense that if we expanded our menu, we would appeal to a larger group of people."

Anton and Dolores nodded in unison.

"Catering Tess Miller's dinner is a good place to start," Dolores said.

"Catering," Anton whined. "It sounds so, I don't know, *banal.*"

"As banal as bankruptcy?" Lina asked.

"No!" The word burst from his mouth.

"My thoughts exactly," Lina said.

"So what are we going to serve?" Dolores asked.

Lina ran her fingers through her neatly cropped hair. She had absolutely no idea.

"We're going to serve selections from our expanded menu. That way we'll get practice as well as publicity."

"And that expanded menu would be what exactly?" Dolores prompted.

"I have absolutely no idea," Lina admitted.

"And to think I didn't bring even one tiny Xanax with me to work today." Anton was gnawing at his thumb again.

"Quit biting your finger," Dolores told him. "We'll figure this out." She shifted her gaze to Lina. "Right?"

Lina's heart squeezed. They looked like baby birds gaping up at her expectantly.

"Right," she said, painting her voice with confidence. "All I need to do is to . . ." she faltered. Her nestlings blinked big, round eyes, waiting for her next words. "Is to . . . um . . . brainstorm." She finally finished.

"Brainstorm? As in the step before writing a paper?" Anton, who was perpetually a sporadic night school student at Tulsa Community College, clutched onto a familiar idea.

"Of course," Dolores added brightly. "Lina probably has about a zillion and a half cookbooks at home. All she needs to do is to go through them and pick out a few great recipes for wonderful meals."

"Then she'll share them with us, and we'll begin our new creations!" Anton gushed. "How ab fab! I can hardly wait!" Then he reached over and squeezed Dolores's hand. "I feel just awful that I was so negative in the beginning. I almost forgot our Baker's Motto."

Dolores and Anton grinned at each other, and then as if they were getting ready to say the Pledge of Allegiance, they covered their hearts with their hands and spoke solemnly in unison:

"In baking we must always rise to the occasion."

Lina thought that she very well might have been in baker's hell, but she kept nodding and smiling. Dolores was partially correct, she did have a wonderful collection of cookbooks at home—all filled with fabulous recipes for breads and pastries. She had very few cookbooks that contained recipes for meals. Actually, she didn't even cook many full meals herself. A little pasta here, a little salad there, and a nice glass of Chianti was her idea of cooking a full meal. Baking was her specialty and her love. Meals were, well, banal.

Out of her element, she admitted to herself. This whole thing was totally out of her element. So, feeling a little like a sparrow struggling to feed the cuckoos in her nest, Lina kept smiling and nodding at her chicks.

"Well, I think we've been absent from the front long enough. Now that we've got a plan, why don't you two handle it for the next hour and close up for me? I'll go home and begin brainstorming."

"Tess said she'd call you on Monday about the menu for the dinner, didn't she?" Dolores asked.

"That's what she said, all right." Lina focused on keeping the panic out of her voice.

"Oooh, this really is exciting. You know, I'll bet there will be lots of local celebs at that dinner." Anton waggled his well-maintained eyebrows. "Not to mention media coverage."

"I imagine there will be." Lina walked briskly from her office.

As she called quick good-byes to her customers and hastily retreated out the door, she could hear Anton telling Dolores that he would certainly need several new, exciting outfits to go with their new, exciting menu.

Her grandmother had told her many times that swearing was common, unladylike behavior reserved only for peasants and men who were not gentlemen. On the other hand, she totally endorsed a well-accented, well-chosen Italian curse as simply showing one's creativity. Standing in front of her bakery Lina let loose with a string of Italian that began with telling the IRS they could *va al diavolo*, or go to hell, and ending with saying they were nothing more than a chronic, flaming *rompicoglioni,* or pain in the ass. Just to cover all bases in between she strung together several "shits" and "damns," in Italian, of course. She felt sure Grandma would have been proud.

When people began staring she shut her mouth and told herself to breathe slowly and deeply. She was an intelligent, successful businesswoman. Hell, she could even curse eloquently in Italian and English, but she tried to keep the English to a minimum—Grandma had been right, it just didn't sound as well-bred (and yes, Grandma would also have appreciated the pun). How difficult could it be for her to come up with a few new menu choices? Even if they were meals and not breads.

She started to twirl a strand of her hair, but caught herself and forced her hand to stay at her side. The problem wasn't that she couldn't come up with some new recipes. The problem, she realized, was that through Pani Del Goddess she had established a solid reputation for preparing breads that were unique and delicious. She couldn't just slap some pesto over pasta and toss a salad on the side of the plate. She wouldn't do it at all if she couldn't do it well. The name Pani Del Goddess meant excellence, and Lina was determined that it would never stand for anything less.

She should call her grandmother; she'd have a stack of ideas that she'd be thrilled to share with her beloved *bambina*. Again.

"But as Anton would say, I'm *sooo* not a baby," Lina muttered to herself. "Good God, I'm forty-three. It's about time I quit running to Grandma."

Lina's dialogue with herself was interrupted by the sound of carefree laughter coming from two women who had just emerged from the used bookstore across the street. She scowled and wished that all she had to worry about was shopping with a friend for the perfect book.

The scowl shifted as her expression turned thoughtful. The Book Place was a wonderful used bookstore with a vast selection of fiction and nonfiction. Lina had spent many satisfied hours lost in their maze of shelves. Surely she could find a fabulous old cookbook in the stacks, something that had been hidden in out-of-print obscurity for years, and

within its pages there would be a recipe that was the perfect blen
Italy and magic and ingredients.

Yes, she thought as she dodged cars and crossed the street, Th
Book Place was the perfect place to begin brainstorming.

Chapter Three

The pile of used books was daunting. She'd found ten of them. Ten old, interesting looking, out-of-print Italian cookbooks. While she was choosing them they hadn't seemed so thick—and ten certainly hadn't seemed to be so many. But now that they were home with her, piled in a neat stack on the glass top of the wrought iron sculpture she used as a coffee table, they appeared to have multiplied.

Couldn't she have narrowed her choices down by a few less books before she'd left the bookstore?

"In baking we must always rise to the occasion," she reminded the enormous, longhaired black-and-white tomcat that perched in the middle of the black-and-white toile chaise. The perfect match made Lina grin. She enjoyed purchasing furniture that properly accessorized her pets, even if the cat didn't deign to notice. Lina did receive a brief look of boredom from his side of the room and a quick swish of his tail in response to the proclamation of her bakery motto.

"Patchy Poo the Pud Santoro," she addressed him formally by his full name. "You are a handsome beast, but you know nothing about baking."

At her feet, the half-sleeping old English bulldog snorted as if in agreement with her.

"Don't be rude, Edith Anne," Lina scolded the dog halfheartedly. "You know considerably more about eating than you know about baking."

Edith sighed contentedly as Lina scratched her behind her right ear. With the hand that wasn't busy, Lina picked up the first book. It was a thick tomb entitled *Discovering Historical Italy.* She let it fall open and began reading a long, complex paragraph about the proper preparation of veal. She blanched and snapped the book shut. Veal was a popular dish in Italy, but to her veal meant baby cows. Mush-brained, adorable, wide-eyed baby cows.

"Perhaps it's not possible to rise to a very difficult occasion without the proper preparation." She said to the now snoring Bulldog. "In baking or otherwise." She closed the book, setting it gently back on the table a little like it was a bomb that might very well explode if not treated carefully.

"I think this particular preparation calls for a nice glass of Italian red," she told Patchy Poo the Pud Santoro. He glanced at her through slitted eyes and yawned.

"You two are no help at all."

Shaking her head, Lina walked away from the table and headed directly to her wine closet. In her opinion, a Monte Antico Rosso Sangiovese was the perfect preparation tool for any difficult situation—baking or otherwise.

"Maybe I can serve enough wonderful Italian wine with my new menu that my customers will get too soused to pay much attention to what they eat." She spoke over her shoulder to her animals as she poured herself a ruby-colored glass of wine, but she didn't need a non-response from her pets to know that her last statement was ridiculous. Then she'd be running a bar and not a bakery, which would give Anton an apoplectic fit. Lina straightened her spine, snagged a bag of double-dipped chocolate-covered peanuts, the perfect accompaniment for the Sangiovese, and marched back into her living room. Planting herself on the couch, she opened her notebook and chose the next book in the pile, *Cooking With Italy.*

The dog and cat lifted their heads and gave her identically quizzical looks.

"Let the games begin," she told them grimly.

* * *

THREE hours later she had finished combing through nine of the ten books, and she had a list of four possible main course recipes: chicken picatta, puttanesca on spaghetti, eggplant parmigiana, and a lovely aioli platter, complete with artichokes, olives, tomatoes, poached salmon and carpaccio.

Lina felt a little thrill of accomplishment as she looked over her list. She was actually enjoying herself. Delving through the musty old books had become an exercise in Italian history and culture—two things that had been a constant part of her upbringing.

Only one more cookbook was left. Lina picked up the slim hardback. She had purposefully saved this one for last. In the bookstore she had been intrigued by the cover, which was a deep, royal blue etched with a gold embossed design. The title, *The Italian Goddess Cookbook,* rested over the golden illustration of a stern looking goddess who sat on a massive throne. She was dressed in a long robe and her hair was wrapped around the crown of her head in intricate braids. In one hand she held a scepter topped with a ripe ear of corn, in the other she held a flaming torch. Underneath the illustration the words, *Recipes and Spells for the Goddess in Every Woman,* flowed in beautiful gold script. The author's name, Filomena, was branded into the cover underneath the embossed print.

"Just one more recipe. Help me to find just one more, and I'll call it a night," Lina said as she ran her fingers over the raised embossing.

Her fingertips tingled.

Lina rested the book on her lap and rubbed her hands together. She must be getting tired. She glanced at the clock. It was only a little past nine o'clock, but it had been a long day.

Lina looked back down at the cover. The gold print caught the lamplight, causing the words *Recipes and Spells for the Goddess in Every Woman* to seem to flicker and glow.

What an unusual coincidence that the woman who baked like an Italian goddess had found an old, discarded copy of *The Italian Goddess*

Cookbook. Her grandmother would have called it *la magia dell' Italia*, the magic of Italy. On impulse, Lina closed her eyes. She believed in the magic of Italy. She'd experienced it in the multicolored marble of Florence's Duomo, the geranium-filled window boxes of Assisi, and the eerie wonder of the Roman Forum at night. She focused her mind on her love for her grandmother's homeland, then she opened the book that rested on her lap, allowing the pages to fall where they chose.

Lina opened her eyes and began reading:

> *Pizza alla Romana, or Pizza by the Meter. This extraordinary recipe comes from Rome. It is proper to allow the soft, supple dough a very long rest—up to eight hours, the longer the better—then place it on a baker's peel two and a half feet long, while rhythmically pounding it with such vigor that it literally dances beneath your fingers.*

Lina blinked in surprise and grinned. A baker's peel! The long, wooden paddle that was used to drop bread into and scoop it out of the oven. Of course Pani Del Goddess had several of them. She kept reading:

> *. . . when the dough has finished dancing, you paint it with oil and then set the peel in the oven where the totally unforeseen occurs: you slowly, slowly withdraw the peel, stretching the remarkably elastic dough to a thin, incredibly light dough of up to an astonishing six foot length—depending upon the size of each individual goddess's oven.*

Well, Pani Del Goddess had several very long ovens. She could stretch the dough to its full six feet! She scanned the rest of the recipe. Included in the book were several different toppings, everything from a light Pizza Bianca, made simply with olive oil, garlic, rosemary, salt and pepper, to Pizza Pugliese, which was a plethora of Italian favorites—eggplant, provolone, anchovies, olives . . . the list went on and on.

"This may be the answer. Why mess with a bunch of different

recipes? Why not have one basic specialty, Pizza alla Romana, with several variations? And it's still baking!"

Reacting to the excitement in her voice, Edith Anne woke long enough to offer a muffled woof of support. Patchy Poo the Pud exercised the innate initiative of a cat and ignored her completely.

Lina patted the dog's head while she studied the dough recipe.

. . . because this dough uses so little yeast and wants a long rising, a goddess can work its preparation into her busy American schedule by making the dough at night with cool water and refrigerating it immediately after it is mixed. Next morning, place it in a cool spot to rise slowly at room temperature all day. Then simply shape and bake it for dinner . . .

Lina ran her eyes down the list of ingredients. Dry yeast, water, flour, salt, olive oil—yes, of course she had everything on the list. She could make the dough that night, let it sit all the next day, then she and the "baby birds" could sample it tomorrow night. Delighted, she began reading the preparation directions.

Before beginning, you will need a green candle, to represent the Earth. The goddess we honor with this recipe is She who breathes life into the flour with which we create our dough, Demeter, Great Goddess of the Harvest, and of Fruits and the Riches of the Earth.

Lina's eyes widened.

As you start preparation, light the green candle and focus your thoughts on Demeter. Then you may begin.

Lina's eyes scanned the recipe. Sure enough, interspersed between instructions for stirring the yeast, and mixing the flour and salt, were otherworldly instructions.

Lina read a line and her brow furrowed.

Was it a spell?

Lina read another line.

It seemed to be more of an invocation, or maybe a prayer. But whatever she called it, the supernatural directions were definitely a part of the recipe. Lina couldn't help but smile. *La magia dell' Italia.* Her grandmother would approve.

Humming to herself, she went in search of a green candle.

Chapter Four

LINA looked around the counter and nodded in satisfaction. She had assembled all of the ingredients and kitchenwares she would need to make the dough. She had even found a small green candle that gave off a vaguely piney scent. It was a relic from the previous Christmas, and she'd had to dig through two boxes of ornaments before she discovered it. Lina opened the cookbook and set it on the counter next to her favorite stainless steel mixing bowl. Then she began:

> *First, light the green candle and focus your thoughts on Demeter, Mother of the Harvest.*

Ever the consummate chef, Lina followed the directions precisely. She lit the candle and let her thoughts drift to the long-forgotten Harvest Goddess. She wondered briefly what lovely, eccentric cooking rituals had been forgotten along with the goddess.

Lina continued reading:

> *Stir the yeast into the warm water in a small bowl; let stand until creamy, about 10 minutes.*

Lina felt relaxed and happy as her experienced hands stirred and mixed.

While the yeast is standing, center your thoughts and take three deep cleansing breaths. Imagine power filtering up the center of your body and traveling along the path of your spine all the way through your head and then pouring out in a waterfall around you to be reabsorbed into your core again. When you feel invigorated, you may begin Demeter's Invocation.

The directions reminded her a little of a new-age relaxation class she had taken once. With a self-amused smile, she set the kitchen timer for ten minutes before beginning the steps of the centering exercise.

She had to admit that in no time she was feeling . . . well . . . if not invigorated, at least very awake and self-aware. Lina went back to the recipe.

When you feel ready, please read the following aloud.

"O most gracious and magnificent Demeter, goddess of all that is harvested and grown, I ask that some portion of Your presence be here with me now. I summon You to enrich the bounty You have already so plentifully provided. I ask also that You breathe a breath of magic and wonder into this kitchen."

The timer chimed and Lina jumped, surprised that ten minutes had passed so quickly.

Mix the flour and salt in a large wide-mouthed bowl while invoking, "Come, Demeter, I summon you with this salt and flour, which are the riches of Your Earth."

The rhythm of the invocation melded harmoniously with the recipe, and Lina found herself eager to read the next lines.

Make a well in the center of the flour; then pour the dissolved yeast, 1 3/4 cups plus 1 tablespoon water, 1 tablespoon oil, and the lard into the well. Speak to the goddess as you gradually stir the flour into the liquid and work to a soft dough that can be gathered into a ball. "I call upon You, O Goddess of the Harvest, and bid You welcome here in the midst of that which You created."

Then knead on a floured surface until soft, smooth, and elastic, 10 to 15 minutes, sprinkling with additional flour as needed. As the dough takes form, recite the following to Demeter: "Power be drawn, and power come, and make me one with thee, O Goddess of the Harvest. Make me greater, make me better, grant me strength and grant me power."

Lina's hands fell into a rhythm as she effortlessly plied the dough against the floured countertop. Her eyes were locked on the words that seemed to come as easily to her lips as the familiar kneading motion came to her hands.

"O Demeter, who is my guardian and sister, I give You thanks. May my summons fall lightly on Your ears, and may Your wisdom and strength remain with me, growing ever finer, as grains ripe for the harvest."

Lina kneaded the dough while her mind drifted. What an incredibly intriguing thought—to couple the magic of an ancient goddess with the perfection of a recipe that had been passed down from mothers to daughters and preserved for generations. It was such a wonderful, natural idea. To call upon the strength of a goddess through baking! Whether it actually worked, whether or not a goddess really listened, was beside the point. It was a lovely, empowering ritual—one that, if nothing else, could serve to focus her thoughts on the positive and remind her that she should take a moment to enjoy the rich femininity of her chosen career.

The sweet scent of the pine candle mixed with the more earthy smells of yeast and flour. The aroma was delicious and heady. Unexpectedly, Lina felt a wave of sensation, fueled by scent, rush through her body. For a moment she was dizzy and disoriented, as if she had been suddenly displaced from her kitchen and transported, dough and all, to the middle of a pine-filled forest. She rubbed the back of a flour-crusted hand across her forehead. Her head felt unnaturally warm, but the touch of her hand re-grounded her and the dizziness dissipated.

It had been a tough day. She shouldn't be surprised that it was wearing on her. She rolled her shoulders and let her head fall forward and backward, causing tired, overstressed muscles to stretch and relax. She would certainly sleep well tonight.

Lina glanced down at the conclusion of the dough recipe. It contained the usual mundane instructions about covering it in a bowl and letting it rise for at least eight hours. Impatiently, she scanned past the recipe to the completion of the invocation ritual.

> **Pinch out a small portion of the dough. Choose a special place—out of doors—where you can leave your offering. Sprinkle it with wine and offer it to Demeter, saying "O goddess of the plentiful harvest, of strength and power and wisdom, I give You greeting, and honor, and thanks. Blessed Be!"*
>
> **Note: You might choose to add your own personal request or praise before concluding the ritual. May blessings rain upon you and may you never go hungry!*

Lina's smile tilted sardonic. The fullness of her hips said that she might consider going hungry once in a while. Not that she was fat, she amended quickly, she was just voluptuous. And voluptuous wasn't particularly "in" today. She huffed under her breath. She would never understand the current generation's obsession with waif-like women who starved and puked everything feminine from their bodies. She was all softness and curves, and she preferred herself that way.

"I'm goddess-like," she said firmly.

With no more hesitation, she pinched off a small piece of the newly-kneaded dough and set it aside while she reshaped and then covered the rest of the large ball. She'd already performed the invocation, it was only right that she should follow through to its conclusion. After all, no good cook ever left a recipe incomplete.

It didn't take long to tidy up her already immaculate kitchen and load her dishwasher. After drying her hands, Lina poured a fresh glass of wine and wrapped the small piece of dough in a paper towel before hurrying from the kitchen. Balancing the glass and dough in one hand, she opened the door to the closet in the hall. Before she had her jacket pulled on she heard the tell-tale slap of Edith's paws on the tiled hallway. Smiling, Lina took the bulldog's leash from its hook.

"It doesn't matter how soundly asleep you are, when this door opens, here you are." Lina laughed as she snapped the leash onto Edith's collar.

The bulldog yawned then snorted at her.

"I know it's late, but I have something I need to finish, and I know the perfect spot."

Far from complaining, Edith was the first one to the door of the condo, and Lina had to juggle to balance the wine without spilling it.

"Easy there, big girl!"

Shifting the ball of dough to her jacket pocket, Lina locked the door behind them. It was early March, and the Oklahoma night was unseasonably warm. The air felt rich and heavy with the promise of spring. Lina let Edith lead her into the heart of the well-kept courtyard. A shadow flitted overhead calling Lina's attention upward. A full moon sat high in the sky, round and bright and the color of whipped butter. She stared at it. What an odd shade of yellow. It lent the familiar surroundings of her English Tudor–style condo complex an ethereal glow, casting mundane hedges and sidewalk edges into new and slightly sinister roles.

"Oh, please. I must be having a *Lord of the Rings* moment," Lina admonished herself. "Dolores was right. I've taken too many trips to the IMAX to drool over Aragorn."

The ritual and the dough-making frenzy had obviously gone to her head if she was imaging sinister shapes around her well-kept condo complex.

"I'll have to tell Anton all about this," she mumbled to herself. "Maybe I can finally convince him to share his Xanax with me."

Actually, now that she was outside and the spell/recipe book was neatly stacked with the other cookbooks in her living room, she was beginning to feel a little foolish.

"Maybe I should have had more wine before this part of the recipe," she told Edith, who flicked her ears back at her and huffed, but kept on winding her way along their familiar path. "Or maybe I'm just exhausted and I need to go to bed."

They were coming to her favorite part of the complex—the grand marble fountain that sat squarely in the middle of the cobblestone courtyard. Year-round it spouted water in an impressive geyser that cascaded down three delicately curved, bowl-like tiers. Actually, it was the fountain that had convinced Lina to purchase the condo. During the summer Lina found the area around the fountain, with its cool cobblestones and old oak shade trees, even more refreshing than the pool, and a good deal less crowded. In the winter months the fountain, like the pool, was heated, and Lina had enjoyed many an Oklahoma winter afternoon swathed in blankets, feet tucked under her, while she read to the musical sound of falling water.

"This is it. The perfect special place," Lina told Edith Anne, who was snuffling around an azalea bush. "Stay there, this won't take long."

She dropped the bulldog's leash. Obediently, Edith planted her wide bottom on the ground, then seemed to reconsider and, with a doggy sigh, relaxed into a full, stretched-out recline, her half-closed eyes watching Lina with sleepy semi-interest.

The nearest oak was also the biggest. Lina approached it carefully in the buttermilk moonlight, careful not to trip over the intricate knots of exposed roots that proliferated the area around the base of the tree. Unexpectedly, they seemed ominous, calling to life visions of grasping tentacles and writhing snakes.

"Stop being ridiculous," Lina said in the tone she reserved for generic perfume solicitors. The sound of her voice dispelled the disturbing vision, and the oak shifted back to its familiar, solid self.

Lina extracted the small lump of dough from her pocket. She looked around the courtyard. No one was stirring; even Edith Anne had stopped watching her and was snoring softly. Lina crouched down and placed the dough ball in the vertex of two especially thick roots that intersected at the base of the tree.

Lina looked around her again. Certain that except for the snoring bulldog she was alone, she dipped her fingers into the glass of wine and flicked red drops over the dough.

It felt good. Lina smiled. It felt right. Still smiling, she wet her fingers again and playfully rained the excellent Chianti Classico all over the base of the ancient tree. Stifling girlish giggles, she continued splattering wine on the gnarled roots until the crystal goblet was empty. Then she squared her shoulders and cleared her throat.

"I would like to say something before closing this remarkable recipe ritual."

Lina grinned at her intentional alliteration, but she quickly schooled her features to appear more sober. She certainly hadn't meant any disrespect, but grinning and giggling at the end of a goddess invocation ritual would probably be considered a faux pas. Lina began her speech again.

"Demeter!" The word came from Lina's mouth with such power that the sound of the goddess's name carried across the courtyard, making Edith stir and flutter her eyes before resituating her stocky body and continuing her nap. Lina swallowed hard and softened her voice. "My name is Carolina Francesca Santoro, and I want you to know that I have enjoyed your ritual very much. I think the dough will make excellent pizza, and I'm looking forward to trying it."

Her impromptu speech reminded her of the reason why she had felt the need to experiment with the recipe, and while remembering Lina was amazed that she had ever forgotten. The lines on her forehead deepened and her shoulders slumped.

"I hope it's good. No, I more than hope it's good—I *need* it to be good. I can't lose my bakery. It's my responsibility; too many people depend on me. Demeter, if you're listening, please send me some help.

In return I'll . . . I'll . . ." Lina stuttered and then blurted, "well, damnit, I don't know what the hell I could possibly do for you in return." She shrugged her shoulders. "And I apologize for my use of common English swear words. How about if I just say, one mature woman to another, that I would really appreciate your help and I would return the favor if I could."

Satisfied, Lina closed her eyes, visualizing the final words of the ritual.

"O goddess of the plentiful harvest, of strength and power and wisdom, I give You greeting, and honor, and thanks. Blessed Be!"

At the words, *blessed be*, Lina felt an overwhelming sense of release, as if—Lina's lips twitched—as if her prayer had been heard and answered. Logically, she knew that wasn't really possible, but she did believe in the power of positive thinking . . . self-fulfilling prophecies . . . feng shui. Her lips tilted upward. She believed in the power of *la magia dell' Italia*.

Lina drew in a deep, cleansing breath, and her eyes sprang open in surprise. Enticing sweetness filled her nose. What was that smell? Lina took another deep breath. It was wonderful! Scenting the soft wind like a wary deer, she sniffed her way around the oak. And came to an abrupt halt. In between a tangle of roots halfway around the tree grew one perfect flower. Its stem was thick and long, the width of a garden hose, and it stretched up almost two feet until it morphed into a huge bell-shaped cup with scalloped edges.

"Oh! Aren't you lovely. It's too early for a daffodil." Lina shook her head and automatically corrected herself. "I mean narcissus." She could hear her grandmother scolding her, *not by their common name,* bambina, *call the* bei fiora—*beautiful flowers—by their formal name, narcissus.*

But by whatever name she called it, the flower was certainly unusual, and for more reasons than just its early blooming. Transfixed, Lina squatted in front of it. The blossom was a luminous, creamy yellow color, as if a piece of the moon had fallen to earth and bloomed that night. She couldn't remember ever seeing a narcissus of that size. If she balled up her fist it would fit neatly inside the cupped bloom. And its perfume! Lina leaned forward and took a long sniff. She hadn't remembered any of her grandmother's flowers smelling like this one. What was that scent? It was illusively familiar, but she couldn't quite name it. Lina took another deep breath. The fragrance made her heart beat and the blood rush through her body. There was something about that fanciful aroma that filled her with a youthful yearning, and suddenly she remembered her first kiss. It had been many years, but she easily recalled that the kiss had contained this same sweetness. She sighed. The blossom smelled like what would happen if moonlight and the innocence of spring had mated to create a flower.

Lina blinked in surprise and huffed through her nose, sounding a little like her dog. She was certainly waxing poetic and romantic. How bizarre and unlike herself—well, unlike herself at forty-three anyway. She used to be romantic and dewy-eyed and blah, blah, love, blah, blah. Until life and experience and men had cured her naïveté. Lina narrowed her eyes at the flower. Romance? Why was she thinking about *that*? She'd sworn off romance on her fortieth birthday. Finished. Through. Ka-put. And she hadn't regretted her decision.

A vision of her last date flashed back through her mind—Mr. Fifty-Something Successful Businessman: divorced twice, four dysfunctional kids—two from each marriage. The best thing that she could say about him was that he was consistent. During their entire very expensive dinner at one of Lina's favorite restaurants he had whined and complained about how much child support and alimony he had to pay his two hateful, money-grubbing ex-wives, who had never understood or appreciated him. Before the main course had been served Lina had found herself empathizing with the ex-wives.

And that experience summed up men in her age range. It was a cliché that was, unfortunately, true. The good ones were taken—or gay. The rest of them were balding has-beens who spent their dates complaining about past choices. Or, like her ex-husband, had chosen newer, more perfect women as their mates. Women who were able to nurture more than stray pets. Women who were able to bear children . . .

Stop it! Lina scolded herself. Why was she thinking about *that*? Her ex-husband was ancient history, as was her desire to date and play the game. Quite frankly Lina would rather stay home and bake a cake. Or walk her dog. Or pet her cat (if he decided he was in the mood for petting).

No, she hadn't regretted giving up on romance. Her eyes refocused on the unusual narcissus. It was just a flower, just a beautiful, early-blooming flower. And she had just had a very long, weird day, which explained why she was feeling odd. Maybe she was hormonal. She made a mental note to ask her mom about *the change* next time they talked.

A teasing breeze stirred the narcissus, bringing another wave of its sweet aroma to Lina. Just one more little sniff. She'd take one more smell, then she'd collect Edith Anne and take herself off to bed where she belonged. Balancing on the balls of her feet, she leaned forward, cupping the heavy blossom in her hands. As she brought her face closer to the flower, the area within the bell-shaped bloom rippled.

Lina blinked. What the hell? She leaned closer and peered into the open cup.

Like water down a sluiceway, shock caused all feeling to drain from her body. She was staring, not into the center of the narcissus, but straight into the face of an amazingly beautiful young woman. The woman's large violet-colored eyes were opened wide, her hair was in wild disarray, and her lovely lips were rounded as if she had been caught in the middle of uttering a terrified *Oh!*

Lina tried to move, but her body refused to obey her. She was frozen, transformed into a living statue. Fear pulsed through her and she felt her heart leap painfully in response, and then it was as if she was being pulled from her body by a giant vacuum cleaner. For a moment she was actually able to look back at the immobile shell that was her physical self before she was yanked forward and into the blindingly brilliant light that pulsed at the center of the expanding narcissus blossom. Lina's mind rebelled as her consciousness whirled down the circular shaft.

She tried to cry out. She tried to stop. She tried to breathe, but there was nothing except the sense of motion and a wrenching feeling of displacement. Just as she was sure she would go mad, Lina felt an enormous tug and she popped from the shaft and slammed into something. Tears swamped her eyes, making it impossible for her to see more than vague, blurred images.

Automatically, she gasped for air. Drenched in vertigo, her arms flailed around until they collided with the grassy earth against which her butt was resting. Struggling to anchor herself, she let her body collapse, arms spread wide as if she was embracing the ground. Lina pressed her face into the grass. She was shaking and panting, and she seemed to be trapped in some kind of silken netting.

"Get it off me! Get it off!" Still panicking she tore at what was entrapping her. "Ouch! *Merda!*"

The distinctive pain of roughly pulled hair penetrated her frenzy at the same instant her vision cleared. She was, indeed, lying against the grass-covered ground. Her hands were tangled in a thick mass of rich mahogany-colored hair that was so long that it fell to her waist.

Her waist. Blinking away tears, Lina gazed down at "herself."

Sucking in a deep breath Lina opened her mouth and screamed her best slasher-horror-movie-girl scream.

Chapter Five

"Calm yourself! There is nothing here for you to fear."

Lina tore her eyes from the body that was decidedly *not* hers. A few feet from where she lay were two women. The one who had spoken was tall, thin and had gray hair that was pulled back into a severe knot. She stood beside the silent one. The silent one sat on—Lina blinked rapidly, her mind not wanting to believe what her eyes reported—an enormous throne. She was draped in cream-colored linen. Her blond hair was wrapped around her head in a series of complicated braids, and an intricate crown of delicately carved golden—Lina blinked again, but the image remained the same—golden ears of corn rested regally atop her head. In one hand she held a long scepter, in the other she had a gilded goblet. The seated woman was beautiful, but her beauty was fierce and serious, what history described as a "handsome" woman. She was watching Lina intently.

"Welcome to my realm, Carolina Francesca Santoro, daughter of man."

Questions warred in Lina's brain and she struggled to shift through the teeming confusion and the lingering sense of physical displacement. She was breathing in short, panicked gulps. Lina glanced down. Through the silky shift she was wearing she could clearly see the mauve-colored nipples of her perfectly shaped breasts thrusting against the thin material barrier.

Even twenty years ago her breasts had never looked like those. Those breasts looked like they belonged on the pages of an airbrushed magazine. Real flesh couldn't be that perfect.

"Oh, God! I think I'm going to throw up," Lina said. Then she pressed her hand against her mouth. That wasn't her voice. Where was the soft mixture of Oklahoma twang and her grandmother's Italian influence? "What has happened to me?" she gasped.

"As Eirene has said, there is nothing here for you to fear."

The queenly woman's voice was deep and comforting. Lina clung to it and willed herself to slow her breathing. Puking wouldn't help things. As her hyperventilation ceased, her mind began working again, and the woman's words registered.

"You said your 'realm.' What did you mean? Where am I?"

Demeter took her time before answering the human. Already she mourned the absence of her daughter's soul. She wanted nothing so much as to call Persephone back and know her child was close to her, protected and safe. But that was the problem. She had kept her daughter too protected. It was time Demeter allowed, or in this case, insisted, that she grow. And the goddess had made a decision; she was bound by her word—even if it had only been given to herself.

"My realm is never-ending—from the smallest garden plot to the vastness of the great fields as they grow ready for the harvest, there you will find what is mine. As to where you are . . ." She hesitated, considering. "Is Olympus a name you recognize?"

In short, jerky movements Lina nodded. "Yes. In mythology it's where the gods lived."

"Why is it that mortal daughters always say gods and leave out goddesses?" The woman who stood beside the throne asked the other.

"That I cannot answer." She shrugged her broad shoulders. "Mortals do not always make sense, especially mortals from Forgotten Earth."

"Wait, stop," Lina brushed the thick hair out of her face, forcing herself to ignore the fact that it was the wrong color, length and texture to be hers. "I need to know where I am, who you are, and what is going on."

In unison the women's heads turned to her.

"Mortal, do you not know to whom you speak?" The gray-haired woman whose name was Eirene bowed her head in the queen's direction. When Lina didn't answer, she frowned, but continued speaking. "You are in the presence of Demeter, Great Goddess of the Harvest."

Demeter did not smile, but her blue eyes softened. "How could you not know me? Was it not my assistance you invoked?"

Dumbfounded, Lina felt her jaw unhinge. It had to be a dream—a horrible, amazing, realistic dream. When she woke up she'd have to remember not to eat whatever she'd eaten before she'd gone to bed. Or maybe it was hormones. Again. She really needed to have a long talk with her mom.

"Carolina Francesca Santoro," Demeter said, sounding disturbingly like her grandmother. "You are not dreaming, nor do you hallucinate."

"Can you read my mind?"

"I am a goddess, and your expression is quite transparent." She gestured at a spot in front of her. Instantly a gilded chair materialized. "Come closer. We have much about which we must speak, and our time is limited."

Unsteadily, Lina stood. Her steps should have been halting and awkward, but her body seemed to have a rhythm of its own. On delicate feet she stepped forward and then sank gracefully into the offered chair.

Demeter gestured, speaking softly to Eirene. "She needs wine."

Lina watched, wide-eyed, as the gray-haired Eirene nodded, turned and seemed to disappear into a fold in the air behind her. Within two breaths, she returned, carrying a goblet that matched the one Demeter held, and a crystal bottle of golden liquid. First Eirene refreshed the goddess's cup, then she filled the goblet and brought it to Lina.

The hammered metal was cold in her hand and the wine was icy and incredibly delicious. Its taste filled her, instantly soothing her harried senses.

"It's wine, yet it's not. It's like drinking sunshine," Lina whispered.

"It is ambrosia. Drink deeply. It will quiet the trembling within you," Demeter said.

Lina obeyed the goddess, letting the cold liquid flash through her body. As she drank she could feel the last of the sense of displacement vanish, leaving her mind clear and surprisingly calm.

Lina met Demeter's steady gaze.

"I'm in Olympus."

Demeter nodded.

Lina glanced down at the stranger's body. "But this isn't me."

"No, you inhabit my daughter's body," Demeter said simply.

Lina took another long drink of the ambrosia. Her daughter's body? Her mind flipped through dusty mental files of leftover useless knowledge from school. Demeter's daughter? Who was she? A name came to her.

"Persephone?" Lina asked. There was something else that came with the name, some vague remembrance of a myth, but the goddess's quick response gave Lina little time to ponder the elusive thought.

"Yes. My daughter is the Goddess Persephone." Demeter nodded solemnly.

"If I'm here"—Lina pointed at herself—"then where is she?" But the chill of dread that shivered through her body answered the question before she heard the goddess's voice form the words.

"You are she, and she has become you."

"Why?" She croaked the question.

"You invoked my aid. My daughter is fulfilling that request."

"Your daughter? But what does your daughter trading places with me have to do with saving my bakery?" Totally confused, Lina struggled to stay calm.

"Foolish child!" Eirene snapped. "Enough of your questions. There is no better way to breathe new life into your insignificant little bakery than for it to be blessed by the personification of Spring."

Lina looked sharply at Eirene. She was confused and out of her element, but she was certainly not going to tolerate that woman's offensive words.

"First of all, I'm not a child. Don't call me one." Eirene's eyes widened at Lina's words. "Second, it might be an 'insignificant little bakery' to you, but you're talking about my life's work, and the livelihood of my employees. I have every right to ask questions and to expect them to be answered."

"How dare you . . ." Eirene sputtered, but Demeter's upheld hand silenced her.

"Enough." Though the goddess's tone was commanding, her expression was open and thoughtful as she studied Lina. "Your points are valid."

Eirene huffed and Demeter tilted her head in her friend's direction. "Carolina Francesca is only demonstrating her maturity and sense of responsibility."

Eirene's mouth tightened into a thin line, but she didn't speak.

"Lina," Lina corrected, drawing the goddess's attention back to her. "My friends call me Lina."

Demeter's brows rose.

"I would be honored if you would call me Lina, too." She said, holding her breath. Had she overstepped herself?

"Then I shall," Demeter said.

"And you shall call her Great Goddess—"

"Or Demeter," the goddess interrupted, flashing an amused look at her friend.

"Demeter," Lina said, "please explain to me why Persephone and I have exchanged places."

"I heard your invocation. It moved me. No one from your world has called to me with such earnest hope in many ages. I chose to answer you."

With her free hand, Lina rubbed her forehead. "But why exchange your daughter and me? Couldn't you have just, I don't know, zapped some new life into my business?"

Demeter's lips almost smiled. "I did. I gave it my daughter."

"I don't mean any disrespect, Demeter, but what does your daughter know about the baking business?"

"My daughter has the wisdom of a goddess." Demeter's face hardened and her tone brought gooseflesh to Lina's arms. "And she is the embodiment of Spring. She will honor your bakery by breathing the freshness of new life into it." The goddess's expression softened. "Have no fear, Lina. You have my word that your business will thrive and prosper. In six months the money you owe the tax collectors will be repaid threefold."

"Six months?" Lina felt like she'd been hit in the stomach. "She's going to take my place for six months? What am I supposed to do while she is being me?"

Demeter appeared to consider the question. "There is a small task you could perform for me. For a woman of your maturity and experience it should be easily accomplished." Demeter's eyes captured Lina's gaze as she mirrored the final words of her invocation. "Let us just say that you are returning my favor."

Lina had offered the deal. The goddess had accepted. And Lina the businesswoman would keep her word.

She nodded stiffly. "Okay. What can I do for you?"

Chapter Six

"You want me to go to Hell!" Lina's head was beginning to throb.

"Do not think of it in your limited, mortal terms," Demeter explained. "Hades is the Underworld. A place where souls spend eternity. There are many realms within the Underworld—most of which are places that hold both beauty and magic."

"And the rest of it is Hell," Lina said. She glanced at Eirene, who was impatiently listening to her exchange with Demeter. If the old woman had had a watch she would have been checking it every minute or so. "I'd like some more wine, please."

Eirene huffed, but she refilled her goblet.

Lina took a long drink.

"You still misunderstand," Demeter said patiently. "There is no 'Hell' in the Underworld. There are just differing levels of reward or punishment."

"Which are all filled with dead people," Lina blurted.

Demeter shook her head sadly.

"Okay, not dead people—the ghosts of dead people."

"Souls, Lina. Hades is filled with souls."

"Just exactly what is the difference?"

"You of all mortals should well understand that difference. Does your soul not quicken within my daughter's body? Does that make you one of the unnumbered dead? Or, as you would call it, a ghost? No, you are simply displaced. That is all that has happened to those who rest in the Underworld. They, too, have been displaced. Some of them will spend eternity amidst the wonders of the Elysian Fields; some will pay for their sins in Tartarus. Others will drink from Lethe, the River of Forgetfulness, and be allowed to be reborn within another mortal body. Some souls will languish beside Cocytus, the River of Lamentation, never able to cease mourning for their lost mortality. Still others—"

"Wait!" Lina blurted. "You've completely lost me. I don't know anything about those rivers or the levels of Hell . . . ur . . . I mean the Underworld. How am I supposed to manage these . . . these . . . dead, displaced souls if I don't even know where they should be or what they should be doing? It seems to me that you have the wrong woman for the job."

Demeter waved off her doubts. "That is all easily understood. Just listen to the voice within your body. There is enough of Persephone's essence left within you to guide you through any difficulty you might have in understanding."

Lina looked dubious.

This time Demeter's lips did turn slightly upward. "Try it, child of mortals. Listen within."

Lina narrowed her eyes and concentrated. Demeter had said there were rivers down there. She'd only remembered ever hearing about one. Styx. As soon as she thought the word, the whisper of a response, like a half-forgotten memory, came to her mind.

The River Styx is the River of Hate. Do not drink from it, it will cause no good end.

Lina yelped in surprise. It wasn't that there was another person inside her head, it was more like she could tap into an information source that was the ghost of a shelf of ancient encyclopedias buried somewhere in her medulla oblongata. Lina appreciated the irony of her analogy and smiled askance at the goddess, who was nodding in understanding.

"And does Persephone have this ability while she's in my body, too? Can she get information from—I don't know how to put it—from the echo of me?"

"The echo of you. That is an excellent description. Yes, she has the same ability. Though she will be mortal, she will not be lost in your world."

"And she's really mortal while she's in my body?" Lina asked.

"Of course. Just as you become a goddess while your soul inhabits my daughter's physical form."

Demeter's words caught Lina in the middle of swallowing a sip of wine, and she choked, almost causing ambrosia to spew from her nose.

"I'm—I'm a goddess?" she sputtered.

"Yes," Demeter said. "As long as you inhabit Persephone's body you are invested with her powers."

"Powers?" Lina repeated stupidly.

"Even in your foolish mortal world you must know goddesses wield many powers," Eirene snapped.

"Merda!" Lina swore in exasperation. Why did Eirene dislike her so intensely? "Could you give me just a little break here? How would you like it if you were suddenly sucked out of your world and plunked down in the middle of Tulsa, Oklahoma, circa the year 2000-something"—she glanced at Demeter and added—"A.D., with a stranger telling you that you had a six-month job to do in a place you thought only existed in fairy tales and bedtime stories. You wouldn't necessarily have to be in Hell to feel like you might just be visiting there."

Eirene blinked in confusion.

"See, it's not so easy, is it?" Lina turned back to Demeter. "What kind of powers?"

"Persephone is Goddess of Spring. She carries life and light with her, and she can share her gifts as she wills," Demeter said.

Lina's eyes widened. "You're sending me down to Hell and I can resurrect people?"

"Not people. Persephone can not return life to dead mortals. I share my realm with my daughter, so she has dominion over growing things: flowers and trees, the wheat of the field and the grass beneath you. They all respond to Persephone's touch," Demeter explained. "She also can create light. Do not ever fear that the Underworld will be a dark, cheerless place. Persephone's presence evokes light."

"So I can make flowers grow and I light things up. What else?"

"Everything you need know is within you. Look deeply, and you will find the powers you seek," Demeter said cryptically.

Lina met the goddess's gaze. She knew evasion when she heard it. Okay, so Demeter didn't want her to know the extent of the powers within her new body.

"I guess I'll just have to discover some things on my own," she said carefully.

"You have a quick mind. You will have little trouble accomplishing your goal," Demeter said.

"Then why six months? That seems like a long time if I'm going to have 'little trouble' accomplishing my goal," Lina said.

"The six months is needed for your bakery to thrive. But do not be concerned about the passage of time—it is measured differently by the gods." Demeter made a vague, dismissive gesture with her hands. "Six hours, six months, six years—it is all the same. Focus on accomplishing your goal, and all will be well."

"And that goal is managing the Underworld?"

Demeter nodded. "That is one way to put it."

"I'm assuming there is some kind of problem down there right now."

"Think of it as a problem with morale." Demeter shrugged nonchalantly. "The Underworld needs the touch of a goddess. It has too long been a place devoid of feminine influence. It is simple. Allow yourself to been seen by the dead. They need to believe that their eternal rest will not be without the love and attention of a goddess. Think of yourself as a figurehead, a symbol of female strength and wisdom. Mortal souls crave the love and attention of an immortal mother. Your very presence will begin to set things to right."

Lina rubbed her forehead again. What was going on down there? Was there the equivalent of a bunch of male spirits sitting around scratching and farting as they watched the mythological version of the Super Bowl while forcing ghostly women to cook tacky, fattening foods for them?

Demeter's no-nonsense voice continued over Lina's mental turmoil.

"Think of it as a large bakery that is in disarray because its proprietress has long been absent. Use your wisdom and experience to put it to order. And know that as you do so, you are returning the favor of a goddess."

"Demeter, the time is short. She must begin her journey," Eirene spoke urgently.

"You are correct, as usual, my friend." Demeter smiled at Eirene and stood, gesturing for Lina to follow her. "Come, I will take you to the entrance of the Underworld."

"That's it?" Lina asked breathlessly. "Those are all the instructions you're going to give me?"

"Are you a child who needs to be led about by the hand?" Eirene asked sarcastically.

"You know, if you touched up some of that gray in your hair your attitude would probably get better. It always works for me," Lina quipped.

Eirene's mouth opened and closed. Once.

Demeter covered her bark of surprised laughter with a small cough. This human woman certainly had a will of her own. She cleared her throat delicately before addressing Lina.

"I have not left you bereft of aid. I have arranged for one of the recent dead to guide you to the Palace of Hades. She will help you with the questions your inner voice does not answer." As the goddess spoke, she was striding quickly through the grassy meadow and Lina had to scramble to keep up with her. "But you must understand that you cannot allow anyone to know that you are not truly Persephone."

"What! But how will I—" Lina gasped.

"It would be an insult," Demeter interrupted her. "The dead deserve more respect than to believe that they cannot be afforded the touch of a true goddess."

"But I'm *not* a true Goddess!"

"You are!" Demeter's intense gaze captured Lina. "I have granted you my daughter's powers. Believe you are a goddess and behave accordingly. And remember, in your world Persephone abides by the same rule. No one will know she is not truly Carolina Francesca Santoro. Now you must give me your word that you will not betray your true identity."

"I promise I'll keep who I am a secret," she agreed after only a brief hesitation. What choice did she have?

Demeter inclined her head in regal acknowledgment of Lina's oath before she continued her trek, leaving behind the grassy meadow and entering a wooded area.

Lina barely had time to wonder what it was she had somehow gotten herself into as she hurried after the goddess's departing form.

They were making their way through a grove of thick trees. The breeze was light and still touched with summer's warmth, but it caused dried leaves to rain from the sturdy branches that formed a canopy of fall colors over their heads.

"It's not spring here," Lina said suddenly.

Demeter glanced over her shoulder at the woman who wore her daughter's body.

"No, as I already explained, time runs differently here, Carolina. Spring has departed from this world, and the resting seasons of fall and winter are upon us, which is why my daughter could visit your world where the growth of spring has just begun."

Lina pressed her lips together. Well, didn't that just figure. It was appropriate that it was spring in the Oklahoma she'd just left, especially since Persephone had just arrived. It reminded her of an old myth. . . .

And Lina turned to stone.

Eirene stumbled and almost bumped into her from behind.

"You must hurry," the old woman said in irritation. "We have no time to—"

She was silenced by the expression on Lina's face. Sensing trouble,

Demeter had already turned when Lina's next words sliced through the air between them.

"The Rape of Persephone." Lina crossed her arms, hugging herself defensively. "I remember the myth now. Hades, the King of Hell, abducts the maiden goddess, Persephone. He rapes her and tricks her into staying down there with him by getting her to eat six pieces of fruit." She searched her memory and came up with the name. "Six pieces of pomegranate. That's why for six months there's fall and winter—because her mother, that would be you, Demeter, went into such mourning at the loss of her daughter that she refused to let anything bloom until she returned."

Lina gulped for air, fighting down her fear. She wasn't an innocent young virgin. She was a mature, middle-aged woman, and she would not be led docilely into a trap. "You're setting me up. You want me to take your daughter's place so that it's not actually Persephone who is raped."

Lina could hear Eirene's shocked gasp at Lina's words, and before she could say more, Demeter covered the space that separated them so quickly that Lina's vision blurred. The goddess took Lina firmly by the shoulders and met her gaze unblinkingly. "You must not believe this lie, Lina," Demeter said.

"I've read the story; it's how it goes."

"Not here, Lina, not in this world." Demeter could feel the girl's body trembling under her hands. She focused the power of her will on Lina's eyes. She had to make this mortal daughter believe she was telling her truth. "I would not allow such a thing to happen. Not to my own daughter, and not to you."

"But I remember it. That's what happens," she insisted stubbornly.

"The stories you know of this realm are only the shadows of truth. Think of them as tales too long repeated by too many gossips. Truth has been twisted and changed and used to explain away mysteries. Think logically, daughter of mortals. Do you honestly believe that I would allow anyone to steal my daughter from me?"

Lina met Demeter's eyes. The goddess filled her vision. Her power was a tangible thing. Suddenly Lina was reminded of her mother, and her grandmother. She recognized in Demeter the protective, earnest tone of another mother who would do anything to ensure that her daughter wasn't harmed. And Demeter had the strength of an immortal to support her maternal instincts.

"When you put it like that it doesn't seem very logical that a goddess would allow her only daughter to be abused." Lina said slowly. "But then again, I'm not really your daughter."

A genuine smile softened the goddess's expression so that Lina saw clearly the love Demeter had for Persephone. "You stand in my daughter's stead. You speak through her lips; you are housed in her form. I would not allow harm to come to you, child."

"And the King of Hell doesn't want to rape me—or Persephone?"

"No, Lina. Hades is a reclusive, somber god. He does not cavort with nymphs; he has no mate, nor has he shown amorous interest in any goddess in"—Demeter scoffed, her handsome face twisted in disdain—"longer than I can remember. His dour existence is consumed with the workings of the Underworld. He cares nothing for love or life. And always remember that you are under my protection. All of the gods and goddesses know it. No one, mortal or immortal, would dare abuse my daughter."

Demeter's words felt logical. The goddess who stood before her exuded power and authority. It didn't seem likely that she would allow her beloved daughter to be harmed. Lina looked deeply into Demeter's clear, guileless eyes and realized with a start that she trusted the goddess.

"Does he know you're sending Persephone down there?"

"Hades will be pleased to have your assistance. Do not worry so, all will be well." Demeter squeezed her shoulders firmly before resuming her trek through the trees. She gestured impatiently at Lina to catch up with her. "It is time for you to meet your spirit guide."

When Lina still didn't move, Demeter turned and raised her distinctive brows questioningly.

"Saying that Hades will be pleased to have my assistance doesn't mean that you've told him I'm coming." Lina knew business rhetoric when she heard it. She'd just fired an accountant who specialized in it. "In other words, he has no idea I'm coming and not a clue that I'm there to mess around with the management of his realm. Right?"

Demeter's expression was wry. "You are experienced enough to understand that not everything can be spoken outright. Especially when dealing with men."

"You're right. I do understand what you're saying. So here's my request. I'd like you to send him word that your daughter is coming for a"—Lina gestured vaguely—"a little vacation. From a purely business standpoint it's always a good idea to keep the lines of communication within management as open as possible."

Demeter considered her request. Perhaps the mortal was correct. Hades should be told of Persephone's coming; even if the dour god didn't deign to bestir himself to welcome her. Still, it was only polite for one god to contact the other when entering another deity's realm.

The goddess raised one hand and pursed her lips, letting loose a series of melodic birdsong. Before the lovely sound had died on the wind, a flutter of wings burst overhead and an enormous raven circled Demeter once before gliding down to perch on her outstretched arm.

"Take the news of my daughter's arrival in the Underworld to Hades," Demeter said to the bird. "Tell him that the Goddess of the Harvest appreciates his hospitality and his protection as Spring visits the Land of the Dead." Demeter threw up her arm and the raven lifted gracefully into the wind, disappearing amidst the trees.

"Does that satisfy your sense of responsibility?" Demeter asked Lina.

"Yes, thank you," Lina said as she hurried after the stern goddess.

Demeter came to a rise in the land that signaled the end of the tree line. There she waited for Lina and Eirene to join her, but Lina's eyes were not on the goddess. They were focused on the incredible sight before them.

"Oh!" The breath left her in such a rush she felt dizzy. "I've never seen . . . this is . . . is . . ."

"It is Lake Avernus." For once Eirene's voice had lost its caustic edge. "Beyond it is the Bay of Naples."

"It's so beautiful," Lina said, at a loss for words to describe the awesome view. The lake stretched before them like a vast liquid mirror the color of sapphires. Light glittered and danced magically over its surface, breathing life to its face so that its perfect, glassy cover sparkled playfully. There were no trees near the lake's edge, but lacy ferns framed it with the soft touch of earthy green. Beyond the lake waited the ocean, its lighter shades of aqua and turquoise making it appear like it was the feminine complement to the darker, land-bound body of water.

"You have only begun to know the wonders of this world, Lina," Demeter said.

Chapter Seven

The goddess's knowing steps found a small dirt path that appeared to circle the lake. Demeter turned to her right and followed the path around a gentle bend, which led directly to the mouth of a tunnel-like opening within a large rock formation mounded near the edge of the lake. As they approached the tunnel, Lina could see that its stone walls had been smoothed and painted with fabulous frescoes depicting gods and goddesses feasting, laughing and loving. But soon the frescoes were swallowed by the darkness within.

Lina's throat felt dry. The darkness was like a tomb.

Demeter's steps didn't falter. She marched into the tunnel. When Lina hesitated, she spoke gruffly to her.

"Well, you must come, too. How else will our way be lighted?" the goddess coaxed.

"Lighted?" Lina repeated, realizing she sounded like an idiot.

Eirene sighed. "You are the Goddess of Spring. Use your powers."

Lina's brow knotted.

"Listen within, *Persephone,*" Demeter enunciated the name carefully. "Your body knows."

Ignoring her mounting frustration, Lina concentrated. Light. If she could make light, how would she do it? *Think!* she told herself. A half-formed idea flitted through her mind. She lifted her right hand to the level of her eyes. It was a lovely hand. The color of new cream, it was smooth and unlined—unlike her own, well-worn forty-something-year-old hand. If she could create light, she would do it like she had done so many other important things in her life—with her hands. And suddenly she knew. She turned her hand, palm up and cast a simple thought down her arm.

I'd like light, please.

With a perky snapping sound, a little globe of brilliance popped from her palm to hover inches above her hand. Enormously pleased with herself, she smiled past the light and into Demeter's eyes.

"That's how I'd make light."

"Well done, Persephone," Demeter said. The goddess nodded in the direction of the seemingly bottomless tunnel.

Squaring her shoulders, Lina stepped forward, leaving the ball of light hovering in the tunnel behind them.

"You must command it to stay with you," Demeter said.

The goddess was standing within the edge of darkness, so Lina couldn't tell for sure, but she thought Demeter might actually be laughing.

"Well, come on! Keep up with me," Lina told the light. Immediately it burst forward, almost hitting her head. Lina jerked back, squinting at its brightness. "With me, not on me." She whispered to the glowing ball, and it settled into a spot just above her right shoulder. "Up higher, you're blinding my eye."

The ball rose a few inches.

"Right there. Good job." The light seemed to wriggle in pleasure at her compliment, which made Lina grin at it. "Okay, we're ready," she told Demeter.

The three of them started forward, this time with Lina and her light leading the way. The tunnel was large and its downward grade was steep, but the walls around them changed very little. The colorful frescoes decorated the dim expanse, appearing incongruous with their bright cheer in the midst of such utter darkness. Lina was just about to ask Demeter who had painted the scenes when the walls around them fell away, leaving only unending darkness in their place. Directly in front of them a grove of trees materialized from the blackness. Lina stared at them.

"Ghost trees," she whispered in awe. That's what they looked like. Though their branches were thick and filled with leaves that appeared to be thriving and healthy, they were white—trunks, limbs, leaves—all the color of milk. They fascinated Lina. Their beauty was unearthly and delicate, and they appealed to her senses at a deep and elemental level.

"It is through this grove that you will find the entrance to the Underworld." Then Demeter raised her voice, calling into the grove. "Eurydice, come forth!"

Lina felt her stomach tighten with nerves. She was just about to meet her first dead person. No! She had to quit thinking about them as "dead," that would only creep her out. She needed to remember Demeter's words—they were just displaced souls, much like her.

Within the grove movement flickered and Lina forced herself to remember to breathe as a slender figure stepped from the tree line and moved purposefully toward them. Lina twirled one long strand of hair around and around her finger while she strained to get a clear image of the figure, but all she could see was a blurred sense of long hair and the flow of a diaphanous garment. Then Eurydice stepped within Lina's circle of light, and she felt the nervousness leave her in a rush of relief. This was no walking specter or *Dawn of the Dead*-like zombie. It was just a pale, frightened looking girl. If Lina had been able to give birth to a daughter, this child would have been her age—probably eighteen or nineteen.

She approached Demeter hesitantly and curtsied low. It was only then that Lina noticed that her body was not as substantial as it had at first appeared. Upon closer inspection, Lina could see that the light actually passed through the girl's body and the silky, toga-like robe she wore. She wasn't quite a shadow or a ghost; she was more like an unfinished watercolor painting that had come to life. Lina felt a rush of maternal sympathy for her. She was so young. What had happened to her?

"Great Goddess, I have awaited your presence as you commanded." Her voice was melodic and sweet.

"You have done well, child. This is the final task I require of you. I ask that you serve as guide to my daughter, who wishes to visit the Underworld," Demeter said.

"I am pleased to serve you in any way, Demeter," Eurydice said. She turned to Lina and inclined her head respectfully. "It is a great honor for me that the Goddess of Spring will join me on my journey to Elysia."

"Thank you for helping me, Eurydice." Lina smiled warmly at the girl. "I've never been to He"—she caught herself just in time and switched words, hoping the child didn't notice her slip—"Hades before."

"Neither have I, Goddess."

Eurydice's voice was shadowed with sadness, and Lina wanted to smack herself in the head for her insensitive comment, but before she could apologize, Demeter spoke to Eurydice.

"Though you have not yet experienced the wonders of Elysium, your soul knows the way and seeks to take you to your eternal destination. As your soul guides you, so you will guide my daughter, and I entrust her to your care," Demeter said, her voice gentle, her expression maternal.

Eurydice bowed her head, obviously humbled by the goddess's trust. Then Demeter turned to Lina.

"It is here I must take my leave of you, Persephone."

Demeter embraced her and Lina was enveloped in the rich, summer scent of ripe corn and windblown fields of wheat.

"May your sojourn in the Underworld bring Spring to Hades' realm, and comfort to those who have felt the absence of a goddess. Fare you well, daughter, my blessings go with you."

Demeter kissed her softly on the forehead, then she turned to go.

"Wait—wait—wait!" Lina stuttered. The goddess was leaving already? Just like that?

Demeter glanced back over her shoulder. "Listen within, Persephone. Your instincts will not fail you."

Lina took a step toward the goddess and dropped her voice. "What if I need more help than that?"

"Trust yourself. Draw upon your inner knowledge, as well as your *other* experiences," Demeter said pointedly. "You life has prepared you well for this endeavor."

Lina's whisper was for Demeter's ears only. "How do I reach you if something comes up that I can't handle?"

Demeter nodded thoughtfully. "Perhaps it would be best." The goddess gestured toward the tunnel from which they had descended. "I will leave my oracle for you at the mouth of this entrance. You only have to look into it to see my face."

"But how can I be sure to find my way back there?"

"You are the daughter of the Harvest. Turn your face upward, and your steps will always lead you to your home," Eirene snapped in her usual, caustic manner. Then she met Lina's clear gaze and Eirene felt herself soften. This woman was, after all, housed against her will in Persephone's body. "Believe in yourself, child. Your strength rests within."

Lina was almost as surprised by the gentleness of the old woman's words as she was by her smile.

"I'll remember, thank you, Eirene," Lina said.

Demeter stepped forward and kissed her lightly on the forehead again. "May you be blessed with joy and magic, daughter."

The goddess turned away with a finality that told Lina not to call her back, even though her heart was fluttering nervously at the thought of what lay ahead. Lina watched the darkness swallow the two women, and she had just begun to think about whether she should send a little of her light to help lead Demeter to the surface when the goddess's staff began to glow with the brilliant golden light of a summer day.

"And she needed me to light the way for her?" Lina muttered. "Not hardly."

"I beg your pardon, Goddess, but we must begin our journey."

Lina turned back to Eurydice. The girl was plucking at the transparent folds of her garment. She gave Lina a shy, apologetic smile.

"I feel compelled to continue. My soul tells me that I have waited as long as I am able."

"Oh! Of course," Lina said, feeling instantly ashamed of herself. Here she was, fretting about Demeter leaving her alone to get started on a temporary job that she had been assured she could complete with no problem, and little, dead Eurydice was . . . well . . . dead. Poor kid. "I'm ready. Let's go."

Instantly, the young spirit re-entered the grove of white trees with Lina following close behind. The little ball of light enveloped them in a soft, clear glow, and as it touched the trees that surrounded them the light caught in the branches and sparkled between the leaves making them shine like they were faceted jewels.

"They're so beautiful," Lina said quietly.

"I think it is your light that makes them appear so, Goddess," Eurydice said in the timid voice of a child.

"Oh, I don't know, I'll bet they have always been beautiful." As soon as she had spoken the words, the limbs above Lina began to ripple, as if in response to her compliment, and more faceted leaves shimmered and glistened in her light. She smiled at her guide and pointed up into the forest of diamonds. "They were here a long time before I came. My light is just allowing them to be seen as they really are."

"Forgive me, Goddess. I did not mean to speak out of turn."

Lina pulled her gaze from the shining leaves. Eurydice had ducked her head, as if she was waiting for some kind of chastisement.

"You didn't speak out of turn. You just made an observation. I want you to feel free to talk to me. Honestly, I'm already missing my"—Lina paused. She'd almost said "life" or "bakery" or "world,"—"mother," she amended, "and I'd really appreciate some conversation to get my mind off her."

"I miss my mother, too," Eurydice whispered.

"I'm sorry. I didn't mean to remind you of . . ." Lina's words failed.

"It is not so terrible, Goddess," Eurydice said quickly. "Though I have been dead but a little while, I think I am already beginning to understand."

When the girl quit speaking, Lina prompted her to continue. "Go on, I'd like to know what you've come to understand."

"The pains of the living world are already fading away. I miss my mother and . . . well . . . others, but I know that I will eventually be reunited with them. I am, after all, still myself." Eurydice held out her arm so that Lina's light shined clearly through her delicate limb. "My body has changed a little, but my mind and heart are the same, which is a great relief to me. What I mean to say is that I have found that the terror of death is worse than death itself." The young spirit finished in a rush.

Lina smiled at Eurydice. "You are very wise."

"Oh, no," Eurydice said, shaking her head quickly from side to side and causing her transparent blond hair to float around her in gossamer wisps. "If I were truly wise I would have avoided my mistakes."

Before Lina could question the girl further, they stepped from the grove of white trees to find themselves standing in front of an enormous ivory gate. Beyond the gate Lina could see a smooth, black path that wound off into the eternal darkness like a thin ribbon of night.

"We must enter here and follow that path," Eurydice said. "It will take us to Charon."

Lina didn't need to pull from Persephone's knowledge; she recognized the name of the Ferryman of the Underworld. She nodded at Eurydice and had just reached up to push open the gate when the ivory wall swung away from her touch. At the same instant, a whir of sound caused the darkness before them to ripple, and a river of mist spewed from the other side of the gate, engulfing Lina in cold, gray vapor. Fear flowed from it like a raging river. Nightmare sounds assailed her senses, reminding Lina of every bad dream she had ever experienced. Her first response was to cover her ears and run away screaming, but the calm core within her took hold and spoke reassuringly into her frightened mind.

They are nothing but false dreams, the harmless mist of nightmare remembrances. You are a goddess; they hold no terror for you. Order them away and they will obey.

Forcing her hands to her sides, Lina stood tall and shook herself like a cat ridding itself of hated water.

"Get away, bad dreams!" she commanded, and breathed a sigh of relief when the mist responded by dissipating into nothingness.

"You made them leave. Oh, thank you, Goddess."

Eurydice had moved close to her side, and now the young girl stood almost touching her. Lina could see the fear in her pale eyes.

"They couldn't have hurt you, Eurydice. They were just the mist of nightmares," she reassured the girl with a quick smile. "Unpleasant, sure, but not dangerous."

"I have never liked nightmares," Eurydice said, looking around fearfully.

"Honey, no one does. That's why they're called *bad* dreams. Don't give them another thought—they're history." The ivory gate had remained open, and Lina pointed at the dark road. "Didn't you say this was the way we had to go?"

"Yes, Goddess."

"Well, then, off we go." Lina stepped through the gate and onto the road with Eurydice following closely behind. Under the soft leather slippers that adorned Persephone's dainty feet, the road felt cool and hard. She crouched down to touch it.

"Marble," she murmured. Lina peered into the distance. "It's made of what looks like a single slab of black marble." She stood up and grinned at Eurydice. "It's not the yellow brick road, but it's sure easy to follow."

"Goddess?" Eurydice looked confused.

"Oh, it's just a saying. It means our way is clearly marked." Lina started walking, Eurydice at her side and the ball of light floating between them. "And I would really like it if you would call me by my name."

"But you are a goddess." She sounded shocked at Lina's request.

"And I have a name. Anyway, goddess sounds so stiff and formal. After all, I am the Goddess of Spring, and spring is anything but stiff and formal." Lina listened within as she spoke and it seemed that the echo of Persephone was pleased by what she had said. Suddenly Lina wondered about the woman whose body she inhabited. What was she like? Lina glanced down at herself. That she was beautiful was obvious, but was she also arrogant and selfish? Or was she a benevolent goddess who treated others kindly?

"Then I will consider it an honor to call you Persephone."

Eurydice's voice broke into Lina's thoughts, but she smiled encouragement to the girl. "Good!" At least it was a start.

They walked on in companionable silence and Lina studied the land around them. She was beginning to distinguish between the levels of darkness on either side of the road. At first glance, it seemed that everything was wreathed in the black of a starless night, but as Lina's eyes grew more accustomed to the lack of light, she could see that there were shadows and shapes within the black. The land that stretched away on either side of them reminded Lina of a dark moor, she could even make out the feather-like shapes of gray-toned foliage and clumps of thick grasses that waved unerringly in the non-wind.

Then a shape flitted past, catching Lina's eye as it swam into focus. It was an old man, bent almost in two with age. He took one limping step toward the road, but his next step was backward, then he took another forward. His rheumy eyes blinked sightlessly at Lina. Just as she was wondering if she should help him, another shape took form out of the darkness. It was a woman. She looked to be about Lina's age and she was crouched on the shadowy grass, cringing in terror from an invisible attacker. Lina's first instinct was to go to her, but the voice within echoed throughout her mind.

You cannot help them. They are Old Age and Fear. Look about you. Grief, Anxiety, Hunger, Disease and Agony will join them.

As Lina watched other spectral forms took shape along side the first two. They were wretched and horrible. The sight of them made Lina's stomach clench.

They are all a part of mortal existence. They cannot be helped. They can only be overcome. Do not tarry here.

Lina realized that she had slowed almost to a stop and Eurydice was staring fearfully around them.

"I think we need to speed up. You have a date with eternity, and I hate to be late for anything, don't you? I think it's rude," Lina said brightly as she stepped up their pace so that Eurydice almost had to jog to keep up with her. She heard Grief wailing behind them and she shuddered, refusing to look back. Instead she focused her attention on several softly glowing shapes that hovered down the path in front of them. Even though she couldn't see them clearly yet, Lina didn't feel any danger or animosity from them, and her inner voice was quiet, which she took as a positive sign.

"Wonder what those are up there?" Lina asked, making light conversation with the silent girl at her side.

"I think they are others like me," Eurydice said slowly.

Lina stifled the instant trepidation she felt. She was, after all, in the Land of the Dead. Did she actually think that she wouldn't come across any dead people? That was a little like thinking she wouldn't find yeast in a bakery, she told herself sternly.

"Well, then we know we're heading in the right direction." She smiled at Eurydice.

"You knew we were on the right path," Eurydice said, smiling shyly back at her.

"That's because I have such a good guide," Lina said, which made Eurydice's smile widen, flushing her pale face with pleasure. Lina kept the warmth of the young spirit's smile foremost in her mind as they overtook the first of the ghostly forms.

It was a young woman, and again Lina found herself thinking that this girl, too, was young enough to have been her daughter. The spirit carried a bundle which she kept hidden and pressed close to her breast, but Lina could tell by its shape that it was an infant. The woman's blank gaze moved from the dark landscape before her and touched on Eurydice without changing expression, but when she noticed Lina, her shadowed eyes widened and her face suddenly became animated.

"Is it truly the Goddess of Spring who walks amidst the dead?" Her voice was thick with emotion.

With only a slight hesitation, Lina answered, "Yes, I am Persephone."

"Oh!" The newly dead woman pressed a transparent hand against her mouth as if to contain her emotions. She took a deep, steadying breath and said, "Then this dark journey is not so hopeless. Not if we walk in the presence of a goddess."

Out of the corner of her eye Lina could see Eurydice smiling and nodding. The whisper of her name passed like a gentle wave through the cluster of glowing spirits that suddenly surrounded them.

"Persephone!"

"It is the Goddess of Spring!"

"She has come to light our dreary journey!"

One by one the spirits turned to Lina. They came in all ages and forms, from old men stooped with age to youngsters who flitted between the shapes of the older dead with the exuberance of youth. Some spirits showed evidence of their wounds, with obvious sword slashes painting their otherwise pale bodies in crimson. Some, like Eurydice and the young mother, were unmarked, but no matter the state of what remained of their physical forms, all of them had one thing in common—the look of delight and newly rekindled hope at the sight of Persephone.

Lina was surprised at her reaction to being surrounded by spirits of the dead. It wasn't scary at all. She could even stand the sight of death wounds, as long as she didn't stare too long and instead focused on the person's eyes. There Lina could see the light that ignited within each soul as she smiled and greeted them with what she hoped was a proper display of caring.

As Lina and Eurydice followed the dark path, the number of dead surrounding them continued to grow. Lina could see that Demeter hadn't exaggerated. The spirits obviously needed her. They reacted to her presence like she was rain and they were a desert plain. Parched, they drank in her smiles and greetings. Voices whispered endlessly around her, murmuring words in languages she shouldn't understand, but did. Feeling a little overwhelmed, Lina tried not to think about the multitude of spirits. Take them one at a time, she chanted over and over to herself. Think of them as eager customers and not as the unnumbered dead.

As if sensing her growing unease, Eurydice stayed close beside her, making sure that she kept the goddess moving forward.

"I can see the marsh just ahead," Eurydice whispered to Persephone. "There we will board Charon's boat and he will take us across the lake to the path that leads to the Elysian Fields. The palace of Hades is at the edge of those fields. It cannot be much farther till we reach it."

Lina was just thanking Eurydice for the bolstering information when the pathway in front of them shuddered, and with a deafening crack, the black marble broke open, exposing an opening in the ground that gaped like a giant's mouth. With gasps of fear, the souls of the dead scattered, leaving only Lina and Eurydice to face the dark maw.

Chapter Eight

"Damnit! Damnit! Damnit!" Lina yelled, too shocked to remember to switch to Italian as the earth at her feet opened. She windmilled her arms to keep from tumbling forward, then hastily grabbed Eurydice by one cool, transparent hand and began to scramble back, pulling the girl with her. She'd only retreated a couple feet when four ebony-colored stallions surged from the opening. Snorting fire in an awesome display of power they converged on Lina and Eurydice.

"Goddess, help me!" Eurydice shrieked.

The girl's terrified voice snapped Lina out of her slack-jawed stupor. She dropped Eurydice's small, pale hand and stepped forward to meet the horses. The lead stallion challenged her with a piercing squeal, his ears turned flat against his massive skull. He was the first horse she approached.

Mentally crossing her fingers that her gift hadn't been left behind in her body, Lina dropped her voice to a playful level and held her hand out to his dangerous looking muzzle.

"Well, hello there you handsome boy."

The horse faltered, mid-fiery snort. His ears pricked forward so that he could be certain to catch every sound she uttered.

Lina smiled. Obviously, her gift belonged to her soul and not to her body. She breathed a sigh of relief. No matter how large or fierce, they were just horses, and like all animals, horses adored her. Lina made soothing clucking sounds with her tongue against her teeth as she caressed the magnificent animal's velvet muzzle.

"You certainly are a big boy," Lina cooed.

"Who dares to disturb the souls of the dead and to touch the dread steeds of Hades!"

The voice broke like a whip over her, and Lina jerked her hands away from the smooth muzzle, glancing guiltily up in the direction from which the deep voice originated.

Lina swallowed hard. She was such an idiot! She'd been so entranced by the horses that she hadn't even thought to look behind them.

The man stood in a brilliant silver chariot the color of moonbeams, holding a large, two-pronged spear in one hand and thick leather reins in his other hand. His massive body was swathed from neck to ankle in night-colored robes. A cloak rippled around him and Lina's little light illuminated its folds so that it shone with shades of deep purple and royal blue. His long hair was tied back in a thick queue. It, too, was black and the light showed its slick sheen. Lina's eyes moved to his face. His coloring was dark and exotic; his skin was a mixture of gold and bronze that gave him the intimidating look of a statue that had come alive. He was staring at her with eyes that blazed above high cheekbones and a strong, well-defined chin. His nose was hawkish. He was stern and angry and . . . magnificent.

God, she thought numbly, he's like an ancient Batman—minus the mask and the Batmobile.

"I'm sorry," Lina said nervously. "I-I didn't mean to disturb anything. The dead were just, well, glad to see me and—"

One of the "dread steeds," obviously annoyed at the lack of attention, blew in her face, obscuring her view of the man. Automatically, Lina clucked reassuringly to him and stroked the muzzle he offered.

"Again, you dare to touch a dread steed." This time the deep voice sounded more confused than angry.

Lina had to shove the stallion's head aside so that she could peer at him from under the horse's neck. "Apparently, he doesn't realize he's a dread steed." She smiled fondly at the horse and it lipped her shoulder.

The other three animals had begun to stretch their heads toward her, too, eager for their share of the attention. "Well, that's not totally true. It's just that I have this *thing* with animals. They like me. A lot." She reached another muzzle and gave it a quick caress. "So I'm sure that they're still dread steeds, just not at this particular moment."

And then the man's words really registered in her mind. He'd said "the dread steeds of Hades." Lina ducked her head behind the nearest horse. *Merda!* That meant that Batman was really Hades. She closed her eyes and counted to three, took a deep breath and stepped back from the knot of horsy affection.

"I'm sorry, it's rude of me not to introduce myself. I'm Persephone, Demeter's daughter. I think she sent word that I was coming for a visit." The man's eyes widened, but he didn't respond. Lina barreled on. "I really didn't mean to disturb the dead. I apologize if I've done something I shouldn't have." Still the god remained silent. Lina's stomach fluttered. "You must be Hades. I hope I haven't come at an inconvenient time."

"I recognize you now, Goddess," Hades said. "And I did receive word of your coming."

Lina felt a little start of surprise. He recognized her? She hadn't expected Hades to know Persephone. Demeter certainly hadn't mentioned anything about the two of them knowing each other.

"You did no harm. It is just that the Underworld is not usually visited by immortals. The dead are not used to the presence of other gods," he said stonily.

Lina tried to smile. His hard gaze made her want to squirm uncomfortably.

"It was my mother's idea," Lina said, and was instantly sorry. She sounded like an insecure teenager. Quickly, she added, "And I thought it would be nice to get away."

Hades raised one dark brow, just as Lina imagined Batman would have done.

"Demeter told me that the Underworld is filled with magic and beauty," Lina repeated truthfully. "I'd like to see for myself."

"There are many wonders in my realm that go unnoticed by the immortals above," Hades said slowly.

"Then you don't mind if I visit?"

Hades studied her with dark, unreadable eyes. But before he could answer the stallion nearest to Lina suddenly laid his ears flat against his head, and with a squeal he bared his teeth dangerously at the small, pale form that had been silently approaching Lina.

With a terrified cry, Eurydice leapt back. Instantly, Lina stepped into the stallion's path, causing the huge animal to pull up short in his attack.

Hands on hips she scolded the massive beast. "That was a very mean thing to do! Eurydice was just coming to me. She wasn't doing anything wrong. I'm ashamed of you. You four have already scared away the rest of the souls. I'd think you'd know better."

Chagrined, the horse hung his head and blinked at Lina with the sad, calf eyes.

Incredulous, Hades watched as the young goddess chastised his steed. What had she done to the horse? Had she cast a spell over him? Hades' gaze took in the other three stallions, each of whom was hanging his head and looking lovingly at Persephone. What kind of magic did the Goddess of Spring possess? He had glimpsed her only a few times in his infrequent forays to the surface. What he had observed was a beautiful, but frivolous, fun-loving young goddess, and he had given her as little thought as he gave the rest of the immortals. Yet the woman before him appeared calm and carried herself with a definite air of maturity. And she had enchanted his steeds. Hades shook his head in disbelief. What was this feeling she had awakened within him? Curiosity? It had been eons since he had felt even mildly curious about another living being. How intriguing . . . the very thought of him finding the Goddess of Spring interesting made him want to laugh aloud. He abruptly made his decision and forced himself to speak before he could change his mind.

"You are welcome in the Underworld, Persephone," Hades said.

Lina looked up in surprise. The god's voice had changed, as had his somber expression. He was looking at her with an intensity that made his gaze feel almost tangible. His eyes were no longer remote and unreadable, they glistened with what she would almost swear was curiosity and, if she hadn't known he was God of the Underworld, something she recognized as good humor.

Batman—sexy, sexy Batman—on a good day when the Joker wasn't bugging him, and so damn male that he radiated power. Demeter's hasty description of Hades had definitely not prepared her for the reality of the god's presence.

"Well, thank you, Hades. I appreciate your hospitality," she said a little breathlessly.

"Come, then. I will show you to my palace." Hades gestured magnanimously to the open space next to him in the chariot.

Lina glanced back at the silent horses. "First, I better make things right with them."

Hades watched as without any hesitation or sign of fear, the goddess stepped into the middle of the massive stallions so that she was surrounded by living horseflesh. An odd little ball of light followed her, causing the animals' slick, black coats to glisten and shine while encasing the goddess in an illuminated globe so that her face was clearly visible and Hades could see her grinning girlishly as she patted each horse in turn. Where was the flighty, self-absorbed Goddess of Spring? This well-composed, horse-loving Persephone was not what he had expected.

"Oh, you're all good boys. Don't be sad. I'm not mad at you."

Hades still found it hard to believe, but his dread steeds nuzzled her and whickered softly. Like they were tame ponies.

Finally, laughing, she emerged from the nest of horseflesh. She felt his eyes on her again, and smiled up at him. "I love horses, don't you?"

The radiant expression on her face caused his stomach to tighten. Had a goddess ever looked at him like that before? His mouth felt dry. He swallowed hard.

"Yes."

Lina thought she could get lost in that one simple word spoken in

Hades' rich, deep voice. For some ridiculous reason, she felt her cheeks warm with a blush, and she turned hastily back to stroke the stallion's slick neck. What the hell was wrong with her? She seriously needed to get a grip on herself. She was a grown woman. There was no reason for her to get all limp-kneed and goo-goo eyed just because Hades hadn't turned out to be a bore or a troll. She glanced at him. Jeesh, he made her nervous. "Reclusive and somber," *merda!* Demeter had failed to add gorgeous.

She needed to start thinking of him as nothing more than an upper-level executive. An incredibly powerful upper-level executive. Business—this trip was meant to be business. Remember that, she told herself firmly.

"I'm ready now." She straightened her shoulders, gave the stallion a final pat, started to join Hades and then stopped. She had just been scolding the horses for their bad behavior, and here she was, reacting to the presence of a handsome man like a silly schoolgirl and forgetting all of her own manners.

"Eurydice," she called, stepping away from the chariot so that she could see the spirit who was standing nervously a little way down the path. "Come on. Hades is going to give us a ride."

Eurydice's eyes were wide and frightened. "Oh, no, Goddess. I could not go with . . ." The young spirit's words ran out, leaving her silent and helpless.

Lina thought she looked like a pale, frightened little fawn.

"Honey, I wouldn't think of going on without you. You've been a wonderful guide and a good friend." Lina turned to Hades. "Isn't your palace on the way to the Elysian Fields?"

Hades nodded.

"So it would be fine for Eurydice to ride there with us?" She asked the god.

Instead of answering her, Hades shifted his attention to the little spirit and spoke directly to Eurydice.

"Do not fear, child. You may join your goddess."

His voice had changed again. Lina thought that now he sounded like a father coaxing a shy child to his side. His expression had softened, too, and gone was the intense look with which he had been studying her. In exchange his face was kind, and he looked suddenly approachable and understanding—and somehow older than he had originally appeared.

"As you wish, my Lord." Eurydice's sweet voice answered Hades. She even managed the shadow of a smile as she skirted around the four stallions to join Lina. "You don't have to worry about them now," Lina told her, forcing her eyes from Hades' shifting face and nodding her head at the horses. "They'll behave."

Eurydice sent the four beasts a nervous glance, and she was careful to keep the goddess between herself and them, even though they gave no sign of striking out at her. They were too busy whickering at Persephone and sending her adoring looks.

The lip of the chariot sat well above the ground, and Lina gratefully accepted Hades' help to climb aboard. His large hand engulfed hers in instant warmth, and Lina was surprised to feel the roughness of well-worn calluses against Persephone's smooth palm. She wondered what work Hades did with his hands, but she didn't have time to ponder the god's habits long because as soon as she pulled Eurydice up next to her, Hades barked a command and the chariot lurched forward, whipped around in a tight circle and plunged back through the jagged opening in the earth. Glancing over her shoulder, Lina caught sight of the crevice closing behind them. She gulped and drew Eurydice in front of her and grasped the smooth ridge that ran along the top of the chariot, effectively locking her within the circle of her arms so that she could be sure the girl didn't tumble off.

Lina's ball of light kept pace with them, hovering just above her right shoulder, but its illumination wasn't needed. Torches blazed from silver wall sconces, lighting the smooth, high sides of the dark tunnel through which they flew.

"It is like the Bat Cave."

Lina realized she'd spoken her thoughts aloud when Hades' head tilted down in her direction and he gave her a questioning glance.

"I was just wondering if there were bats in this cave," Lina said sheepishly.

"Yes, often there are," Hades said.

Lina watched his cape billow behind him. "I'll bet they're big bats," she said wryly.

Hades snorted, sounding much like one of his dread steeds. "Do you fear bats, Goddess?"

"I've never thought about it," she said honestly. "Actually, I don't know much about them."

"It is normal to fear that which you do not know," Hades said.

His tone was still fatherly, and, Lina thought, slightly patronizing. She raised an eyebrow at him. If she'd adhered to that belief system, the events of the past day would have paralyzed her.

"I don't think it's normal; I think it's a sign of immaturity," Lina said.

Hades snorted again, irritating Lina with his condescension. "Thus says a very young goddess."

"Maturity cannot always be measured by years," she retorted. He might be Mr. Tall Dark and Batman, but he was certainly going to be in for a surprise if he tried to treat her like she was young and stupid.

Hades' only comment was a piercing look. He shouted another command to his horses and they increased their speed, making further talking impossible. Lina focused on holding onto the chariot and making sure she didn't lose Eurydice's little spirit body during one of their blindingly fast turns.

Just as she was beginning to think that her hands might have formed permanently into claws from clutching the railing so tightly, Hades raised the two-pronged spear to the roof. A flash of light exploded from the spear's points, causing the tunnel to open and the floor to twist upward. With a thunderous roar the chariot shot from the newly exposed exit and, in a rain of impressive sparks from the hooves of the dread steeds, they slid to a halt.

Lina gazed around her in wordless awe. The first thought that struck her was that it wasn't dark anymore. The sky above them was bright and cheerful. Though there was no sun to be seen, it glowed a palette of luscious pastels—colors that ranged from the softest of violets to Caribbean turquoise and buttercup yellow. She could hear the lyrical calling of songbirds, and the breeze that caressed her face brought with it a sweet, familiar scent. Lina inhaled deeply. Where had she smelled that wonderful fragrance before? Her eyes moved from the subtle beauty of the sunless sky and her question was answered.

Tall, stately trees Lina thought she recognized as cypress lined the path on either side of them, but instead of growing out of marshy land, the area beneath them was carpeted, not in moss or swamp, but in flowers. Huge, moonlight colored flowers, the likes of which Lina had only seen one other time.

"They're narcissus flowers!" Lina exclaimed in surprise.

Hades glanced down at her. "Yes, the narcissus is the flower of the Underworld." The god drew in a deep breath. "I never tire of their sweet scent."

Lina clamped her mouth shut and said no more, but her mind kept circling around the irony of Demeter using the flower of the Underworld to exchange her soul with Persephone's. So, the Goddess of the Harvest had simply answered her invocation? She had just wanted to help out Lina's bakery as if she were performing a divine Good Samaritan act? Demeter had no hidden agenda, like . . . perhaps . . . a send-Lina-to-Hell-in-Persephone's-place plan? She glanced surreptitiously at the god who stood beside her. He didn't seem apt to leap on her and rape her. But he also wasn't the wooden god Demeter had described. In a very short time he had been intense, sexy, intimidating and kind. Definitely *not* a boring, asexual, disinterested god of the dead. What was Demeter really up to? Well, Lina wasn't some foolish young girl who had just fallen off the damn turnip truck. She'd keep her eyes open and her guard up. She had a job to do. She'd do it and then she'd go home.

Hades snapped the reins and the chariot started forward again. This time, Lina was relieved to note, at a more sedate speed. The woods on either side of them were thick and ancient looking. Exotic birds flitted playfully within their boughs and called to one another with melodic voices. The cypress roots were mantled in deep tapestries of the distinctive narcissus flowers, and occasionally Lina would hear the liquid whispering of a stream and catch sight of a crystal pool reflecting the watercolor sky. From time to time Lina thought she saw the flickering shapes of spirits, but when she tried to focus on the elusive images they disappeared, and no other souls traversed the road with them.

"It is so very beautiful," Eurydice said in the hushed voice of a child in church.

"It certainly is," Lina agreed. Then she glanced at the globe of light that hovered above her shoulder. Opening her hand, she held it, palm up, in the direction of the little light. "It doesn't look like we need you now." Instantly, the light reacted by diving into her palm, and with a popping noise it disappeared back into Lina's skin. Her palm tingled, and she had to force herself not to wipe it against her robe. Instead, she smiled brightly at Eurydice and pretended that it was normal for semi-sentient balls of light to pop into her skin.

"See," she told the girl, "you were right not to be afraid. There's nothing horrible or scary here."

The dark god beside them nodded in agreement and smiled kindly at the little spirit. "For such as you, child, death need hold no terrors. You shall spend eternity enjoying the delights of the Elysian Fields, or, if you so choose, you may drink from Lethe, the River of Forgetfulness, and be reborn to live another mortal life."

Lina tried to hide her surprise. Souls could choose to be reborn? She looked at the girl who stood quietly within the protection of her arms. She'd died so young; surely she would want the chance to be reborn and to live a long, full life.

"That sounds wonderful, Eurydice. You could rest for awhile. Maybe loll about the Fields like you're on a mini-vacation—like I am!" Lina grinned at her. "Then drink from the forgetful river and have a whole new life to live."

Lina's grin faded as she watched Eurydice's already pale face blanch to an almost colorless white. Her eyes clearly reflected an inner terror.

"What is it, honey?" Lina asked.

"Why can I not stay with you, Persephone?" Eurydice pleaded desperately. "I don't want to be reborn. I don't want to, even if I forget my past life I might make the same mistakes, might choose the same—" Her voice broke off with a sob and she buried her face in her hands.

Lina looked helplessly at Hades as she wrapped the girl in her arms. The god was studying the young spirit with knowing eyes.

"Be at ease, child," Hades said. "As long as your goddess remains in the Underworld, you will have access to her. Hush now, your tears are not necessary. Elysia is different for each mortal spirit—your Elysia will simply be found at Persephone's side."

Lina smiled her thanks to Hades. Eurydice was just young and frightened. If Hades allowed the girl to stay with her, that would give Eurydice six months to become settled. By the time Lina had to leave, the girl would be so used to the Underworld that she wouldn't be bothered by the absence of her goddess. Maybe Lina could even talk her into being reborn once she relaxed and gained some confidence. Lina wondered what had happened in her short life to cause the girl such pain, and made a mental note to talk with her about it when the little spirit was feeling more secure.

Eurydice raised her face. "Truly? I may stay with Persephone?" she asked Hades.

"Truly. You have the word of the God of the Underworld," Hades replied solemnly.

Eurydice's face blossomed with joy. "Oh, thank you, Hades! I promise to serve my goddess well."

Lina chucked the girl under her chin. "Friends don't serve one another, Eurydice."

The girl thought for a moment before speaking. "If you will not allow me to serve you, will you allow me to look after you and be certain that you are well cared for?"

Lina opened her mouth to assure the girl that she was more than capable of taking care of herself, but Eurydice's desperate expression stopped her words. The girl obviously needed someone on which to focus her attention. Maybe it would be best, at least for a little while, that she be kept busy.

"I'd be honored to have you look after me, Eurydice," Lina said, returning the girl's enthusiastic hug of thanks. "My mother has often told me that I need a keeper." Actually, it was her grandmother who had made the comment on the occasion of the zillionth time she had spilled some kind of food on herself—and she had made the comment in Italian, but Lina refrained from sharing the rest of the sentiment with Eurydice.

"As you will see, child, my palace has many rooms. You shall have one near your goddess." With a flourish, Hades swept his arm ahead of them and the two women looked up. "Behold, the Palace of Hades."

They had come to a place where the road made an abrupt T. The left-handed fork disappeared quickly into the thick forest, but it was the right-handed branch to which Hades drew their attention. It curved gracefully, circling a magnificent castle.

Lina's jaw dropped open. She told herself to close her mouth, but she couldn't keep from gawking like a bumpkin. The castle was built of the same black marble as was the path they had been following. It rose above them, stretching impressive, peaked towers and sweeping, balustraded roofs up into the violet sky. It, too, appeared to be made of a single piece of stone. Tall, arched mullioned windows were gaily lighted from within, giving the huge structure an inviting appearance. From the top of the tallest of the circular towers flew a great, black flag. Lina squinted and shielded her eyes with her hand so that she could see the coat of arms depicted in flashing silver. On one side of the flag was an ornate helmet; on the other was the figure of a rearing stallion. Lina smiled. The stallion looked very familiar.

"One of the dread steeds?" she asked Hades, pointing to the flag.

"Yes, it is Orion." Hades nodded in the direction of the lead horse, who turned his head and pricked his ears at the sound of his name. "He is, indeed, one of my steeds, though today he was only dread in theory."

"I think he is very dread," Eurydice said.

"There you have it," Lina called to the black stallion. Orion tossed his head and nickered in response. "Your reputation is safe."

Hades made a sound of disgust, which Lina ignored.

"Your palace is amazing. I can't wait to see inside," she said.

"It is a wonder that few immortals have experienced."

Hades sounded like a fond parent speaking with pride about a favored child, and it was easy to understand why. Lina had certainly never seen its like. Not in the old oil mansions of Tulsa, and not in the magnificent ancient structures of Florence.

The god pointed the chariot down the road that wrapped around the palace and as they turned the corner Lina gasped. Beautifully manicured gardens stretched in tier after tier behind the palace. Lovely fountains bubbled in happy voices. Hedges were trimmed to form perfect geometrical shapes. Flowers bloomed in profusion. Lina saw many she recognized, orchids, lilies, roses, and, of course, the ever-present narcissus, as well as several plants that were totally unfamiliar, but they all had one thing in common.

"All the flowers are white," Lina said.

Not that they were all the same. She hadn't realized until then how many different shades of white there could be, but all of them blazed before her—from the pure, bright white of newly fallen snow to the subtle iridescence of pearls—each with its own unique pigment range within the lightest of colors.

"It is the color of the Underworld," Hades explained. "White represents the purity of death."

"I thought black was your color."

"And so it is. Each black animal owes allegiance to me. The black of night and shadows were birthed in my realm, as is the black of that little death known as sleep. White and black—the most perfect of colors. They both belong to the Underworld."

"White for the purity of death. When you explain it like that, it makes perfect sense, but until now I wouldn't have associated white with He"—Lina caught herself, cleared her throat delicately as if she'd experienced a tickle, and continued—"the Underworld."

Hades looked pleased as he guided the chariot along a section of the path that branched from the main road. It angled around behind the palace and led to a long, narrow building made of the same black marble, obviously an opulent stable. They halted before it, and four spectral men emerged from the building, each wearing black livery garments bearing the same silver devices as the flag, and each took charge of one of the stallions.

"Treat them well," Hades commanded the ghostly men as he helped Lina and Eurydice from the chariot and gestured for them to precede him to the palace. "They have had an"—he paused, glancing at Lina and raised his dark eyebrows—"unusual day."

Lina blinked, surprised by his teasing tone. Then she said, in a voice staged loud enough for the stablemen to hear, "Well, they certainly scared me. Boy, they aren't called the Dread Steeds of Hades for nothing." She elbowed Eurydice. "Right?"

The girl stifled her smile and nodded vigorously. "Yes, Goddess!"

Hades snorted.

One of the dread steeds nickered like a colt at Lina, causing his stableman to send the goddess a bewildered look. Lina covered her laugh with a cough and quickened her steps to keep the dread steeds from embarrassing themselves.

Chapter Nine

"It's even more beautiful on the inside," Lina said, so fascinated she couldn't stop staring around her.

They entered the palace from the rear, going through an intricately carved wrought iron gate and then crossing a wide hall that led to an impressive courtyard that seemed to have been built in the center of the palace. In the middle of the courtyard there was a huge fountain, as intimidating as Rome's Fontana di Trevi, except that the god depicted rising from the waters in the back of the chariot wasn't Neptune, it was Hades in all of his grim splendor, pulled, of course, by the famous steeds of dread. White flowers grew in clumps around marble benches—the ever-present narcissus, as well as a delicate blossom Lina didn't recognize.

"What is that flower?" she asked the god.

"Asphodel," he said, giving her an odd look. "It surprises me that you did not recognize it, Persephone."

Oops. Lina avoided his keen gaze by bending down and pretending to study the little plant. The Goddess of Spring should know her flowers.

She laughed nervously. "Of course, I recognize it now. It must be the unusual light here that made it appear strange to me." She held out one arm so that the soft, blush-like light glowed off the alabaster of Persephone's skin. "It's so different from sunlight. It makes everything seem somehow changed, even things that should be familiar." She smiled at the irony of implying that the arm she held out was anything like familiar.

"The light in my realm was created by me, and it is as different from Apollo's orb as I am from the God of Light." Hades' voice sharpened and he became instantly defensive.

"Oh . . . well . . ." Lina said uncomfortably. "I didn't mean to imply that I didn't like it. On the contrary, I think it's beautiful. It's just different, that's all."

Hades didn't reply, he just watched her steadily with those intense, expressive eyes. Lina thought it was little wonder that he didn't get many visitors; his moods were like an amusement park ride. Up and down, they changed with dizzying speed. Maybe she'd talk to him about that before she left. She might as well help Hades out while she was there, as well as whatever she needed to do for the dead. Actually, the thought was satisfying. What little she had already seen of the Underworld was far too beautiful to be buried in superstition and misinformation. And Hades was nothing like the uninteresting god Demeter had described. Lina looked slantwise at him. He was a sleek panther of a man, volatile and intriguing. What Hades needed was a good marketing campaign to bring about a change in image. Lina couldn't help smiling secretly to herself. She had always been excellent at marketing.

The three of them walked slowly across the large courtyard. Soon, Lina found herself completely engrossed in her surroundings. Beautiful statuary of nude gods and goddesses dotted the area. They were crafted so expertly from cream-colored marble that they appeared to be living flesh. Lina hoped that her temporary job wouldn't keep her too busy to enjoy the garden. It would be the perfect place to sit, sip wine and daydream.

"After your journey I imagine you would enjoy some refreshments," Hades said suddenly. "I would be pleased if you would join me." Then he added hastily, as if he expected her to refuse him and he wanted to provide her a credible excuse. "Unless you are too fatigued, which would be understandable."

"I'm not tired at all, and I am very hungry," Lina smiled at the somber god, wanting to put him at ease.

"Very well then," Hades said, his expression relaxing a little. "I will have you shown to your room." He nodded at Eurydice. "And you to yours, child, which you can be certain will be near your goddess."

The little spirit grinned happily and Lina felt a rush of warmth for Hades and the compassion he was showing Eurydice. As they continued through the courtyard Lina searched her memory. What did she know about Hades? She couldn't remember reading much about him. He was the King of Hell who had abducted the young Persephone. What else? Persephone's reservoir of knowledge stirred and whispered: *Hades . . . somber, reclusive, stern . . . the gloomy god enriches himself with mortal tears.*

Lina tried not to frown as she listened to her inner voice. He certainly didn't act like Eurydice's tears would in any way enrich him. Actually, it seemed as though the opposite were true. Confused, she shut her mind to Persephone's echo and smiled distractedly at Eurydice who was chattering merrily about the beauty of the white flowers.

The massive courtyard finally ended and they came to two large glass doors, which swung open without Hades touching them.

Magic, Lina thought, trying not to appear startled. She couldn't allow herself to be surprised at magic. She was supposed to be a goddess . . . she was supposed to be a goddess . . . she was supposed to be a goddess. . . . Reminding herself, she kept up the silent mantra. While Lina chanted to herself, Hades stepped aside and motioned for her to enter the palace.

She stepped into a dream.

The floor was the same smooth, seamless black that made up the road and the exterior of the palace, but the inner walls were miraculously changed. They were ebony veined with the palest of white; day and night merged harmoniously together. Silver wall sconces held torches which burned joyously. From tall ceilings hung chandeliers—Lina's eyes were riveted upward—made of faceted stones and candlelight. The flames caught the jewels and sparkled like the sun on water. Directly above their heads was a waterfall of amethyst. A little way down the hall hung another, which looked to be crafted from topaz. Farther on another chandelier winked with the pure green of perfect emeralds.

"Jewels!" Lina shook her head in wonder. "Are the chandeliers really made of jewels?"

"They are. Do not be so surprised, Goddess. Are precious stones not found deep within the earth? And is not the innermost realm of the earth the Underworld?" Hades sounded amused.

"I didn't realize you were God of Jewels, too," Lina breathed, still unable to tear her eyes from the wondrous sight.

"There is much the other immortals do not know of me," Hades said.

"Lord, forgive me for being late. I expected you to arrive at the front of the palace."

The new voice enabled Lina to pull her eyes from the jeweled chandeliers. A man was hurrying down the hall to them. He was wearing a white, toga-like robe, much like the one Hades wore, only less voluminous. He approached the god and bowed deferentially.

"It is no matter, Iapis. I thought the goddess would enjoy entering the palace through the courtyard."

"Certainly, Lord." He bowed again to Hades before turning to Lina. "Goddess Persephone, it is truly a pleasure to welcome Spring to the Underworld."

His bow was precise, but his smile was sincere, and Lina's first impression of him was of an oh-so-perfect British valet, like Anthony Hopkins in *The Remains of the Day*, except that he wore a toga, had more hair and was dead. She smiled graciously, trying to remember to forget the part about him being dead.

"Thank you. From what little I've seen of the Underworld I am already very impressed."

"Goddess, the trunks that your great mother sent have already been unpacked and arranged in your chamber. If you follow me I will show you the way and see that you are settled in." He glanced at Hades. "If that suits you, Lord."

"Yes, yes," he waved his hand dismissively. "You know best in these matters, Iapis. Oh, and find a room near her goddess for this little spirit. She has chosen to stay by Persephone's side."

Iapis nodded solemnly in acknowledgment.

Hades turned to Persephone. "You have only to call Iapis when you are ready for refreshment, and he will show you the way to me." The god inclined his head slightly, spun neatly on his heel and strode quickly away, cloak billowing in his wake.

Lina felt her eyes being drawn after his retreating form. She watched as he disappeared around a corner. The last thing she saw was his cloak. Batman. She couldn't help it. He really reminded her of Batman. And she had to admit that she'd always been ridiculously attracted to Batman, especially the one played by pouting, angst-ridden Val Kilmer. He and Hades had the most sensual lips. . . .

"Goddess?" Iapis said.

"Oh, I'm sorry. I was just so intrigued with the gorgeous . . . uh . . . chandeliers." Lina realized she was babbling, but she couldn't seem to make her mouth stop. "They're so unusual. My breath has been taken away by the beauty of the palace."

Iapis inclined his head in acknowledgment of her compliment, neatly ignoring the fact that her cheeks had suddenly become flushed.

"Hades designed the chandeliers himself."

"Really?" Now she was intrigued.

Iapis motioned for her to precede him down the long hall to their right. Lina walked slowly, and Eurydice stayed close to her side. The servant's voice took on a professorial tone as he walked and talked.

"Indeed. Hades has overseen each aspect of the creation of his palace and the surrounding grounds. There was no detail too minute for my Lord's attention; nothing that was beneath his notice. He has an artist's eye for color and surface, and a fine sense of design. The Palace of Hades is a monument to the God of the Underworld."

Lina pondered Iapis' words. So the stern, brooding, nonsexual, mortal-tear-loving God of the Underworld had fashioned the marvels that surrounded her. He had an artist's eye and a fine sense of design.

Could a passionless, boring god have created such exquisite beauty with loving attention to detail? She didn't know about immortals, but she did have a mature woman's knowledge of mortal men, and she couldn't imagine a passionless man being capable of such an amazing creation.

"I like the flowers that are carved into the walls," Eurydice said, shyly pointing to the crown molding that framed each window and arched doorway under which they passed.

"Yes, Hades is quite fond of the narcissus flower, and has added it to much of the palace detailing." Iapis smiled at the little spirit.

"I'm sorry, seems I've forgotten all my manners today," Lina said. "Iapis, this is my friend"—she paused at the girl's sharp intake of breath when she used the word *friend* and gave her a fond look—"Eurydice."

Iapis stopped to bow to the girl. Eurydice responded with a graceful curtsy.

"I will be taking care of Persephone," Eurydice said, surprising Lina with the determination in her voice.

"I am quite sure that you will do an admirable job," Iapis said patiently. "Perhaps we should meet daily so that you can keep me informed of your goddess's needs."

"Yes, I like that idea," Eurydice said.

Lina kept quiet. She didn't want to tarnish the happy expression on Eurydice's face. Like it or not, she had definitely acquired a keeper.

"Shall we go on, Goddess?"

Lina nodded and continued down the spacious hall. On her right, the wall of windows afforded a wonderful view of the palace's courtyard. She'd already lost count of the number of rooms that branched off to her left, but she had caught glimpses of ornately appointed chambers and an occasional semi-transparent form as it glided around a corner.

Yes, the beautiful Palace of Hades would certainly qualify as a haunted castle. Lina thought about all of the A&E Specials she'd watched over the years: "Haunted Hotels of Europe," "The Top 10 Most Haunted Mansions," "A&E's Haunted Bed and Breakfast List." Another spirit-like figure flitted past the edge of her vision. The Arts & Entertainment Channel would truly love this place.

Iapis guided them down the seemingly endless hall. They made several turns, and Lina felt totally lost. Finally, they came to a halt in front of a large door that was covered with silver overlay fashioned in the form of a blooming narcissus.

"Persephone, this will be your chamber," Iapis announced.

As with Hades, the door opened without the need for Iapis to touch the silver handle.

The sweet smell of blooming flowers welcomed Lina as she stepped into the chamber. Large arrangements of moon-colored bouquets standing in crystal vases dotted the opulent room. One wall had floor-to-ceiling windows which opened out onto a spacious marble balcony. Cream-colored velvet drapes were tied back with thick silver ropes so that the view of the rear grounds was spectacular. A fire crackled cheerfully in a man-sized fireplace. Several wardrobes of dark wood stood against another wall, divided by an impressive dressing table, which was laden with all sorts of women's toilette items. But what drew Lina's attention was the huge canopied bed. It was the most magnificent piece of furniture she had ever seen. The linens matched the velvet drapes and were exquisitely decorated with silver embroidery. The curtains of the canopy were a pale color that reminded Lina of fog—almost insubstantial in their diaphanous delicacy.

"Your bathing chamber is through that door, Goddess." Iapis said, pointing to another, smaller version, of the silver-encrusted entry door. "I have had your clothing and other items put away. Please let me know if all is not to your liking."

"I'm sure everything will be wonderful. Thank you, Iapis. This is an amazing room."

Iapis bowed. "I simply followed my Lord's instructions. When he received word from Demeter that you would be sojourning within his realm he ordered this chamber be prepared for you."

"But if there is something the goddess needs, she will inform me and I will pass that along to you," Eurydice interposed quickly.

"Of course, Eurydice. I will always defer to your knowledge of Persephone's needs."

Lina noticed how neatly Iapis covered his chuckle, clearing his throat and making his voice sound sincere and serious. He really was very kind, Lina realized. She smiled her thanks to him and he inclined his head discreetly in acknowledgment.

"Goddess, will you need assistance in dressing?" Iapis asked.

"Oh, no!" Lina answered hastily, aware of the fact that Eurydice's mouth had already opened. "I can mange just fine on my own. At least this one time." She added, noting Eurydice's disappointed look.

"Very well, Goddess. When you have freshened, you need only speak my name and I will escort you to Hades."

Lina nodded and smiled like that was how she usually summoned people.

"Until then, Goddess, I will leave you to your privacy." He bowed neatly to Lina. "Eurydice, your chamber is just down the hall. Shall I show you there?"

The girl looked nervous and Lina patted her arm reassuringly.

"Go on. I'll be fine. If I need you I can call you," Lina said, without thinking.

"Of course, if your goddess requires your aid, she need only summon you with a word," Iapis said.

Lina breathed a sigh of relief that her slip in wording hadn't been obvious. She'd meant *call* her, like with a cell phone.

"Well, if you are sure you do not need me," Eurydice said.

"Yes, yes, I'll be fine. You go settle into your room," Lina assured her.

"You will summon me if you have need?"

"Yes, child, yes," Lina said, trying to be patient. All she really wanted was a chance to be alone and to collect her thoughts.

"Come, Eurydice," Iapis told the girl, which was the final push she needed to make her leave the room.

Lina could hear them discussing "Persephone's needs" as the thick door swung closed of its own accord. She almost said "I need a drink" aloud, but she was afraid either or both of them would rush back to complete her request.

Chapter Ten

THE wardrobes were filled with clothes—gorgeous, expensive, silky robes in every color imaginable—but all of a similar style. Loose, long skirts, some slit up the side and some not, high waistlines and form-fitting bodices designed by wrapping lengths of fabulous material around and draping the folds over her chest. They were all beautiful and exceedingly feminine, which was in direct contrast to how Lina usually dressed. At home she usually chose comfortable velour sweat suits or shorts and T-shirts, depending on the weather. For work she had several well-tailored, professional looking suits, some with slacks, some with skirts. She tended to choose neutral colors, so that she could mix and match and expand her wardrobe. She let her hand slide across the silky material, enjoying the feel of the fabric as well as the bright, contrasting mixture of colors. When had she started dressing like a corporate matron? Probably about the time she had given up on romance. The thought was an unpleasant realization, and she pushed it aside, refocusing her concentration on the wardrobes.

In the wide, deep drawers there was a plethora of filmy undergarments, as well as delicate leather slippers and long, feminine nightgowns that reminded Lina of something an old-time movie star would have worn.

"Well, they did call them goddesses of the silver screen," Lina whispered as she fingered a particularly beautiful wrap.

The vanity had been stocked with more makeup and hair paraphernalia than a beauty supply store.

"So this is Hell. I've got to remember to be a really bad girl when I get back," Lina muttered, picking through a glittering pool of eye shadows.

The bathroom was another marvel. The bathtub was more like a bathpool, and someone had already filled it to brimming with steaming water that beckoned, making Lina realize just how grubby her journey had made her feel. She'd take a quick bath, change her clothes, freshen her makeup, then she'd call Iapis or Eurydice or both of them, Lina sighed, and be escorted to have refreshments with Hades. What did one eat in Hell, she wondered as she wandered around the huge bathroom.

"Hope it involves more ambrosia," she told a collection of colorful glass bottles of various shapes and sizes covering a marble ledge. Lina pulled the stoppers off each of them, sniffing appreciatively at their oily scents until she found one that she particularly liked, which smelled of lilies, then she poured it into the pool. From another ledge she grabbed a comb and used it to secure the mass of hair she piled atop her head. Undressing quickly she slid into the gloriously hot water and settled gingerly against the bottom with a long sigh of satisfaction.

She could have stayed there forever, but she reminded herself that Hades was waiting for her, and she certainly didn't want Iapis bursting in on her. She hurried through the wonderful bathing experience, promising herself that very soon she would pamper herself with a really long soak.

Rising out of the water she searched for a towel, which she quickly located on a shelf near the huge mirror.

And Lina froze, transfixed by her reflection. No, it wasn't *her* reflection, she reminded herself. It was Persephone, and she truly was a goddess. Of course she had realized before then that her body was different. Of course she'd known that her soul possessed a younger, prettier woman's body. But she'd had no idea . . .

Her slender hand reached up to trace a path along one of Persephone's perfect cheekbones. Her face was stunning. Luminous eyes, a remarkable shade of violet, were framed by thick, black lashes and arching brows. Her lips—Lina touched them—were full and the color of a blush. Lina knew, because as her eyes traveled down the rest of her naked body her cheeks flushed to that same lovely tint. Persephone was lush. Her breasts were high and round, as perfect as the rest of her. Her hand moved lightly over one smooth mound. When the pink nipple hardened instantly in response, sending a sweet, tingling sensation through her body, Lina watched the lovely lips open in surprise as she uttered a little gasp. Was this body ultra-sensitive, or had it just been so long since Lina had allowed herself to have sexual feelings that she had forgotten the thrill of arousal?

And what about Persephone's love life? Was the goddess a virgin? Or did she have many lovers? Lina's gaze continued to study her new body while she considered the questions. The goddess was slender without being gaunt. Her waist curved in gracefully, but her hips swelled, full and sexy. Her legs were long and beautifully shaped; the area between them was covered with a V of soft, dark curls. Her hand moved to touch that inviting triangle.

Lina's eyes snapped guiltily up. She shook her head, laughing nervously at her reflection.

"Oh, for heaven's sake. I have to live with this body. I can't be embarrassed to look at it." Lina grabbed a towel and began to vigorously dry herself, purposefully going intimately over every part of "her" body. "Or anything else." But as she chose a new dress and absently combed through the tangle of her long hair, questions kept circling around her thoughts.

What kind of life had Persephone lived? She must have had a lover—at least one. With this body, how could she have been celibate? Was that really why Demeter had made this exchange? Maybe she wanted to get her daughter away from an undesirable boyfriend. Lina sighed and rubbed her forehead. Too much had happened too quickly. She had no idea if the gods required sleep, but she certainly felt exhausted. She needed to get the refreshments over with so she could come back to her room and really relax and refresh.

Clearing her throat she called aloud, "Iapis! I'm ready for refreshments now."

Within two breaths there was a firm knock at her door.

"Come in," she said.

The door swung open and Iapis bowed to her. "Goddess, please follow me this way." He motioned down the hall the direction in which they had come.

"Thank you, Iapis. I am very hungry."

"I believe you will be pleased with the delicacies Hades has chosen to honor you."

Lina raised her eyebrows. "Hades cooks, too?"

Iapis laughed. "You shall see, Goddess."

Lina bit her lip and followed him from the room. What was she thinking? There was probably no cooking in Hell. Like spirits would need to eat? She remembered Eirene pulling wine from an invisible fold in the air. Goddess of Morons, that's what she was. She needed to keep her mouth closed and her eyes open until she learned the ropes of her new job.

Iapis interrupted her self-chastisement. "Goddess, shall we include Eurydice? I would not want the little spirit to think I am attempting to usurp her position."

"Yes, that's very thoughtful of you, Iapis." Lina raised her voice. "Eurydice! I need you."

Almost instantly a door down the hall opened and Eurydice burst out, rushing to her goddess's side in a flutter of wispy clothing and flying hair.

"Oh, Persephone! I am so glad you called," she gushed, hugging Lina.

"Your goddess thought that you might wish to accompany us so that you could find your way back easily if she called for refreshment at an odd hour."

Once again, Lina was impressed by Iapis' kind treatment of the girl.

"Thank you, Iapis, for putting it so nicely," Lina said.

"Of course." Eurydice nodded her head several times, reminding Lina of an exuberant puppy trying its best to be obedient. "I need to know many things so that I can properly care for Persephone."

With an effort, Lina kept from sighing aloud.

"Persephone, Eurydice, if you follow me, I will be pleased to escort you to my Lord."

Iapis led them through a maze of corridors, all the while explaining, mostly to Eurydice, that even though the palace was large, it was really not difficult to remember one's way around it. Hades had designed it in sections. The frontmost part of it was designated as the Great Hall of Hades, where he held court and heard the petitions of the dead. There was a smaller central meeting area, which was where they were headed. It was linked to the guest wing—where Persephone and Eurydice were staying—complete with two ballrooms. Lina wondered briefly why Hades had bothered to build an entire wing for guests and two rooms for dancing, when he obviously wasn't used to receiving visitors, but she kept her thoughts to herself and let Iapis speak uninterrupted.

"There is an entire wing of the palace designated as Hades' personal chambers. So, as you can see, Eurydice, you need only become familiar with the positions of the different wings of the palace to know where you are."

"Yes, I understand. Perhaps I could be allowed some material with which to draw, so that I might sketch myself a simple map," Eurydice said, looking expectantly at Lina.

"Absolutely. I think that's a great idea. Maybe it could help me find my way around, too. I'm terrible with directions," Lina said. "Iapis, do you think you could find some drawing materials for Eurydice."

"Of course, Goddess. It will be my personal pleasure to be sure your friend has all that she requires," Iapis said.

"Thank you," Lina and Eurydice said together, grinning at each other as their words mixed harmoniously.

Iapis turned another corner and stopped between a huge set of double doors, which, of course, opened without his touch into a large room in which there was one focal point—an enormous black marble dining table. Directly over the table were suspended three massive crystal chandeliers. Lina squinted her eyes against their bright, faceted beauty and suddenly understood that the glittering stones were probably not crystals at all.

"Diamonds," Eurydice said in a hushed voice.

"Yes," Iapis said. "My Lord chose to hang the diamond chandeliers in this room because they cast such perfectly clear light over the dining table and complement the chrysocolla candelabrum."

Lina dropped her stunned gaze from the diamonds to the half dozen multitiered candelabrums neatly arranged across the vast length of the table. They were made of an unusual blue-green stone into which blazing snow-white candles fitted neatly.

"Chrysocolla?" Lina asked. "I don't think I'm familiar with that stone."

"Chrysocolla hides itself well within the earth." Hades' deep voice made Lina jump. She hadn't heard him come into the room. "I enjoy its unique blending of the colors of turquoise, jade, and lapis lazuli, but the reason I chose to display the chrysocolla candelabrums on the dining table is because of the stone's properties." He paused, as if deep in thought.

"What are the stone's properties?" Eurydice asked, her voice barely above a whisper.

Hades smiled warmly at her. "Chrysocolla is a stone of peace. It soothes the emotions."

Eurydice's eyes widened. "I think it is the perfect choice for a dining chamber."

"I agree with you, little one," Iapis said, causing the girl to blush. Then he bowed to Hades and Persephone and gestured to the table. "If you wish to be seated, I will inform the servants that you are ready to be served."

Hades nodded curtly and strode to the table. He pulled out a high-backed chair that sat in front of one of the two place settings near the end of the massive marble expanse, and motioned for Lina to take her seat.

"Thank you," Lina said, smoothing the silky folds of her skirt as she sat. She'd been so entranced by the chandeliers and the candelabrums that she hadn't even noticed the beautiful china and crystal dishware.

Eurydice had followed Iapis from the room, leaving Lina alone with the god. She smiled nervously at him and tried not to fidget. Hades had changed his clothes. His robes were as expansive, and just as black as the toga-like attire, but these were trimmed in an intricate silver-edged design. His hair was still tied back in the same thick queue, but he was minus the cape. Any other man would have looked ridiculous and probably even effeminate in such an Errol Flynn–meets-Zorro-meets-*Gladiator* outfit.

Hades did not.

"I hope your chamber is to your liking."

Good, Lina thought. She'd just make conversation with him. Like he was a normal man.

"It's lovely—just like the rest of your palace," Lina said. "Iapis tells me that I have you to thank for the warm welcome of fresh flowers and a newly drawn bath. Thank you, everything was just perfect. It's like I was an invited guest instead of one who barged in all on her own." She gave him a chagrined smile.

Hades thought he had never seen anything as beautiful as the embarrassed flush that warmed her cheeks, and he suddenly felt himself doing something he hadn't done in centuries. He smiled, leaned forward, captured Persephone's hand and raised it to his lips.

"You are most welcome here, Goddess of Spring."

Lina thought she might fall off her chair. In forty-three years she had never had a man kiss her hand. She wasn't sure of the correct protocol. Did she leave her hand in his? Did she pull it out? Hell! What she really wanted to do was to kiss him back. Instead, she felt her mouth form what was probably a goofy smile.

"Th-thank you," she stuttered.

Hades dropped her hand and looked away from her. Impulsive! He was acting like an impulsive fool. She was a goddess; he could never allow himself to forget that.

Lina watched his expression change and a hardness settle on his features. What was wrong? It wasn't logical, but Lina had a sudden thought that this aspect of Hades—this stern, expressionless god—was a facade he drew over himself as a cover. But why?

Merda, just listening to her thoughts made her want to slap her own face and tell herself to snap out of it! When had her disciplined, well-ordered mind begun having such delusions of romance? She knew the answer already. It had been that damn narcissus. . . .

Uncomfortable silence crouched between them.

Think of something to say, she ordered herself. She took a deep breath and tried again.

"It's interesting what you said about chrysocolla. I don't know very much about the properties of stones." She glanced up at the brilliantly lighted chandeliers. "For instance, I think diamonds are beautiful, but I have no idea about their properties."

"Diamonds are complex gems." Hades' gaze turned upward, too, and as he warmed to the subject of precious stones his voice began to lose its hard edge. "They promote courage and healing and strength. When worn by warriors they can actually increase physical strength, which is why some mortal cultures go to war wearing them set within arm-bands of platinum or silver."

"And all this time I've only thought of them as a girl's best friend," Lina quipped.

"Are they the gem you prefer?" Hades asked.

Lina opened her mouth to give him an automatic *yes!*, but his penetrating gaze stopped her. Something in his eyes said she should think about her answer more carefully. She closed her mouth and reconsidered.

She didn't have many diamonds. Actually, the only diamonds she'd ever worn had been gifts from her ex-husband. She frowned, remembering how her beautiful, expensive wedding ring, with its large center diamond surrounded by a wealth of glittering baguettes, had become a symbol of bondage rather than of fidelity. Her diamond earrings had been a guilt-induced gift given to her after one of his drunken tirades because he found the growing success of her bakery intimidating. The diamond necklace and gaudy cocktail ring had belonged to his mother—a shallow, manipulative woman who had never liked Lina. Every time she'd worn either of the pieces she had felt shackled to her husband's cold, aloof family. Consequently, she'd stopped wearing them long before she'd stopped being his wife.

When she bought jewelry for herself, she never even considered diamonds. She smiled as she thought about the lovely, dangling earrings she'd gifted herself on her last birthday. Yes, they would definitely qualify as her favorite stone.

"Amethyst," she said firmly. "My favorite gemstone is amethyst. What are its properties?"

Hades looked surprised, but not displeased. "Amethyst is a spiritual stone, with absolutely no negative side effects or associations with violence or anger. It is the stone of peace. It calms fears and raises hopes. Amethyst soothes emotional storms. Even in situations of potential danger it can come to your aid. It is a wise choice as your talisman."

"I'm so glad to know that." She grinned at him. "No wonder I've always loved it."

The goddess's beauty stunned Hades. When she smiled, she shined brighter than the diamonds over their heads. His stomach tightened. He had forgotten the power of a goddess's beauty and its overwhelming allure. His response to her was basic, his need raw. He felt his buried passion stir, and desires he thought he had entombed eons ago began to stretch and breathe. Hades felt powerless in the wake of the surge of foreign emotions.

"Amethyst matches your eyes perfectly."

His voice was rough and dangerously sexy. Lina's borrowed body responded to it as quickly as her soul and she looked deeply into the god's eyes.

"Thank you, Hades." This time experience took over and she didn't stutter or blush, she purred.

Hades was overwhelmed by the rush of heat that coursed through his blood. Persephone couldn't possibly know what a temptation she was to him. She was a goddess. She was accustomed to commanding the attention of males, mortals and immortals alike, but she was not accustomed to the Lord of the Underworld. She could not know how painful it was for him to see her there before him, so young and beautiful and desirable. With the return of passion, the old emptiness reared alive within him as the ancient difference between Hades and the other immortals reawakened. He forced his gaze from the velvet trap of her eyes.

"Would you like wine?" he blurted.

"Yes, please," Lina said, confused as he suddenly lurched from the table, shouting for wine like he was in the middle of a fish market. What had just happened? He had complimented her eyes, and she had thanked him. Electricity had passed between them. Even a young woman would not have had trouble recognizing that spark, and Lina was no young woman. She had even thought he was leaning toward her, then pain had flashed over his face and the attraction had been shattered. Lina felt like someone had thrown cold water on them.

Two servants rushed into the room, each carrying a pitcher of wine. Hades glowered, pointing to Persephone.

"Do you desire red or white, Goddess?" one of the servants asked.

"Red, please," Lina answered automatically, not caring whether Hades was serving fish, fowl, beef or pasta for dinner. She just hoped that the red was dark and rich and strong. She took a long drink. Thankfully, it was all of the three.

"Leave this wine and bring more," Hades ordered the servant after he had filled the god's goblet. The two immortals drank without speaking.

Hades studied his empty plate, wishing that he were different . . . wishing that her very presence didn't remind him of why he must remain withdrawn from the rest of the immortals.

"The wine is excellent," Lina broke into the silence.

Hades made a sound somewhere in his throat that might have been a grunt of agreement.

"I like red wine best," Lina said. Now that she had started speaking she didn't seem to be able to stop. She held up the crystal goblet and let the diamond light sparkle through it. "This wine reminds me of rubies."

Hades cleared his throat and allowed his eyes to meet hers again.

"Rubies," he repeated her last word, pouncing on a harmless subject. "Did you know that jewelry set with rubies can be worn to banish sadness and negative thoughts?"

"No, I didn't," Lina said, studying the blood-colored wine. "What else can it do?"

"Ruby-set jewelry can also produce joy, strengthen willpower and confidence as well as dispel fear." Hades noted the irony of his words. Perhaps while Persephone visited his realm he should take to wearing rubies.

"I had no idea jewels could be so fascinating," Lina muttered, looking from the diamond chandeliers to the gleaming chrysocolla candelabrum and then back to her ruby-colored wine. "Actually, I haven't given jewels much thought at all, especially lately."

Hades quirked one dark eyebrow up at her. "A goddess who hasn't given jewels much thought. That would make you a unique goddess indeed."

Lina felt a prickle of warning. Had she said too much? She had been so involved in what Hades was saying she had forgotten to remember that she wasn't herself—as confusing as that seemed.

A stream of semitransparent servants carrying trays laden with food, followed by Iapis and Eurydice, entered the room. Lina breathed a sigh of relief at the distraction. "Oh, Persephone, wait until you see what has been prepared for you!" Eurydice gushed. "I've never seen such delicacies."

Lina was already staring at the trays, and she couldn't agree more with the little spirit.

"It smells fantastic," Lina said, and watched in hungry anticipation as trays filled with color and scent and texture were laid reverently before her. There were clusters of white delicacies that Lina realized were several different kinds of flower petals, all of which had been sugared, crystallized, and frozen in perfect bloom. Olives, ranging in color from light green to black crowded against blocks of cheese that were thick and almost as fragrant as the slabs of warm bread that rested beside them. But it was the fruit that kept drawing Lina's eye. It commanded one tray by itself. Its dark pink skin had been broken open, and fat, red beads spilled forth, begging to be consumed.

"Pomegranates." Her lips felt numb.

"Do you not like pomegranates, Persephone?" Hades frowned at her troubled expression. "I can have them taken away."

Lina glanced up to see the covey of servants peering at her with large, pale faces filled with concern.

Don't be paranoid, she told herself, *it's just a silly coincidence.* "I love them. Everything looks absolutely perfect." She purposefully scooped up several of the drops of red fruit and popped them into her mouth. Flavor burst against her tongue and she sighed with delight. "They're wonderful!" She slurred through the sweet juice.

The servants let out a collective breath of happiness.

"All appears to be to my liking, too," Hades said sardonically. Persephone seemed to have cast the same spell over his servants as she had over his horses. "You may leave the platters. If we need more, I will call for you."

The servants scurried back to the kitchen.

"Aren't you going to join us?" Lina asked Iapis, looking from him to Eurydice. Did the dead eat? She had no idea, but it seemed rude not to ask.

"No, Goddess," Iapis said.

"Iapis and I have much to discuss," Eurydice added eagerly. "We are going to get the drawing supplies."

Lina smiled at the girl, glad that she appeared to be so at ease.

"Go ahead. I'll see you tomorrow," Lina said around another mouthful of pomegranate seeds.

"Oh, but you must call for me when you retire tonight so that I may help you ready yourself for bed!" The panicky edge had crept back into her voice.

"I'll be sure I do," Lina said quickly, not wanting to disappoint the child.

Satisfied with her goddess's reassurance, Eurydice was smiling happily as she curtsied to Persephone and Hades before following Iapis from the room.

"She will become more secure with time," Hades reassured her.

"I hope so. She's going to wear me out." Lina sighed.

"The dead require a great deal of care."

Lina nodded in agreement. "It's like the jewels—I had no idea until now."

Hades smiled, charming and relaxed again. "Which is why I have had the food of the Underworld set before you. Refresh yourself, Persephone, so that the little spirit need not be concerned that her goddess is wasting away here below the world of mortals."

"Ha!" Lina began heaping her plate full. "It's not likely that could happen, not surrounded by"—she gestured with the long silver spoon—"all of this."

"It pleases me that you appreciate the beauty of the Underworld," Hades said, helping himself to the olives.

"Who wouldn't?" she said between bites, and was instantly sorry when she saw his expression begin to change again. She thought suddenly that it was as if he placed a blank mask over his face so that he could cloak his emotions at will. She kept glancing nonchalantly at him, waiting for him to discard the mask and become approachable once more. For the next several minutes they ate in silence, until she noticed that the tension in his shoulders seemed to be easing and his features had begun to thaw. She took a sip of wine, considering. Yes, he definitely appeared more at ease with his fork full. Her lips twisted. He was a god, but he was still male.

"Do you mind if I ask you some questions about the dead?" Lina asked.

His eyes shifted from his plate to her and back to his plate again. He chewed and swallowed. "I do not mind," he finally said.

Lina hurried on. "It's just that I don't know simple things, and I don't want to say something that would embarrass Eurydice, or upset her again, like when I mentioned her drinking from that river, um . . ." She floundered.

"Lethe," Hades provided.

"Right, Lethe. See, that's exactly what I mean. I don't know enough about the Underworld."

"Ask as many questions as you desire," he said.

"Okay, well, the delicious food that we're eating makes me wonder if the dead can eat."

"No, the dead do not thirst and hunger as do the living, but their souls do retain the essence of their mortal life, so they carry with them into eternity their unique needs and desires. You have witnessed some of that with your little Eurydice. She carries with her fears and insecurities from the World of the Living, even though the things that troubled her there cannot touch her here," Hades replied, trying to hide his surprise at her question. Persephone was certainly not what he had expected. Unlike any other immortal he had ever known, she appeared to be honestly interested in his realm and the spirits of the dead.

"That makes sense." She frowned as she nibbled on a sugared white petal. "It's obvious that memories from her life are definitely bothering Eurydice. Poor kid. I wish there was something I could do."

"There is, Persephone, and you are already doing it. The little spirit needs to feel security and a sense of belonging. She would have eventually found those things in Elysia, but you have brought them to her by giving her a place at your side. She feels comfortable now and useful, and much less apt to obsess about lost chances and what might have been."

Hades smiled encouragement to the young goddess. She had done well by the little spirit. Too many immortals would have believed that noticing Eurydice's distress was beneath them. She was no longer among the living; therefore, she could no longer worship them. So the spirit was no longer of interest to them. Persephone's actions thus far told him that she did not adhere to that type of cavalier belief system. Hades watched Persephone ponder his words as she sipped her wine.

The goddess was a mystery to him. She had the beauty of an immortal, but she seemed so different.

"That makes me feel better," Lina said, telling herself firmly that she was talking about Eurydice and not about the warmth of Hades' smile. She was quickly becoming fascinated with the dead—and not just with their god. "Do they sleep, too?"

Hades' eyes crinkled at the edges in amused reaction to her unusual questions. He had never had a conversation like this before, and he was surprised to realize how much he enjoyed talking with the young goddess about his realm.

"They do not sleep exactly as we do, or as do living mortals, but they require rest."

"Are your servants like Eurydice? I mean, did they choose to stay here with you rather than go on to Elysia?"

"Some did, but not out of love for me, as has your Eurydice. For most it is simply that they find comfort in holding fast to the echo of their mortal lives. Others are performing duties as a part of penance for past deeds."

Hades helped himself to the fruit of the Underworld while he awaited her next question. He could almost see her teeming thoughts. She had stopped eating and was twirling a strand of her long hair around one finger, an action that he found strangely endearing.

"So, Iapis must be one of the dead who stays because he loves you."

This time Hades could not help laughing aloud. "Iapis is not one of the dead, Persephone, he is a daimon. But, yes, he has chosen to remain forever by my side."

Lina didn't know what stunned her most—hearing that Iapis was a demon and/or the effect Hades' laughter had on her.

She reacted first to the least volatile of the two.

"Iapis is a demon?" she squeaked.

At the second burst of Hades' laughter the servant's door swung open and several startled heads peeked into the dining room then retreated quickly, but not before Lina registered their shocked expressions.

"I said he is a daimon, not a demon." Hades shook his head at the young goddess.

"Oh, well, of course," Lina sputtered while her mind screamed WHAT THE HELL IS A DAIMON? Thankfully, her inner voice provided an answer. *Daimon—a spirit of a lower divinity than the Olympian gods. They are guardians and semi-deities. They are immortal.*

"Young Persephone, how sheltered you must be not to recognize Iapis as a daimon," he said, still chuckling.

The damn man was laughing at her and looking at her with the same benevolent, fatherly expression he'd used on Eurydice. And he'd just called her "young Persephone!" Like she was a silly little girl! He had no idea he was dealing with a grown woman. One who definitely did not like being the butt of male jokes. Her irritation made her forget that he was God of the Underworld and she was visiting his realm. In that moment he was just another man who had pissed her off. Without stopping to consider the consequences, she narrowed her eyes at him and edged Persephone's soft voice with her own flint.

"I suppose in some ways I have been sheltered. I've been taught to believe that one's guests should not be used as a source of comedic fodder."

Hades sobered instantly as he recognized within her eyes the coldness of a goddess's wrath. He was a fool. He had allowed himself to relax around her and had stumbled into the snare of his own fantasies. Persephone was of Olympus—he must never forget that. He inclined his head in stiff acknowledgment of her reprimand. "I ask your forgiveness, Goddess. There is no excuse for my rudeness."

Without speaking further, he stood, bowed again, and walked from the room, leaving Lina to stare after him and curse sincerely and fluently in Italian.

Chapter Eleven

"IAPIS!" Hades' voice echoed through his vast chamber.

"My Lord." The daimon materialized within two breaths after his name had been spoken.

"Go to her. When she has finished her meal, show her the way back to her chamber. Be certain she has everything she desires." Hades paced restlessly as he talked. "I insulted her."

Iapis stayed silent, but he raised one brow.

"Then I left her there. She had not even finished her meal." Hades raked a hand through his hair, causing some of the shorter strands to come loose. He looked at his loyal friend. "You know I have never been able to do this."

"This?" Iapis asked.

"This! This! This mixing with them. This insane ritual of feint and stab they require to maintain their interest."

"Perhaps you mean conversing with a goddess?"

"Of course that is what I mean!" Hades exploded.

Nonplussed by the god's show of temper, Iapis kept his voice calm and inquisitive. "And was Persephone requiring much, as you call it, feint and stab before you insulted her?"

Hades stopped his pacing and rubbed his brow, considering Iapis' question.

"No," he said truthfully.

"So you had been conversing with her?"

"Yes, yes, yes," he admitted and then reality caught up with him. He had been enjoying himself. She had shown such interest in his realm, and she had been so easy to talk to—so unlike Aphrodite or Athena or . . . his lips curled in a sneer as he thought of the other young goddesses he had known. They were spoiled, manipulative beauties who rarely thought beyond their own needs and desires. When Persephone's voice had hardened at what she had taken as an insult, he had instantly been reminded of those other lovely immortals and his reaction had been automatic. He had absented himself from her presence.

"Did you mean to insult her?" Iapis asked.

"Of course not!" He started pacing again. "I thought what she said was amusing." He gave Iapis a dark look. "She had mistaken you for one of the dead."

Iapis' lips twitched as he tried not to smile.

"I laughed at her and then I spoke to her as if she were a child. That insulted her. She reacted as any goddess would have." Hades hunched his shoulders.

"You say she reacted as any goddess would have. Then may I assume the dining room has been destroyed and she has departed the Underworld?" Iapis said.

"No, she . . . no. She remains and she destroyed nothing." He stopped his pacing and met the daimon's inquiring gaze.

"Then it appears she did not react as any other insulted goddess," Iapis said logically. "What exactly was her reaction?"

"She said that she was not accustomed to being used as comedic fodder," Hades said.

"And what did you say in return?"

"I apologized and left."

"Might I suggest that the next time you apologize and stay, my Lord?" Iapis said.

"The next time?"

Hades could feel the all-too familiar burning sensation building in his chest. He knew that soon it would spread to the back of his throat and he would spend another miserable, sleepless night. Too choleric. That is what Hermes said was wrong with him.

Iapis nodded. "The next time."

"She is different." Hades' voice had deepened and he spoke with a quiet, controlled intensity.

"She is, indeed."

"She does not shun the spirits. She . . ." Hades broke off, remembering her flushed reaction to him, the curiosity in her voice and the warmth in her eyes. His jaw clenched. "I should stay far from her for the rest of her visit."

"My friend"—Iapis rested his hand on the god's shoulder—"why not let yourself enjoy her presence?"

"To what end?" Hades rubbed his chest and shrugged off the daimon's hand. "So that I can taste life, and then when she leaves or loses interest in dallying with me—as she must—I am left with what? It is not enough, Iapis. It has never been enough."

And there it was, Hades thought as he began pacing again, the thing that separated him from the rest of the immortals. Unlike the other gods and goddesses, he longed for something that he had witnessed over and over again between the souls of mortals, but he had not glimpsed once, not even briefly, between immortals.

"My Lord," Iapis said softly, "is it not better to experience even a small amount of happiness, than none at all?"

"I was not fashioned as the rest of them. I do not know how to treat love as a plaything."

Iapis looked into the god's haunted eyes and saw there the loneliness that Hades had kept at bay for countless ages. His spirit ached for his friend. The daimon thought about Persephone. There was something about the young goddess that was unique, something besides her much-lauded beauty and her ability to breathe light into darkness. Hades must not shut out Persephone. If he did, he was afraid that the God of the Underworld would forever be closing the door to any chance of relieving the dark loneliness of his existence.

But how was he to coax Hades out of his instinctive reaction to withdraw from the goddess until her visit was complete? His Lord was not used to visitors. His existence was planned and orderly and set, not at all conducive to disturbances from the other immortals. And the Goddess of Spring was a definite disturbance.

She was also beautiful and vivacious and intriguing.

If only Hades could feel as easy with her as he did with the unnumbered dead. Iapis' eyes widened as an idea took root and grew.

"Perhaps that is the answer, Lord."

Hades gestured impatiently for him to continue.

"Imagine that Persephone is simply one of the unnumbered dead."

"Iapis, that is ridiculous."

"Why?" The daimon threw his hands up in frustration. "You're at war within yourself, Hades! You say you should withdraw from her, yet when you speak of her I see in your eyes a spark that has been absent for an eternity. What if the Fates have been kind and there has been another immortal fashioned as you have been? How will you ever know if you remain sealed from everything that is living? Give the goddess a chance, my Lord."

Before Hades could comment, Iapis cocked his head, as if he were listening to an internal voice.

"She has just called my name."

"Go to her!" Hades commanded. But the moment after Iapis vanished the god shouted his name again.

"My Lord?" Iapis asked, rematerializing.

"Invite the Goddess of Spring to join me in the Great Hall tomorrow. Tell her if she is still interested in learning about the Underworld, hearing the petitions of the dead should provide an excellent source of information for her." Hades spoke the words quickly, as if he wanted to get them out of his mouth before he could change his mind.

Iapis smiled enigmatically. "Very good, my Lord."

"TOMORROW, then, Goddess." Iapis said.

He had almost bowed his way from Lina's bedchamber when Eurydice rushed through the open door and ran straight into his backside.

"Uhf!" He staggered forward, tripped over his own feet, and fell head first onto the floor.

Lina and Eurydice stared openmouthed at each other. Lina smiled. She couldn't help it. Iapis usually looked so dignified and there he was, sprawled on the floor with his toga in the air. A choked laugh slipped from her lips.

A small sound escaped from Eurydice. It was soft and fluid and delightful. It was also most definitely a giggle. And it destroyed the last of Lina's self-control.

Iapis stood, struggling to regain his bruised pride, but the musical sound of feminine laughter more than atoned for any ruffling of his dignity, and he found himself joining them.

How he wished Hades could be there. The god so needed laughter in his life.

"I seem to have found a slight"—still chuckling, he glanced down at the smooth expanse of marble at his feet—"something in the floor which tripped me."

"I think its name is Eurydice," Lina chortled.

Eurydice tried unsuccessfully to stifle her giggles with her hand.

"Then I will have to see that I pay special attention to that slight something."

Iapis' eyes were warm with good humor, and, Lina thought as she watched Eurydice's pale cheeks pinken, perhaps something else. She gazed thoughtfully after the daimon as he bowed to her, and this time successfully left the room.

"Oh, Persephone, I have had such a day!" Eurydice skipped over to the nearest wardrobe. She hummed a lively tune and pulled open drawers until she found the goddess's nightdresses. "Iapis found some wonderful parchment and charcoals and I have already begun a preliminary sketch of the palace."

"That's nice, Eurydice," Lina said. Still considering the warmth she had seen in the daimon's eyes, she wasn't really listening as she absentmindedly nodded and allowed the girl to unwrap her robe and help her step out of it. She held out her arms and Eurydice slipped the long nightie over her head. Lina ran her hand down the length of the material. It was white satin that had been intricately embroidered with narcissus blossoms. It felt like water against her skin.

"Come over to the table and sit down while I brush out your hair. You look exhausted," Eurydice said. She had been studying her goddess and she hadn't failed to notice the dark smudges under her violet eyes.

Lina sank into the padded vanity chair, breathing a sigh of pleasure as Eurydice began brushing her hair with long, even strokes. She hadn't realized how tired she had become. The girl chattered happily about the process of mapping the palace while she worked. The sound of her young voice was almost as soothing as the touch of her hands. Lina felt her shoulders relax and her mind wander.

After Hades had stormed out of the dining room, she had finished her meal and the rest of the bottle of wine. No. The truth was first she had cursed and grumbled about men in general, *then* she had decided that she wasn't going to let another man's lapse in good manners ruin a perfectly good dinner. When she finished the scrumptious meal and the excellent bottle of wine, she had simply said Iapis' name aloud. In what seemed like seconds he answered her call, ready to escort her back to her bedroom. During their walk he had made vague, nonspecific references to the lack of visitors in the Underworld and to how little practice he had in entertaining and conversing with guests. He had said that he hoped she wouldn't judge him, or the Underworld, too harshly or too hastily.

Lina heard the real message loud and clear. The "he" was, of course, not Iapis but Hades. He was obviously apologizing for the god's behavior. The wine she had finished by herself and her riled temper had made Lina want to tell Iapis to take a particularly colorful message (in Italian) back to Hades, but the remnants of her good sense had, thankfully, kept her mouth shut.

Hades was a god and she was staying within his realm. It was not smart to antagonize him and now that she was out of his presence and had time to think about the evening, Lina was regretting her little temper tantrum. Hades wasn't a middle-aged divorcé with sweaty palms who had asked her to dinner so he could whine about his exes and then grope her for dessert. He was a powerful immortal, a being she knew little about.

And, just exactly why had she been so pissed off at him? Okay, he had been moody and unpredictable at dinner, but he had also been interesting and sexy. Iapis' explanation about his god's lack of manners made sense. He wasn't used to visitors. Obviously, his social skills were a little rusty. As an immortal being, just how polite did he *have* to be? She thought about Demeter's imperious manner and Eirene's rudeness. Actually, Hades' temperamental behavior seemed to fit right in with those two.

Eurydice finished brushing her hair, but the little spirit obviously felt Lina's tension because her soft, cool hands began gently massaging her shoulders. Lina sighed happily and closed her eyes, letting the girl's touch soothe her nerves and clear her mind.

She'd really had no reason to snap at Hades. He hadn't been making her the butt of his joke, he'd simply been treating her like the naïve young goddess she was masquerading as, and her silly show of temper had done little to prove his opinion of her wrong. If she wanted him to treat her like a mature adult, she really should try acting like one.

Merda! She'd been there less than a day and she was already messing up. Had she completely lost her mind? She was, after all, in the Underworld to do a job. At least she'd had sense enough to say yes when Iapis had extended the invitation to join Hades the next morning to hear the petitions of the dead. She needed to get her head on straight and think of it as nothing more than just another part of the job Demeter had sent her there to do. She needed to be visible to the dead so that her presence could bring them comfort. It had nothing to do with the fact that she wanted to spend more time with Hades because the dark god intrigued her, which was really ridiculous . . . silly . . . foolish.

Yet undeniably true.

She knew it. As Eurydice soothed her frazzled nerves she could even admit it to herself. Hades fascinated her, but so did everything about the Underworld. She felt drawn to him, but it was probably because she had been displaced and everything in that incredible world was so new and unique. How could she not feel curious fascination about the magic that surrounded her? And that magic naturally included the god in charge. It was a perfectly normal reaction for her to feel compelled to find out more about him.

At least that's what she told herself.

"Persephone, you're almost asleep," Eurydice said. She tugged on her goddess's arm, pulling her toward the canopied bed. "Lie down. I will sing to you. Just as my mother used to sing to me."

Too tired to protest, Lina allowed the young spirit to tuck her into the voluptuous, down-filled bed. Eurydice nestled next to her. Still stroking the goddess's hair, she began to sing a soft lullaby about a child who rode on the back of the wind to a many-colored land of dreams.

"Eurydice," Lina said sleepily.

"Yes, Goddess."

"Thank you for taking care of me."

"You are welcome, Persephone," Eurydice said.

Sleep closed gently around Lina, bringing her dreams of riding the wind while she chased Batman's shadow.

Chapter Twelve

The Great Hall lived up to its name. Lina had thought the dining chamber and her bedroom extravagant, but they paled in comparison to Hades' throne room. The room was enormous, even when judged on the scale of the huge palace. Three colors dominated it—black, white and purple. The floor, walls and cathedral ceiling were all made of the unblemished black of the exterior of the palace, as was the raised dais on which stood a massive throne-like chair, which seemed to have been carved from a single piece of an ethereally white stone Lina did not recognize. On the dais next to the throne there was a tall, narrow table made of the same milky stone. On the table rested a silver helmet which looked oddly familiar to Lina. She stared at it and realized where she had seen it before. It was the same helmet that was emblazoned on the flag that hung over the palace and adorned the uniforms of the stablemen. It winked and sparkled in the candlelight with an otherworldly beauty. She forced her eyes from the helmet to the other color in the room, purple. It came from dozens of chandeliers and wall fixtures, all made of a pure sparkling stone Lina did recognize—amethyst.

Lina hesitated on the threshold of the room, intimidated by its austere grandeur. She felt suddenly small and insignificant and very, very mortal.

"Is something the matter, Persephone?" Eurydice asked.

Lina took a deep breath. She was goddess, she reminded herself. Yes, it was only temporary, but she was goddess nonetheless.

"No, honey, nothing's wrong. I'm just admiring the room." She smiled at the little spirit.

"Ah, Hades comes," Iapis said.

Hades entered the Great Hall from a doorway on the opposite side of the room. His gilded sandals rang against the smooth marble floor, and as Lina watched him she felt her heartbeat increase with each of his steps. He was wearing the cape again. It swirled behind him, accentuating his body's long, powerful lines. His toga-like robes at first appeared black, but as the light from the chandeliers touched him, the material shone like a raven's wing with glints of purple and royal blue. His hair was loose and it fell in a thick black curtain around his shoulders. His chiseled jaw was set and his face was dark, his expression somber. He exuded raw, masculine power.

Lina's stomach fizzed. She had to force herself not to twirl her hair nervously.

Hades took the steps of the dais in one stride. He turned and was about to sit when he noticed the three figures standing just inside the entrance across the chamber. His eyes met Lina's and held.

"Persephone," he said, inclining his head slightly, not breaking their gaze. "I am honored to welcome Spring into my Great Hall."

Lina swallowed, wishing her mouth wasn't so dry.

"Thank you, Hades," she said, pleased that her voice sounded strong and clear. "I appreciate your invitation."

"Please, join me," Hades said. Then, breaking the spell that had locked her eyes to his, he shifted his attention to the daimon. "Iapis, have a chair brought for the goddess."

"Of course, my Lord," Iapis called over his shoulder, and a flutter of activity ensued. Within moments spectral servants carried a delicately carved silver chair to join Hades on the dais.

Lina walked into the room. She could feel the god's eyes on her, and she lifted her chin with pride. Eurydice had helped her dress, and Lina was especially pleased that the violet silk she had chosen reflected the color of the amethyst chandeliers blazing over her head as well as her eyes. But she knew the lovely material that draped her body was incidental. That morning as she had been dressing, she had been struck anew by Persephone's immortal beauty. Lina knew that no matter what turmoil was going on within her mind, she crossed the room with all the beauty and grace of a goddess.

When she reached the dais Hades hesitated, then with a sidelong glance at Iapis he met her as she took the first of the dais steps. He offered her his hand, just as he had when he had helped her into his chariot the previous day. When Lina placed her hand within his, the dark god lifted it slowly to his lips.

"I hope you slept well last night, Goddess."

"Yes, thank you, I did," Lina said, trying to ignore the way her skin tingled at his touch.

"It pleases me to hear you say so," Hades said.

Lina smiled foolishly and nodded. Hades was different today—more powerful and more sure of himself. And there was something else about him, too, a magnetism that today he seemed to have focused on her. Standing so close to him she could feel the strength of his presence, and she found it a little intimidating, as well as very, very sexy.

Admittedly, it had been a long time since she had been around such a tall, virile man. She snuck a look at him as he helped her up the steps and led her to her chair. Okay, so she had quite possibly never been around any man like him before. She watched the cape wrap enticingly around his body as he turned and sat beside her. He definitely looked the part of God of the Underworld.

"Eurydice, you need not remain behind. You may stay with your goddess," Hades called to the girl, who was still standing in the doorway.

Ashamed that she had forgotten about the spirit, Lina whispered a quick thank-you to Hades as Eurydice scampered across the room and up the dais steps to take her place next to Lina's chair.

"Carry on as usual, Iapis," Hades said.

Iapis nodded to the god before disappearing from the room.

"Iapis is going to the front of the palace. There he will announce that I will hear petitions. It will not be long before the first begin to arrive," he explained.

"Do you do this every day?" Lina asked.

"No," Hades shook his head.

"Oh," Lina said. "How often do you hear their petitions?"

"As often as I feel it necessary."

"Oh," she said again, feeling uncomfortable at the shortness of his answers.

Hades watched Persephone brush nervously at her hair, and the little gesture of discomfort made him realize that he had fallen back into acting like he was made of stone. *Give the goddess a chance.* His friend's words rang in his memory. Hades cleared his throat and leaned close to Persephone.

"I can sense the needs of the dead. It is not that I can hear their feelings and desires; it is more like I become aware of their increasing restlessness. I can sense when they need me, and that is when I open the Great Hall to hear their petitions."

"That's an incredible gift—to be able to respond to the needs of mortal souls."

Hades turned his head so that he could look into the goddess's violet eyes. Their faces were very close, and he could smell the sweet, feminine scent that clung to her body.

"It does not repulse you that I am linked so strongly to the dead?"

"Of course not," she said. He suddenly looked so vulnerable that Lina had an overwhelming urge to brush her fingers down his face, to soothe the lines of worry that creased his handsome brow. Instead she reached out and took Eurydice's hand. She squeezed it and smiled up at the spirit, who grinned back at her. "Some of my best friends are dead."

Hades looked from the spirit to the goddess and all at once hope blossomed within his chest with such bittersweet intensity that he made a show of calling for wine to cover his heart-wrenching response.

The servants instantly settled a small table beside them and Hades was able to collect himself as they poured golden liquid into two goblets.

Lina nodded her thanks, sipped, and her face broke into a beatific smile.

"Oh, it's ambrosia! This is so delicious. Thank you for thinking of it."

Fascinated, Hades watched her. Why was she so different? She wasn't repulsed by the dead. She obviously cared a great deal about Eurydice; she even called her "friend." And things that most immortals took for granted, like ambrosia and the opulence of the gods, Persephone delighted in, as if everything was new and interesting to her. She was a puzzle, an intriguing puzzle he was beginning to yearn to solve.

"If it pleases you so much, I will have to remember to serve it often," Hades said. He raised his goblet to her.

Stomach fluttering, Lina tapped her goblet against his. The stilted, wooden Hades who had abruptly left their dinner last night appeared to have been banished. He had been replaced by a charming, powerful god. Her cheeks felt flushed and her body was incredibly warm. His dark, magnetic eyes were mesmerizing. Feeling a little lost, she forced her gaze from his and looked around the Great Hall, reminding herself to breathe.

The light from the chandeliers glinted off the silver helmet that sat on the table on the other side of Hades. It winked with an eerie glow that somehow made it hard to focus on. She felt the god's eyes on her and she looked back at him.

"The helmet is beautiful. I've never seen one like it," she said.

"Thank you. It was a gift from the Cyclops," Hades said, smiling in obvious pleasure at the compliment.

Cyclops? Wasn't that the guy with one eye? *Cyclops, a one-eyed monster who gifted Zeus with thunder and lightning, Poseidon with his trident, and Hades with the helmet—*

Okay! Lina broke into her internal encyclopedic monologue. Whoever he was, she certainly didn't want to get into a discussion about mythological creatures with Hades. So she did what any calm, collected, mature woman would do—she changed the subject. Quickly.

"Your throne is very unusual, too. I don't recognize the stone from which it is made."

"It is white chalcedony," he said.

"Does it have special properties, too?" Lina asked.

"Yes, it banishes fear, hysteria, depression and sadness. I thought it a good choice for this particular room."

"I agree with your choice."

Hades turned his head and leaned toward her again, bringing their faces close together again. "Do you recognize the colored stone in this room?"

"It's amethyst."

"It is the same color as your eyes, Persephone," Eurydice said in a happy voice of discovery.

"Yes, I have noticed that, too," Hades said slowly without releasing Lina's gaze.

His voice had deepened so that it was an audible caress, and Lina felt an answering flutter low in her stomach.

"The dead ask to speak to their god!" Iapis' voice carried his words with formal authority across the Great Hall.

Hades' attention shifted reluctantly away from her, and Lina mentally shook herself. How in the hell was she supposed to think about business with Hades beside her oozing Sex God? She almost wished he'd turn back into Mr. Wooden and Withdrawn. Almost.

She could only hope that Persephone was having better luck staying focused back in Tulsa.

"The dead may enter." Hades' powerful voice commanded.

Lina saw that Iapis was holding the two-pronged silver spear Hades had carried the day before, and with a sound like a crack of thunder, he banged it against the marble floor. One of the shadows from just outside the arched entryway quivered, and then moved into the Great Hall. Lina watched intently as the spirit approached the dais. She was a middle-aged woman. Lina couldn't see any obvious wounds on her semitransparent form. She was, Lina thought, quite attractive. Her hair was piled in intricate braids atop her head, giving the illusion that she was wearing a crown. She was swathed in layer upon layer of draped fabric that fluttered wispily around her as she glided to a halt at the foot of the dais. She dropped into a deep curtsy, which she held until Hades spoke.

"Stheneboia, you may arise."

The woman straightened, but as soon as her eyes widened in recognition of Persephone, she fell back into another deep curtsy.

"I am honored by the presence of Demeter's daughter."

The spirit's breathy voice reminded Lina of a bad Marilyn Monroe impersonator. "Please rise," Lina said quickly, wondering why she felt such an instant dislike for the spirit.

Stheneboia straightened again. Having paid proper respect to the goddess, she ignored Persephone and focused her large, kohl-ringed eyes on Hades.

"I have come, Great God, to ask that I be allowed to drink of the River Lethe and be reborn to the mortal world."

Hades studied her carefully. When he spoke, Lina noted that his voice was filled with the confidence and authority of a god, so much so that the fine hairs on her arms tingled and rose in response to his tangible power.

"It is an unusual request you make of me, Stheneboia. You know that the spirits of suicides are rarely allowed to drink of Lethe."

Lina felt a jolt of shock. The woman had killed herself? Why?

Stheneboia lowered her eyes demurely. "And you know, Great God, that I did not truly mean to die."

She said the title "Great God" like a verbal caress. Lina felt her jaw set. She was actually flirting with Hades!

The spirit's tone turned pouty. "It was a tragic accident. Must I pay for it for all eternity?"

"What have you learned as you have roamed the banks of Acheron?" Hades asked abruptly.

Stheneboia paused, as if carefully arranging her thoughts. When she spoke her words were a slow purr.

"I have learned that I chose unwisely. I will not do so again, Lord of the Underworld."

Hades' eyes narrowed and his deep voice was laced with disgust. "Then you have learned little. You lusted after Bellerophon, a youth half your age. When he rejected your desires, you told your husband the lie that he had tried to rape you. Thankfully, Athena thwarted his attempt to have the youth killed. The goddess was wise to give Bellerophon to your youngest sister. She was more deserving."

"That timid mouse did not deserve Bellerophon!" Stheneboia's sudden rage twisted her attractive features so that her face became hard and cruel.

Hades continued on as if she hadn't spoken. "You did not intend to kill yourself, this I know. You only intended to scare your family and cause them such pain and sorrow that they would reject Athena's matchmaking and send Bellerophon away in disgrace. It was your misfortune that your maid overslept and did not discover you until you had bled beyond saving."

Stheneboia's eyes slid away from the god's penetrating gaze and she pressed one cool, white hand against her brow as if his words had upset her.

"I will choose more wisely in my next life," she said breathily.

"Where is your remorse, Stheneboia?" Hades asked in a stone voice. "You tried to command love with lies and seduction. Love can not survive such poison."

"But you do not understand," the spirit was beginning to sound desperate. "I wanted him so much. He should have wanted me. I was still beautiful and desirable."

"Love can not survive such poison," Hades repeated. "Lust and desire are only a small part of love, but that is another ideal you have yet to learn." Then he shook his head sadly. "I deny your request, Stheneboia. Instead I command that you return to the banks of Acheron, the River of Woe. Perhaps spending more time there will enable you to open your heart to more than your own selfish desires. Do not ask to come before me until another century has passed."

Stheneboia's mouth opened in a wordless scream as a great wind rushed into the chamber and swirled around her like a miniature tornado before picking her up and sweeping her from their sight.

Iapis lifted the spear to signal another spirit forward, but Hades' raised hand halted him mid-gesture. The god turned his attention to Lina.

"What do you think of my judgment?" he asked.

"I thought you were wise," she answered without hesitation. "I don't know the whole story, but from what I heard she did an awful thing, and she certainly wasn't sorry about it. She did make me wonder something, though."

Hades nodded for her to continue.

"If she drank of Lethe she would forget all of her past life?"

"Yes," Hades said.

"But would she still be the same type of person? I mean, is it like wiping everything clean, or is there still a residue of the old self left behind?"

"An excellent question," Hades said with obvious appreciation. "When a spirit drinks of Lethe, memories are wiped completely away and the soul is reborn within an infant's body. But the soul can not help but to retain some elements of personality. Ultimately, the body is just a shell; it is the soul which defines the man or woman, god or goddess."

"Then that just reinforces the fact that you made a wise decision. Stheneboia would have been reborn to make someone else miserable."

"She based her life on lies—most of which she told herself about her true nature. It was not riches or luxury for which her soul yearned; it was love. And love cannot exist with lies and deceit," Hades said.

"You're very insightful about love," Lina said thoughtfully.

Hades paused before he spoke his next words, and as he paused he felt hope stir once again within him. "I have spent eons studying the souls of the dead, and I have come to understand that love is one emotion that mortals know infinitely better than the gods."

Lina blinked in surprise. Mortals knew love better than the gods?

For a woman who had been divorced and hadn't had a decent date in years, his words came as quite a shock.

"Do you really think so?" she asked incredulously.

Hades felt the flicker of hope falter. "Yes, I know it as truth," he said with grim finality before he nodded to Iapis, who cracked the spear against the floor again.

Lina had little time to ponder Hades' reaction to her question. At Iapis' command, another shadowy figure detached from the waiting doorway and Lina watched a pale woman make her way hesitantly across the Great Hall. She was dressed in much more somber robes than Stheneboia had been, but her attire looked just as rich and her dark hair was intricately dressed in a similar fashion. A small coronet circled her head. As she drew closer, Lina could see that she was a plump but attractive woman who looked to be thirty-ish. Then she felt a jolt as she realized that the splash of scarlet on the front of her robes was an open wound, which still seeped blood.

The spirit curtsied deeply.

"Persephone and Hades, I am honored to bow before the Goddess of Spring as well as the Lord of the Underworld."

The woman's voice was strong and regal. Lina smiled and inclined her own head in welcome.

"Greetings, Dido. What petition does the Queen of Carthage have to set before me today?" Hades asked.

"Hades, I beseech your blessing that I may depart the Region of Lamentation beside the River Cocytus and pass into Elysia."

The god studied the spirit thoughtfully. "Have you overcome the grief of your unrequited love, Dido?"

The woman lowered her eyes, not coyly as had Stheneboia, but in a manner that Lina recognized too well from her own past. She lowered them to hide the pain that was still reflected there.

"Yes, Great God. I am finished pining for that which I cannot have."

Lina shifted restlessly in her chair and glanced at Hades. Surely he wouldn't believe Dido.

Hades rubbed his chin and considered the dead queen. "What have you learned from your time of lamentation?"

"That I should have believed more firmly in the strength of love. I should have known that Aeneas just needed time. He was ordered by Zeus to leave me, what else could he do? He was a pious man, a warrior of great faith. It was not his fault. I should have been more understanding, more willing to—" Her words broke on a sob and she covered her face with her hands.

"Dido, you have not overcome your lamentation." The god's voice was gentle.

"But I have!" Dido raised her chin and wiped her face. "It is simply that I am filled with the awe of a child at being in the presence of immortals, and it has made my emotions tremulous." Her shining eyes shifted to Lina frantically, looking for aid from the goddess.

Lina returned the desperate woman's gaze with sympathy. She knew too well how it felt to be abandoned and left to blame only oneself.

"I grant your request, Dido. You may enter Elysia with my blessing."

Hades' words shocked Lina to the core. She found herself staring blankly at the god as the exuberant Dido rushed from the Great Hall.

Again, Iapis moved to raise the god's spear and Hades' motion prevented him.

"You do not agree with my decision, Persephone?" He turned in his throne so that he was facing the goddess.

Lina straightened her spine and met his gaze. You're a goddess . . . you're a goddess . . . you're—no. She stopped the litany. More importantly, she was a woman who had, in real life, loved and been rejected and she understood exactly what Dido was feeling.

"No. I do not agree with your decision."

Surprised by her answer he said, "Could you explain?"

"Dido's not over Aeneas. She's deep in the trenches of hurting and blaming herself. She's still a victim. Whatever lesson the River of Lamentation was supposed to teach her, it hasn't taken hold yet."

Hades felt his anger rise. What did Persephone know of love and loss? She was a young goddess who had always been given everything she desired.

"And how would you know that?"

Lina's eyes narrowed at his condescending tone, but she caught herself before she spat a snide answer at him. To Hades she was only a young goddess. He had no way of knowing her true past and her heartaches. She took deep, slow breaths and got a firm grip on her temper before she began her explanation.

"Well, there were a couple major hints. First, looking away and crying was a dead giveaway. Pardon the bad pun. Second, did you listen to what she said?" Lina barreled on, without giving him a chance to reply. "Her whole little speech was filled with I, I, I and poor me, me, me. Add that to the 'it's not his fault, it's my fault,' and you have one huge victim complex. She doesn't need to go to paradise, she needs to go to the gym, or maybe to a shrink, and work out some of that self-hatred." Lina abruptly shut up, wondering if Hades had any idea what a shrink was.

He cocked his head sideways and looked at her as if she was a very interesting science experiment. Then he did something that really pissed her off. He smiled. And chuckled.

She set her jaw and dug deep, trying to find her own voice somewhere in Persephone's youthful sweetness, and she was rewarded by a steely tone with a satisfyingly sarcastic edge.

"Check into one thing, Hades. This Aeneas guy. I'll bet you one of your diamond chandeliers against one of Demeter's golden crowns that he's in Elysia. And that would be the same Elysia Dido just manipulated her way into. I'll also bet that he's a new arrival, which is what has instigated her sudden interest in moving into Elysia."

Hades' chuckle died and his eyes flattened. "Perhaps the young Goddess of Spring would like an opportunity to do more than observe and comment. The next judgment is yours, Persephone. Fate will, in turn, judge how well you choose."

Lina nodded tightly. Two words passed through her mind. *Oh* and *shit*.

Iapis struck the god's spear against the marble floor, and it rang its somber knell like it was heralding the end of the earth.

This time not one, but several shadows disengaged from the entryway and approached the dais. Lina counted almost a dozen spirits. Her heart pounded and her sweaty hands gripped the armrest of her chair. This wasn't one or two lonely petitioners, it was an entire herd. They were all women, but were of various ages, and their spirit bodies were in varying states. Some of them were almost as substantial in form as was Eurydice, and some were so transparent, they were practically nonexistent. They moved as a group like frightened sheep, at first hesitant and unsure, then they caught sight of Lina in her chair next to Hades, and a definite change came over them. They lost their timidity. As one they walked purposefully forward, their steps becoming more eager the closer they drew to the dais. When they were at the foot of the stairs they stood silently, gazing in open fascination at her. Then one spirit, a woman who was obviously the oldest of the group, dropped to her knees and bowed her head. The rest of the women followed her example.

For what seemed to Lina to be a long time, no one spoke, then Hades' strong voice cut the silence.

"What petition have you brought forth today?"

The oldest woman raised her head. She spoke her response to Hades, but her shining eyes never left Lina.

"We have no petition, Great God. We have come in supplication to the Goddess of Spring, thanking her for answering our orisons. We have been too long without the presence of a goddess." The old woman motioned with her hand, and several of the younger women stood and moved forward. They carried within their skirts bunches of freshly cut flowers, which they placed at Lina's feet.

Hades was looking at Lina with one brow quirked upward. He remained silent, apparently remaining true to his word and allowing her to handle the situation.

She cleared her throat and forced her hand to stay clamped to the arm of the chair when it really wanted to twirl frantically at her hair.

She was a goddess, she reminded herself for the zillionth time, and goddesses didn't pull nervously at their hair—at least not in public.

"Well, this is certainly a surprise. I do appreciate you coming, and the flowers are lovely." She tilted her head toward the little spirit who stood by her side. "Eurydice will put them in water for me, and I will cherish them."

The women smiled and made happy, breathless sounds. Lina began to relax. They seemed like nothing more than happy well-wishers. Even a baker from Tulsa couldn't mess this up.

"You will not be leaving the Underworld soon, will you Persephone?" the old woman asked.

"No," Lina said firmly. "I will not be leaving soon." Six months was certainly not "soon."

The spirits whispered together in happy relief.

"We are so pleased, Goddess . . ." The old woman began, but her words trailed off as an amazing sound floated through the chamber.

Lina blinked in surprise. The sound surrounded her. Music. It was incredibly beautiful music. Entranced, she listened to notes that rose and fell like an impossibly complex birdsong. As the sound moved closer it became musical water. Some of it glided smoothly over pebbles in a clear brook, some tumbled along the slick bank of her hearing and still other notes cascaded powerfully over a rhythmic waterfall of tinkling sound.

"Iapis?" Hades' voice intruded on the music, causing Lina to frown and wish he would just be still.

"My Lord I do not—"

The daimon was interrupted as the musician entered the Great Hall. He walked toward the god's dais and the women parted to let him through. Lina studied him, still amazed at the beautiful music he produced. He was an average, normal looking young man and he was playing a small wooden harp that was gilded with gold. The gold was reflected in his hair and in the fine cloth that draped over his body leaving one tanned, muscular shoulder bare. He continued to pluck magic from the harp as he approached the dais. He was humming a lilting melody, and Lina was surprised when she noticed that his attention was not directed at Hades or at her. Instead his eyes blazed at a spot directly to her left.

"Why does a living man dare enter the Underworld?" Hades' voice sliced through the music, instantly silencing it.

Lina felt a shock of recognition. No wonder he looked so normal to her. He was alive.

"Who are you?" Hades thundered.

The answer came from the little spirit standing to the left of Lina.

"He is Orpheus. My husband."

Chapter Thirteen

Eurydice's voice was brittle with shock. Lina's eyes flew to her face. The girl was staring at her husband. Her eyes had gone huge and round. Her face was completely devoid of color.

"By what right do you enter the realm of the dead?" Hades demanded.

Orpheus tore his eyes from his wife. He bowed low, first to Hades and then to Lina. Then he ran his fingers lightly across the lyre, as if testing its readiness. When he spoke his words were accompanied by gossamer notes, and his voice was the magic that held them together:

O Hades, who rules the dark and silent world,
to you all born of a woman must come.
All lovely things at last return to you.
You are the debtor always paid.
A little while we tarry upon earth.
Then we are yours forever and ever,
but I seek one who came to you too soon.
This bud was plucked before the flower bloomed.
I tried to bear my loss, but oh, oh, I do love her so
and the pain of her loss is killing me slowly.

Love is too strong, a too tempting god.
I beg you return to me what was mine.
Then weave again her sweet life's refrain,
which ended too quickly,
I ask this small thing.
That you will lend her back to me.
Yours again when her life's span is full she shall be.
Because oh, oh, I do love her so
and the pain of her loss is killing me slowly.

Orpheus' words ended, but his fingers kept plucking a soft, sweet version of the melody of his song. Lina felt her heart ache and break. His music moved her like she had never before been moved. Her cheeks felt wet and she touched her face, wiping off the tears she hadn't realized she was shedding.

She looked at the silent god sitting beside her. His face, too, reflected the grief of the mortal's song. Hades began to speak, and then he stopped. His head turned slowly until his dark gaze met Lina's tear-filled eyes.

"The choice is yours. I gifted you with the next judgment, but even if I had not, Eurydice has pledged herself to your service. Only you can release her; therefore, twice over you are granted the power to decide her fate. Choose wisely, Goddess of Spring." Hades said in a voice that mirrored the emotion in Orpheus' song.

Lina drew in a shaky breath, feeling for the first time the awesome responsibility that went with being goddess. Eurydice's future rested on her decision. She turned in her chair so that she faced the girl.

Eurydice's slender body had gone very still. The only movement that came from the girl was from the tears that washed wet trails down her colorless face and dripped steadily onto the gauzy fabric of her gown.

"How did you die?" Lina asked softly.

But Eurydice didn't answer her. Instead the tune Orpheus played changed to a darker melody, underscoring his words.

"Only one month after our wedding day we were taking a moonlit walk. She became separated from me, lost in a sudden fog. She chose the wrong path. Instead of leading her back to me, her loving husband, it led her to a nest of vipers where she met her untimely death."

Although Orpheus didn't sing, his words still sounded lyrical. Lina felt them create a spell of sadness around her. She wept anew over the tragedy of Eurydice's death. So that was the wrong choice the girl had made, and the loss of her young husband was the price she had paid for that choice—a price that still weighed heavily on her soul. So heavily, Lina noted, that Eurydice had been struck speechless with grief at Orpheus' appearance.

Lina reached out and grasped the little spirit's hand. Eurydice's hand was cold and Lina could feel the silent tremors that shook her body.

"I free you," Lina said through her tears. "You may return to your life with your husband. Now I understand your sadness, and I am so happy I can do this for you."

Eurydice gasped in surprise. Her body trembled visibly and her mouth twisted in grief.

"Oh, honey! Don't worry about me. I'll be just fine. Iapis will take good care of me, as will Hades." Lina squeezed the girl's hand, glancing at Hades for support.

The dark god was watching Eurydice closely.

"Persephone has spoken. I bow to her decision. I have but one condition." Hades' gaze speared Orpheus. "Eurydice may return to the Land of the Living only if you do not look back at her; you must trust that she follows you. When you turn from this palace you may not gaze upon her again until she has departed my realm and stands firmly once more in the mortal world."

"I will adhere to your will. She will follow me, of that I have no doubt." Orpheus bowed low to Hades and Lina. "Hereafter I will sing praises to you extolling your benevolence." His eyes captured Eurydice and his words turned to liquid music:

Follow me, follow me . . .
Together forever we shall be . . .
You belong to me, you belong to me . . .
Together forever we shall be . . .

Orpheus strummed magic from his lyre. With one last piercing look at his wife, he turned, and, singing his Siren's song, he walked from the Great Hall. Eurydice began to follow him as if he held her on an invisible tether. She stumbled down the stairs from the dais, righted herself and continued with jerky steps after her husband. She glanced once over her shoulder. Lina was shocked at the glazed expression in the girl's eyes. Eurydice looked as if she were in agony.

Orpheus, his music and Eurydice drifted from the Palace of Hades.

Hades spoke into the sudden silence. "Petitions are closed for today."

Iapis stuck the spear against the marble floor and the group of women bowed to Lina once more before they faded out of the entryway, leaving her alone with Hades and Iapis.

None of them spoke.

Lina couldn't get out of her mind the expression on Eurydice's face as she followed her husband from the room. The girl had looked—Lina wrapped a strand of hair around and around her finger—trapped. Eurydice had looked trapped. Now that Orpheus and his seductive music were gone, and Lina was replaying the scene in her head, it felt wrong. Her intuition was screaming that something was very wrong.

"I'm going to go back to my room now," Lina said, trying to sound nonchalant. She smiled briefly at Hades. "Thank you for inviting me. I found it very interesting." She hurried down the dais steps, holding her breath and hoping that Hades didn't stop her. She called to Iapis, who was still standing in the entrance to the Hall. "Could you show me back to my room? I think I'm going to take a nap. The excitement of the petitions has worn me out."

Lina saw Iapis' eyes travel questioningly over her shoulder, but he must have received the go ahead from Hades, because he nodded convivially to Lina and led her from the Great Hall. When they were out of Hades' hearing, Lina stopped and pulled at the daimon's sleeve so that he had to face her.

"Something's wrong with Eurydice. I can feel it. Well, I didn't while Orpheus was playing his music, but as soon as he was gone everything changed," Lina said.

"What is it you wish, Goddess?" Iapis asked, lowering his voice.

"I need to follow them." Lina didn't realize what she was going to say until she had spoken, but the words felt right. "I have to watch and make sure that I made the right decision by letting her go back to him."

Iapis nodded solemnly. "We would not want her to be hurt."

"No, we wouldn't."

"Come this way," Iapis said decisively. He led Lina quickly to the front of the palace. "There is the pathway." He pointed to the path of black marble. "She is not far ahead of you."

"Thank you, Iapis." Lina hugged him impulsively before she hurried down the path.

"The Underworld is opened to you, Goddess," Iapis called after her. "You may come and go at will. Eurydice belongs here. She, too, has access to this realm. But Orpheus is a living mortal. Once he passes through the Gates, he may not return as long as he is living."

"I'll remember," she called over her shoulder.

"PERSEPHONE follows Eurydice?" Hades asked the daimon.

"Yes."

Hades paced the empty Great Hall restlessly. "Orpheus was hiding something. His music spun a web of seduction, but his words were false. The little spirit did not want to follow him."

"I agree, Lord," Iapis said fiercely.

Hades stopped his pacing. "You care for Eurydice." It was not a question.

"I do," Iapis said.

"Are you certain?"

"Eurydice makes me laugh. I have not laughed in eons."

"Do you know her heart?" Hades asked softly.

"There has not yet been time, and she is so young," Iapis said helplessly.

Hades nodded. "Women are difficult."

"They are indeed."

"Bring me the Helmet of Invisibility. I will follow Persephone. It may take my intercession to right this error."

Relief flooded the daimon's face. "Thank you, Lord."

Hades' eyes warmed and he grasped Iapis' hand. "You need not thank me, my friend."

Iapis rushed to the pillar that held the Helmet of Invisibility. He grasped it firmly in his hands. As always, its weight was a surprise to the daimon. It appeared so lightly wrought, yet it was, indeed, a heavy burden to bear. He brought the Helmet to the Lord of the Underworld.

Hades took it from the daimon. Then he paused, considering.

"Iapis, I need you to look into something."

"Of course, Lord."

"See if Aeneas has recently entered Elysia."

"It shall be done, Hades."

The god nodded. Then in one swift motion, he placed the Helmet of Invisibility over his head. The pain that lanced through his body was excruciating. He pressed his lips together and refused to give in to the agony. It would pass, he reminded himself—nothing worthwhile comes without a price. He breathed deeply against the pain until his senses were his own again.

Iapis watched the god's body ripple and then disappear. He spoke to the empty space before him, "Bring them back, Lord."

Hades' answer floated to the daimon from across the room. "I shall. . . ."

Chapter Fourteen

LINA fell into a rhythm of hurry up and slow down. She managed to keep Eurydice's back just at the edge of her sight, while staying out of the reach of Orpheus' music.

"Doesn't he ever get tired?" She muttered to herself. When she considered the situation with a clear head, versus one filled with the compelling notes formed by a magician masquerading as a musician, it hadn't been difficult to see the drug-like effect Orpheus' music had on everyone and everything that heard it. The dead paused in their pilgrimages to Elysia as he passed. Flowers and trees swayed toward him. Even Lina found herself smiling ridiculously if she got too close to his voice.

"Ugh. He reminds me of too-sweet candy. He seems great at first, but pretty soon he'll just make me want to puke." Lina talked to herself, taking comfort in the nonhypnotic sound of her own voice while nodding briefly to the surprised spirits that curtsied and bowed as she hurried past them. "I should have been wiser. I should have paid more attention to Eurydice than to that singing boy. And I shouldn't have been so damn cocky after that whole Dido thing." She bit her lip in frustration.

The sky ahead of her was changing and a chill of trepidation shivered through her. She knew all too well that the fading light signaled the end of the bright, cheery part of the Underworld. She was retracing the path she and Eurydice had traveled from the upper world.

Lina ordered herself not to think about the bad dreams and the darkness. If Eurydice was going through it again; so would she.

Ahead of her she heard maniacal barking. Then the faraway music grew louder and the fierce barks changed to puppy-like grunts and whimpers. Lina shook her head. What the hell—she cringed at the unintentional bad pun—was Orpheus doing? Steeling herself against his compelling song, she picked up her pace until she was jogging at a steady beat. Persephone's long legs carried her swiftly forward. Her breathing was deep and even. She smiled in satisfaction. Persephone's body wasn't just young, it was also in great shape.

The road angled abruptly to her left and she stagger-stepped down to a walk. Blocking the pathway directly in front of her was a humongous dog.

The creature raised its head and growled a menacing warning. Lina blinked, trying to clear her vision, but the image remained.

"The damn thing has three heads," she gasped.

The "damn thing" growled.

Lina tightened her jaw. It was just a dog. Sure, the biggest dog she had ever seen. And it had—*merda!*—three heads.

The creature snarled a warning. Saliva dripped from its triple jowls.

Jowls?

Lina's face split into a relieved grin as soon as her stunned mind processed what she was seeing. The dog was nothing more than a giant version of Edith Anne, complete with slobber and under bite—times three.

Her laughter caused three sets of stubby ears to perk in her direction.

Lina hurried forward, speaking in what she liked to think of as her "doggie voice," (which was *much* different than her "cat voice"—cats didn't tolerate baby talk of any sort).

"Hey there you big, adorable thing!" she cooed.

Three tails wagged tentatively.

"Aren't you a wonderful surprise. And to think I was just missing my Edith Anne. Well, I guess I'll just have to make you my big, bad

Doggie From Hell while I'm here." She was within touching distance of the multiheaded creature.

"Arrwoo?" said the beast.

"Edith always liked her ears scratched. Bend down here and let's give it a try." She reached her slender hand up toward one of the six ears. The creature tilted its nearest head in her direction.

Lina scratched.

One of the beast's heads sighed and leaned into her hand, almost knocking Lina over. The other two heads whined piteously.

"There's a good doggie." Lina grinned, patting the middle head's slobbery nose, causing the third dog to yelp like a needy puppy. "Oh, come here. How about a scratch under that chin?"

While Lina cooed and petted and cajoled she searched her mind for a name.

Cerberus—Watchdog of the Underworld—his job is to eat souls that attempt to escape and stop living people who attempt to enter Hades' realm.

"Well, you're falling down on the job, big boy," Lina said.

The dog whined and all three heads gave her pitiful, big-eyed doggie looks.

"Don't feel bad, Orpheus fooled me, too."

Three tails beat the air.

"Okay, here's the deal. I'm going to follow the shyster musician and Eurydice. You just be sure that Mr. Goldentongue doesn't get past you again." Lina tried to meet all three sets of eyes. "Understand?"

Cerberus squirmed and woofed.

"I've seen enough Lassie reruns to know a doggie 'yes' when I hear one. Be a good boy, ur, boys. I'll see you on my way back." With a final ear scratch Lina left the Guardian of the Underworld wriggling and yapping like a happy puppy(s). She hurried so that she was soon jogging with a quick, but steady pace.

"I should cease being surprised by her actions," Hades murmured to himself. He watched Persephone bespell Cerberus as she had his steeds.

Safe within the Helmet of Invisibility, he had followed the goddess closely enough to hear her berate herself about allowing Orpheus' music to sway her judgment. She was much wiser than she knew. Hadn't he felt the pull of the mortal's words, too? And he was a mature god, experienced in commanding his realm.

True, she was a goddess, but she was really just a child. Even so, she continued to show amazing insight and maturity. For instance, his instinct was telling him that Iapis would report that Aeneas had indeed just entered Elysia. How had Persephone recognized Dido's deception when all he had observed was a lovely feminine soul unaccustomed to being in the presence of immortals? And then she had stood up to him, not with the blinding temper of an irate goddess, but with logic and insight and, he chuckled remembering the bet she had proposed, wit. Before she had come to his realm, he would have never believed it of Persephone, but there was definitely more to her than a shallow young goddess.

Persephone fondled Cerberus and Hades felt a sudden surge of jealousy for the attention she was lavishing on the slobbering, three-headed creature. The God ground his teeth. He wanted her to touch him. It shocked him, but he could not deny it. He was beginning to wonder if what Iapis had said was true, that perhaps it was better to experience even a small bit of happiness than none at all.

The very thought made his hands sweat.

As she jogged down the road, Lina decided that she'd have to come back and visit the three-headed dog. Maybe she'd bring him a treat. Edith Anne loved Bacos. Surely Hell's kitchen could fry her up a little bacon snack. She thought about the creature's size—okay, maybe she'd have them fry up a *big* bacon snack.

The road took another abrupt turn and Lina slid to a halt, scrambling back from the edge of a lake that seemed to want to swallow her feet. Its waters were thick and black, almost oily. She looked to either side. Darkness surrounded the lake so that the water seemed to stretch endlessly before and beside her.

Lina shivered.

She was a goddess. She thought each word carefully.

Light the recesses, her mind whispered.

With a gasp of relief she raised her hand and commanded, "I need light!"

The ball of brilliance popped from her palm and hovered expectantly above her.

"What is your desire, Goddess?"

Lina jumped and made a squeaky sound she was sure wouldn't qualify as goddess-like. Out of the darkness beside her a skeletal man materialized. He was wearing gray robes that dragged on the ground. He carried a long, hooked staff that reminded Lina of the rods gondoliers used to push their boats down the Grand Canal. But that's where his resemblance to anything mortal or romantic ended. This man was a grim being whose large, amber-colored eyes glowed with a strange luminescence. Lina did not have to delve into her memory to give him a name. He could be none other than Charon, the Ferryman of Hades.

"I want to follow Orpheus and Eurydice. Did you take them across the lake?"

"Yes, Goddess."

"Then I want to go, too."

"As you command, Goddess." He made a sweeping gesture and suddenly a boat appeared nudging the bank at their feet.

Telling herself not to think about sinking boats, bottomless lakes or the scary stuff that might be lurking just below the surface, Lina climbed into the little craft, taking a seat near the middle of it. Charon stepped into the boat and leaned forward to touch his staff against the bank, but he stopped mid-motion and stood very still as if he were listening to whispered words. He nodded his head with the briefest of motions, paused and then he finally pushed them away from the shore.

"The passage is not long, Goddess."

Lina nodded and tried unsuccessfully to relax. She kept her eyes focused on the distant shoreline. She didn't look down at the water. Unbidden, a memory came to her from the scene in *Lord of the Rings* when Frodo and Sam crossed the Dead Marshes. She shivered, afraid if she looked into the water she would see reflected faces of the dead. Her only consolation was the ball of light that hovered loyally close to her shoulder.

SHE looked afraid, so afraid that he almost tore the Helmet off his head and betrayed his presence. Then he remembered her reaction when he had chided her for being young and sheltered. Likely she would not look kindly upon his interference and the subterfuge of the Helmet. Persephone would not be pleased that he had hidden himself and followed her. But his heart whispered for him to take her in his arms and protect her from her fears. As always, Hades listened to his mind, but for the first time in his existence, he yearned to follow his heart.

Charon felt his god's presence. He knew when Hades boarded the boat. Charon also knew that Hades wished to keep his presence hidden from the goddess. The Ferryman was nothing if not discreet. So Hades stood at the opposite end of the small craft, his eyes never leaving Persephone. He saw how she clutched the seat on which she sat so tightly that her delicate knuckles whitened. She held her spine rigid, as if she could brace herself against her fear. Her little light illuminated the space surrounding her so that she appeared to be floating in a halo of brightness that was almost as brilliant as her beauty.

The boat hit a wave causing it to rock dangerously. Persephone's body shuddered in response.

Carefully and quickly! Hades' anger burst through his thoughts to Charon. The Ferryman bowed his head in acknowledgment and shivered at the force of the god's fury. With the Lord of the Underworld standing vigilant attendance, the remainder of the passage was smooth and swift.

"FOLLOW the path that leads there, Goddess." Charon pointed ahead into the darkness. Lina stepped from the boat to the shore. "The Gates of Hades are just beyond. Through them you will find the entrance to the world above."

Lina realized she didn't really need his direction. Demeter had been right, it was as if her body felt the way to the world above. But she smiled politely at the Ferryman.

"Thank you, Charon. I know my way from here." She took a couple of steps, stopped, and turned back to the tall man. "You will be here when I come back, won't you?"

Charon almost smiled. "Yes, Goddess."

"Good."

Lina and her circle of light moved away from the lake. Under the shroud of invisibility Hades followed.

The ivory gates loomed before Lina. Thankfully, there was no sign of the eerie fog of a bad dream. Jogging through the gates she narrowed her eyes, trying to catch sight of Eurydice's ghostly form, but she saw nothing except velvet layers of darkness. Lina stopped and strained to listen. She could hear music, but it sounded far away and indistinct.

Please, please don't let me be too late, she prayed silently as she broke into a sprinter's run.

Lina passed through the grove of opaque trees in a blur. Then she spotted the tunnel, and, she breathed a sigh of relief, within it she could clearly see the silhouettes of two figures. One was several yards ahead of the other.

Lina ran silently and swiftly, covering the distance that separated her from Eurydice in a single breath.

The music was so sweet. Lina felt her shoulders begin to relax and her steps falter. She should just rest awhile and then . . .

Do not listen to his music! The words shouted within her mind, and with the power of a goddess they chased away the cloying notes of Orpheus' song. Suddenly clear-minded, Lina was able to hear something that had been hidden beneath the spell of music until that moment—the sound of Eurydice's sobs.

As if sensing her presence, the girl looked over her shoulder. When she saw Lina her face grimaced with the strength of her emotion. Lina could see that Eurydice was still struggling against the lure of Orpheus's song. Even though they were almost to the lip of the tunnel, the little spirit still stumbled and dragged her feet, pulling back with everything inside of her against the magical lure of her husband's music. With a powerful effort, Eurydice silently mouthed two words to her goddess, *help me.*

Orpheus stepped into the sunlight of the World of the Living.

Hades raised his hands to pull off the Helmet of Invisibility and do something he had never before done: he would revoke his word by refusing to allow Eurydice to leave the Underworld.

But before he could act, Persephone moved. She grabbed Eurydice's hand and held it in such a tight grasp that the little spirit was able to keep from stepping from the edge of the Underworld and into the light. Then, in a voice pitched to impersonate Eurydice's naïveté, she called to the musician who stood with his back resolutely facing them.

"Oh, my goodness! Orpheus, look! This sunlight makes my robe completely see through! And I have absolutely nothing on underneath it."

With a victorious shout, the arrogant young musician spun around, but the look of triumph vanished when he realized that he was staring at his wife and the Goddess Persephone. Both women were still safely within the dark mouth of the Underworld.

"NOOOOOO!" His shriek of rage echoed through the tunnel. He lunged forward.

Unseen, Hades threw his hand up and issued a silent command.

When the musician's living body tried to pass into the shadowy entrance of Hades' realm, the air surrounding him seemed to solidify. Orpheus set his square jaw and kept trying to move forward, but the invisible barrier prevented him. The harder he struggled, the more firm the barrier became.

"You belong to me!" His words were no longer seductive or magical; instead they had become hard and cruel.

Eurydice shrank back from him as if she was afraid he would strike her. Lina was filled with a wave of righteous anger.

"You sound like a spoiled brat. You can't own another person's soul. Go back to your world. Leave Eurydice at peace in hers," Lina said.

"Never! She will always be mine!" Orpheus shouted.

Lina shook her head. She had known his type of man. He would never be content with simply loving a woman. His kind had to control and bully and subjugate. She felt the anger expand within her, lending power to the words she hurled at Orpheus. "Go away, boy!"

The command slammed into the musician, lifting him off his feet and tossing him end-over-end away from the tunnel, carrying him back farther and farther until he disappeared completely from sight.

Apparently she'd discovered another one of Persephone's goddess powers. Lina smiled grimly. One shouldn't piss off a goddess.

Unaware that she was being shadowed by the invisible God of the Underworld, Lina wrapped an arm around Eurydice, who was sobbing quietly. Supporting her slight weight, Lina turned away from the World of the Living and led Eurydice through the welcoming darkness of the tunnel and into the glade of white trees. Once within their shielding canopy, Eurydice collapsed onto the soft, dark ground. The girl had quit crying, but she was panting like she had just run a marathon.

"You c-c-came for m-me!" She struggled to talk while she fought to bring her breathing under control.

Lina sat beside her and hugged her fiercely. "Of course I did. I knew something was wrong. I'm sorry I let you go—it was his music. At first I couldn't think clearly because of it, but as soon as Orpheus left with you, I understood that you didn't want to go with him."

"N-no!" She shivered, but drew strength from the embrace of her goddess. "I did not want to go with him."

"That wrong choice you said that you made. It wasn't taking the path that led to your death, was it?" Lina asked.

"No!" Eurydice said. The strength of her voice grew as she continued to speak. "It was him! He was the wrong choice I made. I was so incredibly wrong. I met him one day and the next I pledged myself to him. I was blinded by the magic of his music. I did not look into his heart." She trembled, but forced herself under control. She needed to say it. She had been silent too long. "If I had looked into his heart, I would have seen that it was filled with cruelty. I did not understand until it was too late. It began with little things. He did not like my hair when I wore it a certain way. He asked me to change it. I did." Eurydice's words came faster and faster. "Then it was my clothes. Then my friends. I tried to tell my family, but they could only hear his music. They gave me to him willingly, believing that my hesitation was simple, maidenly reserve. After we were married he would not even allow me to visit my family. He could not bear it if I was not always by his side. He wanted to consume me. When I tried to get away from him, even if it was just to have a moment of privacy, he struck me. He struck me again and again. Life with him was a prison." Eurydice's eyes were bright, but her tears had stopped. "When the fog separated us, I simply ran from him. I did not know about the nest of vipers. But I was glad of their bite. I welcomed the release."

"You are so brave." Lina touched the girl's damp cheek.

"Do you really think so, Persephone?"

"I know so. On that you have the word of a goddess."

Eurydice's smile flashed. "Then I must believe it." Her expression changed, and became introspective.

"What is it, honey?" Lina asked.

The girl was staring down the path that led back to the Underworld. "I have to go. I don't belong this close to the World of the Living. It does not feel right."

Lina nodded understanding. She could see the need in the little spirit's eyes. This time Eurydice's steps were confident as she hurried through the grove of milk-colored trees. Lina followed her more slowly. When they broke through the trees, Eurydice glanced over her shoulder at Lina, who had stopped.

"Will you not return with me?" Eurydice's voice had become frightened again.

"Yes, don't worry. I'm coming"—she hesitated—"but, honey, would you mind going on ahead of me?" Lina pointed behind her. "I need to do something first, and I don't want to ask you to wait for me."

"But you will return to the Palace of Hades?"

Under the Helmet of Invisibility, Hades held his breath, waiting for Persephone's answer.

"Of course! I just need to have a quick talk with Demeter."

Hades and Eurydice breathed sighs of relief.

The girl understood Persephone's need to speak with her mother. In many ways the goddess had taken the place of her living mother. She nodded and smiled. "I can return ahead of you to the palace."

"You won't be afraid to go by yourself?"

"No. I belong here. I am not afraid."

Lina hugged her again. "I won't be long."

Eurydice grinned and skipped through the ivory gates. As Lina re-entered the grove of trees, she heard the girl's voice echoing through the limbs. "I will see that a meal is made ready for you. You will be hungry when you return and I must make certain that . . ."

Lina smiled wryly. Eurydice would be fine.

FEELING like a voyeur, Hades shadowed the unsuspecting Persephone. He should not continue to follow the goddess. Eurydice was free; she was returning safely to his palace. That had been his reason for donning the Helmet of Invisibility and going after them. And it had been a credible reason. Now he should return to his palace. His task was completed.

But he didn't turn back. He couldn't. Not yet. He wanted to watch her as she hurried so gracefully through the trees. The ball of light touched her lovely features like a bright caress. He envied that light.

She passed through the tunnel quickly, barely pausing before raising her hand and calling the light back within her. Then she stepped from the entrance to the Underworld and into the soft glow of a beautiful pre-dawn morning. Hades followed her.

Persephone looked around quizzically. Hades wondered if she was worried that Orpheus might still be lurking near. No, he reminded himself. The musician had been cast away by the power of the goddess's righteous anger. Persephone would know that he would be far from there. But she was obviously searching for something. She walked away from the tunnel and down the little path that was lined in frothy ferns. Occasionally, the goddess stopped and peered amidst the greenery as if looking for a lost trinket. Then she would sigh, mumble something unintelligible, and move on.

The path tilted gradually up and soon Persephone stood near the high bank of Lake Avernus. The goddess smiled and breathed in deeply, obviously appreciating the view.

Hades wanted to shout that Avernus would seem as nothing when compared with the wonders of Elysia. There were beauties in his realm that were far more spectacular than an ordinary lake in the simple, mundane light before dawn. He ground his teeth together. He wanted to show the magnificence of his realm to her and to watch her face brighten with the discovery.

"There you are!"

Persephone's voice sounded relieved and she rushed over to a pillared marble basin which stood to one side of the path. Resting within the basin was a large glass ball. Its interior was murky, like it had been filled with thickened cream. Hades recognized it instantly as the oracle of a goddess.

Persephone stood in front of the oracle. She hesitated. To Hades it seemed that she was almost uncertain of what to do next. Then she closed her eyes, as if she needed to concentrate very hard. When she opened them a moment later her full lips lifted in the briefest of smiles. With no more hesitation, she passed her hands over the crystal three times, causing the inside of the globe to begin to swirl.

"Demeter," Persephone spoke to the oracle. "I almost messed up. Badly."

The face of the Goddess of the Harvest materialized within her oracle.

"You use the word almost, which must mean that you righted your error," Demeter said, her voice sounding a little hollow and unnatural as it echoed from the oracle.

Persephone sighed. "Yes, but if I hadn't, my mistake would have cost a lovely young girl a lifetime of misery."

"Being goddess does not mean perfection. We must each use our best judgment. Sometimes mistakes are made."

Persephone pulled at a long strand of her hair and twirled it around her finger.

"I don't want to make mistakes that cause others pain."

Hades forced himself to turn away. He strode quickly back through the tunnel. He had intruded upon the goddess's privacy too long. His conscience would not allow him to continue to listen to Persephone's conversation with her mother. Hades yanked off the Helmet of Invisibility. It was not meant as an eavesdropping device. It was to be used with discernment, not selfishness. He was ashamed of himself. Had he not just berated Stheneboia for selfishness and deception?

He had never before behaved in such a manner. He was not a callow youth. He understood that sneaking and spying would not win a goddess's heart.

Hades stopped.

Was that what he desired, to win Persephone's heart?

He raked a hand through his hair. He wanted her. His body had begun to ache for her. For eons he had thought that his difference had in some way hermetically sealed him from the common lusts of the gods. He avoided women, be they mortal or immortal, because his very nature had been fashioned so that meaningless passion and brief dalliance was not enough for him. Age after countless age he had witnessed in the spirits of the dead that which mortals knew so well, the eternal bond forged by soul mates. Bearing witness to that unique, unforgettable depth of joining had soldered the difference that had already been imprinted into his nature. Anything less than mating for eternity would never satisfy him.

Oh, he had tried—centuries ago. His stomach still tightened when he thought of his one brief mortal lover, Minthe. He had come upon the maiden during one of his rare visits to the World of the Living. She had been gathering flowers for her first fertility ritual and his appearance had seemed an answer to her prayers. He had made her his, there in that fragrant meadow, and there he had visited her often until she vowed that she loved him and that she would leave her home and cleave only to him.

Looking back, he was amazed by his own naïveté. He still shrank away from the memory of her hysterics when he had finally revealed himself to her as Lord of the Dead. In his mind he could see it all happening again. Minthe's blind flight from him as she hurled herself over the cliff, and how he had snatched her from the air before she could end her own life. Instead of condemning her to an eternity of lamentation within his realm, Hades had called forth his immortal power and changed her form into the sweet scented, ever-growing herb that retained her delicate beauty, as well as her name.

Unlike mortal women, goddesses did not fear him, but they also did not understand him. They scorned him, thinking him somber and stern because he ruled the Underworld. Until Persephone, no goddess had ever bothered to visit his realm. He scoffed. Truly, he had never had any desire to offer an invitation. Goddesses had no real loyalty, no real ability to love. Look at Athena, she even betrayed her precious Odysseus by allowing him to be led astray for twenty years before returning home to his faithful wife.

It had been easy to convince himself that there was no mate for him. Mortal women must die to reign forever beside him, so they feared him and shrank from his love. Goddesses were immortal; therefore, they could never truly belong to him.

He had been content to rule his realm and live surrounded by the beauty of the Elysian Fields and the wonders of his palace.

But no longer.

Hades' lips twisted in self-mockery. The God of the Dead desired the Goddess of Spring.

Even within his head it sounded impossible.

Then he remembered the goddess's brilliant smile and the childlike wonder with which she responded to his realm. Yet she consistently displayed a maturity that belied her youthful appearance. She was different from the other goddesses—that she had proven. But was she different enough to love him?

How to woo Persephone? He paced back and forth across the black path while he considered. Then a sudden idea halted him. His smile was fierce with victory. Hades brought his fingers to his lips. His whistle pierced the blackness, traveling with mystical speed all the way back to his palace.

Chapter Fifteen

"In other words, there is no magic wand, or whatever, that you can wave over me that will guarantee that I make the right decisions. Even if it means my mistakes might cause others a lot of misery." Lina knew she sounded exasperated. What was the use of being a goddess if she was still fallible?

Demeter's expression was kind. "Wisdom does not come with immortality, *Daughter*." The goddess emphasized the word to reinforce to Lina the role she must play. "It comes with experience. And you have had many years of excellent experience in your life. Listen to your intuition. Use your mind. Believe in yourself. If you do make a mistake, learn from it." The glass began filling with murky wisps of cloud-like tendrils, obscuring the goddess's face. "Return to Hades with my blessings, Daughter." Her voice faded and her image disappeared.

Lina sighed. Basically, she was on her own.

"I hope Persephone's having an easier time at Pani Del Goddess," Lina grumbled.

The instant she spoke, the vapor within the glass ball began to swirl again. Then, as Lina watched in amazement, the cloudiness cleared to reveal a scene that caused her stomach to tighten with an unexpected wave of homesickness.

Lina bent closer to the oracle, totally engrossed in what she was seeing.

Pani Del Goddess was definitely having a good day. The little bakery was filled with customers. Actually, Lina blinked in surprise, it was packed. She peered though the magical orb, counting the familiar faces and realizing that they were in the minority. She didn't recognize most of the customers.

They certainly looked happy. There was a lot of talking and laughing going on along with—Lina blinked again, then her face broke into a pleased smile—they were eating what she was sure she recognized as Pizza alla Romana, the pizza that had summoned Demeter.

There were also several new signs placed along the wall behind the pastry cases. In bold script one read PIZZA DEL GIORNO—*Pizza of the Day*—QUATTRO STAGIONI—*Four Seasons, with all your favorites: tomatoes, artichokes, mushrooms, olives, three cheeses and prosciutto.* Another proclaimed the VINO DEL GIORNO—*wine of the day*—PEPPOLI, CHIANTI CLASSICO RISERVA. It was the third sign that confused Lina. All it said was TUBS OF AMBROSIA CREAM CHEESE LIMITED TO THREE PER CUSTOMER.

Ambrosia cream cheese? What was that?

Then Lina gasped and felt her face flush hot as she watched herself saunter through the swinging doors from the kitchen and enter the bakery. Lina shook her head back and forth, back and forth, back and forth in a repeated motion of denial.

What had Persephone done to her? She wasn't wearing one of her well-tailored business suits. She had on a little silk wraparound skirt that was bright fuchsia and a flowy short sleeved shell the color of honeydew melons. The skirt was short. Very short. And fuchsia! She didn't even own anything fuchsia! The shell veed dangerously low to expose Lina's deep cleavage. Openmouthed, Lina stared at her own body. The long length of leg that the skirt revealed was tanned, as was the rest of her body—which, in her opinion, Lina could see entirely too much of. And she had lost weight.

Lina narrowed her eyes and studied herself. No, maybe she hadn't actually lost weight. She looked toned and healthy. Her curves were all still there. They were just tighter and more well-defined. And her hair was different. It was longer—a couple of inches longer. How could that be? Hadn't she only been gone a day or so? Lina looked again. Yes, it was definitely longer. It rested on her shoulders in messy, indistinct curls, giving her a naughty, windblown look.

A man waved at Lina's body and she responded with a saucy smile and a toss of her hair. The man—*merda!* He wasn't just a man, he was an incredibly young man—hurried over to the object of his attention. Lina gaped as she watched herself flirt outrageously with a young, handsome, young, muscular, *young* man who was quite obviously very well acquainted with her. He couldn't have been much older than twenty-five.

The young handsome man bent and kissed Lina's body's mouth. Right in the middle of the bakery. Right in front of everyone.

"I don't F-ing believe it." She was too shocked to curse correctly in Italian or English.

Persephone laughed and spun playfully away from her suitor. For a split second she looked up and winked. Right at Lina.

Lina gasped and jerked back like she'd been slapped. At once the glass began to swirl and become cloudy. The image of Pani Del Goddess dissipated like smoke.

"Problems with the oracle, Goddess?" A deep voice spoke from behind her.

Lina whirled around to find that she was facing a man. An amazingly beautiful man.

"Persephone! I did not realize it was you."

"Hello," Lina said breathlessly, her shaking hand covering her pounding heart. Who was this gorgeous man?

A name drifted enticingly through her mind like an erotic whisper—*Apollo.*

Lina fanned her hot face and tried to pull herself together.

"You startled me, uh, Apollo."

The god lounged against the side of a large boulder. He was wearing a short leather tunic that was carved with a chest plate that met an unusual looking skirt-like wrap slung low around his muscular hips.

But the "skirt" in no way made him appear effeminate. Except for a pair of sandals the rest of his body was bare. Very bare. Apollo was made of long, golden lines of muscle. His smile was smooth and attractive. Lina couldn't help staring. Actually, she thought staring was probably required in her particular situation.

The god nodded his head at the oracle. "Talking to Demeter?"

"Um, yes."

"She is visiting Hera. I think the two of them are planning something new with which to plague Zeus." He dropped his voice to a conspirator's level and his eyes gleamed. "Gossip has it that the Thunder God is besmitten with a mortal maiden . . . again." Apollo scratched his strong chin in consideration. "I believe the hapless girl's name is Io." He shook his head and laughed, making his brilliant blue eyes sparkle mischievously. "I will never understand Hera's temper. We all know Zeus has an appetite for beauty, yet he has chosen only one wife. She should not waste her time on frivolous jealousies."

Lina lifted one perfect eyebrow. "You don't consider fidelity in marriage important?"

"I believe finding pleasure is important, as you know very well, Persephone." His look was intimate as well as seductive.

Ohmygod. Had Apollo been Persephone's lover?

"I would be honored to remind you of any number of pleasurable delights, Goddess of Spring."

He pushed himself from the bank and moved with a feral grace toward her. Lina's mouth went dry. He looked like he was going to take her in his arms. Lina lifted one hand out in front of her like a stop sign. Yes, he was the most handsome man she had ever seen, but she wasn't the type of woman who would kiss a stranger—despite what Persephone might be doing in her world.

Apollo watched her body stiffen and her jaw clench. He was well-versed in seduction and he knew how to get past a goddess who was dabbling in coy flirtation. In a fluid motion he changed his intent. Instead of taking her luscious young body in his arms he captured her outstretched hand and bowed gallantly over it. Like the consummate gentleman he was not, he kissed her hand lightly. Still holding her hand, Apollo looked deep within her eyes.

"I have watched you frolic in the meadows as I have driven my chariot through the sky. Your body moves with more grace than the flowers that bend delicately in the morning breeze. We would make a good match, you and I—the God of Light and the Goddess of Spring."

Lina almost laughed aloud with relief. Now here was something she was used to dealing with—a slick guy with a ready line. She batted her long lashes at the handsome god and sighed with an excess of maidenly delight. For good measure she even added a little Oklahoma twang to her breathless response.

"Oh, Apollo, I'm so glad you finally asked."

The god's lips began to turn up in victory, but her next words caused his expression to freeze.

"Imagine—marriage to the God of Light! I simply couldn't be more thrilled! Just wait until I tell Mother." She gushed, squeezing his hand and bouncing up and down like a giddy school girl.

"Marriage?" His deep voice had gone suddenly hoarse.

Lina beamed an innocent smile into his sapphire-colored eyes.

He dropped the goddess's hand like it was a flaming torch and took a step back, retreating from her bubble of personal space.

"It is not wise to rush hastily into marriage." He cleared his throat as if the word *marriage* was stuck there.

She told her face to frown prettily.

A flash of gold over Apollo's right shoulder caught her attention and interrupted the pithy reply she'd planned. She glanced behind him and felt her mouth round in pleasure.

"Oh! They're amazing." Forgetting about the suave god she turned her full attention to the four horses that had just trotted into view. They were harnessed to a golden chariot that blazed with such a brilliant light that it made her eyes tear. And the horses! They were the same blinding golden color with manes and tails of silver-white. The four slid to a halt, snorting and stamping their delicate hooves.

Apollo glanced over his shoulder. His consternation at the goddess's mention of marriage vanished as he saw his escape.

"Yes, Hadar, yes. I come!" He returned his gaze to Persephone. He had meant to rush away, and considered himself lucky that he had such a ready excuse. Marriage? What had Persephone been thinking! But the rapturous expression that filled her beautiful face gave him pause. She was truly spectacular. Apollo felt a familiar heavy tightening in his loins. "I did not realize you were interested in horses, Persephone."

"I love them," she said without looking at him.

"Come, I will introduce you." He held out his hand to her. Absentmindedly, she took it and hurried eagerly toward the horses, pulling him with her. Apollo's brow wrinkled. It was as if she had forgotten about him. An odd feeling passed through the god. Never before had a goddess forgotten about him—especially not a young goddess who had just tried to snare him in marriage.

The four mares pawed the ground and blew through their noses restlessly. With a flourish, Apollo presented them to Persephone.

"Persephone, Goddess of Spring, I am honored to present to you the mares that draw the light of the sun across the sky. They are Hadar, Aquila, Carina and Deneb," he said, pointing in turn to each horse.

Persephone dropped into a prima ballerina's graceful curtsy. "I am so pleased to meet each of you. Your coats are the most amazing color! You take my breath away."

The effect of her voice on the horses was immediate. Four pairs of ears pricked forward. Hooves ceased their restless pawing. The mare who stood nearest to the goddess stretched her muzzle tentatively in her direction, whickering like a colt.

"Oh, you beauty," Persephone laughed and caressed her.

Apollo felt stunned. He watched the goddess move from horse to horse, clucking and murmuring and whispering strange endearments to each of them. His mares, who were usually aloof and proud, reacted to her with true warmth. They lipped her face and pressed close for her caresses. They all but wriggled and wagged their tails for her attention.

The mares' reactions amazed him, but he was equally surprised at

Persephone. He had never seen this side of her. She had been a goddess with whom he had flirted and had even enjoyed an occasional tryst—always begun and ended at his discretion. He had thought she had no interests beyond growing flowers, frolicking with nymphs and hosting sumptuous feasts. Today she was different. She had not fallen willingly into his arms. His eyes narrowed as he thought about her actions: *She* had actually toyed with *him*. She hadn't truly been interested in marriage. And now she appeared completely enamored with his mares.

She was magnificent.

Apollo was still watching Persephone and trying to decide what could have caused the change in the young goddess when a shrill scream of rage split the air. His mares reacted instantly. They bowed their necks and shook their heads, answering the scream with squeals of anger. The God of Light spun around, ready for battle.

A huge black stallion reared and pawed the air above him. Apollo recognized the wrath-filled creature as one of the dread steeds of Hades. His teeth were bared and his eyes blazed fire. Apollo's horses answered with their own show of rage.

"Stop it this second!" Lina's command dashed cold water on the horses' displays of anger.

Apollo stepped silently to the side, intrigued by this new Persephone. Hands planted firmly on her shapely hips she marched from his golden mares straight to the black beast. He watched, eager to see what she would do next.

"Orion, what in the world is wrong with you?"

She positioned her body so that she could berate all of the horses together. Her back was turned to Apollo affording him an excellent view of her very shapely rear end. He mused that it looked even rounder and more pleasantly inviting than when last he'd seen it. Or perhaps he had never before looked closely enough.

"And you four! What were you going to do, pick on Orion when he is clearly outnumbered?" She shook her head in disgust.

Five horses dropped their heads and looked like repentant school children. Orion took a halting half step toward the object of his affection, stretching his muzzle out to her. She gave him one more hard look before capitulating.

"What are you doing here?" She asked, trying not to smile as he nuzzled the side of her face. Then she noticed that he had been outfitted with a bridle and an attractive saddle made of leather dyed as black as his coat. Tucked into the crownpiece of the bridle was one perfect narcissus blossom. Lina felt a little thrill of pleasure. "Did he send you to get me?"

Apollo was irritated at the obvious delight in her voice. He? Surely she didn't mean Hades.

One of the golden mares nickered. Persephone tilted her head at Apollo's horses.

"Looks like I have to get going. It was wonderful to meet all of you. I hope we see each other again soon."

The goddess moved to the black steed's side and grabbed a fistful of mane, obviously preparing to mount and leave. Apollo couldn't believe it. She'd said good-bye to his horses, but she hadn't spoken another word to him.

"Allow me to aid you, Persephone," Apollo said, moving quickly.

"How rude of me, Apollo. With all this"—she waved her delicate hands at the horses—"excitement I totally forgot about you. It was really nice to meet you, too."

"Meet me." Apollo smiled suggestively at the lovely goddess. "It is not as if we were strangers before today."

Persephone blushed an attractive pink. "Oh, of course not. I didn't mean . . . I'm just . . . discombobulated."

Apollo threw back his head and laughed. "Discombobulated? From hereafter I am going to think of you as Goddess of Surprises rather than Goddess of Spring." He touched the side of her face gently. "And I *will* think of you. Often."

Lina felt the warmth of his hand on her face. His body was so close to her that she thought she could hear his heartbeat—or maybe that was her own. His eyes were such a vibrant shade of blue, the perfect match for his sun-colored hair and his golden skin. Without realizing it, she leaned into him.

Orion snorted.

Lina jerked back.

Apollo smiled knowingly. Before she could refuse him, he took her waist in his hands and slowly lifted her onto the impatiently waiting stallion's back, being careful to brush her body firmly against his own as he did so.

"When will I see you again?" Apollo asked when she had arranged her seat and placed her feet in the stirrups.

"I don't have any idea. There's a lot I have to do." She nodded her head behind her in the direction of the entrance to the Underworld.

"You sojourn with Hades?"

Apollo's incredulous tone irritated Lina. "I am vacationing in the Underworld."

Apollo laughed again. Orion's ears flattened to his head and Lina worried that he would bite the god.

"Vacationing with the dead? I have never heard of such a thing."

"I am finding that the Underworld, as well as its god, has been vastly underrated. Have a nice day, Apollo." Lina nudged Orion. The steed spun on his back hooves and lunged forward into a gallop, eager to return home with his treasure.

"I will be here every dawn, Persephone!" Apollo shouted after her.

Lina leaned forward, grabbing two fistfuls of Orion's mane. She ignored the Sun God, concentrating instead on keeping her seat, even though Orion's gallop was smooth and a childhood in Oklahoma had taught her to be an excellent rider. Apollo was handsome, seductive, and interesting. But she—unlike Persephone—had a job to do and would not let distractions get in her way. Nor did she—again unlike Persephone—want to create a situation that might cause embarrassment for either of them when their bodies were re-exchanged.

The breeze whistling past Orion's head brought with it the enticing scent of the narcissus blossom. Without realizing it, Lina's lips turned up in a wistful smile.

Chapter Sixteen

ORION'S fluid strides covered the distance from the entrance to the Underworld to Hades' palace in what seemed like minutes. Even the ferry ride was faster and easier with the big horse beside her. As the palace came into view Orion slowed his pace to a gentle canter. Without having to be guided, the stallion carried her around the side of the palace and directly to the stables. A uniformed stableman jumped to attention at their appearance, catching Orion's bridle and holding him steady while Lina dismounted.

"Thank you," she whispered to the stallion, kissing his silky muzzle. Orion nuzzled her affectionately. "It was a wonderful ride." Before she gave a final pat to his sleek neck, Lina reached up and pulled the narcissus from his bridle. She hesitated just a second, then tucked it behind her right ear before she turned to the stableman. "Do you know where Hades is?"

"Yes, Goddess. He is at the forge. You may follow that pathway. It will take you to Hades."

Lina smiled her thanks to him and started down the path. She knew Eurydice would be waiting inside with her meal, and she was hungry, but first she wanted to thank Hades for sending Orion to her. She thought that she also might ask him if he would mind if she rode the horse occasionally. The stallion was definitely a horse-lovers dream come true.

The path curled around the stables. It was lined with a hedge of roses the color of cream. She took deep, even breaths, enjoying their fragrance as it mixed with the tangy sweetness of the narcissus behind her ear. The little path angled to her left, and Lina could see that it led toward a small building that sat a little way from the main stable. From it a rhythmic clanging drifted to her on the wind. It was metal pounding on metal, proclaiming that she was heading in the right direction.

The door to the building was slightly ajar, just enough so that Lina could slip silently into the dimly lighted interior. She blinked, trying to adjust her vision from the brightness of outside. She heard a strange *whooshing* noise, which was followed by more clanking. In the far corner of the building flames from an enormous, openmouthed furnace flared, licking the air and adding sudden bursts of light to the darkness.

A man stood before the furnace, magnificently silhouetted against the orange fire. His back was to Lina. He was almost naked, covered only by a loincloth-like wrap that fit snugly around his hard buttocks. With long, powerful strokes he hammered a flat metal object held firmly in place by an ancient looking pair of tongs. With each fluid movement his muscles tensed and released. His body was slick with a glossy sheen of sweat, highlighting the strong ridges of his well-shaped form. His hair was tied back in a thick, dark queue.

Lina felt a jolt of recognition. It was Hades. Of course she'd already thought of him as handsome, and she had definitely been attracted to him . . . but . . . but . . . *merda!* She'd had no idea just how scrumptious he was. Until then he had always been so . . . fully dressed. Her mouth felt dry. He was so . . . so . . . not dressed. And muscular. And absolutely the sexiest thing she had ever seen. Apollo had been almost as scantily clad, but seeing Hades nearly naked was different. The God of Light was handsome, but his beauty was a tame kitten compared to Hades' wild and feral masculinity. Seeing him so gloriously sweaty and under-clothed called awake fantasies within Lina that she thought she had permanently put to sleep.

Fantasies . . . charmed like a cobra, Lina stared at the god. Fantasies . . . she felt an ache deep within her body. It had been so long.

Her thoughts flew free. If only Hades would stroke her with the same intensity with which he was working metal against metal. He looked so incredibly powerful. Lina shivered and imagined hot, sweaty flesh against hot, sweaty flesh. If only . . .

When she was younger Lina had dreamed about being passionate and unrestrained in bed; she had longed for it. Instead of finding a partner who matched her desires, she had married a man who thought quantity in bed equated to quality. So they "did it" a lot, quickly, and with boring regularity. Her husband didn't have the imagination or the inclination to experiment with passion. At some point in her marriage Lina's fantasies had died in a bed of boredom, and by that time she had hardly noticed their passing. Of course she had had lovers before and after her husband, not many—but enough. Long ago she had resigned herself to the fact that she seemed only to attract men who were more cerebral than sensuous. Her love life had been a bust.

So it was with unexpected intensity that Hades' body resurrected her youthful fantasies.

Not realizing he was being watched, Hades wiped his dripping face with the back of one hand and straightened, stretching his back to first flex and then release his massive shoulders.

A little aching sound slipped from Lina's throat.

His head snapped around, and he saw her. She was standing near the doorway with a peculiar look on her beautiful face. Pleasure flushed his already heated body; she was wearing his narcissus in her hair.

Lina licked her lips and cleared her throat. "Um, I didn't mean to disturb you."

"You haven't." He set aside the tongs and wiped his hands on a piece of cloth. Her voice sounded odd, like she was having trouble breathing. Perhaps the return ride from the World of the Living had taxed her strength. Concerned and wishing to put her at ease, he made a welcoming gesture with his hand. "Please, come in."

Lina walked toward him, trying to keep from staring at his chest. His bronzed skin was slick and inviting. Muscles . . . she wanted to moan with pleasure and run her hands up and down his sweaty torso. *Act your age!* she mentally scolded herself.

"I wanted to thank you for sending Orion after me."

She seemed breathless and maybe even a little jittery, which he found strange. What was bothering the goddess? "He was happy to be of service to you."

Lina's hormones shouted that they wished Hades would *service* her, but her voice was better behaved. "If you wouldn't mind, I would love to ride Orion again."

"I would not mind." Hades hesitated. *Keep talking, don't stand there like a mute fool,* his mind commanded. "I am quite sure that Orion would be pleased. Of course, there are three other steeds who will be clamoring jealously for your attention, too," he said, wiping the back of his hand across his brow again.

His movement caused a single bead of sweat to slide from his neck. Lina watched as it traveled with agonizing slowness down his chest and over the well-defined ridges of his abdomen to disappear enticingly under his loincloth.

Her mind refused to formulate a response. All she could do was stand there, speechless, and stare at the damp path the drop left on his glistening skin, wishing with X-rated intensity that she could follow it with her tongue.

"Persephone? I only meant to jest with you. Of course you may ride Orion," Hades assured her. Why was she not speaking? It was certainly not like her to be silent.

"Th-thank you." Lina's eyes snapped up to his face. "I'm sorry. I guess my thoughts are elsewhere."

Hades nodded with sudden understanding. "Of course, it has been a difficult day." He looked down at her sheepishly. "I asked Iapis to report to me if Aeneas had entered Elysia."

"Really?" Hades' words pulled her interest from his body. "And what did he say?"

"I appear to owe you a crystal chandelier. The warrior's soul is, indeed, resting in the Elysian Fields. And, just as you predicted, he has only recently entered the Underworld."

Concern wrinkled her smooth brow. "What are you going to do about Dido?"

The god sighed and wiped another trail of sweat from his cheek. "I will not rescind my decision. I suppose I must have Iapis keep watch on her and . . ." he broke off. The goddess's instincts about Dido had been correct. Why not get her input? He gave her an appraising look. "What would you suggest I do, Persephone?"

Lina felt a little flutter of pleasure; Hades valued her opinion. "Well, I don't think it's wise to leave them in Elysia together. Dido will never get over him like that." Absently, she tugged at one long lock of hair as she considered what to do with the spirit. "I'm assuming that you don't want to send Aeneas out of Elysia?"

"No. The warrior has earned his paradise."

"And you already said you won't send her back to that lamentation place, so I think the only reasonable answer is to let her drink from," she hesitated, making sure she had the right name, "the River Lethe. You said that when they drink from Lethe, souls forget their lives, but remain essentially the same type of people. So send her back for another lifetime. Maybe she really did learn something during her lamentation, something that Aeneas' presence would overshadow, but without any memory of him—" Lina gestured abstractly with her hands. "I guess what I'm trying to say is that maybe she'll do better the second time around."

Hades' smile made his eyes dance. He wanted to throw his arms around her and shout for joy. "Persephone, how is it that a goddess who is so young is also so wise?"

Lina's heart thudded at the warmth of his expression. "You shouldn't judge me by how I look. There's a lot more to me than just a pretty young face."

Hades couldn't stop himself from reaching out and touching that lovely face. "You are correct again. Of all the gods, I should know better than to judge others on appearance and rumor."

His fingers were hot and Lina wanted to turn her face into his palm and press herself against him.

"I'm far from perfect," she said, her voice hardly above a whisper. "I made a mistake in my decision about Eurydice."

"But you were wise enough to correct your mistake. You saved the little spirit. All is as it should be now." As he spoke, his hand moved from her face to touch the moonlight-colored bloom she had tucked behind her ear. Hades glanced from her eyes to the flower. "I hoped that you would approve of Orion's decoration."

Lina sounded out of breath when she answered him. "He looked very handsome with it tucked in his bridle; it's a beautiful flower."

Speak your thoughts aloud! Hades' mind spurred him on. He drew a breath and said, "It is, indeed, a beautiful flower, but it pales in comparison to your loveliness, Persephone." Almost as if it acted on its own, his hand moved from the blossom to trail down the side of her throat, caressing her smooth skin with gentle fingers.

The goddess's breath caught and a little surprised "oh!" sound broke from her lips. Instantly, Hades stopped, his hand hovering near the curve of her neck. His eyes met hers.

"Would you rather that I did not touch you?" His voice sounded rough and foreign.

Persephone blinked twice—quickly.

Hades tightened his jaw and turned away from her. What a fool he'd been! He had read the look in her eyes. He had not seen desire or acceptance there; instead, he had clearly seen shock and confusion.

"Wait!"

Hades took another deep breath, steeling himself. He turned to face her.

"It's not that I don't want you to touch me. I'm just . . . it's just . . ." Lina forced herself to stop babbling. Then she started over in a more controlled, rational tone. "Demeter told me that you weren't interested in women, and it's a well known fact that you don't cavort with nymphs or chase after goddesses, so it's a surprise to me that you're so . . . so . . ." She sighed, frustrated at her inability to explain. "Hades, you are definitely *not* the boring, dour god that Demeter had described to me."

Hades' body became very still. His eyes met hers and held and she read good-humored surprise reflected within their expressive depths.

"The rumor *was* correct," he said slowly and distinctly, his lips curving up. "I did not cavort with nymphs or chase after goddesses because I had met none who interested me."

"Oh," Lina said, unable to look away from his penetrating gaze. Sexy—he was just so damn dark and sexy.

"Until you entered my realm," Hades said with finality.

He stepped forward, and in one swift motion, took her in his arms. Lina felt herself melt into the simmering heat of his sweat-slickened body as he bent and pressed his mouth against hers. Her lips parted and for one delicious moment the kiss deepened. Then, too soon, he released her. She felt dizzy, like she had been underwater for too long and couldn't catch her breath.

"There is more to me than appearance and rumor." Hades echoed her earlier words.

"I believe you."

Hades bent to taste her sweetness again. Lina moaned huskily against his mouth and the sound inflamed him. The full globes of her breasts burned into his chest. He felt his willpower begin to dissolve as his passion for her consumed him.

The shudder that passed through his body became her own, and Lina slid her hands up his bare chest and wrapped them around his neck.

"Don't stop," she whispered. She took his bottom lip between her teeth and bit down teasingly.

With a groan of unleashed desire, Hades cupped her buttocks and lifted her from her feet so that her softness was pressed firmly against him. In two strides he had her pinned against the wall of the forge. One hand slipped up to entrap her breast. The sweet, enticing nipple puckered against his palm and he molded and stroked it. Beneath his other searching hand he found an opening in her silky robe and his hot fingers grasped her naked skin. His pulse thundered in his ears as his world narrowed to exclude everything except his raging need for her.

Caught between the hard coolness of the stone wall and the hard heat of Hades, Lina felt that she was being consumed by him.

Eurydice burst into the forge like a Fourth of July sparkler.

"Persephone! There you are! Oh—" She broke off, her eyes widening as she took in the rumpled, flushed condition of her Goddess and the dark intensity with which Hades had her pressed against the wall.

"*What is it!*" Hades roared, causing the floor of the forge to shake in response.

"Forgive me!" Eurydice's pale face blanched, and she backed fearfully toward the door.

Fighting to catch her breath, Lina pushed firmly against Hades' chest. The god stared down at her. His eyes still burned with need.

"You're scaring Eurydice," she hissed, and, Lina added silently, he was scaring her, too. She had never witnessed the raw power of a god's desire. It definitely had the ability to excite, but it was also overwhelming.

Slowly, through the fog of his passion Hades recognized the fear that flashed through Persephone's eyes. By Zeus' beard! He didn't want her to fear him. Hades blinked, and with a sigh like a storm wind, he moved back, setting her gently to her feet as he suppressed the hot tide within him.

"The spirit may not yet depart," Hades snapped the command and the door to the forge closed before Eurydice could scuttle through it.

The little spirit turned slowly to face the god. Her voice trembled. "It was foolish of me to interrupt. Please forgive me, I . . . I . . . did not realize."

Lina thought that Eurydice looked like she was close to dissolving into tears. "Don't be silly, honey, there's nothing to forgive." She smoothed her hair and tried to ignore the heat that still tingled up from her breasts, through her neck, and into her cheeks. "I was just thanking Hades for sending Orion after me."

Beside her, Hades snorted, "I'll have to send the stallion after you more often."

Lina's gaze met Hades', which sparkled with a mischievous sense of humor, and something else, something that she thought might be tenderness. He brushed the side of her cheek with the tips of his fingers before reluctantly turning his attention to Eurydice.

"Calm yourself, child," Hades said.

Eurydice gave the god a dubious look.

He smiled reassuringly at Eurydice, his voice full of fatherly concern. "Why is it you were searching for your goddess?"

Eurydice looked from Hades to Persephone, who nodded encouragingly at her. The little spirit's expression began to relax and she smiled tentatively back at the dark god. "Iapis asked me to find Persephone. The Limoniades are calling for her."

"Are they indeed?" Although he hated the interruption, he couldn't help but be pleased that the spirits in his realm were not simply accepting the goddess, they were actively seeking her out.

Eurydice nodded enthusiastically, "Iapis said they would not begin the gathering until the goddess joined them."

Lina looked from Hades to Eurydice while she quickly accessed Persephone's memories. *Limoniades—nymph-like spirits of meadows and flowers.* So the spirits of flowers were calling her for a gathering, and Hades and Eurydice looked pleased about it. Lina tried to appear as if she knew what they were talking about. Gathering? What could they be gathering? She frantically asked her built-in memory file.

"It is only logical that they would desire the presence of the Goddess of Spring," Hades said.

In Olympus, forest nymphs are responsible for the gathering of many things: herbs for potions, grapes for wine, flowers to bedeck the palaces of the immortals—

Her internal monologue was interrupted by Hades' voice.

"It is, of course, Persephone's decision," Hades said, obviously surprised at her hesitation.

"Well, I . . ."

"Oh, please, may I watch?" Eurydice rushed forward and grasped her hand. "I have never witnessed the gathering of nectar for ambrosia. Nor have I even seen a nymph, not in the flesh or in the spirit." Eurydice beamed at her.

Lina smiled at Eurydice's infectious exuberance. "Of course you may watch." She felt a trickle of relief. Gathering nectar for ambrosia couldn't be that difficult. She'd just follow the lead of the Lemonade-whatever-their-names-were nymphs.

"Thank you, Persephone!" Eurydice danced to the door.

"May I watch, too?"

Lina looked up at Hades, surprised by his question. He was, after all, God of the Underworld. He had the power to command anyone within his realm; he certainly didn't have to ask her permission. Yet there he stood, doing just that. A little half smile played around his full lips. Sweat still beaded his bare skin, making the bronze muscles of his chest look erotic and exquisitely touchable. Lina felt a tug deep within her, an elemental response to the virile beauty of the dark god.

"No, I don't mind," she said breathlessly.

"Good. It pleases me to watch you," Hades said. Then he repeated his earlier gesture by gently touching the blossom tucked behind her ear. When he withdrew his hand, he allowed his fingers to brush the side of her face in the whisper of a caress. The goddess still shivered under his touch, but this time Hades saw only the reflection of his own desire within her eyes.

"Hurry, Persephone!" Eurydice called from the doorway without looking back at her goddess. "I can't wait to see the Limoniades."

Hades sighed again, quelling the frustration he felt at having to share Persephone. But would he really have it any other way? No, he wanted the goddess to be accepted within his realm, and with that acceptance went the responsibility of sharing her attention. Reluctantly, he moved from her side to reach for a length of dark material that hung from the wall behind him, which he wrapped, toga-like, across his body.

"I'm coming," Lina said, hurrying to catch Eurydice as she scampered through the door and along the pathway. Hades strode beside her, and Lina felt his presence like he was a live wire, humming in time to her own electricity. She was energized by his closeness and by the lingering thrill of his touch. How long had it been since a man had made her feel breathless and excited? Too long, she told herself, ignoring the little voice of reason that counseled her to think about what she was rushing into, that reminded her that she was only there to complete a job and that she didn't know anything about immortals, or the Limoniades, or nectar, or . . .

The path turned abruptly around the corner of the stable and then it opened onto the expanse of the palace's rear gardens. Lina stumbled to a halt, drawing a deep, surprised breath.

Shapes made of incandescent light filled the first tier of the trellised lawn. As Lina came into sight, the glowing forms trembled, and then with a noise that sounded very much like the coo of doves, they surged forward until they surrounded Lina, Eurydice and Hades. Lina stared at them in wonder. Naked women! Her mind registered that the lights hovering and cooing around her were fashioned in the shapes of hundreds of naked women. They were tiny and delicate, the tops of their bright heads barely reached Lina's shoulder, but each one was unique and beautiful in her own right—like flakes of snow, or petals on a flower. And sprouting from the back of each spirit was a pair of sparkling, gossamer wings that looked as fine as mist.

Eurydice giggled. "Why are none of them dressed?"

The echo of Eurydice's youthful laughter rippled through the Limoniades like water over a pebbled brook.

"Look closer, child," Hades' deep voice answered Eurydice. "They are dressed in light and laughter and the brilliance of their souls. It is the only dressing spirits of flowers and meadows require."

"I think they're perfect," Lina said.

The sound of the goddess's voice sent a wave of excitement through the group, and several of the spirits twirled and leapt in glee.

"Join us, Goddess of Spring. Bless the gathering of nectar, which will become the ambrosia of the Underworld."

They spoke with one melodic voice that was magnified magically on the soft breeze.

"Come with us, Persephone. The flowers await the Goddess of Spring."

Their voices were enchanting. Instinctively, Lina's body responded. She stepped away from Eurydice and Hades, joining the Limoniades. Musical notes and the whir of hundreds of wings engulfed her. On feet that felt like air, Lina moved with the spirits out into the flower-filled grounds.

The Limoniades began humming. It was a sound that thrummed through Lina's blood, reminding her of the feel of warm summer nights, the smell of newly cut hay and the taste of fine dark chocolate. Entranced, she watched the glowing forms separate and descend upon the listening blossoms. Wings blurring, they hovered above the ground like elusive hummingbirds, and then, as one they dipped their fingers within the open blooms.

Lina watched the nymph spirits draw beads of golden drops from the flowers. Hades was forgotten. Eurydice left her mind. The only thought that filled her body was how very much she would like to join the Limoniades.

"Yes! Call the nectar to you. Take your rightful place as Goddess of Spring amidst the Limoniades."

The whisper within Lina's mind sounded restless and impatient. It was the final goad she needed. Her heart drumming in time with the song of the Limoniades, Lina approached a cluster of milk-colored tulips. Their stems were long and thick and their blooms opened to expose the crisp yellow of their pistils.

She needed to call the nectar to her. Lina squinted her eyes, dipped her finger into one of the tulips and concentrated. The first blob of golden liquid spurted from the bloom with such force that Lina yelped in surprise as it flew into her hand and disintegrated into a sticky mess.

The deep base of Hades' chuckles framed the light, trilling sound of laughter that trickled through the watching Limoniades. Lina glanced over her shoulder at the god. His eyes sparkled at her. She tossed her long hair back and sent him a saucy look. Then, a thought drifted through her mind. . . . She felt alive and sexy and incredibly, amazingly seductive. With a wicked smile Lina caught Hades' gaze. She arched one brow up, raised her hand and let her soft, pink tongue slowly lick a trickle of the sweet, syrupy nectar from her middle finger. The Limoniades responded with appreciative coos and trills as Hades froze, slack jawed and speechless.

"Gently, Goddess, gently," the Limoniades purred. *"The nectar already desires to come to you. You need only coax it, not command it. It is not a god. . . ."*

Without looking at Hades' reaction to the nymphs' words, Lina stifled a smile and turned back to the cluster of tulips. She tickled another blossom with the tip on one slender finger and sent the gentle thought to it that she might like the nectar to come to her, please.

A pearl of gold drifted from the center of the flower to perch on the tip of her extended finger. Lina smiled triumphantly at it.

"The gathering, Goddess. Join the gathering."

Still smiling, Lina gazed around her. Each spirit nymph was creating a pile of glowing golden drops beside her as she flitted from flower to flower, calling the nectar forth.

Okay, Lina thought. She could do that. And she began weaving her own pile. Without stopping to think or understand or question, Lina used Persephone's perfect voice to harmonize with the spirits of the flowers, and when she joined the Limoniades in their song, Hades' garden seemed to inhale with a tangible sense of joy and then erupt into glorious full bloom. Every flower opened itself. Every blossom dripped golden drops of nectar, aching to be harvested.

Amidst it all, Lina shined.

Hades couldn't take his eyes from her. In his entire existence he had never desired anything as much as he desired Persephone. He was becoming consumed by her, and the thought made his immortal soul shiver.

What would happen when she left? She would, he reminded himself. She was the Goddess of Spring. She belonged to the world above. He was the dark God of the Underworld, scorned by everything living.

Everything except Persephone. But for how long?

The ache within him pulsed and took on a life of its own. And the god gave name to it, finally understanding what it was that caused him such elusive, unending pain—what it was that Persephone had awakened along with hope.

Loneliness.

Hades clenched his jaw against his inner turmoil and turned blindly away from the sight of the lovely young goddess frolicking joyously amidst the spirits of his realm.

He ran right into Eurydice. Hades stifled his groan of frustration as he caught the little spirit and kept her from tumbling to the ground. He forced his stiff face into the semblance of a smile. "I was not looking, child." He changed his path of retreat, but Eurydice's voice gave him pause.

"But, you aren't leaving? What shall I tell Persephone?" she asked in her sweet, shy voice.

"Tell her," he ground his teeth, "that I had the business of my realm to attend." Eurydice's eyes were large and round and they seemed to reach into his soul. Her disappointment was obvious, as was her concern for her goddess. The god raked a hand through his hair. "And tell your goddess that I wish her to ride with me on the morrow."

Eurydice's face lit in a smile. "Persephone will enjoy that very much."

Will she enjoy it enough to stay with me? the god wanted to rant and rage and roar. Instead he pulled the familiar mantle of sternness over his features and made certain that when he spoke his voice was free of his seething emotions.

"I will send Iapis to escort her to the stables after daybreak."

"Yes, Lord."

Hades strode away, muttering under his breath about goddesses and young girls.

As soon as he was out of sight, Iapis materialized beside Eurydice.

She glanced at the daimon, her look betraying no surprise at his sudden appearance.

"How goes it?" Iapis asked her.

"I am pleased," Eurydice said, sounding wise beyond her years.

"Do you think he took my advice and thought of her as one of the dead?"

"Not for long," Eurydice said enigmatically, remembering her goddess's flushed face and the heat with which Hades' eyes followed her. "Not for long . . ."

The daimon smiled and took the little spirit's hand in his. Raising it to his lips, he kissed her gently. Eurydice's pale cheeks pinkened slightly, but her large eyes gazed steadily at him. She returned his smile.

Chapter Seventeen

"Good-bye! Thank you!" Lina waved to the Limoniades as the glowing spirits faded into the distance, taking their shining golden drops of nectar with them. Their farewell coos tumbled musically on the wind.

"That was wonderful to watch, Persephone." Eurydice was all smiles as Lina rejoined her at the edge of the gardens.

"I'm so glad they called me. It was an amazing experience," Lina gushed. She felt giddy and energized, like she'd had too many double-shot cappuccinos before breakfast. "Oh, Eurydice, this world is incredible." She grinned, slinging an arm around the spirit and hugging her. Lina glanced around them. "Hades left?" she asked, trying to sound nonchalant.

"He had to attend to the business of his realm. But," she added quickly as the goddess's shining face dimmed, "he commanded me to request your presence at the stables on the morrow."

"Riding Orion again." Lina's smile turned dreamy as she thought about the black stallion. She would definitely look forward to the morning ride—almost as much as she'd look forward to seeing Hades. Her mind skittered around, jumbling images of the god's sweat-beaded body, the sensuous song of the Limoniades and the way Hades' lips had burned against hers. Lina's young borrowed body tingled erotically.

"That horse frightens me," Eurydice said.

Lina blinked, refocusing on Eurydice's pale face. *Merda!* She needed to stop letting her mind wander.

"He's nothing to be frightened of. Really, he's like a puppy in my hands," Lina said breezily, trying not to think about Orion's master, and how *un*like a puppy he felt under her hands.

"I think I'll just stay away from him," Eurydice said.

Lina told herself that's probably the attitude she should have about Hades. He was too damn dangerously attractive. She should just stay away from him. But the low ache in her body murmured that she wouldn't.

She definitely needed to get her mind off Hades.

"Hey, how about we go find me something to drink?" Lina wiggled her eyebrows at Eurydice. "All this nectar-gathering has made me thirsty for ambrosia."

Eurydice tittered, "It has also made you sticky."

Lina glanced down at herself. Shiny speckles of golden dots were sprinkled like dew all over her body. She touched one of them and then put her finger to her mouth. It tasted like sugarcane mixed with honey mixed with something like caramel or maybe butterscotch. It was delicious. But Eurydice was right, she was a mess. And she certainly was not going to think about how it would feel to have Hades lick the sweet drops off her body.

"I need a shower. A cold one," she muttered.

"You wish to be caught in a cold rain?"

Lina laughed. "Not exactly. A shower isn't just rain from the skies. It's kind of like bathing, only you're standing up and water is being poured over you."

"Oh, that sounds like my mother's bathing ritual, although she did not like her water cold," Eurydice said.

Startled, Lina asked, "Really, what kind of bathing ritual did your mother have?"

Eurydice grinned impishly. "I could show you. It would probably be an easier way to get the nectar off of you." She touched one of the drops and it trailed long, gooey tendrils from her finger back to the goddess' skin. "They might make your bathing water a sticky mush."

"Eurydice, you are a genius. Tonight I put myself in your capable hands."

THE little spirit had turned into a mini drill sergeant. From the second they reentered the palace she had been firing orders and directing a bevy of flitting servants. She wouldn't allow Lina to do anything except sit on the edge of the vanity chair and sip ambrosia.

"The goddess would prefer to bathe on the balcony."

Mid-gulp of ambrosia, Lina sputtered. Bathe on the balcony? What was Eurydice thinking? The spirit was using the voice that Lina was rapidly coming to recognize as her formal, she's-my-goddess-you-better-mind-me tone as she tapped one slender foot thoughtfully against the marble floor. Without giving Lina a chance to speak, Eurydice barreled on.

"Yes, mother always used our inner courtyard. No! Not there!" She snapped at two male servants who were struggling to carry a large basin into the bathing room. "She pointed to the door in the middle of the wall of windows. "Take it through there."

"Um, Eurydice, why are we going out on the balcony?"

"You are not to worry, Persephone. All will be perfect." She frowned at one of the servants who jostled the basin a little too roughly against the marble floor of the balcony.

"Goddess," Iapis entered the room and bowed politely to Lina before turning his attention to the spirit. "You have need of me, Eurydice?"

"Yes," Eurydice said, hooking her long, wispy hair behind her ears. "The goddess is going to bathe on her balcony, and—"

Here Lina had to interrupt. "Wait, I think it's a lovely idea for me to bathe on the balcony—I mean, the view is spectacular—but I'm really not comfortable with, well," Lina dropped her voice so that the daimon and Eurydice had to lean forward to hear her. "I don't want a bunch of guys seeing me naked." Even if they were dead guys, she added silently.

Eurydice squinted at her as if she didn't fully understand what she was saying, but Lina was relieved to see Iapis nodding his head.

"It is also true of the Goddess Artemis. She will not allow her nakedness to be glimpsed by any mortals except for her handmaidens. But that problem is easily remedied, Persephone. I shall simply command that all spirits stay away from your wing of the palace and the surrounding grounds."

Eurydice gifted the daimon with a smile filled with warmth, and Iapis looked inordinately pleased with himself. Lina felt like she had been caught in the middle of a well-meaning tornado. It was whirling her around and around, and was determined to spin her clothes off.

"I really don't want to cause any trouble," Lina said helplessly.

"It is no trouble at all," the daimon assured her.

"You are the Goddess of Spring," Eurydice said.

Apparently, that was the final word on everything.

Resigned, Lina settled back, deciding not to care if she got nectar all over the silk-lined chair. She was, after all, the Goddess of Spring. She watched the whirlwind of preparation for her bath. They appeared to like cleaning up after her. Eurydice shook her head severely at an insubstantial servant who had failed to retrieve the correct number of towels from the bathing room. Or maybe they were just scared of Eurydice. At least the little spirit didn't seem to have been traumatized by the day's events. Lina sipped her ambrosia, considering. Had it only been that morning that Orpheus had descended into the Underworld? It felt like it had happened so long ago. How could she only have known Hades for a couple of days? What was it that Demeter had said? Something about the passage of time being measured differently by the gods. Her instincts told her that Demeter's words rang true. The passage of time was different in the world of the gods, as different as her borrowed life. Her heart felt different, too. The veneer of cynicism that had muffled it the past several years didn't seem to have transcended worlds. Lina's stomach tightened. To lust after a god . . . wouldn't that be the ultimate stupidity?

"Goddess, I will leave you to Eurydice and the maiden servants. Let your mind be eased—no mortal male will gaze upon you." Iapis bowed to her.

"Iapis!" A sudden thought made Lina call him back. "You said no *mortal* male would see me, but what about Hades? Where is he?" Lina pretended that she didn't know her cheeks were blazing with hot color.

Iapis' face remained impassive. "The Lord of the Underworld has gone to the Elysian Fields. He spoke of seeking out Dido and escorting her to the River Lethe."

Even though Lina was pleased at the news that Hades had followed her advice, she frowned and pointed out the open glass doors to the balcony and beyond.

"Aren't the Elysian Fields that way?"

"Some are, Goddess." Then his eyes flashed with understanding. "I will go to my Lord and guide him back to the palace by a different route. Rest assured, Persephone, Hades would not wish to disturb your privacy."

"Oh, no, of course not," Lina said hastily.

"Enjoy your bath, Goddess." Iapis bowed again.

Eurydice followed him to the door.

"If your goddess requires anything else, you need only send one of the maidens for me, and I will see it done," Iapis said.

Eurydice tilted her head in acknowledgment. "That is most gracious of you, Iapis," she said, stepping into the hall. There she lowered her voice so that Persephone could not hear her. "Did Hades really go to Elysia?"

"Yes," Iapis whispered.

"But you will not stop him from returning through the gardens?"

Iapis answered with a slow, knowing smile and a wink. Eurydice had to clamp her pretty lips together to keep from giggling.

EURYDICE was chattering happily as she helped Lina out of her nectar-speckled robes. They were standing in the middle of the spacious balcony that looked out over the glorious rear grounds of the palace. Grounds that were decidedly empty of all spirits, male or otherwise, Lina noted. Directly in front of her was the basin Eurydice had ordered the servants to bring. Beside it was a small table covered with bottles and sponges. Sitting closer to the basin than the table was a short, fat stool. Near the edge of the balcony was a chaise lounge that Eurydice had insisted the servants drag out of Lina's bedroom. On the chaise sat an intricately carved wooden tray, which held sumptuous pomegranate fruits, their skins already opened and spilling forth their garnet-colored seeds. And, of course, there was also a crystal bottle filled to brimming with chilled ambrosia. Lina grinned. A goddess could certainly never have enough ambrosia.

The balcony itself was, like the rest of the palace, opulent and unique. It didn't just extend out and around the wall of windows. It curved gracefully, like one half of a Valentine's Day heart, until the balustrades opened to a circular marble staircase, which spilled out into a flower-lined path, which led, like spokes in a wheel, to the first tier of Hades' gardens. It was her own private entrance to paradise.

Lina gazed out on the amazing scene while Eurydice unwrapped her clothes from around her. She hadn't been exaggerating when she'd said that the view was spectacular. And there was something about the light—it had begun to change. The pastel sky was darkening and the colors were deepening from pink to coral and violet to purple. Suddenly, torches flared alive all throughout the gardens, causing Lina to jerk in surprise.

"There is no need to worry, Goddess." One of the maidens who had stayed to assist Eurydice spoke up with the voice of a child. "The torches light themselves. There is no mortal man in the gardens to look upon your nakedness."

"What is your name?" Lina asked the young spirit.

"Hersilia," she ducked her head shyly.

"Thank you, Hersilia, for reminding me not to be so silly." Lina smiled at the servant.

Eurydice unwrapped the final layer of silky fabric from around her waist and bent to help her off with her leather slippers.

"Now just step into the basin, Persephone," Eurydice directed her.

The marble basin felt cool against Lina's bare feet, and she decided that it was a little like standing in a giant cereal bowl. The lip of the bowl came up to her knees. She was about to say that she felt like a naked Fruit Loop when Eurydice climbed on top of the stool.

"You may bring me the urn."

The waiting servants formed an unlinked chain from the balcony, through the glass doors and into the bathroom. From there they began passing hourglass-shaped clay urns filled with water, which, to Lina's delight, Eurydice poured in steaming waves over her head.

More servants dripped soap onto sponges soft as cotton balls. Slowly, gently they began cleaning her skin. Lina's initial response was to stay very still, with her arms held at a rigid T away from her sides.

Then Eurydice began to sing, softly at first, but soon the other spirits joined with her and sweet, feminine voices filled the balcony.

Pale, beyond porch and portal,
crowned with hair of silk, she stands,
she who gathers all things mortal
within her soft, immortal hands.

Their song was slow and sensual, like the beat of bolero, and it stirred something deep within Lina. Intrigued, she accessed Persephone's memories. *They sing ancient praise to the beauty of the goddess. They do you great honor.* They did her great honor. . . . Suddenly it didn't matter that she was wearing a borrowed shape. She was alive and beautiful and filled with the exquisite power of a goddess. Lina let her body go loose. She drew a deep breath and exhaled all the stress and cares and inhibitions of her mortal life. Her ivory skin tingled and she began to sway gracefully with the tempo of the song.

Her languid lips are sweeter
than love who pines to greet her
no mortal man shall meet her
the goddess solitary stands.

The hot water sluiced over her naked body, a river of silk the soapy sponges traveled along. Lina turned and laughed and reveled in the sensations cascading down her skin. She felt the evening air lick her sleek sides. It was warm, but in contrast to the heat of the water it brought gooseflesh rising on her skin and caused her nipples to pucker erotically. Her laughter was infectious, and soon the maidservants joined her and the sounds of song and joy drifted through the palace and the gardens of the God of the Dead.

WITH slow, thoughtful steps Hades followed the snaking path that led from the forest, which separated his palace grounds from the Elysian Fields. The path took him through the third tier garden. He was glad that he had listened to Persephone's advice. Dido had been easy to find. All he had had to do was locate Aeneas. Her spirit had been nearby, pining miserably as she obsessively shadowed the warrior's every move. She hadn't wanted to drink of Lethe, such was the strength of her unrequited love, but Dido's soul belonged to Hades, and what he commanded she must do. As always happened, when she drew near Lethe, her spirit had quickened. The river's seductive voice had entranced her, making her transition a gentle one. But it was not the memory of Dido that slowed the god's steps. It was Persephone. The goddess haunted his senses. Though he had only held her in his arms briefly, he could still feel the satin of her skin against his . . . taste the sweetness of her mouth . . . smell the scent of woman that clung to her body.

He could still hear her laughter. Hades swore under his breath. Was this what love was like? Must he be consumed with thoughts of her?

The laughter came again. Listening carefully, Hades halted. Then he drew a relieved breath. The sound wasn't coming from his imagination.

It was being carried from the palace by the warm evening breeze. Now he could discern different voices along with Persephone's. Some were laughing, some were singing. All were delightfully female. When Hades began walking again, his stride was no longer slow and thoughtful.

Entering the second tier, Hades scanned the rearview of his palace. Daylight had darkened to evening and the flickering torchlight that periodically illuminated the gardens did little to aid his vision. As usual, the palace windows were gaily lit, and Hades thought he could see graceful, curving shapes outlined against the wall of windows that belonged to Persephone's chamber. He thought it odd that they appeared to be on her balcony. Hades increased his stride.

When he reached the stairs that would take him up to the first tier, he was sure that he could hear the splashing of water. Taking the stairs three at a time, he climbed quickly up to the level of his palace. Here the greenery and flowers wound around in labyrinthine twists and turns, and Hades did not have a clear view of Persephone's balcony until he was very close to the edge of the gardens. The god stepped around an ornamental hedge and stopped like he had slammed against an invisible wall.

Persephone was naked. She stood in the center of a large marble basin, looking like an exquisite statue that had come to life. The stray thought passed through Hades' numbed mind that he suddenly understood Pygmalion's obsession with Galatea. Then his mind seemed to cease functioning completely and he became nothing more than a receptacle for the desire that scorched through his blood.

Eurydice was pouring trails of steaming water over Persephone while semitransparent maidservants lathered her skin and hair. The goddess laughed and teasingly splashed water at the spirits, who were humming a slow, seductive tune between breathless, girlish giggles. The evening light was muted, but Persephone's body was silhouetted against the wall of glowing windows. Hades could see the flush that swept her ivory skin. His eyes ravished her body. His fingers tingled as he remembered how the delicate curve of her neck had felt under his too-brief caress. Hades' gaze lowered to her breasts. The soft globes were full and heavy. Their blush-colored nipples were taut, begging for the touch of his lips and tongue. His loins tightened and throbbed achingly with the heat of his lust. He ground his teeth together to keep from giving voice to the moan of frustrated desire that was building within him. But he did not turn away, he did not stop gazing at her. He could not.

Persephone's waist curved in, and then swelled to flare into well-rounded hips. Her legs were long and shapely. Hades' eyes were drawn to the inviting V of dark hair that formed at their junction. The curling triangle glistened with water, which dripped down her inner thighs.

As if sensing him, Persephone's chin went up and her gaze shifted from the laughing servants to rove over the distant gardens. Hades was sure he would be discovered, but his dark cloak blended like night with the shadow of the hedge and the goddess's eyes passed unseeing over him.

Eurydice poured a final stream of water over Persephone and then the little spirit called for a maidservant to bring her towels. They helped the smiling goddess step from the basin and began drying her body.

Now was the time for him to turn away. Persephone's laughter floated to him and his eyes refused to leave her as they sought glimpses of her nakedness. His conscience told him he should go, but the voice of newly awakened desire and longing and loneliness drowned it out.

The servants finished drying Persephone's body. Her hair drifted around her in long, damp tendrils, which Eurydice gathered and piled loosely atop her head. Then the spirit poured a thick liquid from a tall glass bottle into her hand and began gently massaging the oil into her skin. Two other maidservants joined her. Hades watched Persephone's eyes close. A sensuous smile curved her lips as the slick hands of the maidens anointed her body. Hades' breathing quickened. The glistening oil caught the flickering lights that shined through the windows of her bedchamber, and soon the goddess's body glowed with a wet, luminous invitation.

The throbbing ache in his loins was unbearable and Hades' hand sought his engorged flesh. His breathing turned ragged as he stroked himself, quick and hard, never taking his eyes from Persephone's body. His focus narrowed until she was all that existed in his world. He imagined that it was his hands that were slick with oil caressing her breasts, cupping her luscious buttocks, traveling up her ivory thighs to find her moist core. There he wanted to bury himself, to pump his need into her and to be surrounded by her velvet heat. His orgasm ripped from his body, exploding with such hot intensity that it drove him to his knees. There he remained, knelt within shadow, alone, struggling to regain his breath. And, still, his longing eyes locked on the goddess.

"Persephone . . ." Her name was a harsh whisper on his lips.

Chapter Eighteen

Lina felt like a well-fed kitten. Her body was in that wonderful place between relax and replete. Every bit of stress had been massaged from her muscles. Her skin was so incredibly smooth that as she lounged across the chaise and nibbled pomegranate seeds she absently stroked her fingers across her body, which seemed to hum with pleasure.

"Youth, beauty, and the power of a goddess—Persephone has it all," she said, and then looked guiltily around. No, she was totally alone. Just as she'd asked. After her shower and fabulous oil massage, Eurydice had dressed her in the shimmering narcissus nightdress and Lina had curled up on the chaise. When the little spirit asked if there was anything else she required, Lina had drowsily told her that the only thing she wanted was to lie on the chaise, drink ambrosia and eat pomegranates. Then she was going to go to sleep.

Eurydice had clapped her hands together like the bossy headmistress of an all girls school and hastily shooed the maidservants from the balcony, announcing that Persephone required privacy. And then, to Lina's surprise, Eurydice had actually followed the servants from the chamber, saying that she had an appointment with Iapis to go over her preliminary sketches of the palace, but she promised to bring by what she completed for the goddess's approval in the morning.

Iapis and Eurydice again. Lina tugged at a lock of long hair and twirled it around her finger. If she wasn't mistaken, the daimon's interest in Eurydice was more than friendly. Maybe she should speak to Hades about it.

Hades . . . thinking of the god brought the restlessness that was simmering just below her skin to the surface. She poured herself another glass of ambrosia. What was up with him? Why had he suddenly disappeared? He'd told her very clearly that he was interested in her, then he'd kissed her. Kissed her, hell! He'd pinned her against the wall and ravished her thoroughly. Remembering his passion made her shiver. Hades was the personification of dark and dangerous—a living, breathing Batman. She licked her lips and swore she could still taste him, or maybe that was just the ambrosia? Both were certainly delicious.

Lina closed her eyes, letting her fingers trail from her throat down, brushing over her already aroused nipples. She breathed a moan. *Merda!* Persephone's body was young and responsive and . . .

Lina's eyes snapped open. "And very, very horny," she said in a frustrated voice. "Or maybe it's more me than her. Or a combination of what happens when a forty-three-year-old woman who hasn't had sex in"—she stopped and counted back in her mind—"who hasn't had sex in almost three years is put into the body of a nubile young goddess and then is tempted by a handsome, Batman look-alike. Up! Time to get up and walk it off."

She stood, too fast, and felt all bubbly and slack-kneed. The ambrosia had definitely gone to her head . . . as well as to other sensitive spots. Her lips twisted in chagrin and a pretty pink flush heated her cheeks. Jeesh, she had it bad. Well, she'd tried the cold shower, and it definitely hadn't worked the way she'd planned. She sighed and trailed her finger across the smooth marble railing of the balcony, thinking of Eurydice's idea of a shower. It had been a heavenly experience. But it had done nothing to dispel her fantasies about Hades. Actually, it had accomplished the opposite. Her body had been bathed and massaged, pampered and preened. She felt like a royal concubine who had been prepared for her sultan.

So where the hell was her sultan? Pun definitely intended.

Lina shook her head and rolled her eyes. "You've had entirely too much ambrosia." With finality she set her half-empty glass on the flat top of the railing and started purposefully, if a little wobbly, for the circular staircase that wrapped down to the palace grounds. She'd take a nice brisk walk in the garden. That would clear her head and make her sleepy enough that she would remember that bed was a place in which one slept more often than one had hot, sweaty sex with a dark, handsome god.

In an ambrosial mist, Lina followed her private path to the first tier of the palace gardens. When she reached the entrance she stood very still, soaking in the magical view of the torch lit grounds. The Underworld was such an incredibly lovely place. The sky had continued to darken, but it was not black, as was the night sky in the world above. Instead, it was slate gray, illuminated by several brilliantly lit stars, each haloed with iridescent color that reminded Lina of the pearlized belly of a seashell. The unusual sky caused everything to be bathed in soft darkness, as if this part of the Underworld was a sweet dream.

"Those stars are the most beautiful things I have ever seen," Lina said to the silent sky.

"They are the Hyades."

Hades seemed to materialize from the shadows of the garden.

Lina's hand flew to her throat. She could feel her heart pounding there. "You scared me!"

"I did not mean to startle you, but I was just thinking of you and when I heard your voice I wanted very much to join you."

Lina bit her bottom lip and tried to clear her wine-fogged mind. He was wearing that damn cape again. And, even more dangerously, he had traded in the voluminous length of material he usually wrapped around his body for a much more revealing outfit. He had again chosen to wear black, but that night it was in the form of a short, black leather chiton that appeared to have been molded to his chest. It ended in panels just over his hips. Beneath, he wore a fine, pleated tunic, the color of thunderclouds, which left almost all of his muscular legs exposed. Lina wrenched her eyes up to meet his. He was watching her with a dark intensity she felt tingle through her blood.

"You've been on my mind, too. I'm glad you're here," she said, and reminded herself to breathe as he moved with feral intensity closer to her.

His body was like a furnace; she could feel the heat that radiated from him. Hades took her hand and raised it slowly to his mouth. His lips seemed to burn a brand into her skin. He didn't release her hand. Instead, he traced a circular path across it with his thumb. The cooling wind brought his scent to her. He smelled of the night and of leather mingled with man. It was an erotic, dangerous scent that made her stomach tighten and shiver. It made her think of sweat-slicked, naked skin. Without conscious thought, she breathed more deeply and leaned toward him. His eyes flashed and the teasing breeze caught his cape so that it rose behind him like wings. She was submerged within the intensity of his gaze. She could feel his passion ignite. This Hades was not the smart, sexy god she had been getting to know. Once again he was the being who had possessed her in the forge. He loomed before her, an infinitely powerful immortal—seductive, alluring, overwhelming, and a little frightening. She still wanted him. His presence was magnetic, but her mortal soul was struggling to maintain some semblance of control. Lina forced her mind to work, grasping at something, anything she could say to him.

"You said the stars are Hyades. I don't understand," she finally managed.

Hades lifted his eyes from hers to gaze at the night sky.

"You don't understand because you know them only as the bright nymphs they are in the world above. What most immortals do not know is that a group of forest Hyades tired of their earthly duties. They begged Zeus to allow them to become mortal so that they could die and be relieved of the burden of immortality."

His voice was as deep and as hypnotic as his eyes. Entranced, Lina stared at him as he wove the tale. He was a dark flame that drew her soul inexorably to him. Batman. Definitely Batman. And, ambrosia or no ambrosia, what sane woman would *not* be into Batman fantasies?

"Zeus granted the Hyades their wish and that same night they entered my realm. I was so moved by the iridescence of their souls that I proclaimed that their great beauty could light all of Elysia. The nymphs were intrigued by the idea and they came as one to petition me. As Zeus before me, I, too, granted their wish, and they have illuminated the night sky of the Underworld ever since."

Lina forced her eyes from the magnetic god to look up at the stars that were really the spirit of nymphs.

"What are you doing here, Persephone?"

The raw emotion in the god's voice stopped Lina's breath, and her gaze flew back to his. What had happened to him tonight? And how could he be so powerful and yet look so vulnerable at the same time? She shook her head and gave him the only answer she could.

"I drank too much ambrosia and I thought a walk in the garden would help sober me up."

Hades stared at her a moment longer, then he blinked, raked one hand through his hair and expelled one long breath. Slowly, the tense lines of his face began to relax. "Too much ambrosia? I understand that feeling all too well. It makes your head cloudy and your knees weak."

Relieved that he seemed more normal, Lina smiled. "Glad to hear I'm not the only one it's happened to."

"A walk does help." He returned her smile, and bowed gallantly to her. "I would be honored if you allowed me to escort you."

He was her dashing Hades again, and she grinned, curtsied and realized that she was wearing nothing but a thin silk nightgown. She cleared her throat.

"I, uh, seem to be underdressed for an evening stroll."

Hades' eyes glinted darkly as they roamed from her flushed face down to her silk-draped body. In one graceful movement he unclasped his cape, and with a swirling motion that reminded her of a matador, wrapped it around her shoulders.

"Better?"

Encased in his warmth and scent, she could only nod.

"Then I may escort you?"

"Absolutely," she said.

He smiled and pulled her arm through his. Hades led her slowly into the night-shrouded grounds. They didn't speak; they just accustomed themselves to the feel of one another. Hades chose a wide path that bisected the gardens. Lina gazed around her in awe. The unusual gentleness of the Underworld's night cast a magical glow over the sleeping flowers and hedges, so that even though many of the blossoms had closed, the flowers still dotted the landscape with splashes of snowy color.

"I can't decide whether I think they're more beautiful during the day while they're in full bloom, or like this, looking like sleepy children," Lina said, reaching out to trail one finger gently over the closed blossom of a milk-colored day lily. At her touch, the folded flower burst into full bloom. Lina bit back a startled cry. She had to remember that she was Goddess of Spring. Obviously, she shouldn't be surprised when she made a flower bloom.

"Now you can have both beauties together," Hades said.

Lina's brow furrowed. "No, I don't want to wear them out." She thought for a moment before waving her fingers at the flower. "Go back to sleep," she told it. With a sound that was very much like a sigh, the lily closed.

She turned back to Hades to find him watching her with an expression she couldn't read. Before she could ask him what was wrong, he took her hand, the one that had touched the flower, and turned it so that it rested, palm up, in his own, then he raised the tips of her fingers to his mouth.

The touch of his lips made her stomach shiver. She wanted him to kiss much more than her hands.

Too soon, he released her hand and said, "You are a very kind goddess."

She wasn't really Persephone, but Hades made her feel like she truly was a goddess. Instead of wrapping her arm through his again, Lina slid her fingers down his arm so that she could hold his hand. His lips quivered, then turned up in a pleased smile. He squeezed her hand, and they resumed their walk.

"I would like to show you something," Hades said suddenly. "Something that is very important to me."

Lina glanced up at him and their eyes met briefly. Then he looked away, and Lina could see the tense line of his jaw.

"If it's important to you, I would love to see it."

His jaw unclenched and he squeezed her hand again. "It is this way."

The first tier ended and Hades led her down the stairs to the second level. Earlier that day when she had been collecting nectar she really hadn't been able to pay attention to anything except calling forth the sticky liquid, and Lina would have liked to have stopped to take a closer look at the fountains and statuary, but the God's pace quickened. Obviously, he was anxious to get to whatever he wanted to show her. Curiosity piqued, she lengthened her stride to match his.

On the third level Hades chose a path that branched to their right. It wound in little S curves down the side of that tier. Gradually, the well-tended gardens gave way to large pine trees. Their sharp scent reminded Lina of holidays and home.

"I love the way pine trees smell," Lina said.

Instead of answering, Hades pressed his finger against her lips. "Ssssh," he whispered. "We do not want them to know we are here."

Before Lina could ask who he meant, Hades pointed to a cluster of large stones.

"We must wait behind those."

Intrigued, but completely confused, Lina let him pull her down next to him as they crouched behind the jagged rocks.

"What's going on?" Lina whispered.

Hades changed position so that he could see over the top of the nearest boulder. He gestured for her to do the same. She peeked over the rock.

On the other side of the cluster of rocks the land angled sharply down until it met the bank of a river. Lina blinked several times to make sure her eyes weren't fooling her, but the water remained the same, sparkling like liquid diamonds in the magical light of the Underworld night. Everything was very quiet around them, and Lina could hear the sound of the river. Its voice laughed and sang the words of a strange language. She didn't understand the words, but the sound was compelling, and she felt a sudden desire to rush down the bank and wade into the water so that she could be immersed in its bright laughter.

Hades' firm hand enveloped her shoulder. His lips almost touched her ear as he spoke quietly to her. "Do not listen to the river's call."

Lina focused on his voice and almost instantly she felt the river's allure slide away.

"I should have warned you. The call of Lethe can be very strong." Hades' breath was warm and Lina leaned into him. He shifted his position, put his arm around her shoulders and drew her in front of him so that she was half resting intimately across his lap. She leaned back against his chest and tilted her head toward him so that he could catch the whisper of her words.

"This is Lethe, the River of Forgetfulness?"

Lina felt him nod and she stared at it, unbelieving. So this was the famous river that caused souls to forget their lives and readied them to be born anew.

"Is that what is so important to you?"

"In a way," he whispered, "but there is more."

"Why do we have to be so quiet?"

"We do not want the souls to know that we are here. Our presence would be a distraction. For this the dead do not need us."

Lina felt a rush of excitement and she searched the banks of the river. "I don't see any dead."

"Watch and wait" was all he would say.

Lina settled back against him. Hades wrapped his arms tightly around her. It felt incredibly good to be so close to him. The bite of pine lingered in the air, mixing with the heady male scent of Hades. Once she tuned out its compelling call, the river's voice was lilting and melodic. Lina felt immersed in an experience of the senses. Her entire body felt aroused and ultra-sensitive. The god's hand rested on her forearm and his thumb was tracing lazy circles over her skin. She shivered under his touch.

"Is my cloak not warm enough?" he murmured, his breath licking against her ear. "Are you cold?"

She shook her head no, and turned in his arms so that she could see his face. He surrounded her. His body was hard and strong and he radiated heat through the leather of his breastplate. His bare arms encircled her. She opened her mouth to tell him that it was his touch that made her tremble and that . . .

"There." His whisper was urgent. He leaned forward, moving her with him. Hades pointed and Lina's eyes followed his finger.

Two figures were approaching the river from the opposite side. As they drew closer Lina could see that they were holding hands. The bright water reflected off their bodies, showing them to be an ancient-looking man and woman. They moved slowly, allowing their shoulders and hips to brush against one another. Every step or two the man would raise the woman's wrinkled hand to his lips and hold it there while she gazed tenderly at him.

Lina felt a little uncomfortable spying on them, but she was also mesmerized by the obvious adoration the two felt for one another. Finally, the couple reached the river's edge. They turned to face each other. The man rested his hands on the woman's shoulders.

"Are you quite certain?" His voice was cracked with age and emotion, but it carried clearly across the river.

"Yes, my love. I am certain. It is time, and we will find each other again," she answered him.

"I have always trusted you. I cannot doubt you now," he said.

As the old man drew the woman gently into his arms and kissed her, Lina felt her eyes fill with tears. She blinked quickly to keep her vision clear. The couple ended their embrace, and then with their hands still joined, they knelt beside the river, bent down and drank the crystal water. Instantly, their bodies began to shine. Their hair and clothes whipped wildly around them as if they had been caught in a fierce wind. Then they began to change. Lina gasped as she watched years fall away from the couple. Their images shifted from old age, to middle age, then young adulthood, and finally they glowed with the vibrancy of teenagers. There the metamorphosis paused. Stunned, the two gazed at each other. Then the man threw back his head and shouted with joy. Again, he pulled the woman into his arms and she wrapped herself around him, laughing and crying at the same time.

Tears spilled from Lina's eyes—that must have been how they had looked when they had first fallen in love. While they were embracing their bodies became brighter and brighter, until Lina had to use her hand to shield her eyes against the light. Then they exploded, as if two stars had just burst, raining a shower of sparks into the water. From the center of each of the explosions twin dots of fist-sized lights were formed. They hovered over the water, acclimating themselves to their new senses. Then they began to float downstream, carried by their own special breeze. Lina stared after them. The two globes of light remained close together, so close that, as they moved farther away, there appeared to be no visible distinction between them. The river curved to the left and the lights followed it, disappearing from sight.

Lina wiped at her eyes and sniffled. "What will happen to them?" she asked in a broken voice.

"What you saw them become is how the soul appears after all memories and all links to the body are removed. Their souls will follow Lethe to its beginning. There they will be reborn as infants to live new lives," Hades said.

Lina swiveled in his lap so that she was facing him. "But will they be together again? If they're reborn as new people with no memory of their previous lives, how can they find each other?"

"Soul mates will always find each other. Do not weep on their behalf. The woman spoke the truth; they will be together again."

"Do you promise?" Lina's voice trembled with emotion.

"I promise, sweet one. I promise."

Slowly, warring against eons of solitude, he cupped her face in his hands. Hades made his decision. He had to try. He would be lost if he didn't. Hades gazed at her while his pulse beat erratically. Taking a deep breath, he let his thumbs wipe away her remaining tears.

"This is what I wanted to show you—to share with you—the bond of soul mates. Once you have seen it, it is something that you will remember always. It may even change you. It has surely changed me."

Gently, Hades bent to her. First he kissed the closed lid of each of her eyes, then he placed his lips over hers. The kiss began as sweet and hesitant, but when Lina's arms slid up around his shoulders and she opened her lips to accept him, Hades automatically deepened the kiss. She was there, a reality in his arms. This time he did not have to imagine that he touched and tasted her. His desire for her, which had not truly been sated, surged through his blood. With a moan of pleasure, he met her tongue with his own. She was soft and she tasted of ambrosia and heat. His hands slipped inside the covering cape and found her waist. Hades caressed the curve of her hip, following the path his fantasy had taken. He buried one hand in the silk of her hair and he felt her breath quicken as his other hand roamed up and down the length of her thigh. The silky slip of a nightdress offered little barrier. She shifted in his lap, so that the hard flesh of his erection pressed firmly against the curve of her buttocks.

The sound deep in his throat was low and feral. How had he lived so long without her? He desired her with a fire that was burning him alive.

His hand traveled back to the luscious curve of her waist and continued up. He could feel the round fullness of the side of her breast, and in his mind he again saw the puckered nipples glistening wet with water and oil. His fingertips found the hard bud and he rolled it gently through the thin silk.

Persephone made a choked gasping noise against his mouth.

The sound penetrated the red haze of lust that fogged his brain and he wrenched himself back from her. His cape had been pushed aside and Persephone's body lay across him, trembling and exposed. Her hair was disheveled and her lips were red and swollen. By all the gods, what was wrong with him! Had he lost total control of himself? He hadn't wanted it to happen like this, even a callow fool knew better than to maul a goddess in the middle of a forest. Uttering a curse he stood, lifting her abruptly to her feet. She had dried pine needles and smudges of dirt on her nightdress and she looked achingly young and alluring as she gazed up at him, a confused smile tilting her sensuous lips.

Hades was filled with shame. He still wanted to press her to the ground and take her right there. He brushed frantically at the pine needles that clung to her robe, muttering nearly incoherent apologies.

The force of the God's passion stirred a desire in Lina so intense, so fierce, that it was a little frightening. But as she watched the lust that drained from Hades' face being replaced by an expression that could have been either anger or embarrassment, she brought her breathing under control and commanded her mind to function again. She'd never had a god for a lover, but she was certainly no virgin, and she shouldn't be reacting like one.

"I did not mean to bring you here to . . . to . . ." He shook his head miserably and continued to wipe at her dress. "To rut you like a beast."

He wasn't angry, she realized with relief. He was mortified. Lina grabbed his hand and tugged on it until he met her eyes. "Hades, stop. I'm fine. What is this all about?"

"A goddess deserves more than a tussle on the bare ground."

Her smile was slow and sensuous. "I can't speak for other goddesses, but I was enjoying that tussle." She slid her hands up to rest against his leather breastplate. She could still feel the furnace-like heat radiating from him. "And I wasn't sitting on the bare ground. I was sitting on your lap."

Hades expelled his breath in an audible sigh. The haunted expression in his eyes made him look decades older. Gently, he touched the side of her face. His voice was thick with restrained emotions. "Truly, I did not bring you here to seduce you, but I find that I cannot keep my thoughts away from you . . . nor my hands. I desire you above all things, Persephone, may the gods help me," he finished in a rush.

"Then may the gods help both of us, Hades," Lina said. And when his lips met hers she refused to think of Demeter and tomorrows.

Hades broke the kiss gently, while he was still able to control himself. She was so soft and so open to him. That she desired him was obvious, but Hades wanted more than to possess her body. He wanted her soul. With a gesture that was incredibly tender, he straightened his cloak around her shoulders and wrapped her arm through his.

"The night grows cold. We should return to the palace." He brushed a long lock of hair from her face, noting the disappointment that flashed through her eyes. Good, he thought. He wanted her to desire him and yearn for him, until it was more than his body that she craved.

He led her back to the path that would take them to the palace. Lina's thoughts were spinning. Her body still felt overheated, and her heightened physical sensitivity somehow merged with the incredible beauty of the scene she had witnessed between the soul mates. The poignancy of the lovers' devotion stayed with her. Under her hand she could feel the pulse of Hades' blood, which was steady and strong. He had brought her there to witness the rebirth of the soul mates, but he hadn't used it as a seduction device—if that had been his intention, he could have taken her right there on the ground. But he hadn't. Hades obviously wanted more from her than sex. Her soul quickened even as alarm bells rang within her mind. Love—he had shown her his idea of love. Hadn't he already said that he believed mortals understood love better than the gods? Did the gods have soul mates? She had no idea. All she knew about the immortals was what she had inattentively read decades ago. What she did remember was that the ancient gods were fickle, that they discarded lovers at their whim. That didn't fit with what she was learning about the god who walked by her side.

She glanced up at his dark profile. Who would ever believe that she had found such desire and romance in the Land of the Dead? As if he felt her gaze he looked down at her. Hades' lips twitched and then curved up.

"You look as if you have many questions playing through your mind. You know I have already given you leave to ask me anything, and I promise you that this time I will remember my manners and not insult you as my guest."

Lina felt herself blush and she hoped that the dreamy darkness hid her suddenly pink cheeks. She had completely forgotten about snapping at him and his instant withdrawal from her. It seemed like it had happened an age ago, and that they had been two totally different people then. She leaned into him, loving the strong feel of his arm and the way he bent attentively over her.

"It was a magical thing we watched tonight," she said.

"Yes, it was the most perfect type of magic—that which is created naturally by the soul and not contrived by the gods."

"The gods don't bring soul mates together?"

Hades snorted. "No. Mortal souls find their own match; they do not require the meddling hands of the gods."

His words brought another question to her mind.

"Can the dead fall in love?" she asked, thinking of the shy looks Eurydice had begun giving Iapis. "Or is it only soul mates that have the ability to love after death?"

"You can answer that question yourself, Persephone."

Lina glanced sharply up at him, but his tone was instructional and not patronizing.

"Think, Goddess. What is it that loves? The body or the soul?" He prodded.

"If you're asking about real love, and not just lust or infatuation, I'd have to say the soul."

Hades nodded. "The body is just a mantle, a temporary covering for our true visage."

"So that means that the souls that exist in Elysia, or even in your palace, can fall in love?"

"Any of the unnumbered dead who are capable of it may find new love." Hades frowned. "But you should know that not all souls are capable of that emotion."

"Are you talking about mortal souls, or do you mean the souls of the gods?"

Hades stopped walking and turned to face her. They were standing very close and her hand still rested on his arm. The god hesitated before answering her. Then his fingers brushed her cheek in a familiar caress.

"I cannot speak for the other gods, only for myself. My soul longs for its eternal mate." He bent and brushed his lips against hers. He gestured to the space behind her. "It seems we are back where we began."

Lina looked over her shoulder and blinked in surprise. They had stopped at the mouth of the little path that led to her balcony.

Without speaking, Hades cupped her face in his hands in such a gentle gesture that Lina expected the kiss to be sweet and brief. When his lips met hers she realized that she had been very mistaken. The god took his time tasting her, splaying his fingers into the thickness of her hair until he was caressing the sensitive nape of her neck. Lina ran her hands up his arms, thrilled anew by their muscular strength. He nibbled at her bottom lip before ending the kiss. Still holding her he spoke against her mouth, "Will you ride with me tomorrow?" His voice was husky with desire.

Heart fluttering, Lina nodded.

"Yes."

"Until tomorrow then." He released her reluctantly, brushing a strand of hair from her face. Then he bowed to her, turned and strode away.

Lina climbed the steps to her balcony and entered her room on shaky legs. As she sagged onto the bed she caught a reflection of herself in the mirror situated over the vanity across the room. Her cheeks were flushed and her hair looked wild. Hades' cape had fallen down around her waist and her sheer nightdress was smudged, a couple of pine needles clung to the side of her hem. And even from across the room she could see the clear outline of her aroused nipples.

"Misericordioso madre di Dio!" she said, using her Grandmother's most potent exclamation. "You're forty-three years old," she told her

reflection. "And you haven't felt like this since . . . since . . ." She shook her head at her strange, youthful image. "Since never. No man has ever made you feel like he does. And he wants eternal love." She squeezed her eyes shut. "Oh, Demeter. What am I going to do?"

Chapter Nineteen

"Honey, I think you have the makings of a real artist." Lina studied the charcoal sketch on the parchment. She had expected Eurydice's map to be a crude little drawing, but when the spirit unrolled the parchment Lina had immediately been impressed by the quality of her work. The palace blueprint was laid out with strong, clear lines, each section labeled in a flowing script, but what impressed Lina the most was the meticulous detail with which Eurydice had symbolized each section of the palace. To mark the main dining room she had reproduced in miniature the ornate table, complete with candelabrum. The Great Hall had been labeled with a dais on which she had drawn Hades' throne. She had even sketched in the flower-filled courtyard and outlined the massive fountain in its center.

"Do you really like it?" Eurydice asked breathlessly. "It is not completed yet. There are still many finishing touches I should add."

"I love it. Have you always been an artist?"

Eurydice's face was animated with excitement. "Yes! I mean, no, not actually an artist. My father did not believe drawing was a proper pastime for a young lady—even as a hobby. But I used to draw things in secret. I sketched pictures of flowers on dry patches of ground with a sharpened stick. I dipped a bird's quill in my mother's dye and drew animals on old rags." She grinned impishly at Lina. "My father would have been very upset if he had known."

"Well, I think being an artist is the perfect pastime for a lady, and I give you wholehearted permission to draw and draw and draw," Lina said.

"Thank you so much, Persephone!" Eurydice did a happy skip-step. "I cannot wait to tell Iapis. He said he thought that I drew very well, and that he could find more supplies for me if I wished to keep sketching."

"Did he?" Lina raised her eyebrows suggestively.

Eurydice's face, already luminous, took on a decidedly pink hue. "Yes, he did. I thought he was just being kind, because he is always so kind, but if you agree with him then I know it must be true."

"Tell Iapis I said to load you up with supplies. You are now officially Personal Artist to the Goddess of Spring." Lina raised her arm regally to punctuate the proclamation.

Eurydice's eyes grew round with wonder. Impulsively she threw her arms around Lina, hugging her tightly. "You are the most wonderful goddess in all the world!"

Lina laughed. "That is exactly the opinion I expect from my Personal Artist."

"You must task me with a commission. What shall I draw for you?"

"Shouldn't you finish the map first?"

"That will be done soon. Then what would you like me to draw?" she demanded eagerly.

Lina thought for a moment. Then she smiled. "The narcissus is quickly becoming my favorite flower. Why don't you draw me a big, beautiful picture of a narcissus?"

Eurydice's face glowed as she curtsied deeply to her goddess. "Your artist will do your bidding, Goddess of Spring."

Lina inclined her head in her best goddess-like gesture, pleased at how happy she had made Eurydice. "I will try to wait patiently for your first commission."

The little spirit popped up from the curtsy. "Oh! My first commission!"

Two firm knocks sounded against the door to Lina's room. Eurydice danced to open the door.

"Iapis!" she gushed. "Persephone has declared that I am her Personal Artist!"

Lina observed the daimon closely. His expression was warm and open as he congratulated Eurydice, and his eyes never left the girl's face. Lina's grandma would say that he looked very much like a man who was on his way to being well and truly smitten. Lina noticed that Eurydice touched the daimon's arm twice during her excited recitation. The girl's body language definitely said she was returning his interest—no, Lina corrected herself—she was going to have to stop thinking of her as a girl or a child. Eurydice was a young woman who had already been unhappily married once. In actuality the body Lina currently possessed didn't look to be much older.

"Goddess, may I commend you on your excellent taste in artists?" Iapis said gallantly.

Grinning, Eurydice hovered at his side.

"Thank you, Iapis. I think we are just beginning to discover Eurydice's talents."

Iapis smiled fondly at Eurydice. "I must agree with you, Goddess." Then he bowed to Lina. "Hades awaits you at the stables. He asks that I relay to you that Orion is growing impatient."

Lina's stomach gave a jolt at the mention of the god. "Well, then, it's a good thing I'm ready. I wouldn't want to keep a dread steed waiting."

"They scare me," Eurydice said.

"Remember, just think of them as big dogs," Lina told her. The spirit and the daimon hurried after her as she walked briskly down the hallway and through the courtyard, fully aware that now she was the one who felt like dancing happily.

"Was your bath satisfactory last night, Goddess?" Iapis asked.

Lina was glad that she was walking ahead of him. She knew the expression on her face would give away just how satisfactory last night had become.

"Yes, it was lovely. Thank you."

"Persephone said she slept very well," Eurydice added.

Lina smiled. She had slept wrapped in Hades' cape, falling in and out of teasingly erotic dreams.

"It pleases me to hear it," Iapis said to Eurydice. "Especially after the restless night my Lord spent. I do not believe Hades slept at all."

"Perhaps you should try bathing him as I did Persephone," Eurydice said.

Lina quickened her pace, letting the soft breeze that drifted through the courtyard cool her flushed skin. Her body already felt like a spring that had been tightly wound. She definitely didn't need to start visualizing Hades' naked body being bathed and covered in oil. Lina hurried past the central fountain and the lovely sculptures, relieved when she finally reached the wrought iron gates.

"I think I will stay here, Persephone," Eurydice called from behind her. The little spirit pointed to a cluster of narcissus flowers. "I can begin some preliminary sketches while you are riding with Hades."

"And I must procure the proper supplies for your artist," Iapis said, but his eyes never left Eurydice.

"Behave yourselves. I'll be back soon," Lina said.

The pair waved her away and she hadn't taken more than a couple of steps from them when she looked back to see that they already had their heads together. Eurydice's girlish giggle was followed by the deep sound of the daimon's laughter. She was going to have to remember to talk to Hades about them. Iapis seemed like a good guy—if guy was the right word to use when referring to a semi-deity—but what exactly were his intentions? Eurydice was recovering from a bad relationship, not to mention the fact that she was newly dead. That had to make her doubly vulnerable. Didn't it? No matter what, Lina was definitely responsible for her and she didn't want to see her hurt. Iapis should be told to take it slow. Eurydice needed to be treated carefully and with respect.

An ear-splitting neigh brought Lina up short and she stopped her inner tirade. Orion was standing outside the stable. His mane had been combed and braided with ribbons the color of moonlight, which was the exact color of the narcissus tucked under the crownpiece of his bridle. He caught her eye, arched his neck and snorted, taking a few frisky side steps to show off. Beside him stood another stallion that could have been his twin, except that the other horse's night-colored coat was broken by a single white splotch on his forehead in the shape of a lopsided star. The two steeds were almost as magnificent as the god who held their reins. Hades was scowling impressively at his lead stallion.

"Settle down you great foolish beast!" Hades told Orion. "You see that Dorado is not making such a fuss."

Lina hurried to join them, trying not to be obvious about staring at the way the god's arms and shoulders bulged as he pulled Orion to order. He was wearing another short tunic which exposed an excellent amount of his arm muscle as well as most of his legs. His black cloak billowed around him. Batman. A delectable, ancient version of Bruce Wayne. Lina fought the urge to fan herself.

"Don't scold him. I've decided that he's incorrigible, but loveable," she said, heart fluttering. Laying her cheek against Orion's soft muzzle when he nuzzled her in greeting, she averted her eyes from Hades. "You're just glad to see me, aren't you, handsome boy?"

Hades thought he knew exactly how the stallion felt; he had the ridiculous urge to strut and shout at the sight of her. Persephone was swathed in a long length of fine linen with a skirt that was full enough so that she could ride comfortably. When the breeze stirred it pressed the semisheer fabric against her body, outlining the swell of her breasts and the delectable curve of her waist, making Hades wish that he had thought to call up more wind. He watched jealously as she caressed Orion, even though he felt like a shallow clod for being jealous of a horse.

Dorado nickered at the goddess and looked bereft. Instead of doing the same Hades said, "Persephone, I do not believe that you have been formally introduced to Dorado. He does not lead as well as your Orion, but he is the swiftest of the four." He patted the horse's glossy neck affectionately.

Lina rubbed Dorado's head. "It's nice to meet you, Dorado. Faster than Orion, huh?" She slanted a sassy look at Hades. "I guess that means that we won't be able to run away from you."

Hades swallowed past the sudden thickness in his throat. Just being close to her made him feel powerful and helpless, hot and cold, all at the same time. He was probably going mad—and he didn't care. Moving close to her so that the sides of their bodies pressed against each other, Hades caught her teasing gaze with his own. "No, you will not be able to escape me."

Lina felt like she was falling into his eyes. Escape from him? Not likely. She wanted to climb under his skin.

Orion butted her back and snorted. She laughed, breaking the spell between them.

"Okay, impatient boy!"

"The beast is not impatient. He is jealous," Hades said, sending the stallion a black look, which Orion pointedly ignored and lipped innocently at his goddess's shoulder.

"Jealous?" Lina pretended to be taken aback. "Just because I petted Dorado? That's very silly of you," she cooed to the horse.

"You have no idea how silly," he muttered, but he wasn't talking about Orion. "Come," he took her elbow, guiding her to the horse's left side and helping her mount. "The Elysian Fields await the presence of the Goddess of Spring."

THEY rode side by side, following the black marble road. The steady clip of the horses' hooves mingled with the lyrical sound of songbirds calling to one another from the boughs of the imposing cypress trees that lined their pathway. The fragrance of narcissus blooms perfumed the air. Every so often they would pass spirits, sometimes in groups, sometimes a solitary soul walking alone. But all of the reactions were the same. First, the spirits would step off the road, giving the dread steeds a wide berth. Then the realization of who was riding the steeds would hit them. The dead bowed solemnly to their dark god, all the while keeping wide eyes fixed on Persephone. The men would smile at the goddess and bow to her, some of them even called greetings to her, but it was the women whose reactions moved Lina the most. When women recognized that they were in the presence of the Goddess of Spring, their faces became alight with joy. Many of them addressed her by name and asked for her blessing, which Lina readily gave. Some even dared to approach Orion so that they could touch the hem of the goddess's robe.

Lina couldn't believe what a difference her presence seemed to make to them. She had to admit that Demeter had been right—for whatever reason, the spirits of the dead needed to know that a goddess still cared for them. It was an awesome responsibility, but it made Lina feel needed and cherished. If, just by being visible in the Underworld, she could spread happiness and hope, then Lina was very glad to be there.

At first she worried that Hades would be upset, or even threatened by all the attention she was receiving. But though he said little in words, his pleased, relaxed expression spoke volumes. The dark god was obviously glad that the dead responded so joyously to her.

Eventually, the road climbed sharply uphill. They topped a rise and Lina pulled Orion to a halt.

"It's like someone divided it in two, and then painted it—one side dark, the other light." She shook her head in disbelief, even though she knew her eyes didn't lie. The road they were on stretched in front of them as the dividing line in a radically different landscape. It was the most bizarre thing Lina had ever seen.

"Painted different colors, dark and light, that is an apt description of it," Hades said. He pointed to their left where the land reached down into a vast darkness ringed by a distant red line of fire. "That is the flaming River Phlegethon, which borders Tartarus, where darkness reigns." With his other hand he gestured to the brightness to their right. "And there you see Elysia, where light and happiness exist perfectly together and the only darkness that is there is what is required for the spirits to rest peacefully."

Quickly, Lina accessed Persephone's ghostly memory. *Tartarus,* the voice whispered within her mind, *the region of the Underworld where eternal punishment is meted out. It is a place of hopelessness and agony. Only evil dwells there.*

It was Hell. Lina couldn't take her eyes from the dark abyss. Suddenly she felt chilled. The darkness seemed to reach for her, like tendrils from a malevolent creature.

"Persephone!" The sharpness in Hades' voice drew her attention from the void of Tartarus. She met his intense gaze. "You may roam anywhere within my realm, with or without me at your side—except for Tartarus. There, you may not enter, nor may you travel near its boundaries. The realm itself has been tainted by the corrosive nature of its tenants."

"It's awful there, isn't it?" Her face felt bloodless.

"It must be. You know that there is great evil in the world. Would you have it go unpunished?"

Lina thought about her mortal world. Snippets of news stories flashed in her memory like nightmares: the Oklahoma City bombing; the horrors of grown men and women who abused and killed defenseless children; and, of course, 9/11 and the cowardice of terrorists.

"No. I would not have it go unpunished," she said firmly.

"Neither would I. That is why I command that you do not enter its borders."

Lina shivered. "I don't want to go there."

Hades relaxed his stern expression. He nodded toward the brightness that illuminated the right side of the road. "What I would like to show you is a little of the beauty of Elysia."

With a conscious effort, Lina turned her back on the horrors of Tartarus, smiled at Hades and patted Orion's warm neck. "All you have to do is lead the way. We'll follow you."

Eyes sparkling, the god gathered Dorado's reins in his hand. "It is well that you follow me. You ride the slower steed."

Lina narrowed her eyes at him and she drew out her words in her best John Wayne imitation. "You shouldn't talk about my horse, pilgrim."

Then she pointed down the hill. "See the big pine at the edge of that field down there?"

Hades grinned at her and nodded. "Dorado and I will reach it first. He is the faster horse."

"He may be the faster horse, but he's certainly carrying more dead weight," Lina quipped. "Oops, that's probably a bad pun to use in the Underworld, but—YAHH!" She yelled, catching the grinning god off guard. Orion responded instantly by leaping forward and lunging past Dorado to fly down the embankment. The wind whistled past her cheeks as the stallion ran. Lina leaned into his neck and he increased his speed until the world blurred by her. Close behind, she could hear Dorado gaining on them. "Don't let them catch us!" she shouted into the stallions flattened ears and Lina felt him respond with another burst of speed. Then they were past a tall, green shape that was the pine tree and Lina straightened in the saddle, whooping with victory as Orion slowed to a snorting, prancing trot before he stopped. Breathing hard, Dorado slid to a halt beside them.

Lina laughed aloud at the expression on Hades' face.

"The fastest horse, huh? Don't ever underestimate the power of a resourceful woman."

"I believe you cheated," Hades said in mock seriousness, trying unsuccessfully to hide his smile.

"I like to think of it more as using all my resources to win than actually cheating."

"I had no idea you were so competitive."

"There's a lot you don't know about me, Lord of the Underworld," Lina said, still stroking the stallion's neck. "I am not your typical goddess."

Hades snorted. Orion snorted back at him. Dorado tossed his head.

The god gave his horse a couple quick pats. "Don't feel bad, old steed. We will have our day of victory." Adding in a staged whisper, "We must keep a close eye on her—the goddess is wily," Hades said, more to himself than Dorado.

"Uh-huh," Lina agreed and they both laughed.

"Persephone!" A young voice called. Lina turned to see who had spoken.

"Oh, it is the Goddess of Spring! I knew it!" A lithe figure broke from the grove of pines that ringed the lovely little meadow in which the horses stood. She was followed quickly by several others who skipped and danced with excitement toward Lina. The entire group was made up of young, beautiful women. Their flowing wraps were draped alluringly around their strong, young bodies. If they hadn't had the semi-substantial look that marked them as spirits of the Underworld, Lina could have believed that she had stumbled into a sorority toga party.

Hades kneed Dorado so that he was close to her, speaking in a low voice for her ears alone. "They are maidens who died before they could marry. They tend to frolic a great deal before choosing to drink of Lethe."

When the group got close to the two horses, they slowed, making an obvious effort to contain their excitement so as not to get too close to the fearsome steeds. The spirit who had called her name dropped into a deep, graceful curtsy, which the rest of the maidens mimicked. When she rose she was the first to speak. "I heard that you had been seen, and with all my heart I wanted to believe it. Oh, Goddess! It is so wonderful to have you with us."

A chorus of "Yes! We are so pleased!" followed her little speech.

"Well, thank you. I am having a wonderful visit," Lina said.

The first maiden frowned. "You only visit? You mean to leave us?"

The meadow was silent as if every blade of grass and leaf on each tree listened for her answer.

She didn't know what to say.

"Persephone may stay in the Underworld for as long as she wills it." Hades' voice, rich with feeling, broke the silence.

Lina's breath caught at the sudden rush of pleasure his words brought to her. She pushed aside the oh-so-serious-and-responsible thought that reminded her that she could not stay, that she was there for only six months. Instead she smiled at the god, and thought how very much she would like to kiss him again.

"Then you have no reason to rush on. Come dance with us, Goddess!" the maiden called.

Lina tore her eyes from Hades. "Dance with you? But there isn't any music," she told the young spirit.

"That small detail is easily remedied," Hades said. "Our goddess requires music!" He commanded with a flourish. The breeze took his words and swirled around them with an odd whistling noise that grew to a crescendo that melted unexpectedly into the melodic sound of musical instruments. The god inclined his head graciously to her. "Now you have music."

"So it seems." Lina's heart was beating so loudly she was sure everyone could hear it over the music. Dance? She didn't know how to dance with those girls.

"Yes! Oh, please."

"Now you can dance with us!"

"Come frolic to the music of the god, Persephone!"

"But . . . I . . . well . . ." Lina looked around helplessly. "What will I do with Orion?" she floundered.

"You will leave him here with Dorado and me," Hades said, already dismounting. He strode to Orion's side and lifted his arms so that she had little choice but to slide down into them. Hades held her close for a moment, and then he whispered, "Please dance for me here in Elysia. No goddess has ever done so."

Lina looked up into his eyes, saw the desire as well as the vulnerability that he was feeling, and she knew she had no choice. She had to dance for him.

"I would be happy to dance for you," she said.

"My dread steeds and I will await you." He paused, and then added, "eagerly."

"Okay. Well." She brushed at her robes, pretending to straighten that which was already straight. "I won't be long."

"Persephone! We already have the circle formed!" a maiden called to her.

"Oh, good," Lina said, starting toward the waiting group. Sure enough, they had formed a loose circle in the middle of the meadow. Lina was so nervous that she felt vaguely nauseous. Dance with a group of dead maidens? It was just something that her life experiences had not prepared her for. Her hands felt sweaty. This wasn't like the nectar gathering; she didn't have an example to follow. They were expecting her to show them. Should she break into an imitation of one of John Travolta's disco solos from *Saturday Night Fever*? She was going to mess up. She was going to make a fool out of herself. Hades and everyone would know that she wasn't a goddess. She'd be found out as a fraud.

Cease this nonsense!

The echo within her mind startled her so much that she almost cried aloud.

Your body knows the dance. Relax and trust it.

Lina glanced down at herself. She had forgotten that she wasn't wearing her forty-three-year-old skin. She was young and lithe and in such amazing shape that she could probably eat Godiva chocolate non-stop for days and not have to worry about zipping her jeans.

"Goddess?"

Lina looked up to see all the maidens watching her with openly curious expressions on their pretty faces. She probably looked like a moron standing there staring down at herself.

Lina smiled, straightened her shoulders, and let her legs begin walking again. "I was just admiring the . . . uh . . ." She looked down again, "clover in this meadow. It's lovely, don't you think?"

All of the heads nodded energetically, reminding Lina of dashboard ornaments.

"It is our special meadow. We like clover and green, growing things, so it has arranged itself to please us," the first maiden said.

"Well, I like it, too," Lina said, joining the circle.

You begin in the center. Her internal voice directed.

Lina took a deep breath and moved to the center of the circle. Then she did the only thing she could think of doing. She closed her eyes and concentrated. The music filled her and automatically her body began to sway. Her arms raised themselves and she spun in a slow, lazy circle.

The music was wonderful. It reminded her of something wild and feminine. Her body matched itself to the music as she began to trace intricate steps with her long, supple legs. Her hips turned and swayed. Her arms painted images in the air. She wasn't a forty-three-year-old baker. She wasn't a young goddess. She was the music.

Lina opened her eyes.

Faces glowing with pleasure, the maidens circled around her, trying to match her movements. They were beautiful and many were obviously talented dancers, but the difference between their mortal dance and that of Persephone's was clear, even to Lina. Persephone moved with the inhuman grace of a goddess. Lina's heart swelled with joy at the power she felt within her. This must be how a prima ballerina felt at the peak of her career. She leapt and twirled and shouted with joy.

She could have danced forever, but one of the maidens stumbled and then collapsed into a laughing heap in the middle of a bed of clover. Soon after, several of the other girls were obviously struggling to keep up the dance. Lina quelled her disappointment, and with a glorious final twist and flourish she brought the dance to an end. While the girls cheered and clapped, she sank into the deep curtsy of a prima ballerina. Then the spirits surrounded her, gushing their thanks and asking when she would return to frolic with them again.

As they giggled and talked, Lina tried to unobtrusively search the background for Hades. She found Orion and Dorado first. They were grazing contentedly not far from the pine tree that had served as their finish line. Her eyes traveled back. Hades was standing under the tree. He was leaning against it, his arms crossed nonchalantly and his body relaxed. But his eyes were bright and his hot gaze was locked on her. His lips were tilted up in just the hint of a smile. When he saw that she was watching him, he slowly raised his hand to his lips and then gestured toward her, as if sending her a kiss.

It was the most unabashedly romantic thing that a man had ever done for her.

"Well, ladies, it has been wonderful to dance with all of you. We'll have to do it again very soon, but Hades and I must move on," Lina said, extricating herself from her circle of admirers.

Several of them shot shy glances at the waiting god, and then there was much whispering, of which Lina could only catch the words *Persephone* and *Hades* linked together. Giggling and waving good-bye, the maidens disappeared into the pines.

Hades walked away from the tree to meet her in the middle of the meadow. For a moment neither of them spoke. Then, he reached out and brushed a damp strand of hair from her face.

"I have never watched anything as graceful as your dance," Hades said.

Lina suddenly felt more breathless than she had been while she was twirling and leaping to the music.

"You must be thirsty," he said.

Until then Lina hadn't realized that she had been thirsty or sweaty, but in actuality she was both.

"Very."

"There should be a spring near here." He took her hand and started toward the opposite side of the meadow. "Things never stay completely the same in Elysia, but they do tend to reflect the same elements."

"So it's kind of like a changeable fantasy?" Lina asked, letting her hand trail over the clover that was knee-deep at that end of the meadow. Instantly, tufts of white flowers sprang from between the shamrock-shaped leaves, emitting a perfume that smelled of summer and freshly mowed lawns.

"Yes, a little." Hades smiled at her. "Elysia is divided into different parts, but those parts can mingle and change, according to the desires of the spirits."

"Different parts? You mean like there's one place for people who have been really, really good, another for people who have been mostly good, and another for people who were just ordinarily nice?"

Hades' laughter filled the meadow. "You say the most unexpected things, Persephone. No, Elysia is divided into different realms. One is for warriors. One is here"—he gestured around them—"for maidens to come and frolic. And there are several others. Royalty exists in one. Another is for shepherds." His smile turned lopsided and Lina thought he looked twelve years old. "Oddly enough, shepherds do not like to mingle with others."

"Who would have guessed?"

"Exactly."

"So they can't mix? What if a warrior wants to court a maiden? I'd think even the most dedicated warrior would get tired of only doing manly things after awhile."

"They may mix, but it is rather difficult." Hades paused, considering. "But perhaps it should not be difficult. Perhaps they do not realize what they are missing because they have been so long without." The god stared off into the distance, deep in thought.

"Can you make Elysia rearrange itself according to your will?" Lina asked.

Hades' gaze returned to her. "Yes."

"Then have the meadow of the dancing maidens placed next to the warriors' practice field. The rest should work itself out."

Hades barked a laugh. "I think you are correct."

They entered the forest of pines and after some searching, Hades found a small path. They followed it until it crossed a stream that bubbled and tumbled over smooth rocks. Hades left the path and led Lina downstream and around a bend where the water pooled into a little sandy-bottomed basin before continuing its trek by splashing noisily over one side of the rocky ledge.

"For you, Goddess, only the best in drink and dining," Hades said with a rakish smile.

"You may be kidding," she said, hurrying to crouch at the edge of the pool, "but all that dancing has made me incredibly thirsty, and right now water looks better to me than ambrosia."

She cupped her hand and drank of the clear liquid. It was so cold that it made her teeth hurt. She sighed happily and slurped another handful. After she drank her fill, Lina kicked off her soft leather slippers and let her legs dangle into the icy pool. Hades reclined next to her, leaning against a fallen log. The wind sloughed in the trees above them, surrounding them in the scent of pine and sap. The mystical Underworld sky cast an opaque glow over everything. Rose-colored glasses, Lina thought dreamily, so this is what the old cliché meant.

"Demeter told me that the Underworld was a magical place, but I would never have believed that it held so much beauty," Lina said softly. "If the gods really knew how wonderful it was down here, you'd have a constant stream of visitors."

Hades shrugged his shoulders and looked uncomfortable.

Lina studied him, and almost didn't press him further. Then she remembered his words from the night before. He wanted more than simple sex from her. She knew that, and in order for there to be more between them, they would have to be able to talk. About everything and anything. And, quite frankly, she was too old to play college dating games with all the silences and misunderstandings that went with them. She was a grown woman, and she needed to be able to say what was on her mind.

"If you didn't want visitors, why did you build such a huge palace with all those empty rooms just waiting to be filled?"

He considered the question. How much should he admit to her? He certainly didn't want to tell her that he had never before been involved with a goddess, sexual or otherwise, that he had spent an eternity longing for something more than the frivolity that satisfied the rest of the immortals. He remembered the last time he had visited Mount Olympus. Aphrodite had teased him with an open sexual invitation, and he had not responded to her offer. Later he had heard her smirking with Athena as the two goddesses discussed what part of his body must be dead—along with his realm. Thinking about their cutting words he felt a rush of anger. His body was not dead. It was simply attached to his soul, and his soul required more than the insincere attentions of a self-serving goddess.

What could he say that wouldn't make her bolt away from him? He glanced at her. She appeared to be waiting attentively for his answer.

He had to be as honest with her as possible. He couldn't lie or dissemble. A lasting relationship could not be based on falsehoods. He released a long sigh.

"Sometimes I have wondered myself why I built it. Perhaps I was hoping that some day I would learn to overcome my"—he struggled, trying to find the right word—"my difference."

"Difference? What do you mean?"

"I have always found it difficult to interact with other immortals," Hades said slowly. "You must know that I am shunned because I am Lord of the Dead."

Lina began to deny it. Then she remembered the look on Demeter's face when she spoke of Hades, and the offhanded way she discarded him as unimportant . . . uninteresting. The memory made her suddenly very angry.

"They just don't know what you're really like."

"And what is it that I'm really like, Persephone?"

Lina smiled at him and said exactly what was on her mind. "You're interesting and funny, sexy and powerful."

Hades shook his head, staring at her. "You are a constant surprise."

"Is that a good or a bad thing?"

"It is a miraculously good thing."

She was a goner. She couldn't resist him, and she didn't want to. "I'm glad."

"You are not like any of the other immortals. You know how they are . . . so filled with their own importance, constantly striving to outdo one another, never satisfied with what they have." He shook his head and leaned forward so that he could brush her cheek with his fingertips. "You are honest and real—what a goddess truly should be."

Honest and real? A true goddess? Lina wanted to crawl under a rock. She wasn't even who she was.

"I . . . you . . . I . . ." Lina babbled, not sure what she should say.

Hades didn't give her a chance to collect her thoughts. He slid forward and pulled her into his arms. Her mouth was still cold from the spring water. He wanted to drown in her. He plunged into the softness of her lips. If only he had known about her earlier. How could he have spent so much time without her? The goddess wrapped her arms around him and pressed her breasts against his chest. Hades moaned. His desire for her was a molten, throbbing need.

Lina jerked and screamed. Flailing water everywhere she scrambled to pull her long, bare legs from the little pool. Leaping up Lina rushed around behind the god so that he was between her and the water's edge.

"Something rubbed against me." Her voice shook as Oklahoma experience flashed visions of water moccasins and snapping turtles through her mind.

Hades patted one of her hands that clutched his shoulder, trying to pull his thoughts together. He could still feel the imprint of her breasts against the supple leather that covered his chest and his body still surged with hard longing.

"Persephone, nothing in Elysia would harm you."

"There!" Lina was ashamed that the word came out as a squeal. She pointed to a dark shape that flitted under the water. "There's something in the pool."

With a sigh Hades stood and walked the few feet to the bank. He crouched down and peered into the clear water.

All of Lina's senses were on high alert. "Be careful," she said. "It might be a snake."

Hades shot her a bemused look over his shoulder. "Why would you fear a snake?"

Lina twisted a thick strand of hair around her finger. *Snakes are closely allied with Demeter. They are nothing to fear.* Her internal voice chastised her.

"I know it's silly, but I've never liked them," she said miserably.

The god's wide brow wrinkled in confusion, but a splash from the pool called his attention. Lina cringed back, not wanting to see the slithering reptilian body.

When Hades looked at her again a small smile played around his lips. "You cannot possibly fear this creature."

"I don't really like turtles, either," Lina said quickly, keeping her eyes averted from the dark shape that had just surfaced in the pool. "Especially snapping turtles."

Hades chuckled and motioned for her to join him. "Come. You like animals."

Lina didn't bulge. "I do. I like mammals. I like birds. I don't even mind fish. I do not like reptiles. I know it sounds narrow-minded, but—"

An odd barking noise came from the water. Lina peered past Hades to see a little creature floating on its back.

She gasped. "You're not a snake!"

The otter barked at her again, kicking the water with his adorably webbed paws.

Lina hurried to join Hades. She crouched next to him, leaning in against his side. "I think it's the cutest thing I've ever seen."

"Don't tell Orion," Hades said. "He believes that he is your favorite."

Lina pushed her shoulder against his before she reached across the water to tickle the otter's belly. "Orion is my favorite horse. This little guy can be my favorite otter."

At her touch, the otter went into a frenzy of puppyish yips and snuffling sounds, wriggling so much that he sprayed water all over before swimming to the ledge and disappearing down the little waterfall.

"I didn't mean to scare him."

Hades smiled at the goddess's disappointed expression and wiped beads of water from her cheek.

"You did not scare him, sweet one. The otters of Elysia are notoriously shy. Even I have never before seen one this close. I certainly have never touched one."

Lina looked wistfully after the cute creature. "Can't you get him to come back? You are a god."

Hades laughed. "As a wise god, I know when it is best not to tamper with the natural order of things. And you would have more luck than I at charming the little beast. You are the animal sorceress, not I."

"I'm not really a sorceress," Lina said. "I just like animals, and they like me, too."

"Mammals," Hades corrected her, brushing a long strand of hair back from her face.

Lina tilted her head so that her cheek nuzzled his hand.

"Perhaps it is only me you have bespelled, sorceress." Hades rubbed his thumb across her full bottom lip.

"There's no one I'd rather work magic on," Lina heard herself say as she leaned forward to meet his kiss.

When something butted her in the back, she didn't jerk around in surprise or scream. She simply reached up and patted Orion's muzzle.

"You know, the uninformed would believe that the Underworld would be the perfect place to find peace and quiet."

Hades scowled at the stallion. "They would be incorrect."

Orion snorted and tossed his head at the god, then he nuzzled Lina again, breathing warm, horsy breath on her neck and making her giggle. Lina grabbed a handful of silky mane, and Orion raised his head, pulling her to her feet.

Lina looked down at the god, who was still glaring at the horse. She bent down and took his hand and tugged at him until he rose reluctantly to his feet.

"Would you like to see more of Elysia?" Hades asked.

Lina raised up on her tiptoes and brushed his cheek with a kiss. "I would love to see more of your realm."

Her words brought Hades a surge of happiness and he bent to kiss her swiftly and possessively before he lifted her to Orion's back.

Chapter Twenty

THE day passed delightfully. Elysia was an endless adventure where beauty and harmony had been melded perfectly together. And everywhere they went, souls of the dead responded to Persephone's presence. She was moved beyond words by the happiness that she saw on the faces of the spirits as word passed throughout the Underworld that there was a goddess abiding among them.

Hades stayed close to her side, often guiding Dorado close enough so that he could touch her. The reaction of the spirits to Persephone's presence filled him with a bittersweet pleasure. The dead respected and feared him. Some were even intensely loyal to him, but he had never evoked within them the love and joy Persephone's presence did. He did not feel envious of the goddess's effect on his realm. He understood it. How could he not? She had awakened the same feelings within him. Again, he wondered how he had existed so long without her. He could not bear to think what would happen to him or to his realm if she chose not to remain.

Daylight had faded and the night sky was beginning to twinkle with the souls of the Hyades when they finally neared the rear grounds of the palace. Hades nudged Dorado close to Orion and reached over to take Persephone's hand. She smiled at him. Hades' hand felt warm and strong, and she was content to lace her fingers through his and day-dream about the wonders of the day as they entered the familiar pine forest. When they reached the bottom tier of the gardens, Hades pulled Dorado to a halt, causing Orion to snort and stop short.

"There is one last thing that I would like to show you today, if you are willing."

"Of course," she said.

"We must walk," he pretended to whisper.

Lina dropped her voice to a conspirator's level. "What will we do with"—she waggled her fingers at the two stallions who had their ears cocked back, obviously listening—"them."

"Leave them to me."

He dropped athletically from Dorado's back and then held his arms out to help her dismount Orion. She slid against his body, loving the erotic feel of having muscular horseflesh on one side of her, and a hard, hot god pressing against the other. Hades leaned down and nibbled the sensitive lobe of her ear before whispering, "I believe it is time to be rid of our chaperones." Then he straightened and barked the command for them to return to the stables in a voice so powerful that the leaves on the trees surrounding them whipped wildly in response. Orion and Dorado reacted instantly by plunging into the palace grounds.

Lina raised her brows at him. "I'm impressed. I didn't think they'd go so easily."

Hades lips twisted. "They were just surprised. I rarely command them to do anything. Actually, they are rather spoiled."

"Then they'll be mad at you later."

"Probably." He laughed and linked his fingers with hers. "What I want to show you is this way." He led her to a path that skirted the edge of the gardens. They walked beside rows of ornamental hedges trimmed into curling cones. Sleeping flowers shadowed the hedges, and Lina was careful not to let her fingers pass too close to any of the closed blossoms. When Hades stepped from the path and entered the line of cypress trees that ringed that side of the gardens, she couldn't contain her curiosity any longer.

"Where are we going?"

"Not far. To a field there." He pointed ahead of them.

All Lina could see was more of the huge trees, but they were close enough to the palace that the land was still well-ordered. The ground beneath the trees was grassy and free from brambles and debris. The night forest had been emptied of the songbirds' trilling melodies, and Lina began to feel intimidated by the vast silence.

Speaking in a whisper she said, "What's in the field?"

Hades squeezed her hand. "You do not have to be quiet tonight."

"Oh," she said feeling a little embarrassed. Raising her voice to a normal level she repeated her question. "What's in the field?"

"Fireflies."

"Fireflies?"

The god nodded.

The one last thing that he had to show her of the mysteries of the Underworld was fireflies? She'd seen fireflies before. Lots of them.

Reading her expression he grinned mischievously and said, "I believe that you will find these fireflies unique."

Lina shrugged and kept her mouth shut. Maybe the real Persephone would have thought a field of fireflies was unique, but it would take a little more than summer bugs to raise the eyebrows of an Oklahoma girl, especially after the wonders she had already seen that day.

"Ah, here is the break in the trees. Watch your step, we must cross this small gully first."

Lina's attention was focused on stepping across the little ditch, so she didn't look up until she was actually standing in the field. When she did her eyes widened with surprise.

The field was filled with light, but it wasn't the familiar butter-yellow firefly light she had grown up chasing. It was light the color of moonbeams, lace, and . . .

"Narcissus flowers!" She gasped. *"Misericordioso madre di Dio!* They're making narcissus flowers."

Hades' soft chuckle sounded happily self-satisfied. "Few outside of the Underworld have witnessed their like. So, Goddess of Spring, do you approve?"

Lina stared at the field. What must have been thousands of fey fireflies were hard at work. And they were spinning flowers. From the middle of tufts of ordinary-looking green foliage a group of the tiny insects would swarm, then they would begin flying in a sparkling spiral, around and around until, like miniature comets, their glowing tails took on form and mass, leaving behind a perfect narcissus in full bloom.

"It's incredible. Is this how all of the narcissus are made?"

"All of them that exist in the Underworld. Occasionally, a group of fireflies will get confused and drift too close to the opening to the land of the mortals. Sometimes they create a flower in the world above, but I try to prevent that. As you may have noticed, the fragrance of my narcissus bloom is different than those in the World of the Living. Mortals find it too intoxicating."

Lina remembered the night she had bent to breathe in the scent of a very unusual narcissus bloom.

"I can see how that might cause problems," she said faintly.

As if the sound of her voice had just registered on their small consciousness, several of the closest groups of fireflies paused in their flower building. Then, like they all had the same thought, in one glowing flock they flew to Lina. They hovered in front of her spinning in sparkling circles and making strange little chirping noises that Lina thought sounded a lot like soprano-singing crickets.

"What do they want?" Lina whispered out of the side of her mouth to Hades.

The god tilted his head and then smiled. "They want you to create flowers with them."

"Really?" she said, undecided about what to do.

"Really," he said. Hades let go of her hand. "Go to them. I will wait for you."

She pretty much had to. She was supposed to be Goddess of Spring. Building flowers would definitely be a part of her job description. And, as she stood there pondering what she should do, she realized that she wanted to join them, very much.

Just touch them and wish the blossom into being. They will bloom. Her internal monitor told her.

Lina stepped into the field. The long grass swayed softly against her calves. The fireflies danced in dizzying circles around her, chirping happily. Lina approached a clump of green that wasn't grass and wasn't flower. Hesitantly, she stroked the wide, flat leaves with her fingertips, thinking about how much she would like it to bloom. In a burst of bright light that reminded her of a fireworks display, a brilliant white blossom exploded from the center of the plant.

She bent and inhaled the unique fragrance. Lina laughed aloud. She had created that beautiful flower. The joy of youth and new beginnings filled her. Without thinking, she followed the lead of her body and did a graceful pirouette and a little leap step to the next cluster of greenery. The fireflies haloed her body as she caressed the flower alive and then danced to another bloom.

Hades stood at the edge of the field and filled his eyes with her. How could anyone be so lovely? He felt a ferocious desire to have her, and through that act to finally gain true belonging—the kind of belonging that he had born witness to so many times as he had watched it reflected in the eyes of soul mates.

She spun and danced and called the narcissus flowers alive. And wasn't she doing the same to him? The Lord of the Dead, the god who had considered himself immune to love, had fallen in love with the Goddess of Spring. No matter how ridiculous or ironic it seemed, it had happened. And he didn't want it to end. The decision was made. He wanted to do more than to watch the ghosts of love—he wanted to experience love for himself.

He rubbed his chest automatically, anticipating the burning, but it didn't come. Even though Persephone made his body ache and his blood pound, she did not make his choler flare. His hand stilled and he tried to remember the last time he had felt the burning in his chest. Hades blinked in surprise. It had been the night he had offended her and walked out of dinner. Not since then. He smiled. She was not only the breath of spring; she was also balm for a weary soul. Perhaps his loneliness had truly come to an end.

Lina felt his eyes on her and as another narcissus burst into blossom, she looked back to where he waited. He stood at the edge of the meadow, tall and dark and silent, watching her with an intensity that sent a thrill through her blood.

But why must he always just watch? Suddenly she wanted more for him. A wonderful thought came to her. She'd been frolicking with maidens and nymphs since she'd arrived. It was definitely Hades' turn. Smiling happily, she danced up to him, trailing a mist of glittering fireflies in her wake. She grabbed his hand.

"Come on! Make flowers with me."

His eyes were shadowed with sadness. "I am the God of the Dead. I cannot create life."

"You can if I help you," she said with more confidence than she felt and tugged at his hand.

"No, I . . ." He sighed. "Persephone, I can refuse you nothing." Reluctantly, he allowed her to pull him into the meadow.

Surrounded by the sparkling fog of fireflies, Lina led Hades to a clump of not-yet-narcissus. She motioned for Hades to stand behind her, then she reached back and slid her hands down the underside of his arms until his hands enveloped hers and his arms encased her. She splayed her fingers wide, as if she had just thrown a ball.

"Lace your fingers beside mine." His nearness caused her voice to be a husky purr. "And think about how much you would like to make the narcissus blossom."

Lost in her, Hades let her guide his hands. He did wish he could make the narcissus bloom, but even more he wished that he could make this goddess his own, that she would stay beside him and relieve his loneliness for an eternity.

His fingers began to tingle as the magic within Persephone's body merged with his own. Incredulous, he watched as the brilliant narcissus burst into being beneath their joined hands.

Lina shouted with joy and turned, face blazing with joy. "We did it!"

Hades' arms wrapped around her and he looked into her glittering eyes. "Together, Persephone. I could not have done it without the Goddess of Spring. I wish I could find words to tell you what great pleasure it gives me to share my world with you."

His voice was serious, his expression earnest, and she felt completely lost in his eyes. Hades wanted more from her than a quick kiss, or even a quick affair. She knew that she should make a little joke and dance away from him. But she couldn't make herself. She burned to be with him as badly as he ached for her. She kissed him, pressing herself against the hard length of his body.

Abruptly Hades ended the kiss. Resting his forehead against hers, he concentrated on controlling his ragged breathing. He would not grope her in the woods again. Persephone deserved more than that. She deserved all that he could give her.

"It is late. We should go back to the palace now," he said, kissing her forehead gently.

She looked up at him. "I'm not tired."

"Nor am I."

"And I'm not ready for the day to end."

"Then it shall not." He took a deep breath. "You have not yet seen my private quarters. Would you like to?"

Lina saw how difficult it was for him to ask. She felt her heart pounding—a heart that was not truly her own, inside a body that didn't belong to her. But her soul did, and it wasn't simply her body that desired him. She loved his sweetness and sense of humor. She loved the sound of his laughter. She loved his power and his passion, and the care and wisdom he showed in his dealings with the spirits in his realm. Lina touched his cheek, and admitted the truth to herself. She loved him.

"Yes. I would like to very much."

Joy flashed over his face, followed quickly by desire, and he bent and kissed her again, hard and fast. Then he reluctantly released her from his arms, took her hand in his, and began to retrace their steps. Lina heard a high-pitched buzzing behind her, and she and Hades turned.

The fireflies were hovering in a huge cluster at the edge of the field. All of them were turned toward Lina.

The god laughed. "Persephone will return. She is not leaving the Underworld."

Their frantic buzzing eased a little.

"I'd love to come back and make more flowers with you," Lina assured them, and their buzzing changed to happy chirps. Smiling, Lina and Hades continued on their way. "It's nice that they like me so much."

"All of my realm adores you, Persephone," Hades said.

Lina glanced up at him. "Just your realm?"

The god's lips tilted up. "No, not just my realm."

She squeezed his hand. "Good."

It was as they stepped from the trees into the ornamental garden that Lina heard the sobbing.

"Someone's crying," Lina said. Peering around in the gentle darkness she tried to discover who it was.

"There," Hades said.

He was pointing ahead of them in the direction of the road that passed in front of the palace and led farther into Elysia. Lina could barely make out a blur of human-sized brightness near the edge of the road.

"I think we should see what's going on." Lina looked up at the god for confirmation. "Don't you?"

"Yes. It is odd that a spirit would cry in Elysia." He explained as they started toward the blotch of light. "The dead might miss family and loved ones from the Land of the Living, but by the time they are ferried across Styx and enter Elysia, their souls are filled with joy, or at the very least, peace. The ability to cease longing for the living—or at least the ability to understand that all partings are only temporary—is built into the mortal spirit. Those who have earned an eternity in Elysia find that they are content."

As they got closer to the spirit the brightness took shape. Lina could see that she was a pretty young woman with long, upswept dark hair and a plump figure. She was sitting at the edge of the road, face in her hands, weeping with such passion that she did not even notice their approach. Instinctively, Lina motioned for Hades to stay back, and she walked to the woman's side. Just before she touched her shoulder, Lina noticed that the spirit's body looked unusually dense. If she hadn't had the typically pale luminescence of the dead, Lina would have believed that she was a living woman who had somehow gotten lost and stumbled into the Underworld.

"Honey, what's wrong?" Lina asked softly.

The woman jumped, and raised a tear-stained face to peer with frantic brown eyes at Lina. Instantly she recognized the goddess, and began to bow her head. Then she caught sight of Hades, and her hand went to her mouth. She changed the direction of her bow, but ended up bobbing back and forth, not sure which of the immortals to acknowledge first.

"I did not mean to disturb the gods!" she cried, wiping her eyes. Climbing awkwardly to her feet, she began backing hastily away from Lina. "Please forgive me."

"No." Lina held out her hand in what she meant as a calming gesture. The woman jerked to a nervous halt, staring at her outstretched arm. Lina thought she looked like a frightened mouse. She sighed and modulated her voice to the tone she used to reassure young animals. "Don't go. You didn't disturb us. Hades and I were taking a walk and we heard you crying. We were concerned, not angry."

She seemed to relax a little.

"What is your name?" Hades asked in the pleasant, fatherly voice he used with Eurydice.

She glanced nervously at him. "Alcetis."

"Tell us why you were crying, Alcetis," Lina said gently.

Alcetis looked down and spoke to her feet. "I am so very lonely. I miss my husband and my family desperately." She pressed the back of her hand against her mouth, trying unsuccessfully to stifle a sob.

Lina's worried gaze found Hades. She saw that he, too, looked surprised at the spirit's words. Then she saw him tilt his head to the side and his face took on a listening expression. In a moment his eyes seemed to darken and he pressed his lips together before speaking to the spirit.

"It was not your time, Alcetis," Hades said in a voice shadowed with sadness.

The spirit drew another ragged, sobbing breath. "No, it was not. But I had to come."

Hades frowned. "You did not have to. It was your choice."

Alcetis raised her dripping face. "Do you not understand? He asked others. They would not. I had to."

Completely confused, Lina shook her head. "Wait, *I* don't understand. What are you two talking about? Has some kind of mistake been made?"

"Alcetis, tell Persephone why you have entered the Underworld," Hades said.

Alcetis took a deep breath and wiped her face with the sleeve of her burial robe. "I have only been married a short time. My husband's name is Admetus." The spirit's damp face brightened as she said the name and she almost smiled. "Yesterday at dawn the arguers prophesized the Admetus would die before the sun set. My husband immediately petitioned Apollo, and the God of Light concurred. Indeed, the prophesy was true. The Fates had finished weaving Admetus' life, and at dusk his mortal string would be cut. But my husband has long been a favorite of the God of Light, and Apollo heard my husband's cries. He granted Admetus a new fate. He would be spared if someone would agree to die in his place. First, Admetus went to his parents, who are old and not well, but they refused. Then he went to his brothers. They, too, would not die in his stead. He asked his closest friends, assuring them that he would see their families well cared for, but the answer was always the same. No one was willing to die for him. In despair, he returned home to await his fate." Alcetis paused, looking searchingly at Lina. "I could not let him die."

Hades' jaw clenched, but when he spoke his voice betrayed no anger. "And he let you die for him."

The spirit turned wide, wet eyes to the god. "He wept and rent his garments. His sadness was great."

"But not great enough to stop you," Hades said.

"You must see that I had no choice. I had to take his place." Alcetis began weeping again.

"That is why you feel such loneliness and pain. It is not your time. Your life's thread is still spinning. Your soul knows this and you cannot find peace." Hades spoke solemnly, as if a great weight pressed down upon his words.

"Well, this can't be right," Lina said. "Look at her—she doesn't even have the same kind of body as the rest of the spirits."

"That is because she is not like the rest of the spirits. She is misplaced, outside of her allotted fate."

"Then it sounds to me like you need to fix this," Lina said firmly.

"She is here because a god meddled in a mortal's life, something that happens far too often, and for far too many selfish reasons. I do not believe in interfering with the lives of mortals."

"But she's a part of your realm now. You're not technically meddling. You're doing your job."

Hades spoke through gritted teeth. "Persephone, do you not remember what happened the last time you made a judgment about sending a spirit back to the Land of the Living?"

Lina flinched as if he had slapped her. "This is different, and I can't believe that you are heartless enough not to see that." Her voice was ice.

"Oh, please!" Alcetis threw herself on her knees between the two immortals. "I did not mean to cause strife between the King and Queen of the Underworld."

"What is it you called Persephone?" Hades said, fast and sharp. "What title did you give her?"

Trembling, the out of place spirit answered the god. "I called her Queen of the Underworld, but I did not give the title to her, Lord. I simply repeat what she has been named in the world above." She managed to smile shyly at Lina. "It is well known that she is now reigning at your side."

Lina was struck speechless. Queen of the Underworld? People were really calling her that? She looked at Hades and the dark god captured her gaze. His eyes flamed and his face seemed to burn with transparent joy. As he spoke, Lina could not look away from him, and she forgot to breathe.

"Pronounce your judgment, Persephone. I bow to your will."

And then he did, almost imperceptibly, bow his head to her.

Lina forced her eyes from him. She smiled shakily at Alcetis. "Then my judgment is that you return to the mortal world and your husband to finish living out your fate. And tell your husband that he can continue following whatever new thread the Fates have woven for him."

With a happy cry, Alcetis jumped to her feet and took Lina's hand. She kissed it, then held it to her wet cheek. Through shining eyes she beamed at Lina.

"Oh, thank you, Queen of the Underworld. My children and my children's children shall make sacrifices to you every spring until the end of time."

"That's really nice of you, but you should know that I prefer a little wine and honey scattered around the ground. I don't so much like the blood sacrifices," Lina said quickly.

Alcetis curtsied deeply. "I will always remember your kindness, Goddess."

Chapter Twenty-one

Hades had been very quiet after Alcetis disappeared back down the road that would return her to her mortal life. Lina watched him with little sideways glances. He was holding her hand, but his face was inscrutable. He was definitely making her very nervous. Were they still going to his room? Had she misunderstood his reaction to hearing her called the Queen of the Underworld? Could it have been an emotion other than fierce happiness she had thought she had seen? But then why would he have allowed her to pass a judgment that he was clearly against? Her mind felt like it was filled with fireflies.

They entered the palace through the rear courtyard, and turned to the left away from the direction of Lina's room. They walked past the entry to the dining room. Finally, Hades stopped in front of a huge door into which had been carved the rearing image of Orion and the helmet from the Great Hall.

Feeling nervous, Lina pointed at the door. "It's a good likeness of Orion. He looks very ferocious."

Hades snorted. "I think a new rendition is needed—one which shows him nickering softly to his goddess."

Relieved by his banter, Lina gave him a playful nudge with her shoulder. "Oh, he's still thought of as a dread steed. Eurydice certainly avoids him."

Hades shook his head. "I'm afraid his reputation of being a fierce, solitary creature has been forever shattered." He turned to her and took Lina's chin in his hand, tilting her face up. "But he does not mind. His gain far exceeds his loss." He kissed her gently, and murmured against her lips. "Will you join me in my chamber?"

"Yes." Her stomach tightened.

Hades opened the great door for her and she stepped into the god's private world. The first thing she noticed was the enormous bed that was centered in the room. It was canopied by a gossamer net of sheer silk that hung in luxurious folds all around it. Lina could see that the bed itself was covered with thick white linens so that the whole thing looked like it was a cloud that had lost its place in the sky. It was opulent and sexy and very, very inviting. Lina realized she was staring at the bed, and letting her imagination wander. She felt her cheeks grow warm.

Yanking her eyes away, her attention was drawn to the impressive pair of chandeliers that hung from the domed ceiling. They appeared to have been made from black glass, and flames from hundreds of candles danced and glistened in their unusual surface.

"Your chandeliers are always so beautiful. Are these really made of black glass?"

"Obsidian," Hades said. Pressing his hand intimately into the small of her back, he led her into the room. "Although when it has been cut and polished it does resemble glass."

Lina smiled at him. "What are its properties? I know they must be special if you chose this stone for your room."

"Obsidian's powers are that of protection, grounding, divination and peace." He glanced up at the winking light. "And I find it soothing."

"Well, it definitely works with your color scheme." Lina gestured at the rest of the vast chamber. The predominate colors were black, white and silver. But instead of making the room austere and cold, the dramatic differences fit well together, as if the god had found a way to comfortably wed light and dark.

"Would you like some wine?" Hades asked. He was nervous and he wondered if she could hear the pounding of his heart.

When Persephone nodded, Hades hurried over to a squat table that sat between two white satin chaises and poured two glasses of wine from a bottle that had already been opened and placed in an iced container.

Lina smiled her thanks and took the crystal glass that was filled with golden liquid. Its fragrance drifted to her and Lina's smile widened.

"Ambrosia!"

"Rumor has it that you are fond of it." His lips twitched.

"Rumor should also have it that sometimes I'm overly fond of it."

"That is our secret." He smiled. Then he cleared his throat and raised his glass to her. "To new beginnings."

"To new beginnings," Lina repeated, touching her glass against his. As they drank their eyes stayed locked together.

Then Hades placed his glass back on the table. Without hesitation, Lina placed hers next to his. The dark god took a deep breath. Then he closed the small space between them and took her in his arms.

"You are haunting me, Persephone. I cannot breathe without thinking of you."

He captured her lips in a hungry kiss. Their bodies pressed together. All she could think was, oh-thank-you-finally! His hardness pulsed against her and she responded with liquid heat. Lina's hands roamed up and across his chest, the width of his leather chiton, and Lina wanted to curse in frustration. She had no idea how to get the thing off him. While his deep kisses sizzled through her blood, she directed her fingers until she finally found the ties that laced the leather together low on his side. She tugged and pulled, and they loosened enough for her to slip her fingers within so that she could stroke the hard muscles of his waist and abdomen.

Hades moaned against her mouth. His hand moved down to cup her curved bottom as he pressed her more firmly against him. Heat flooded his body as he felt her move against him in response.

She nibbled on his bottom lip teasingly. Then she pulled back, but only far enough to meet his eyes.

"Take me to bed, Hades." She sounded breathless.

He swallowed, trying to clear the dryness in his throat, and nodded. Then he led her to his bed. Hades parted the silk curtain for her, but he did not follow her within. Lying back against his pillows, Persephone looked beautiful and ultimately desirable. At his hesitation, the goddess smiled questioningly up at him.

"I must tell you something first." Hades' voice was thick with emotion. "I have never before done this."

"You mean you have never brought a woman to your bedroom before?"

"It is true that I have never brought a mortal woman here, but that is not all that I have never before done."

Lina's eyes widened. "You have never made love?"

Hades' laughter sounded forced and nervous. "I have made love, just never with a goddess."

Lina sat up. She wished desperately that she could admit to him the irony of their situation. He was nervous for the same reason she was feeling a herd of butterflies stampeding around in her stomach.

"Truthfully, I haven't been with anyone in quite a while." She reached and touched his hand. His fingers wrapped around hers. "And I can promise you that no god has ever made me feel the way you do."

He sat next to her on the bed, looking at their joined hands.

"When Alcetis called you the Queen of the Underworld I was filled with unspeakable pride. To think that others believe that you might belong to me, that you could be content reigning at my side. I cannot conceive of anything that would bring me more joy."

She released a long sigh. "I would be proud to be called Queen of the Underworld, but I don't know . . ." She faltered, trapped between her promise to Demeter and her need to tell Hades the truth.

He cupped her face in his hands. "It is enough for now that I know that the idea is not repellent to you. Time will take care of the rest."

She placed her hands over his. "How could your wonderful realm repel me? I adore it," she said hoarsely.

His smile was dazzling, and Lina wondered how it was possible that the other immortals did not see him as she did. Then she was suddenly, fiercely glad that they did not. If they knew, then he wouldn't belong to her; he'd be like the rest of them. Hades kissed her gently, but she could feel the tension in his body through the corded muscles of his arms.

When he spoke his voice had deepened with his breathing. "Show me how to bring you pleasure. Just the thought of you, just a glimpse of your skin, makes my blood heat. But I know desire is not so simple for women." Despite his taut nerves Hades managed a chuckle. "And even with my limited experience I have learned that goddesses are, indeed, much more complex than gods. Teach me how I can flame your desire, Persephone."

Lina's mouth felt dry and she ran her tongue over her lips, feeling a shiver of pleasure as Hades' gaze became riveted on her mouth.

"You could start by undressing," she said breathlessly.

With no hesitation, Hades pulled off his already loosened chiton, unwrapped his short undertunic and the linen loincloth that Lina had found so enticing when he was dressed only in it at the forge. Tossing his clothes away he stood before her naked. He was magnificent. The rich luster of his skin gilded his muscles, making him look dark and exotic. She had never seen such a beautifully made man. Her eyes traveled down his body and her breath caught in her throat. He was already fully aroused.

Lina felt a heady rush of pleasure at the knowledge that the power of a god was hers to command. She stood, resting her palms against his bare chest. Then, slowly, she drew them across his skin, loving the feel of the hard, well-defined ridges of his chest and arms. When her hands moved down to his lower abdomen, she felt a tremor run through him.

"One thing that all women like is to believe that their touch is arousing," Lina said huskily. "It gives us pleasure to know that even though our bodies are less powerfully built, one small touch from us can make a man tremble and moan."

She took his hard flesh in her hand and stroked it caressingly. A moan that sounded almost painful came from deep within Hades' throat.

Lina's smile was a seductive tease. "Am I hurting you?"

"No!" He gasped. "Though I believe you could slay me with one touch. All I need do is to think of you . . . to see you . . . to smell you and I become engorged, aching, longing for your touch."

His words sent a bolt of heat through her body. She released him so that she could tug at the lacing on her left shoulder that held her robe together. She shrugged the top off, leaving her breasts bare. It only took her a moment to pull loose the ties over her hips, and with a small, sensuous movement she caused the material to slide from her body. Then she stepped into Hades' arms.

"Your skin is so hot. I love the way it feels against mine," she said between kisses.

"Wanting you makes me feel that I am on fire," Hades whispered against her lips as his hands explored the deep curve of her hips. Then he turned and fell back, pulling her with him onto the bed. "Show me more, Persephone. Teach me how to set you afire, too."

Lina rolled off of him, so that they were lying on their sides, facing each other. She hardly knew where to start. She already felt so hot and wet that for a moment she almost pulled him on top of her. Then she took a deep breath and stopped the impulse. No, he wasn't like her ex-husband or any of her other disinterested lovers. This time it was going to be different. Hades was different. In him she had what all women really desired—a man who honestly wanted to please her, and was willing to listen and learn so that she would, indeed, find that pleasure. All she had to do was show him what she desired.

And that was much more difficult than she had imagined. What did she desire? She closed her eyes and collected her thoughts. All of her adult life she had wanted a man who would cherish her enough to care about her pleasure as much as his own. She had to be honest with Hades, as well as with herself. She must break down the barriers her previous lovers had required her to erect. Lina shivered. She was ready. She opened her eyes.

Lightly, she touched the spot where her neck met her shoulder, and with a voice that sounded suddenly shy she said, "To me, it's the little things that matter. For instance, I like to be kissed here."

Hades propped himself up on his elbow, then he bent to the curve of her neck. Kissing and nipping her gently, he ran his tongue around the sensitive area.

"I would also like it if you caressed me while you kissed me. Let my body become accustomed to your touch," she whispered.

When her breathing deepened, he followed the seductive line of her shoulder down to her breasts, which he cupped gently in his hands.

"Oh, yes, there, too," she moaned as he rained kisses on the soft mounds.

"Will it give you pleasure if I lick and kiss your nipples?" Hades' voice was husky with desire.

"Yes," she said, burying her hands in his dark hair.

As he teased and sucked his hand traveled down. First he caressed the length of her leg, molding his touch to her curvaceous muscles. Remembering that she desired him to pay attention to the small things, he teased the velvety area behind her knee. Then, following the unspoken cues of her body, he drew hot circles on her inner thigh. She opened to him and guided his hand to her core, showing him how to caress her sensitive bud, whispering breathless encouragement when his touch moved with her rhythm.

The wave of her orgasm came hard and fast. She gasped his name as exquisite electricity began deep within her and radiated throughout her body.

Hades held her close, his own desires temporarily forgotten in his amazement that he had been able to evoke such a passionate response from her. He wanted to shout with happiness. She knew him for who he was, and she desired him and had given herself to him.

She opened her eyes and looked up at him. He was smiling at her and stroking the hair from her face. Her breathing had not even returned to normal when she began kissing him again.

"I think that the best lovemaking is mutually satisfying," she said breathlessly, pressing him gently back against the bed. "It is a dance of give and take, where even though your partner's pleasure can become your own, it shouldn't exclude you from having your needs and desires fulfilled as well."

She stroked his muscular body, kissing and tasting the saltiness of his skin until his breathing was ragged. Sweat glistened on his body and all of his muscles strained and tensed as he fought to control his desire. Quickly, she wrapped her arms around him.

"Don't hold back anymore. I want you inside of me—and I want to feel all of your passion."

With a growl, he rolled so that he was on top of her. Holding himself up on his hands, he stared into her eyes as he plunged into her body. Her wet heat surrounded him and it took all of his force of will to hold back the explosion that raged to be released. Possessing her was better than his fantasy, better than anything he could have imagined. He held very still for a moment, trying to regain control. Then, with a whimpering sound, she thrust up to meet him and he responded, matching her passion with his own until he was lost to everything but the sensation of her. Feeling her tighten rhythmically around him, she drove him over the edge. As the spasms of pleasure coursed through him, Hades buried his face in her hair and said one word over and over.

"Persephone . . ."

A sweet, familiar scent awakened her. Hades was standing beside the bed smiling. He was naked, except for the snug loincloth wrapped low around his waist. He was holding a chilled glass of golden liquid in one hand and a silk robe in the other.

"Good morning," she said, sleepily.

"Good morning. I thought you might be thirsty." He nodded at the crystal wineglass. "Also, Eurydice brought those things for you." He gestured over his shoulder at a table that was laden with pomegranates and a mouthwatering assortment of cheeses and breads.

Lina thought he couldn't possibly have looked more adorable standing there nervously, trying to act like he was used to having a goddess in his bed.

"Thank you." She sat up and stretched. The sheet fell down around her waist, and his eyes devoured the sight of her bare breasts.

Entranced, Hades placed the glass on the table and knelt before her, taking her breasts in his hands and kissing her nipples. Although his touch was gentle, Lina couldn't help flinching. Her body was incredibly, wonderfully satiated, but also very, very sore.

The god pulled back. "I am hurting you?"

"I'm just feeling a little . . . sensitive. Seven times in one night is, well, unusual."

Hades actually blushed as he draped the silk robe over her shoulders and smoothed her hair. She did look rumpled, and she had a red bite mark on the curve of her neck. Had he been too rough with her? Last night he had thought that he had pleased her, but this morning she seemed almost disgruntled. She stood up, a little gingerly, and shrugged into the robe. By all the gods! Had he hurt her?

She gave him a distracted smile, and sat gingerly before she descended hungrily on the laden table. She did not notice how the god flinched in response at her obvious physical discomfort. Hades silently damned himself for an inexperienced fool.

As Lina ate, she felt her energy level return to normal and the aches of her well-used body dissipate. Responding to her revived good humor, Hades' nerves evaporated, and they ate breakfast like lovers, with their knees touching, feeding each other choice tidbits from their own plates. He was just explaining to her how he had fashioned the chandeliers that hung gracefully from the ceiling above them when two firm knocks sounded against the door.

"Yes! Enter," Hades called.

Iapis entered the room, holding a square, flat box in his hand. He bowed first to Hades and then to Lina.

"Good day, Hades, Persephone." His eyes danced and he tried unsuccessfully to hide a delighted smile. "I have brought that which you requested, my Lord." He handed the box to Hades.

"Excellent, thank you, Iapis."

Seeing the daimon reminded Lina that she had been neglecting Eurydice lately, and she felt a twinge of guilt.

"Iapis, could you take a message to Eurydice for me?" Lina asked.

"Of course, Goddess."

"Tell her that I would love to see what she has been sketching."

Iapis smiled. "She will be pleased, Goddess."

"Good. Have her bring her work to my room later today. And please tell her that I am looking forward to seeing her creations—and her. I've missed her lately."

Lina thought she saw a telltale flush darken the daimon's cheeks before he nodded, and, still smiling, bowed his way from the room.

"He's certainly in a good mood," Lina said, drumming her fingers against the table.

"He likes seeing me happy," Hades said, kissing her hand.

Lina felt herself grinning as foolishly as the daimon had been. Then she mentally shook herself.

"I don't think that's all there is to his jolly expression. I've been meaning to talk to you about that daimon of yours."

Hades raised an eyebrow at her.

"I think he's interested in Eurydice," Lina said.

Hades' grin reminded her of a little boy caught with his hand in the cookie jar. "I think you are correct."

"Then I need to know his intentions," she said firmly.

Hades nodded, his expression instantly sobering. "I see. Of course you would be concerned. I believe I can speak for Iapis. His intentions are honorable. He truly cares for the little spirit."

"You will see that he is careful with her? She has been through a difficult time. It's hard for a woman to love again after she has been hurt."

Hades touched her cheek gently, wondering suddenly if the goddess was speaking only about her loyal spirit.

"You may trust me. Always. I will watch out for Eurydice as if she were the Goddess of Spring herself."

"Thank you. It's not that I don't like Iapis—I do. I just worry about Eurydice."

"You are a kind goddess who cares for those who love you," Hades said. Then he looked down at the square box sitting beside his hand. He slid it across the table to Persephone.

"This is something I made the first night you were here. I could not sleep. All I could do was to think about you, about your smile and your eyes." He gestured for her to open the box.

The little clasp unlatched easily and Lina lifted the lid. Nestled in a bed of black velvet inside the box was a chain made of delicate silver links from the middle of which hung a single amethyst stone that had been carved and polished into the shape of an exquisite narcissus blossom.

Lina felt tears fill her eyes. "Oh, Hades! It's the most beautiful thing I've ever been given."

Hades stood and moved behind her, taking the necklace from its case so that he could place it around her neck. It hung perfectly, just above the swell of her breasts.

"Thank you. I will always cherish it."

The god pulled her into his arms. "The night I made it I was filled with emptiness and longing, but now you are here with me and the black hole within me exists no more. The mortals were wise; you are Queen of the Underworld. I cannot imagine my life without you. You have brought eternal Spring to the Underworld, and to the heart of its god. I am in love with you, Persephone."

The tears that had been pooling in Lina's eyes spilled over and she couldn't speak.

He wiped her cheeks with his thumbs. "Why do you weep, beloved?"

"Things are just so complicated."

Hades' brow furrowed. "Because you are Goddess of Spring?"

"That's part of it."

"Tell me truly, Persephone. Do you weep because you cannot imagine remaining in the Underworld?"

The god tried to keep his voice neutral, but Lina could see the p reflected in his eyes.

"I want to be with you," she said, trying not to sound too evasive.

"Then I cannot conceive of any difficulty that we cannot overcome together." He hugged her fiercely.

Resting within the strength of his arms, Lina squeezed her eyes closed, willing her tears to stop. Crying wouldn't help.

She did love him, but that was only a small piece of the truth he needed to know. She wanted to tell him everything. She had to.

But she had given her word, and first she must talk to Demeter.

Chapter Twenty-two

“YOU say she is not in her chamber?” Hades snapped at the daimon.

“No, Lord. The goddess is gone.”

“And Eurydice does not know where she is?”

“No, Lord. Eurydice has been busy with the paintings she is to show her goddess later today.”

Hades paced. Persephone had told him that she needed to soak in a hot bath and then take a nap. Yes, she had appeared distracted, but he had told himself that the goddess was just tired. He had given her time to herself while he had presided, in an unusually distracted manner, over that day’s petitions of the dead. Most of them had come to see Persephone, and were visibly disappointed that the goddess did not appear. His jaw tightened. He did not blame them; he wanted nothing more than to see her as well. He could still smell her scent on his skin, and when his mind wandered, he could feel her soft heat against him.

Where had she gone? And why hadn’t she told him? What was she thinking? He raked his hand through his hair. After eons of solitary existence, his desire had been too fierce; he had been too rough with her. Perhaps he had hurt her. Or perhaps his lovemaking had not satisfied her. Had she compared him to her other immortal lovers and found him wanting? He clenched his fists. Just the thought of another god touching her caused him to feel ill.

"Find her, Iapis," Hades growled.

The daimon bowed and disappeared.

OKAY, Lina admitted to herself, she was worried. She chewed her bottom lip.

"Merda! Why does it have to be so complicated?" Orion's ears tilted back to catch her words and he whickered in soft response.

"I do love him," she said aloud. "So now what are we going to do?"

She knew what *she* had to do, which was why she'd evaded Hades and sneaked off with Orion.

"I think my cover story was excellent, though," she told Orion. "And I'm sure Iapis will only be a little annoyed when he finds out that the huge wineskin of ambrosia that Eurydice insisted he fill to the brim was for Cerberus."

At the mention of the three-headed dog, Orion snorted in disgust.

"Oh, he's not that bad. Perhaps a closet alcoholic, but at least he's loveable. Anyway, you know I like you best." She patted the horse's glistening coat. Orion arched his neck and shifted from a trot into a rolling canter. The dark road passed quickly beneath them. Lina's faithful ball of light hovered over her right shoulder, keeping pace with the stallion. In the distance, she could see the milky outline of the grove of ghost trees.

She wondered if Hades had noticed her absence yet. She hoped not, but if he looked for her, Eurydice would tell him that Persephone had wanted to bring Cerberus the treat she had promised, and the stablemen would report that she had taken Orion for a ride. Hades shouldn't worry. She didn't want him to. She didn't want to cause him any pain.

Their night together had been a new experience for her. Hades had awakened feelings in her that had, until then, just been wisps of dreams and fantasies. And it wasn't just about the sex. Lina sighed. That would have been easy to deal with. She could have a torrid, steamy affair with him, and then be satiated and pleased with herself when it was time for her to leave.

No, it hadn't just been the sex.

The memory of the soul mates haunted her, as did the look on Hades' face when he had declared his love for her. She had wanted to respond with the same words, but she wasn't free to pledge herself to him—not yet—not until she dealt with Demeter. And it had broken her heart.

Lina hadn't meant to love him. She had gone to the Underworld with the best intentions; she'd had a job to do. Period. She hadn't been interested in romance or love or sex. And, quite frankly, the Underworld was the last place she had expected to find any of those things. *Merda!* Demeter had described Hades as an asexual bore. Lina had been totally unprepared for the truth.

She twirled a strand of Orion's satiny mane around her finger as the stallion navigated quickly through the grove of ghost trees. She was definitely in the middle of a mess. She loved him—that Lina was sure of—but a nagging thought wouldn't leave her alone. While she was with him, while she could touch him and look into his eyes, it was easy to believe that he loved her, too. *Her*—Carolina Francesca Santoro—and not some flighty young goddess. And hadn't he been the one to point out that true love had more to do with the soul than the body? So why should it make any difference to him that her real body was that of a forty-three-year-old mortal? In theory it shouldn't.

Orion shot through the dark tunnel toward the broadening speck of light spilling from the world above.

It was undeniable that she had been lying to Hades. Even though she hadn't meant to deceive him into loving her, would he believe that when he learned the truth? Would he understand?

And, most importantly, would he still love her?

Orion galloped out of the tunnel and into the soft light of a cool early morning. She pulled the stallion to a halt, got her bearings and then guided him toward the marble basin which held Demeter's ball-shaped oracle. She slid from his back.

"Just hang around and be good. Hopefully, this won't tal[illegible] long."

"SHE has ridden Orion to feed a treat to Cerberus?"

The daimon nodded, looking slightly annoyed. "I filled the wineskin myself. She brought that great brute ambrosia!"

At any other time that would have made Hades laugh. Now doubts stabbed him in the heart. "But she told me she was exhausted. She was going to bathe and rest. Why would she go for a ride instead?"

"Only Persephone can answer that, Lord."

The growing sense of unease that had been gnawing at him since that morning blossomed. He must have hurt her. Had he frightened her? Or had he declared his love for her too soon? His chest tightened. She had not proclaimed her love in return. He remembered her tears. Silently cursing himself for his inexperience, he turned to the daimon.

"Bring me the Helmet of Invisibility!" he commanded.

LINA studied the oracle. It rested, still and benign, a simple milky-colored glass ball. But it was a conduit to a goddess who had the power to shape her future. Lina closed her eyes, admitting to herself that she wasn't just worried, she was scared. How could it work? She was a mortal, from another time and place. He was an ancient god. She felt tears of frustration well in her closed eyes.

Stop it! Pull yourself together! She had to tell Demeter everything. She couldn't avoid it any longer.

PERSEPHONE wasn't with the dog, although Cerberus had been happily licking at the well-mauled wineskin she'd fed him. She hadn't passed him returning to the palace, so Hades continued down the road. When he reached the boatman, Charon reported that he had ferried the goddess and her steed across Styx.

Hades admitted the worst to himself. Persephone was definitely returning to the Land of the Living. Hades felt a familiar burning begin in his chest. She was leaving him without saying good-bye? He did not want to believe it. He wouldn't believe it until he confronted her and she told him herself. With the speed of a god, Hades followed the dark path that would lead him to the world above and the Goddess of Spring.

LINA took a deep breath, and opened her eyes. Concentrating on the goddess, she passed her hands three times over the oracle.

"Demeter, we need to talk," she said.

The orb began to swirl and almost instantly Demeter's handsome features swam into focus.

"When a daughter calls upon her mother, the tone of her voice should be more welcoming than grim," Demeter said, softening the reprimand with a small, motherly smile.

"I didn't mean any disrespect, but I do feel rather grim," Lina said.

Demeter frowned. "What is troubling you, Daughter? I have heard only positive reports about your work. The spirits are pleased that the Goddess of Spring is sojourning in the Underworld." And that was quite true. Since the arrival of the goddess everyone believed to be Persephone in the Underworld, the unceasing, annoying petitions to Demeter from relatives of the dead had ended. Instead, sacrifices of thanksgiving had increased. The mortal must be making her presence known and doing an excellent job of impersonating a goddess. Demeter couldn't imagine what could be bothering her.

"Things have taken an unexpected turn."

Demeter's frown deepened. "Do not tell me you have been discovered."

"No! Everyone still thinks that I'm Persephone." Lina paused, chewing on her bottom lip. "But my problem does have to do with that."

"Explain yourself," Demeter said.

"I've fallen in love with Hades, and he loves me too, and I need to tell him who I really am and figure out how to fix this mess," Lina said in a rush.

Demeter's eyes turned to stone. "This is not some kind of mortal jest you make?"

Lina sighed. "No, this is absolutely not funny."

"You are truly telling me that you and Hades have become lovers?"

"Yes."

"Then a god has dallied with your affections," Demeter shook her head sadly. "I am to blame for this. I exposed a mortal to the whims of a god. Forgive me, Carolina Francesca Santoro, my intention was not to cause you pain."

"No," Lina protested. "It's not like that. He wasn't taking advantage of me. *We* fell in love—with each other."

"Fell in love? With each other?" Demeter's voice went hard. "How could that be? Hades believes that you are Persephone, Goddess of Spring. He has no idea that he has been making love to a mortal woman. Think, Carolina! How could you believe that it is you he loves?" She made a rude noise and her handsome face twisted. "Love! Are you really so naive? Immortals *love* differently than mortals. Surely even in your world you have heard tales of the excesses of immortal *love*."

Lina lifted her chin and narrowed her eyes. "I am not a child. Do not talk to me like I have the fickle emotions of an inexperienced girl. I know the difference between love and lust. I know when a man is using me, just as I know when he is treating me honestly. The lessons were hard, but experience taught me the difference."

"Then you should know better," Demeter said.

Lina's face burned as if Demeter's softly spoken words had struck her. "You don't know him. He's not like the rest of you."

"Not like the rest of the immortals? This is naive nonsense. He is a god. The only difference between Hades and the rest of the gods is that he is reclusive and has chosen to place the dead above the living."

"And that's part of what makes him so different." Lina took a deep breath; she didn't want to betray Hades' confidence, but she had to convince Demeter. "I am the only goddess he's loved."

Demeter's eyes narrowed. "Is that what he told you? Then here is your first lesson in immortal love. Never believe anything a god says when he is trying to gain access to the bed of a goddess. What he told you was only what he thought you needed to hear so that you would give yourself to him."

Refusing to believe Demeter's words Lina shook her head from side to side, but the goddess ignored her and continued her barrage.

"What did you believe? That you and he would be together for eternity? Forget that you are a mortal. Forget that you are from another world. Even if you were truly the Goddess of Spring, did you honestly believe that Hades and Persephone would be mated, that their names would be linked for eternity? The idea is absurd! How could Spring exist in the Land of the Dead?"

"Then Spring doesn't have to exist there. I will. Me—the mortal, Carolina Francesca Santoro. I'll stay in the Underworld and love its god. Just re-exchange me. Give me back my body and return this"—she gestured at herself—"to your daughter."

"I cannot. You are not of this world, Carolina." The anger drained from Demeter's face. "You knew your time there was temporary. I did not pretend otherwise."

"There has to be a way."

"There is not. Both of us must abide by the oaths we have given."

"Can't I even tell him who I am?" Lina asked hopelessly.

"Use your mind, Carolina, not your heart. What would the Lord of the Dead do if he knew he had wooed, not the Goddess of Spring, but a middle-aged baker from the mortal world? Would he open his arms to your deceit?" Demeter held up a hand to silence Lina's protests. "It matters little that you did not intend to deceive him. You say that I do not know Hades, but all immortals know this much of him: the Lord of the Dead values truth above all things. How would he react to your lie?"

"But he loves me."

"If Hades loves, it is Persephone, Goddess of Spring, who has won his affection," Demeter said with finality. "And consider for a moment how the spirits of the Underworld would feel if they learned that the goddess who has brought them such joy is only a mortal in disguise."

Lina flinched. "It would hurt them."

"Yes, it would."

"I cannot tell anyone."

"No, Daughter, you cannot." Lina closed her eyes and Demeter watched the woman in her daughter's body struggle to accept the pain of her words. "Remember this, when you have returned to your rightful place, *Persephone* will just consider Hades another god with whom she dallied. And no matter what you believe has passed between you and he, Hades will eventually feel the same. Listen to the voice that is within you and you will remember that this is simply the way of immortals."

When Lina opened her eyes, her gaze was resolute.

"I'll return to the Underworld and finish my job. You said my time is almost over?"

Demeter nodded.

"Good. I'll be ready to go when you say so."

"I knew I made a wise choice in you." The goddess's image began to fade. "Return with my blessing, Daughter," she said, and she was gone.

Lina turned away from the oracle. Her eyes passed over the beauty of Lake Avernus without actually seeing. She didn't cry. She held herself very still, as if the lack of movement could protect her against further pain.

CLOAKED in invisibility, Hades had, at first, stayed within the mouth of the tunnel. His initial reaction to finding Persephone had been relief. She wasn't leaving him. She was only speaking to her mother's oracle. He could not hear what she was saying, but as he watched, his relief was rapidly replaced by concern. Persephone was visibly upset, she almost looked frightened.

Was that why she hadn't told him she meant to speak with Demeter? Was she afraid of her mother's reaction to their love? Had she been trying to protect him? Surely, she was aware that he was a powerful god in his own right. But perhaps she wasn't. Persephone was very young—she behaved with such maturity that it was easy for him to forget just how young—and he had kept himself separated from the rest of the immortals for a very long time. Did she believe that he only wielded power in his own realm?

He watched as her face paled. Demeter was wounding her. Anger surged through him. Still wearing the Helmet of Invisibility, he strode toward his beloved.

Demeter's hard voice drifted to him from the oracle.

"Remember this, when you have returned to your rightful place, Persephone will just consider Hades another god with whom she dallied. And no matter what you believe has passed between you and he, eventually Hades will feel the same. Listen to the voice that is within you and you will remember that this is simply the way of the immortals."

Hades stopped short. Had he heard her correctly? He was just another god with whom she had dallied? Incredulous, he listened to Persephone's reply.

"I'll return to the Underworld and finish my job. You said my time is almost over?"

He had only been a job to her?

"Good. I'll be ready to go when you say so."

She wanted to leave him. Invisible to her, Hades watched the goddess he loved turn from her mother's oracle and stare off into the distance. Her eyes were dry. Her face was stone. She looked like a stranger.

No! He wouldn't believe it. He had heard only part of their conversation. He must have misunderstood. He knew Persephone. His Persephone could not deceive him. As his hand lifted to remove the Helmet of Invisibility, a sound drew his attention. Together, he and Persephone turned to face the god who strode from the path that curled around Lake Avernus.

Apollo's handsome face was alight with pleasure. His lips curved in a warm smile of welcome.

"Ah, Persephone, it pleases me that you accepted my invitation. We all knew that too much time in the Underworld would cause the Flower of Spring to yearn for the sun again."

With a growing sense of numbness, Hades watched as Apollo took Persephone's unresisting body in his arms.

Unable to continue watching, the Lord of the Underworld turned his back on the two lovers and silently returned to the realm of the dead.

Chapter Twenty-Three

It didn't take Apollo long to realize that holding Persephone was like hugging a corpse. He pulled back and studied her pale face.

"What's wrong? More problems with Demeter?"

Persephone shook her head. When she blinked, two perfect teardrops fell from her eyes and made glistening tracks down her cheeks. He was just considering whether he should kiss her or materialize a drink for her when a black monster burst from around the path and thrust his body between them.

"Be gone, beast from the pit!" he yelled as he staggered back, trying not to fall.

The stallion turned and bared yellow teeth at him.

"It's okay, Orion. Apollo doesn't mean any harm."

The sadness in her voice touched the god. He peered around the black brute who was nuzzling Persephone. The goddess caressed the horse absently. Tears leaked down her face, but she took no notice of them.

"Orion! I need to speak with your mistress." Eyes blazing, the stallion turned his swiveled head to face Apollo. He held his hands out in an open gesture of peace. "I wish only to offer her aid."

Orion seemed to study the god, then he blew through his nose and lipped the goddess's cheek before moving a few feet down the path where he grazed while keeping one black eye focused on the God of Light.

Apollo took Persephone's limp arm and led her to a bench carved from bare rock. The goddess sat. He made a spinning motion with his hand and a clear goblet appeared suddenly in a shower of sparks. He offered it to Persephone.

"It is only spring water," he said when she hesitated. "I thought you might need its refreshment."

"Thank you," she said woodenly. The water was cold and sweet. She drank deeply, but it didn't begin to quench the emptiness within her.

Apollo sat next to her.

"What has caused you such pain?" he asked.

She didn't answer for so long that he thought she wasn't going to respond. Then she spoke in a voice that was filled with such hopelessness that the god felt his own chest constrict.

"My own foolishness—that is what has caused me such pain."

Apollo took her hand. "What can I do to help you?"

She looked at him then, and the god felt as if her eyes could see through to his soul.

"Answer a question for me. What is it that loves—the body or the spirit?"

Apollo smiled and began to respond with a witty reply, but he found he could not. Once again, she surprised him with her candor. Since their last meeting, the Goddess of Spring hadn't been far from his thoughts. His eyes met hers. He could not belittle her obvious pain, so he answered honestly.

"Persephone, you ask this question of the wrong god. As you know, I have had much experience with lusts of the body. I feel desire and I slake it. But love? That most elusive of emotions? I have witnessed it bring an undefeated warrior to his knees, and cause a single maiden to wield more power than Hercules, but I cannot say that I have ever truly experienced it." Wistfully, he touched her cheek. "But looking at you makes me wish otherwise."

The light was growing. It signaled the coming of dawn. His chariot had to be near, and his time was short. Apollo could see that, though he was close beside her and offering her comfort and compassion,

Persephone was not even looking at him. She was staring at the mouth of the tunnel which led to Hades' domain. His hand dropped from her face.

"You love Hades!" He did not bother to hide the surprise in his voice.

Persephone's eyes snapped to his. "And why do you find that so shocking? Because I am Spring and he is Death? Or is it because immortals don't really know how to love?"

"I just didn't think it possible," Apollo said.

"It's probably not." The temporary fire in her voice was gone, and the hopelessness had returned. She lurched to her feet. "Orion!" The stallion moved with supernatural speed to her side. Without another word, she flung herself astride the horse and dug her heels into his sides. Orion leapt forward, leaving Apollo to stare openmouthed at the dust that rose from his iron-clad hooves.

"Persephone and Hades? How could that be?" he murmured.

HADES was at his forge. He stoked the fire to a level that was almost unbearable and striped down to his loincloth. He wouldn't work on a horseshoe. That would not satisfy him. He needed something else, something larger. He would fashion a shield, wrought from the strongest of metals. Something that could protect a body, if not a soul.

He fed the coals until they screamed with the voice of searing heat. Then he thrust the naked sheet of unformed metal into them and pulled it out when it hummed with readiness. He began pounding it to his will.

On and on Hades worked. His shoulders ached and his blows coursed through his body, and still he could not pound the pain from his soul. He did not blame her. She was just a young goddess. He should have known better. He had been wise to set himself apart from the immortals. She had simply proven how wise he had been. His way had worked for age after age. He had been foolish to deviate.

He felt her presence the moment she entered the forge. Absently he wondered if he would always know when she was near him. How could his soul be linked to hers even though she did not love him? It would bear consideration. Later. When he was alone again, when he could think of her without feeling such raw yearning. Now he must end it. He must return to his old ways before he humiliated himself further. And before she caused him irreparable pain.

"I wish you knew how incredibly handsome you are when you work at your forge."

When she entered the room he had stopped pounding metal against metal, and her voice sounded too loud in the echoing silence. He could not force himself to speak.

"Hades?" She cleared her throat and continued, even when he didn't respond. "I'd love to see more of Elysia today. Would you escort me?"

Her voice. It was so young and sweet. For a moment his resolve wavered. Then he remembered how easily she had allowed Apollo to take her into his arms. When he turned slowly to face her, Persephone did not meet his eyes. Hades felt a little more of his soul dissolve.

"I am afraid our travels have come to an end. As you can see, I have work I must complete."

Lina felt her stomach roll. The man who turned from the forge to speak to her wasn't her lover. He was the cold, imperious god she had met when she had first come to the Underworld. No—she studied him more carefully and realized her initial impression had been wrong. He wasn't even that familiar.

"But, I thought you liked teaching me about your realm," she said inanely.

He laughed, but his voice held no warmth and his eyes were flat and cold.

"Persephone, let us stop this—"

"But," she interrupted him, shaking her head. "Last night . . . I don't understand."

The look of naive shock on her face sliced through him. It was all a cruel pretense! He wanted to scream his pain, and with the anger of a god he hurled the hammer across the forge. When it landed, sparks exploded and the floor beneath them shook. His eyes blazed and his voice thundered.

"Silence! I am Lord of the Dead, not a lowly teacher!"

Lina felt her face lose all color. "All this time you've just been pretending to—"

"DO NOT SPEAK TO ME OF PRETENDING!" The walls of the forge vibrated with the intensity of the dark God's rage. Before he destroyed the chamber in which they stood, Hades brought the force of his anger under control. Through tightly clenched teeth he hurled sarcasm at her. "Have you not been *vacationing* here, Persephone? Masquerading as Queen of the Dead?" His laughter was cold and cruel. "You may be young, but both of us know you are far from inexperienced. Yes, our *lessons* were amusing, but you must realize that it is time the charade end, and, as I sense your visit is also concluding, my timing is perfect. Unfortunately, I have allowed our dalliance to take me too long from my duties. If I do not find time to speak with you again before you depart, let me wish you a pleasant return trip to the Land of the Living. Perhaps you will sojourn in the Underworld another time, perhaps not."

He shrugged nonchalantly, and then turned his back to her, closed another hammer within his shaking fist and resumed his rhythmic pounding. He didn't need to see her leave, he felt it. Soon sweat poured down his face, mixing with his silent tears, and still he kept on beating against the unspeaking metal until the ache in his arms mirrored the pain in his soul.

"I don't belong here." Lina's lips felt bloodless, and she spoke her thoughts aloud to assure herself that they could still form words. It didn't do any good to tell herself that Demeter had been right, that Hades' treatment of her was the norm for one of the immortals. She wasn't really a goddess, and so it was her mortal soul that grieved, and her mortal soul that couldn't understand.

Lina fled the forge without caring where her feet led her. She just wanted to be away. She skirted the stables and passed quickly between rows of ornamental shrubbery, but instead of keeping to the paths in Hades' gardens, she plunged into the surrounding woods. Finally, through the tumult of her mind, she recognized that she was retracing the path to the firefly meadow, and instantly changed direction. Her mind cringed away from the sweet memories of that night. She couldn't bear to go there.

She didn't notice the spirits of the dead except as vague, distant images that might have whispered her name. Her eyes were too blurred with unshed tears, leaving her vision as unfocused as her thoughts. Somewhere in her mind she realized that she was grateful that none of them approached her. She couldn't be their goddess today.

As she passed, the dead paused. Something was wrong with Persephone. Her face had lost its color. Her eyes were glazed and she did not seem to be able to hear them. She moved with the numb steps of the newly dead. Concern for their goddess began to flicker throughout Elysia.

Lina kept walking. She'd be all right. She'd make it. Time would help it not to hurt so badly. The three sentences were a familiar litany. They had become her mantra when her husband had left her for a younger, more perfect woman who could bear him children. They had helped her through the shattered dreams and the sleepless nights that had followed. They had kept her strong through the series of disappointing relationships afterward. And they had soothed her when she had realized that she probably would never love again.

She'd be all right. She'd make it. Time would help it not to hurt so badly.

A mischievous breeze brought with it the intoxicating fragrance of narcissus blossoms and she winced, recoiling from a bed of flowers in front of her. She changed direction, picking her way around the beautiful blooms, choosing her path according to which way led past fewer flowers.

Her hand rose to her chest where the amethyst narcissus dangled from its silver chain. What had his gift really meant? It wasn't a token of his love, his speech at the forge had made that painfully obvious. Lina blinked her eyes rapidly. In her mind she still heard the echo of his uncaring words. Her fingers caressed the beautifully wrought outline of the narcissus. Payment for services rendered; that's all the gift had been. Hades—a different kind of a god? Her self-mocking laughter came out like a sob. Her hand closed over the jewel and she tugged, snapping the delicate chain.

"Demeter was right. I should have known better." Lina hurled the necklace to the ground and kept walking. She didn't look back.

She'd be all right. She'd make it. Time would help it not to hurt so badly.

The only notice Lina took when the landscape began to change was to feel relief that there were no more narcissus blossoms to avoid. There were also fewer spirits of the dead hovering in the periphery of her vision, and that, too, brought her relief. Vaguely she acknowledged that it was growing darker, but the trees were very tall and dense. They could easily be shutting out the pastel light of the Underworld's day. And she had been walking for quite a while—at least she thought it had been quite a while. She didn't feel tired. Actually, she didn't feel much of anything. The thought almost made her smile. Demeter needn't have been concerned. The gods underestimated the resiliency of the mortal spirit.

She should probably start back to the palace. Eurydice would be waiting to show her the sketches. She would enjoy the upbeat company of the little spirit, and then she would take a long bath. Not a shower on the balcony—her mind skittered away from the thought—just a long, relaxing soak. For the time that remained to her in the Underworld, she would simply avoid Hades. That shouldn't be difficult. He had made it clear that he was too busy to bother with her. Instead of pining over the god, she would spend time with Eurydice, but she'd be up-front with the spirit about the temporary nature of her visit. She'd also warn her to be careful about falling in love with Iapis. He seemed trustworthy, but so had . . .

Her mind shied from the rest of her thought.

he would ride Orion into Elysia and let the spirits see the Goddess ing. But she would be more careful with them, too. They deserved to know that hers was only a temporary visit. She could tell them that Persephone would continue to care for them from the world above, and then all she could do was hope that the real Goddess of Spring would follow through with her word.

Deciding on her course of action felt good and she was so preoccupied with her thoughts that she did not notice that she had come to the forest edge until she stumbled from the tree line. Confused, she looked around her, trying to make sense of what she was seeing. The trees had ended, as had the grass and the ferny ground cover. The land was barren; the cinnamon-colored ground cracked and eroded. Directly in front of her flowed a river of seething flames, perfectly silhouetted against a background of inky darkness.

Lina stopped breathing. Tartarus—she had stumbled into the edge of Hell.

Turn around. Retrace your path. Her mind knew the logical thing to do, but her stunned body would not obey her.

And then she heard it, the whisperings from the blackness beyond the river of fire. Like threads of hate they called to her, weaving a net of dark remembrances: every mistake she'd ever made, every lie she'd ever told, every time her words or actions had caused others hurt. Her mortal soul cringed. Lina whimpered and staggered under the weight of her own misdeeds. She fell to her knees.

The oily darkness leaked from the bank of the blazing river. It licked at her with tendrils of hate.

She wasn't a goddess. She was a mortal woman—middle-aged, plain of appearance—a failure in relationships. No man loved her. Why would anyone? She couldn't even bear children. She was a failure as a woman and a wife. Being alone was what she deserved.

Slowly her soul began to peel away from Persephone's body and Lina felt herself begin to disintegrate.

"HADES, you must come." The daimon had to shout over the incessant pounding to gain the god's attention.

Hades straightened and wiped the sweat from his face. "Whatever it is, you must deal with it. I do not wish to be disturbed."

"It is the dead. They ask to speak with you."

Hades' expression was dark and dangerous. "Then they can petition their god when I hold court."

"I do not believe you will want to wait for court to hear what they have to say," Iapis insisted.

"Leave me in peace! What they have to say could not interest me today," Hades snarled.

Unmoved by the god's show of temper, Iapis met his eyes. "They say there is something wrong with Persephone."

Hades was pulling on his tunic when he burst from the forge. The sight before him brought him to a sudden halt. Spreading down the landscaped tiers of his formal gardens were countless spirits of the dead. They stood quietly, side by side: young girls, maidens, mothers, matrons and crones.

An ancient crone and a maiden Hades recognized as one Persephone had danced with in the meadow, detached themselves from the forefront of the group and approached him. The women curtsied deeply. The crone spoke first.

"Great God, we come to you because of our love for the Goddess of Spring. Something is amiss. The goddess is not herself."

"We saw her walking through the forest," the maiden said. "We called her name, but she did not hear us, nor did she see us."

"It was as if she were dead," the old woman said.

A dagger of fear pricked the god's heart. "Where was she last seen?"

"There," the crone and the maiden turned, raising their hands to show the direction.

They were pointing toward Tartarus.

"Saddle Orion!" Hades commanded in a voice that carried to the stables.

Then the god closed his eyes and took a deep, calming breath. He blocked out the voices of the dead and focused his entire being on

Persephone. He found the link that tied their souls together, the link that had told him when she had entered his forge, and then told him when she had departed. But it was like a thread that had been cut. Their connection had been severed. Fear mushroomed within him.

"Bring Cerberus," Hades commanded Iapis. The daimon nodded and disappeared.

Hades turned back to the spirits of the women. "You did the right thing coming to me."

The crone and the maiden bowed their heads, as did the multitude behind them.

Hades' gaze searched the faces in the throng surrounding him.

"Eurydice! Bring me an article of Persephone's clothing. Something she has worn recently."

Instead of instantly obeying his bidding, the young spirit approached him. Her eyes met his and he felt the light touch of her hand on his arm.

"You must bring her back to us, Hades." Her voice was choked.

"I will," he said, and strode to the stables.

ORION plunged through the forest close on the heels of Cerberus. The three-headed dog hunted silently, following the scent of his goddess. Hades' hands were slick with sweat, and they gripped the steed's reins tightly. The stallion needed no urging to stay on the dog's trail, which led inexorably toward the dark realm of Tartarus.

His thoughts warred within his mind. He must have wounded her terribly if he had driven her to the dark realm. He hadn't meant to hurt her. His own pain and jealousy had made him forget her youth. Persephone couldn't possibly know into what she was heading. Not even being a goddess would afford her protection against the utter despair that reigned in Tartarus. Desperately he tried to remember if she had been wearing the amethyst narcissus when he had last seen her. Yes, he thought she had been. A trickle of relief cooled his panic. The amethyst would help to protect her. It was a powerful jewel that he had fashioned specifically for her. Its protective properties were vast.

Hades tried not to imagine what might be happening to Persephone. As God of the Underworld, he knew only too well the horrors of Tartarus. It was the eternal dwelling place of the damned. Only the souls of mortals who had completely embraced darkness were condemned to that region. He loathed it, but he acknowledged the necessity of a place to house immutable evil.

And that was where his beloved had gone.

Orion came to a halt beside the dog. Cerberus was snuffling through dried leaves and pawing at something that flashed silver in the dim light. Hades dismounted and picked up the object. It was Persephone's amethyst necklace. She had no talisman to protect her.

"Faster, Cerberus!" he commanded.

The dog redoubled his efforts and Orion responded in kind. They broke through the forest of trees. Cerberus had come to a halt beside the fiery bank of Phlegethon. The dog was whining piteously and all three heads were nudging what Hades thought might be the collapsed body of a dead animal. Then Orion pierced the air with a heart-wrenching scream and plunged down the bank toward the dog. As the horse slid to a halt, Hades recognized the body.

"No!"

He flung himself from Orion's back and pushed Cerberus' massive body aside. Persephone had collapsed upon the cracked earth. Her arms were wrapped around her legs so that her knees pressed into her chest and her body had formed a rigid ball. Her eyes were open, but her pupils were fully dilated and she stared unseeing into the darkness beyond the flaming river.

Hades followed her gaze. The blackness of Tartarus was leaking from its banks. He looked down. Fingers of darkness had slithered from Phlegethon and they soaked the ground around Persephone.

Fury pulsed through the god. Quickly, he bent and knotted the broken chain around Persephone's unresisting neck. The amethyst narcissus began to glow. Then he raised his arms and the air around him began to swirl. In a voice magnified by anger and love, he commanded the grasping darkness.

"Away! You have no right to harm this goddess!"

The dark tendrils shivered, but they did not loosen their hold on Persephone.

"I am Hades, Lord of the Dead, and I command you. Do not touch her!" The god roared, casting all of his formidable power against the malignant fingers of evil.

The darkness drew back and then with a sizzling sound it dissipated like a thief retreating into the night.

Hades fell to his knees beside Persephone. He grasped the goddess's shoulders and turned her rigid body to face him.

"Persephone!"

She did not respond. Instead she continued to stare unblinkingly into the darkness beyond Phlegethon. Her face was deathly pale and her skin was cool to the touch. She was gasping in short, panting breaths, like she was having difficulty breathing.

"It is gone. It cannot harm you now. Look at me, Persephone."

Still she did not acknowledge his presence.

"Persephone! You have to listen to me." He shook her until her head bobbled and Cerberus whined his distress.

The goddess's lips moved.

"Yes! Speak to me," Hades cried.

"Too many mistakes. I can't . . ." Her voice cracked, and her words became inaudible.

"You can't what?" Hades prompted, shaking her again.

"Can't find my way. My body isn't here. I've disappeared."

The emptiness in her voice terrified Hades. Her face was blank. Her eyes were glazed. The Persephone he knew was not there. It was as if an echo of her spirit was speaking through a shell.

And suddenly nothing mattered to him except bringing her back. He didn't care if she thought of him only as a job her mother had charged her to complete. He didn't care that Apollo was her lover. He didn't even care that she was going to leave him. He cared only that she was herself again.

Hades cupped her cold face in his hands. "Your way is here. You must come back to those who love you."

Persephone blinked.

"Come back to us, beloved. Come back to me."

She took one deep, rasping breath and Hades watched as her hand lifted to grasp the glowing amethyst flower. Then she blinked and struggled to focus on his face.

"Hades?" she croaked his name.

Dizzy with relief, he pulled her into his arms. "Yes, beloved. It is Hades, the foolish, arrogant god who loves you."

"Take me away from here," she sobbed, and buried her face in his chest.

Chapter Twenty-four

The women watched silently as the Lord of the Dead carried their goddess into his palace. Though the god's face was grim, Persephone's arms were wrapped securely around his broad shoulders and her face was pressed into his neck. Relief passed through the spirits. She would be herself again. The god's love assured them of that. Like wind sloughing through willow branches they murmured softly to one another and departed the palace grounds.

"Eurydice!" Hades bellowed as he entered the palace. The spirit materialized instantly with Iapis at her side. "Draw the goddess a bath. Make it very hot."

"Yes, Lord," she said and disappeared.

Iapis kept pace with Hades. "What can I do?"

"Go to Bacchus. Tell him I must have his most potent wine. Something to soothe the soul of a goddess." Hades said.

"I will, Lord." Before Iapis disappeared he touched Persephone's head. "Be well, Goddess," he whispered, and was gone.

Hades carried Persephone quickly to her chamber. Fragrant steam was already escaping from the bathing room and Hades entered the moist fog to find Eurydice hurrying around, pulling thick towels from shelves and choosing soft, plump sponges.

There was a well-cushioned chair near the mirrored wall. Reluctantly, Hades placed Persephone in it. Her arms slid lifelessly from around his shoulders and she sat very still. Her eyes were closed. Hades knelt beside her.

"Persephone, you are home now," he said.

A tremor passed through her body.

"Beloved, can you hear me?"

She opened her eyes and looked at him.

"I can hear you." Her voice was flat and expressionless.

"Do you know where you are?" he asked.

"I'm at your palace."

"Yes," he smiled encouragement, ignoring the dead sound of her voice.

Iapis materialized in the room. He held a crystal bottle of ruby-colored wine and a matching goblet. He poured the wine and an intoxicating scent drifted from the glass. It smelled of grapes and meadows, of ripened wheat and summer nights under the full moon.

Iapis offered the goblet to Persephone. "Drink, Goddess. It will revive you."

She tried to hold the glass, but her hand was trembling so violently that she almost dropped it. Hades wrapped his hand around hers, guiding the wine to her lips. She drank deeply. The magic of the immortals' wine began warming her almost instantly. Soon, the trembling in her hands subsided so that she could drink without the god's help.

"Go, now," Eurydice said, taking charge. "The goddess needs her privacy to bathe."

Hades stood, but hesitated to leave the room.

"My Lord, I will call you when she is ready," Eurydice assured him.

Still Hades hesitated. "Persephone, I will not be far away."

The goddess looked up. "You don't need to worry. I'm back now," she told him.

Even though her voice was expressionless, Hades nodded and he and Iapis reluctantly left the room.

* * *

HADES paced in the hallway outside her chamber. How long did it take to bathe? Would the spirit never call him? He wanted to thrust open the door and order Eurydice from the room. Then he would make Persephone listen to him. She had to hear his apology. He was a stupid, inexperienced, jealous fool. Hades sighed. She knew him. It shouldn't be difficult to get her to believe that he had blundered into such a terrible mistake.

The door opened and Eurydice stepped into the hall. She closed the door gently behind her.

"How is she?" Hades asked.

Eurydice looked up at the god, searching his face before she answered him. When she did she sounded much older than her years.

"She is sad, Lord."

Hades raked his hand through his hair. "I have caused this."

"Yes, you have," she said simply.

Hades nodded tightly and turned to the door. Eurydice's pale hand halted him.

"Be patient. Treat her carefully. It's hard for a woman to love again after she has been hurt."

Iapis materialized beside Eurydice. He slid his arm around her and the little spirit leaned into him.

"It's hard for a woman to love again after she had been hurt, but it is possible, Lord," the daimon told his god.

Hades watched them walk slowly away. They fit well together. He turned back to the door, took a deep breath and entered Persephone's chamber.

The goddess was wearing a sheer silk chemise the color of candlelight. She was curled up on a chaise that sat in front of the wall of windows. Part of the velvet drapes had been pulled back and Persephone seemed to be studying the night-cloaked gardens while sipping Bacchus' wine.

"Your gardens really are very beautiful," she spoke without looking at him.

He crossed the room and stood beside her chaise.

"Thank you. I am glad . . ." His words faded. He didn't want to make inconsequential conversation with her. Eurydice had warned him to be patient and careful, and he would. But he must also speak his heart to her. He sat beside her on the chaise.

"Please forgive me. I am a fool," he said.

She turned to face him.

"I knew you were going to leave me, so I wanted to break with you first. I thought it might save me pain. I thought I could go back to how it was before I loved you. I was wrong. I was selfish. I did not think of your feelings. Like an aging, solitary monster, I thought only of myself."

Lina put up her hand to stop his words. "Don't say any more. You're a god. You were simply acting like a god."

Hades clutched her hand. "No! I am not like the others. Everything I said to you in the forge was a lie. I was angry. I was hurt. It is hard for me to understand that you can be with me, and share yourself with Apollo, too. I . . ." he faltered. "It is I who am not accustomed to the way immortals choose and then discard their lovers."

"Hades, Apollo is not my lover."

The god studied her face. "I saw him take you into his arms."

Lina blinked in surprise. "You were there?"

"I followed you. I heard Demeter remind you of the way immortals love, then I watched Apollo hold you."

"If you had watched a little longer, you would have seen that that's all that happened. I don't want Apollo, Hades. If what Demeter had said to me hadn't upset me so badly, I would never have let him touch me at all."

Hades wiped his hand across his brow. "You don't desire Apollo, too?"

"No."

He bowed his head. "Then the pain I caused you was truly for no reason. I do not know if you can forgive me, but please believe me when I say that I do love you, Persephone."

She turned her face away from him. "You don't love me, Hades. You love what you think I am. You don't really know me at all."

"How can you say that to me?" He grasped her chin and forced her to look at him.

"You just love the goddess, not the woman inside her soul."

"You are wrong, Persephone, but let me tell you what I love and then you may decide for yourself. I love your curiosity about everything. I love how you see my realm with new, wondering eyes. I love your sense of humor. I love your kindness and your honesty. I love your unbridled passion. I love the way you bespell animals. I love your loyalty. I especially love your stubbornness, because it was your stubbornness that did not let an ancient god remain trapped within his own denial and loneliness." Tears fell from Persephone's eyes and Hades brushed them gently away. "Now you tell me, what is it that I love—the goddess or her soul?"

"But you don't know . . . you can't really know," she said brokenly.

"I know that I feel your presence before I see you. Something has happened to me, and it has little to do with anything physical. For the first time in an eternity, I understand why soul mates cannot be separated, even after death. It is because their hearts beat in tandem. While I was waiting outside your door, I could feel your heart breaking within. Let me heal it, Persephone, and in the mending of your heart, I will save myself."

"Is it possible that you really do love my soul?" Lina whispered.

Hades smiled at her as he felt the fear inside him begin to thaw. "Death is completely enamored with Spring. If that is possible, then anything is possible, beloved."

She melted into his arms and their lips met. Hades meant for the kiss to be soft and reassuring, but Persephone opened her mouth and pressed herself against him, demanding more. His desire for her flared and he moaned her name as he crushed her barely clad body against his chest.

"Make love to me," she gasped. "I need to feel you inside me."

He lifted her in his arms and carried her to the bed, but as he began to strip the clothes from his body, she stopped him.

"Let me," she said.

She sat on the edge of the bed and Hades stood in front of her, forcing his hands to remain at his sides while she undressed him. He was wearing a shorter version of his voluminous robes, and she slowly unwound the linen from his muscular body. She slid her hands down his chest; his skin felt hot and slick to her touch. At his abdomen she bent forward and replaced her teasing hands with her mouth. He sucked in his breath as her tongue feathered sensation over his skin. She couldn't get enough of him. She felt like she had been awakened from the dead, and she needed his passion and his love and his touch to keep her anchored there with him. She loosened his loincloth and slid it from his hips. Then she stroked his hardness in her cool hands, all the while moving her mouth slowly lower. When she swallowed him his body spasmed and swayed.

"Your mouth is like a silken trap that has captured me," he moaned. He thought his knees might buckle.

She drew back and met his eyes. "Do you want to be free?"

He lifted her into his arms and held her tightly against his body. "Never," he breathed into her hair. "Never, beloved."

She led him to her bed. While she stroked him he explored her body. The chemise was so thin that it felt like she had been wrapped in mist. He found her nipple, teasing and suckling it through the transparent material. He remembered the touches that brought her pleasure, and he did not need her to guide his hand. She responded to him as if they had been lovers for centuries.

Suddenly she sat up and pulled the chemise from her body. When he moved to take her back into his arms, she stopped him.

"What is it, beloved?"

"I want you to do something for me."

"Anything," he said.

"I want you to make love to me with your eyes closed. Pretend you cannot see my body." She peered into his face as if she were searching for an answer written there. "Can you make love to me without looking at me?"

He smiled and closed his eyes. Blind, he opened his arms to her and she fell into his embrace.

Surrounded by her scent and touch, Hades existed in a world of Persephone's sensations. Without seeing her, he had to pay more attention to her small sounds and follow the flow of her hips and the movement of her body. When her breathing quickened and his name sighed from her lips he did not need to see her flushed face to know he was bringing her pleasure. In his soul he felt her need and Hades responded with caress after caress. And then he filled her body and they rocked together in an ancient rhythm that needed no sight or sound—only feelings.

LATER she nestled against him, her head resting on his shoulder. He didn't know it yet, but he had helped her to make her decision, and now that she had made it, she felt at peace. Whatever happened next, she would survive it. Nothing could ever be as terrible as the black nothingness of Tartarus. With Hades' help, she had found her way free of that ultimate nightmare, and now she must be free of all the lies remaining in her life. She wasn't willing to hide the truth from him any longer. Demeter's anger be damned, she would tell him. He deserved to know everything. He loved her soul.

"Hades, I have to tell you something."

The god smiled. "May I keep my eyes open?"

Lina laughed softly. "Yes."

She sat up so that she was facing him, the silk sheet wrapped around her naked body. Hades grabbed a few pillows from the disheveled bed, and propped himself comfortably against the padded headboard. He raised his dark eyebrows questioningly.

"I didn't mean to go to Tartarus. It was an accident. I was too upset to realize where I was until it was too late."

Hades frowned. Just the thought of how close she had been to losing her soul made his stomach tighten. "I know, beloved. You don't have to explain it to me. It was my fault. If I hadn't hurt you—"

"Sssh . . ." Lina leaned forward and pressed a finger against his lips. "Let me finish."

The god looked uncomfortable, but he remained silent.

"Tartarus was," she shivered, "horrible. It called to me. It knew things about me—every bad thing I've ever done, or even ever thought about doing. Every mistake I've made. It caused me to lose myself. I could feel it capturing my soul. There was nothing I could do." She took his hand and laced her fingers with his. "Then I heard you. You called me back. *Me,* Hades. The real me—the soul inside the body."

"I had to get you back. I love you," he said.

"And I love you, too. But you need to know more than that. I am not who you think I am. I am not—"

"Enough, Persephone!" Demeter's voice cut through Lina's words. "Your time here is finished. You must return."

Appalled, Hades shot from Persephone's bed. Giving no thought to his nakedness, he faced the goddess who had materialized in the middle of his beloved's chamber.

"What do you mean by this intrusion, Demeter?" he challenged. "This is not your realm. You have no right to trespass here."

"You dally with my daughter, Lord of the Underworld, and I have come to reclaim her. I am her mother. That is all the right I need."

"You are not my mother." Lina enunciated the words carefully so that there could be no mistaking what she was saying. She stood next to Hades, clutching the sheet to her breasts.

Demeter sighed. "Let us not play these childish games, Daughter. Your adventure has ended. It is time you return to your own reality."

"I know I can't stay, but I won't leave without telling him the truth. He deserves to know. He loves *me.*"

"You are being a young fool," Demeter said.

"As you know very well, I am not young. And let me tell you once and for all, I am not a fool, either." She faced Hades and looked into his eyes. "I'm not really Persephone. My name is Carolina Francesca Santoro, but most people call me Lina. I am a forty-three-year-old mortal woman who owns a bakery in a place called Tulsa, Oklahoma. Demeter exchanged my soul with her daughter's." She glanced at Demeter and her mouth twisted into a sardonic smile before she looked back at the god. "She said she would help me out with a problem I was having, and in exchange I needed to do a little job for her in the Underworld."

The god's eyes widened.

"Remember when you overheard her reminding me how immortals love? She wasn't *reminding* me, she was explaining it to me because I'm a mortal. The whole thing was new to me."

"You are not the Goddess of Spring?"

"No, I am definitely not the Goddess of Spring," Lina said. She was so relieved to finally be telling the truth, that she didn't notice that Hades' face had gone expressionless.

"So it has all been a lie," Hades said.

"I wanted to tell you, but I gave my word to Demeter that I would keep my real identity a secret." Lina tried to touch his arm, but Hades flinched away from her.

"The things you said to me . . . what we did together. It was all pretense?"

"No!" Lina felt her stomach knot as she watched Hades withdraw into himself. She reached out to him, but again he moved away from her. "I meant everything I said, everything I did. It's just this body that is a lie. Everything else has been real. I love you; that is real."

"How can love be based on a lie?" he said coldly.

"Please don't do this," she pleaded with him, trying to reach the man inside the god. "Don't let us part like this. We can't be together. I have to return to my own world, but let's not make hurtful words what we remember when we're apart."

"Do not beg for his love like a common mortal, Carolina," Demeter's voice interrupted Lina. "There is enough goddess within you that you should have more pride."

Lina spun to face her. "You caused this! He does love me; he just feels betrayed because of your insistence on maintaining a lie. I don't blame him—how could he feel any other way right now?"

Demeter raised on arched eyebrow. "You believe he loves you,

Carolina Francesca Santoro? Then let us test your belief in this immortal's love."

With a flick of her wrist, Demeter showered Lina in golden sparks. Lina felt her body tremble and she was suddenly horribly dizzy. She closed her eyes, fighting against nausea. Then there was an odd settling feeling, like she had just stepped back into a comfortable pair of jeans. Before she opened her eyes she knew what she would see.

Across the room, the full-length mirror—the mirror she had preened in just that morning—reflected a new image. Lina's body was her own again. Gone was the lean young body of the goddess. Lina's curves were fuller, and she was older and decidedly not perfect.

"You *are* a mortal." The god sounded strangled.

Lina shifted her gaze from the mirror to Hades. He was staring at her, his face a mask of shock and disbelief.

"Yes, I am a mortal," she said. Squaring her shoulders she dropped the sheet, exposing all of herself to him. "And I am also the woman who loves you."

Hades averted his face, and refused to look at her. "How could you have lied all this time?"

"And what good would the truth have done?" Demeter broke in indignantly. "You would have shunned her as you do now." Her tone turned sarcastic. "At least you finally possessed the body of a goddess, Lord of the Dead. The irony is that you have a mortal to thank for it. No true goddess would have you."

Hades clenched his jaw. While Demeter had been speaking his face had become very pale. When his eyes met Lina's she saw only anger and rejection reflected in their darkness.

"Leave my realm," he commanded in a voice that raised the hair on Lina's arms.

"Come, Carolina. Your time here is finished." Demeter moved to Lina's side and covered her with her cloak. Without another word, the Palace of Hades faded from around them.

Chapter Twenty-five

THE chime over the front door of Pani Del Goddess jingled merrily, letting in another stream of customers as well as a rush of cold air.

"Burr," Anton shivered dramatically. "Oh, poo! Winter is really coming. It's just so hard on my skin."

"The weatherman is predicting an unusually snowy season. You'd better stock up on moisturizer and get some sensible shoes," Dolores said, pointing down at Anton's feet.

"What's wrong with these?" Anton pouted, turning his feet this way and that so that the entire bakery could admire his glossy black eel-skin, pointed-toe, mock cowboy boots with their two and a half inch heels. "Lina," he called from across the room. "Do you think I need new shoes?"

Lina looked up from the cappuccino machine. She wanted to say that she didn't care about his shoes or the weather, or . . . but Anton's expectant expression reminded her that she had to pretend. She had to keep pretending, no matter how she really felt.

"Honey, I think your boots are perfect. But just remember, my insurance doesn't cover falls outside the bakery."

Laughter fluttered through Pani Del Goddess. The customers grinned and placed their orders. Everyone was happy. Business was booming. In the two weeks Lina had been back, she had been amazed at the changes Persephone had made during her six months. The Goddess of Spring had truly worked magic. Her advertisement campaign had been miraculous. New customers filled the shop day and night, most of them clamoring for anything on which they could spread the incredible new ambrosia cream cheese that was offered exclusively through Pani Del Goddess. Persephone's creation had definitely been a hit. And that wasn't all that the goddess had changed. Instead of going in the direction of catering, as Lina had been thinking they should, Persephone had steered Pani Del Goddess into a whole new realm of business ventures, via the Internet. She packaged a wide variety of their specialty bread, gubana, added a small tin of ambrosia cream cheese and shipped it all over the United States. For an outrageously high price. Their new Internet service was booming. Persephone had even hired an additional full-time employee who did nothing but service their Net orders.

It amazed Lina. It had taken a goddess from an ancient world to see the potential in something as modern as the Internet. The IRS debt had been repaid threefold. Just as Demeter had promised. All was well.

And Lina was so miserable she thought she was going to die.

No, she couldn't think about dying, or death, or spirits, or the Lord of the Dead . . .

The bell over the door jingled again.

"Hello, handsome," Anton teased.

"Hey there, Anton. Nice boots." A deeply masculine voice said.

Anton giggled happily.

Lina ground her teeth together and readied herself, glad she had the cappuccino machine between her and him. At least he wouldn't try to kiss her hello.

"Good evening, Lina."

"Hi, Scott." She sighed and looked up at the gorgeous young man. He was tall and muscular. His blond hair was neatly cut and his deep blue eyes gazed down at her with open adoration. He was wearing a perfectly tailored business suit, complete with red power tie. The suit did nothing to camouflage his amazing body. Actually, the long Italian lines accentuated the young man's incredible physique. Not for the first time, Lina thought he could have been a young Apollo—if the God of Light had come to Earth as an up-and-coming Tulsa attorney.

It wasn't hard to understand why Persephone had been attracted to him. That didn't surprise Lina. What she didn't understand was why he was so obviously smitten with her in return.

"I still have those front row tickets to Aida. I thought I'd come by and see if you'd changed your mind. I really don't want to go without you," Scott said.

"Thank you, but no. I really can't."

"Why, Lina? I don't understand. Just two weeks ago—"

"Not here. Not now!" Lina interrupted him, mortified that the bakery had gone silent and everyone was watching their little scene while they pretended not to be.

"Then where and when, Lina? You've been avoiding me for two weeks. I deserve an explanation."

Knowing he was right didn't make her feel any less miserable, nor did it make her decision less certain. Scott was handsome and incredibly sexy. Add to that he even seemed to be an honestly nice guy. But she didn't feel anything for him. It would have been easier if she could care for him. Losing herself in his youthful infatuation had seemed, fleetingly, like a good idea. She'd even tried going out on a date with him—once. When he touched her, she felt nothing except the empty ache within her. Scott couldn't make her forget.

"Come on," she said. Rushing out from behind the counter she grabbed his arm and led him to the door. As she stepped out of the bakery, she could hear Anton sighing mournfully and saying, "What a waste . . ."

The evening was chilly, and Lina should have already put up the little café tables and chairs that sat on the sidewalk outside the bakery, but as she struggled to find some barrier she could erect between them, she was glad she hadn't. She sat down at one table, and Scott took the chair across from her. Before she could say anything, he slid it around so that they were sitting close together. Seeing her shiver, he took off his jacket and wrapped it around her shoulders. It was warm, and it smelled faintly like expensive aftershave and virile young man. He would have taken her hand, but she kept it out of reach in her lap.

"Scott," she began, honestly wishing that the sexy way his muscular chest looked in his dress shirt could make her feel more than an aesthetic appreciation for his well-toned physique. "I told you before. It's over between us. I wish you would respect that and just let it alone."

Scott shook his head. "I can't. There's no reason for it. Just two weeks ago everything was fine. Everything was better than fine. And then one day I wake up and, *wham!* It's all over. No explanation. After almost six months, you dump me and you won't even tell me how I screwed up."

"That's because *you* didn't screw up. *Merda!* I told you before—it's me, not you." He's perfect, Lina added silently. Young and handsome and successful and attentive. He needed to go find a nice young woman and settle down in the suburbs with a big mortgage, 2.5 kids and a dog.

"Tell me again. I don't understand how you can suddenly be so different. What is it?"

"You're too young for me, Scott," Lina said earnestly.

"Would you please stop it with that crap! I'm twenty-five, not fifteen. I'm not too young."

"So let's say it's not that you're too young. Let's say the problem is that I'm too old."

"You are not," he leaned forward and pulled her hand from her lap, holding it in both of his. "I don't care that you're forty-three. You're beautiful and sexy, but it's more than that. Your heart is young. You sparkle, Lina. When we were together, you made me feel like I was a god."

Lina smiled sadly. "Not anymore. I'm not like that inside anymore." She stood up and pulled her hand from his. Then she slipped his jacket from her shoulders and gave it back to him. "I can't give you what you need. I don't have it inside of me anymore. Please, just leave me alone."

He shook his head. "I can't. I'm in love with you."

"Okay, here's the truth, Scott. I'm in love with someone else."

Scott straightened in his chair and the skin on his face tightened. "Someone else?"

"Yes. I didn't mean for it to happen, but it did. I'm sorry. I didn't want to hurt you."

His handsome young face flushed and Lina watched as he erected a barrier of pride between them. Scott stood up. His jaw was set, but his eyes were sad.

"I hadn't realized there was someone else, but I guess I should have known. You're too amazing to be alone. I apologize for bothering you. Good-bye, Lina."

"Good-bye, Scott," she said to his retreating figure as he walked away from the bakery.

Feeling seventy-three instead of forty-three, Lina slowly reentered the bakery.

Anton, Dolores, and just about every other face in the store looked up at her expectantly, but when they saw that she was alone, they looked quickly away.

"I think I'll call it quits early today," Lina said.

"Oh, no problem, boss lady." Anton smiled at her and gave her arm a motherly pat.

"Yeah, we can take care of locking up," Dolores said. "You need some time off. You've been working really hard."

Anton nodded. "Why don't you sleep in tomorrow, and then go for a nice massage and a facial. You know, from that place you found a few months ago. Remember, you said that they knew how to treat you like a goddess."

"Want me to call and set up an appointment for you?" Dolores asked.

"No, I'll be fine," Lina said, grabbing her purse and her jacket. "But you're right. I think I need to sleep in tomorrow." She tried to smile at them, but her lips didn't form much more than a grimace.

"Oh, by the way, we're almost out of the ambrosia cream cheese. You better make some more soon. Or . . . you could let us in on your secret recipe," Dolores said, waggling her eyebrows at her boss.

"Yeah, we've already promised not to sell it to terrorists, or to Hostess, even though it would breathe new life into their dreadful Twinkies." Anton shuddered dramatically.

Lina rallied her sense of humor. "A girl has to have some secrets of her own." She winked at Anton and slung her purse over her shoulder. "I'll see you tomorrow afternoon, and I'll have a new tub of ambrosia cream cheese with me." She tried to swing jauntily through the door.

Her employees watched her go. As soon as she was out of sight, they met behind the counter and put their heads together.

"Something's wrong with her," Dolores said.

"Well, of course there is, she broke up with that young stud," Anton said.

"It's more than that." Dolores sighed. "She liked Scott, but I never got the feeling that he meant more to her than a good time. Breaking up with him shouldn't make her this sad."

Anton thought about it and nodded. "You're right. It is something else. She's not herself—again. Remember how weird she acted last spring?"

"Of course I remember, but she was worried about losing the bakery."

"Well, she saved Pani Del Goddess, and it did her good. She changed her whole image. She bought different clothes, started roller skating along the river. I swear she lost ten pounds."

Dolores nodded. "She even changed her hair."

"*And* she started dating young men. Adorable young men," Anton said.

"So, what's the point? That's all old news. What does that have to do with what's going on with her now?" Dolores asked.

Anton shrugged his shoulders. "Could be some kind of delayed stress reaction. Or maybe a tragic split-personality syndrome that is manifesting in her middle-age."

Dolores rolled her eyes at him. "You've got to stop watching so much Discovery Health Channel. How about this: it could be that she worked herself too hard and now she needs a vacation."

"Oh, poo! You always spoil the dramatic effect," Anton said.

"Let's just agree to keep an eye on her and take as much work off her shoulders as we can. Okay?"

"Okay."

Chapter Twenty-six

"Yes! Yes! Yes! I know—I love you, too." Lina struggled to get in the door, past her over-enthusiastic, slobbering bulldog. "Edith Anne, will you behave? Let me take off my coat and put down my purse." The bulldog backed off half a step, still whining and wriggling. Patchy Poo the Pud jumped down from his perch on the chaise and was rubbing himself against her legs, complaining in indignant meows that she wasn't giving him enough attention, either.

"Crazy animals," she muttered, hanging up her coat. "Okay, come here." She sat in the middle of the hall and let Edith climb into her lap while she scratched Patch under his chin. The bulldog licked her happily. The cat purred. Lina sighed. "Well, at least the two of you missed the real me." Her pets looked as well-fed and healthy as they had the night before Demeter had transported her away, but from the moment she'd reappeared in the middle of her living room, the two of them hadn't wanted to let her out of their sight. They followed her from room to room. Patchy Poo the Pud had even gone as far as to sit outside of the bathroom and yowl if she didn't let him in with her. "You two need to relax," she told the adoring creatures.

But secretly she liked it that they were so pleased that she was back. At least she wasn't a disappointment to them. Everyone else kept looking at her like she'd suddenly grown a third eye. No, that wasn't it. People didn't treat her like she was doing anything weird, they were treating her like she *wasn't* doing something, like they kept expecting more from her.

How had Persephone been more like Lina than Lina was like herself? She sighed and gently pushed Edith Anne off her lap. Persephone was a goddess. Of course people wanted Lina to be like her. Who wouldn't rather be around a goddess?

Hades . . . Her thoughts whispered his name before she could stop herself. Hades had liked being with her more than he had liked being with any goddess.

She shook her head.

"No," she reminded herself. "That's not true. He only wanted to be with me as long as he thought I was Persephone." She remembered the look on his face when he had seen who she really was.

"No!" Lina stopped herself, she wouldn't think about that.

She had to pull herself together. She'd been moping around like a jilted schoolgirl for two weeks. She'd been hurt before, why should this time be any different? It wasn't like she was going through another divorce.

Lina stared, unseeing, down the hall. It wasn't like a divorce. It was worse. Why did she feel like part of her—the best part of her—was missing?

Lina remembered the night she and Hades had watched the soul mates drink from the River Lethe. He had told her that soul mates would always find each other again. But what happened if they were separated by time and worlds? Did their hearts turn into wastelands? Did their capacity for happiness erode until they were just walking shells, going through the motions of daily living but not really feeling alive?

That wasn't what was happening to her. Hades couldn't be her soul mate. He had rejected her. She'd just done something she should have been too old to have allowed herself to do. She'd fallen in love with someone she couldn't ever have. She'd made a mistake. She was simply going to have to get over him and get on with her life.

She'd be all right. She'd make it. Time would help it not to hurt so badly.

Edith Anne whined while Patchy Poo the Pud rubbed a worried circle around her legs.

Lina pushed the sadness away from her heart and straightened her shoulders. "Okay, you two. Let's make some ambrosia cream cheese."

IT didn't matter how many times she read it, it still gave her a weird feeling. The paper that the note and the recipe had been written on was from her private stationary that had CFS printed across the top in the Copperplate Gothic Bold she liked so well. The words were written in her favorite blue pen, and the handwriting was identical to her own. But she hadn't written it. She'd found it taped to Edith Anne's dog food bin the day Demeter had brought her back. She'd almost ignored it. After all, it had been in her own handwriting. She'd thought it was just an old note she'd written to herself reminding her to get more dog food, or dog treats, or other items of dog paraphernalia. Then the salutation registered in her mind, *Dear Lina,* and her eyes had moved quickly to the closing, *Here's wishing you joy and magic, Persephone.*

Lina had taken the note into the living room and read it. Then, just as she did now, she thought how bizarre it was that she and Persephone's handwriting was identical.

Dear Lina,

Six months is almost completed. It feels to me that I have been here so much longer—time passes differently in your world. Mother will call for me soon and I want to be certain that you have the recipe for the ambrosia. Our customers love it, and I would not want them to be disappointed.

How odd! I just realized that I called them "our" customers, but I do think of them as that. Your mortals are good people. I shall miss them.

I shall not miss your wretched cat or that horrid slobbering dog, al-

though the black-and-white beast has finally deigned to sleep with me, and yesterday the dog did bark protectively at a stranger who tried to accost me while I was frolicking beside the river.

Perhaps I shall miss them after all.

Remember to have fun with your life, Lina. You have been richly blessed.

Here's wishing you joy and magic,
Persephone

The cream cheese recipe was written neatly on the back of the note. Lina studied it one more time. She didn't want to follow it, but Persephone had been right, their customers did love it, and she didn't want to disappoint them either.

She refilled her glass of pinot grigio, leaving the bottle on the counter next to the crock that she'd already filled with softened cream cheese. She didn't need to double check the calendar to see if there was a full moon. All she had to do was to glance out the kitchen window. There was no escaping it. A round white moon was hanging brightly in the clear night sky.

"Just get it over with. It's not like you're a stranger to magic." She grabbed a measuring cup from the cabinet. "And stop talking to yourself."

She put the recipe on the counter and began the steps it would take to make ambrosia cream cheese.

Persephone's recipe was wordy. Lina sipped from her glass of wine while she read it.

Fill that pretty yellow pot—the one that is the exact color of wild honeysuckles—with cream cheese. Let the cheese soften. (And Lina, do not use that atrocious low fat concoction others use. Its taste borders on blasphemy.)

Lina couldn't help smiling. She and Persephone had the same attitude about cooking with low fat ingredients.

Next add one cup of your favorite white wine to the cream cheese and mix thoroughly. The specific type of wine is not important, as long as it is not too sweet. (Lina, I have grown quite fond of the lovely Santa Margherita Pinot Grigio I found in your cooler. I certainly hope Mother gives me time to replenish your supply before she exchanges us. If not, I offer my apology for depleting your supply.)

Lina chuckled. "Apology accepted." She had been totally out of white wine when she returned.

After adding the wine to the cream cheese, drink what remains in the rest of the bottle yourself. (Lina, don't underestimate the importance of this step.)

She poured herself another glass of wine after she added the cup to the cream cheese. She tried not to gulp, but she was in a hurry to get done.

The more she drank, the easier it was for her to admit it, Persephone did sound like fun. Lina read the rest of the recipe with a wine-induced smile.

During the night of a full moon, take the mixture and place it under the old oak tree. You know the one. It is in the courtyard next to the fountain. I sprinkled a little of the magic of Spring there (do not be surprised if you see a nymph or two, although they seem to be very shy about showing themselves in your world). Before you leave the mixture there, you must dance three complete circles around the tree while you focus your thoughts on the sweet beauty of the night. (Lina, there are no particular dance steps you must complete. Simply listen to your soul and frolic! I think your body may surprise you. . . . It has certainly surprised me.)

Lina groaned and re-read the line. *It has certainly surprised me.* She didn't even want to guess what Persephone meant by that, but the searing looks Scott had given her, and the fact that he had a hard time keeping his hands off her, gave her a pretty good idea.

Well, it wasn't like she'd been particularly chaste in Persephone's body, either. She didn't want to think about that, though. She returned her attention to the end of the recipe.

> *Retrieve the finished mixture the next morning. You must dilute it ten times for mortal consumption. (Lina, be careful. I can only imagine what would happen if Anton sampled some of it while it was full strength.)*

"No kidding," Lina muttered. "Talk about a nymph. He'd probably sprout wings and fly." She laughed.

Then she caught herself. Persephone had just made her laugh—twice. And she wasn't even there. No wonder everyone loved her so much.

"Well, kids," she said to Patchy Poo the Pud and Edith Anne. "I'm going to finish up this last glass of wine, then I'm going to take this honeysuckle-colored crock, put it under an old tree, do some quick frolicking before I pour myself into bed." She hiccupped and her pets stared at her with accusatory eyes. They always seemed to know when she'd had too much to drink.

Lina wrapped an arm around the crock and started blearily for the door. Edith Anne, of course, stood directly in her way.

"Don't fret, old girl. I'm not going anywhere without you." That was one good thing about her dog being so umbilically tied to her—she didn't have to bother with a leash anymore. "We'll be back soon. I promise," Lina told Patchy Poo the Pud, who was watching her with eyes that were somehow disdainful and worried at the same time.

The night had gotten colder, and Lina wished she had grabbed her coat, but the cashmere turtleneck Persephone had added to her wardrobe was snug and warm—even if it was a delicate pink color that Lina thought would look better on a teenager than a middle-aged woman, no matter how many compliments she got whenever she wore it.

Forget it, she told herself. She didn't have the energy to worry about her wardrobe, and if she didn't want to go on a major shopping spree, there wasn't much she could do about it. In six months Persephone had replaced every single item in her closet. Everything. From shoes to jackets to a whole new line of sexy silk panties and matching bras.

"Where did the girl find the time?" she asked Edith Anne. The dog made a snuffling noise while she kept pace at Lina's side.

Lina shook her head. "I don't know either. I think she needs to be renamed the Goddess of Shopping instead of the Goddess of Spring."

Lina giggled. Quite frankly, she was a little drunk. She needed to be for where she was headed.

She followed the little brick path that led from her condo to the centrally located courtyard. She heard the fountain before she saw it. Six months and two weeks ago, it had had a calming effect on her. Now as she came closer to the courtyard, her stomach clenched.

Thankfully, the area was deserted. Lina glanced at her watch, twisting her wrist so that the dials could be illuminated by the light from the full moon. 10:45 PM. How had it gotten so late? Steeling herself, she approached the old oak—the same oak under which she had discovered the beautiful narcissus.

It looked much as it had six months before. Then the branches had been bare except for buds of new growth waiting to open. Now the branches were almost bare again. There were just a few leaves the color of paper grocery bags clinging to its boughs. Lina cast her eyes down. Thick, gnarled roots crisscrossed the ground at its base. Slowly, Lina walked its circumference, studying the shadows.

Except for dirt and roots, the area around the tree's base was empty. There was no hidden flower that smelled of first kisses, moonlight and springtime. What had she expected? Frowning at herself, she tucked the crock of cream cheese and wine in a semi-flat niche between two roots near the trunk of the tree. Then she stepped back.

In her mind she could see Persephone's directions. *Before you leave the mixture there, you must dance three complete circles around the tree while you focus your thoughts on the sweet beauty of the night.* Okay, she rubbed her hands together. I'll think about how pretty the night is—I'll dance around the tree—and I'll be done.

She looked around her. Except for Edith Anne, who sat a few feet away from her watching attentively, the courtyard was still deserted.

"Good," Lina muttered. "They'd think I was crazy."

Edith huffed at her.

"Don't worry, this won't take long."

Think about the beauty of the night, Lina told herself. She looked up. The moon really did look pretty, sitting up there like a glowing silver disc lit from within.

Lina took a tentative step, lifting her arms over her head she half turned. Moonlight filtered through the branches of the tree and stroked the cashmere that covered her arms, making them glow a silvery blush color that reminded Lina of the breast of a dove. She skipped over a root, surprised at how gracefully her body responded.

She passed once around the tree.

A soft breeze blew through the branches of the old oak, and the dry leaves whispered an autumn melody. Lina lifted her arms and twirled. She raised her face to the sky, letting the moon caress her skin. The night felt rich and beautiful and magic-filled.

She passed twice around the tree.

Lina pointed her toe and swung her leg forward. It seemed that she heard the humming of women's voices in harmony with the sound of the leaves. From the corner of her eye she saw familiar shapes join her in the dancing circle. They glittered and glowed and their wings made a melodic humming noise. Arms spread Lina leapt and twirled and reveled in the beauty of the night.

She passed a third time around the tree.

Lina stopped. She was breathing hard and her breath showed in the cool air like little puffs of magic smoke. She looked around, but the nymphs that had danced with her had disappeared. Edith Anne waddled past her, sniffing curiously around the base of the tree. Cocking her ears forward, she peered up into the oak's branches.

"They're gone," Lina told her. "Come on, old girl. It's time for us to go, too."

The dance had left her body feeling more alive than it had in two weeks. Maybe she should dance more. Anton and Dolores had questioned her several times about why she had suddenly stopped rollerblading along the river. Lina thought about it. *She'd* never rollerbladed—ever. But Persephone obviously had quite often. And she hadn't needed Anton and Dolores to tell her that. Her body was a full dress size smaller. Her legs were fit and her butt was firmer than it had been when she was twenty.

Lina let herself back in her condo. Before she could change her mind, she walked straight back to her bathroom, kicking off her shoes and stripping off her clothes until she stood totally naked in front of her full-length mirror.

She looked good, and not just for a woman in her forties. Except for the dark smudges under her eyes, her skin looked firm and healthy. She still wore her hair as Persephone had worn it—shoulder length with loose, messy curls. Her breasts weren't perfect and perky, but they were full and womanly. Her waist curved in nicely and her hips swelled down to tight thighs and well-defined calves.

She smiled at her reflection. She was pretty and smart and sexy and successful—everything a man should want.

"It's past time you got over him, Lina," she told herself.

With a sense of finality, she clicked off the bathroom light and tucked herself into bed. She felt the mattress sag as Patchy Poo the Pud curled into his place near her hip. She heard Edith Anne sigh as she turned twice and then flopped down in her doggie bed. Lina closed her eyes and before she fell asleep she made a promise to herself. Beginning tomorrow she would start over. Persephone had been right—she was richly blessed.

* * *

PERSEPHONE had been brooding when she felt the stirring of her magic being used. As nonchalantly as possible, she excused herself from Hermes and Aphrodite's tiresome conversation. The immortals waved her aside and continued their argument about whether the Limoniades, nymphs of the meadows of flowers, or the Napaeae, nymphs of the glens, were the most beautiful. They didn't mind that the young Goddess of Spring was leaving the conversation. She was an expert on forest nymphs, yet she had been uncharacteristically reticent and had had nothing amusing to say on the subject. They hardly noticed her absence.

Demeter did.

"Daughter, where are you going?"

Persephone paused and schooled her face into an aspect of innocent boredom before she turned to face her mother.

"Oh, Mother, you know I cannot bear to be indoors while the flowers are blooming. The meadows call me."

"Very well, child. I expect to see you tonight at the Festival of Chloaia."

"Of course, Mother." Persephone bowed and left her mother's throne room.

Demeter watched her daughter depart with a mother's sharp eyes. The Great Goddess was ready to admit to herself that exchanging the mortal for her daughter had been a mistake. Oh, her plan had had the desired effect. Persephone had matured. To Demeter's surprise she was even being called the Queen of the Underworld, and the relatives of the dead had quit their ceaseless petitioning. But at what price? Since her daughter's return the Goddess of Spring had behaved in a more sober manner. She rarely hosted feasts and had stopped consorting with semi-deities. But she was also moody and distracted. Much of the young goddess's sparkle had dimmed. Demeter worried about her. And she also worried about the mortal woman.

Carolina Francesca Santoro seemed to have taken up permanent residence as a nettle within the goddess's conscious, and it was not a comfortable arrangement. Demeter could not forget the look of raw pain on the mortal's face when Hades rejected her. She had caused Carolina a great hurt, and that had not been her intention.

Then there were the disturbing rumors. The immortals whispered that Hades had gone mad. He would see no one. It was even said that he had refused to grant Zeus an audience when the god had entered his dark realm.

"Eirene," she called her old friend to her side. "Something must be done about Hades."

"Again?" Eirene asked.

"Again," Demeter said.

THROUGH her mother's oracle Persephone watched Lina dance around the oak tree. She smiled when the little nymphs joined her. Lina's body twirled and leapt with a grace that Persephone recognized as not completely mortal.

"Her body remembers," the Goddess of Spring whispered to the oracle. "It has been touched by the presence of a goddess, and it will never be the same. . . ."

Just as she would never be the same, Persephone finished the thought silently. Carolina had departed her body, but she had left behind an essence of herself. Absently, Persephone stroked the amethyst narcissus that hung between her breasts. The chain had been broken, but the goddess had left it knotted around her neck. She could remove it and command it repaired, but she had been loath to part with it. In some way, its touch soothed her.

Lina finished the dance and returned to her home. Persephone watched as she stood naked before the mirror. Her smile echoed the mortal's. She was proud of the changes she had wrought in Lina. Persephone still remembered the burn of tired muscles and the satisfaction it had given her to watch Lina's body grow more fit and flexible. She had molded it into a vessel fit for a goddess. When Lina slid into bed, Persephone could almost feel the warm, soft body of the cat pressed familiarly against her own hip.

The oracle swirled and went blank.

"What is it, Daughter? Why do you and the mortal seem so unhappy?" Demeter's voice caused Persephone to jump guiltily. "No," Demeter continued before her daughter could answer with a ready excuse. "I do not want empty words meant to salve my feelings. I want truth."

Persephone met her mother's eyes. If Demeter wanted the truth, she would give it to her. "I miss it, Mother. I did not intend to, but I fell in love with Lina's world. It is so vibrant and messy and *alive.* And they did not know I was a goddess. They did not know I was your daughter, yet they embraced me."

"Was it not Carolina that they embraced?" Demeter asked gently.

"No. I wore her body, but the soul was mine."

Demeter shook her head sadly. "Carolina said the same thing to me, only I did not listen to her. I believe that was a mistake."

"What if there was a way to correct your mistake?"

"This time I would listen."

Persephone smiled fondly at her mother. "Good. I have an idea."

Chapter Twenty-seven

"Are you sure you want me to leave early? I really don't mind staying," Dolores said.

"No, honey." Lina waved a linen napkin at her. "I insist. It's not busy and we're going to close in thirty minutes. Anton and I can handle it."

"Well, if you're sure . . ." Dolores said dubiously.

"Oh, go on! Lina and I will be fine alone. Who do you think I am, Mr. Incompetent?" Anton huffed.

"I have never called you Mr. Incontinent—at least not within your hearing." Dolores dissolved into snorting giggles at her own joke.

Anton drew himself up into his full Southern belle glory. "Ah'll nevah be niiice to you again!" he said, raising his fist in the air.

Lina laughed. "I don't think Scarlett would have worn those boots."

"She would have if she had been gay," Anton said smugly.

"Okay, ya'll, I'm leaving." Dolores opened the door and then hesitated, smiling back at Lina as she said, "It's nice to hear you laugh again, boss." Then she hurried out into the Oklahoma evening.

Surprised by Dolores' words, Lina stared at the closed door.

"It is, you know," Anton said, touching her arm.

"Thanks," Lina patted his hand. "It feels good to laugh again." They smiled at each other. "I'll take care of closing up out here. Why don't you finish the dough in the back? It should be ready to be separated and put into the bread pans."

Anton nodded and scampered through the French doors separating the kitchen from the café. Lina was taking the PIZZA DEL GIORNO sign from the wall so that she could change it to read the next day's special, when the front door jangled open.

"I'll be with you in just a moment!" she called without turning around. "You're in luck; I still have one pizza of the day left. It's a lovely three cheese blend with garlic, basil and sun dried tomatoes."

"It is one of my favorites, but I have been dreaming of a thick slice of warm gubana with butter spread over it."

Lina froze. That voice. She knew that woman's voice as well as her own. Lina turned and was struck anew by the goddess's beauty. She was wearing jeans and a snug knit sweater, and she had her long hair pulled back into a thick ponytail, but her casual clothes did nothing to dispel her unique loveliness.

"Hello, Lina."

"Hello, Persephone."

Persephone smiled. "That is one thing we can count on—we would recognize each other in the middle of a teeming crowd."

"I—" Lina ran her hand across her brow as if she was trying to wipe away her confusion. "I didn't expect to see you. This is a surprise."

Before Persephone could respond, the door chimed again. A tall, handsome woman stepped regally into the bakery.

Persephone sighed and glanced over her shoulder.

The woman chose a table near the front window. She sat as if readying herself to hold court.

"I had a feeling Mother would follow me," Persephone said.

Anton breezed from the kitchen.

"Ohmygod, who knew we would get a rush right before closing?" Like a feather, he fluttered up to Demeter. "May I bring you something?"

The goddess raised one eyebrow at him. "Wine. Red."

Anton tilted his head, considering. "Is the house Chianti okay?"

"If Carolina has chosen it, I will abide by her will."

"Oh, sweetheart, you are right about that. Our Lina knows her wines," he cooed. "Anything else?"

"Anton!" Lina suddenly found her voice. "You can go back to the dough. I'll take care of both of these ladies."

Demeter raised her hand to silence her. "No. I am enjoying this"—she returned Anton's considering gaze—"young male. You two must talk. He shall attend me."

Anton shot Lina a *so there* look.

"Can't I tempt you with something more than wine? We have an ab fab pizza today. I promise to heat it for you with my own lily white hands."

"Pizza?" The goddess spoke the word as if it was a foreign language.

"Cheese, tomatoes, garlic, basil—it's to die for."

"Create it for me." Demeter said with an imperious waft of her hands.

Anton smiled smugly. Before he turned away he said, "Sweetheart, what is your name? I don't think I've ever seen you in here before."

Lina opened her mouth, but Persephone shook her head, motioning for her to keep quiet.

"You may call me Robin Greentree."

"Well, Ms. Greentree, may I just say that on anyone else that outfit would look like a silk muumuu, but on you it looks like something a goddess would wear. You are perfectly majestic."

"Of course I am," Demeter said.

"I'll have your wine right out." Anton hurried back to the kitchen. As he passed Lina and Persephone he said, sotto voce, "I can't resist an old queen."

Persephone covered her laugh with a polite cough. Lina scowled at him.

"Robin Greentree?" Lina whispered after Anton had disappeared back into the kitchen.

"Mother has a rather eccentric sense of humor, especially about names. Do you know in some languages my name sounds just like 'corn'?"

"I am across the room, but I am not deaf."

"Of course, Mother," Persephone said.

"Sorry, Demeter," Lina said.

The two women shared knowing looks that turned into smiles.

Persephone studied the bakery with keen eyes. "Dolores isn't here?"

"I let her go early."

Persephone nodded. "She works hard. She deserves time off."

"It's hard to get her to take time for herself." Lina and Persephone spoke the words together.

They stared at each other.

"Yes . . ." Persephone said.

"Yes," Lina echoed.

"Here's your Chianti and some bread with spiced olive oil." Anton placed the red wine goblet and a bread basket in front of Demeter. "Your pizza will be out in a jiff." He swished past Lina humming "Shall We Dance" from *The King and I* and fluttered his fingers amiably at Persephone.

Persephone laughed. "I've missed Anton."

"Well, he certainly grows on you."

"Stop wasting time!" Demeter snapped.

"Mother! Please. Drink your wine. Your pizza has to cook. Try to be a little patient." Persephone sighed and turned back to Lina. "Being the daughter of a goddess is not easy."

"I know," Lina said.

"Yes, you do." Persephone looked down at the counter and took a deep, cleansing breath. "I needed to come back."

Lina's face was a question mark. "Why?"

The goddess met her eyes. "I am not happy. I miss my bakery—our bakery—your world," she stuttered.

Lina glanced at Demeter, expecting her to react to her daughter's words, but the goddess continued to sip her wine silently.

"I don't understand."

"Is there nothing you miss about the Underworld?" she asked imploringly.

Lina felt her spine straighten. "What do you mean?"

Persephone searched the mortal's eyes. "We cannot lie to each other."

"I'm not trying to lie to you," Lina said. "It's just that it . . ."

"It hurts," Persephone finished for her. "I know. I tried not to think about everything I missed, too. I thought it would be easier if I chose not to remember."

Lina nodded, struggling to keep her emotions under control.

"I will begin." Persephone's smile was wistful. "I miss the bakery—its busy efficiency, the way it smells and sounds, and how it is a gathering place for so many different types of mortals. And I miss little things, like how Tess Miller has to have her glass of white wine precisely at the same time every day. I miss her little dog, even though he shocked Tess so badly when he snubbed me that she threatened to take him to the pet psychic. Animals do not react to me as they do to you." Persephone wrinkled her brow at Lina. "You know, the connection you have with animals is very odd."

"Yes, I know."

"I think what I miss most is the way everyone looked to me to solve problems. They did not see me as a younger, incompetent version of my mother. No one ran to her after I made a decision to double check that I was being wise. They respected me and trusted my judgment."

"You showed excellent judgment, Persephone," Lina assured her. "The bakery is thriving. Everyone is happy. *Merda!* You even managed to get me into shape."

Persephone gave her an assessing look. "Your body was a comfortable place to live, Lina. Do not underestimate your own beauty." The goddess grinned and Lina was reminded of a cat regarding a bowl of cream. "That is another thing I miss. Mortal men are so very *appreciative.*"

"Scott," Lina said dryly.

"Scott," Persephone purred. "I found him to be an interesting dalliance."

"He fell in love with you."

"Of course he did." Persephone shrugged her shoulders. "He will recover and be a better man for the experience. Knowing how to please a goddess is something all men should learn."

The idea made Lina smile.

"I even miss those two creatures who live with you, especially the cat," Persephone admitted.

That made Lina laugh. "Patchy Poo the Pud is awful, but loveable."

"Horrid beast," Persephone teased.

Lina nodded.

"Now it is your turn to remember. What is it you miss about the Underworld?"

"I miss Eurydice," she said with only a slight hesitation. "The little spirit was like a daughter to me. I worry about her."

"What else?"

"I miss Orion. I know he's supposed to be a dread steed, but he reminded me more of an overgrown black lab puppy."

"And?"

"I miss the way the sky looked. Daylight was like a watercolor painting that someone had breathed into life. I realize that sounds ironic because I'm talking about the Land of the Dead, but it wasn't dark and gloomy there, at least not after you got to Elysia. Actually, it was the most incredible place I've ever been, ever even imagined." Lina let her mind wander. Now that she had started talking she didn't want to stop. "Did you know that the night sky is lit by the souls of the Hyades so that when evening comes to Elysia everything looks like a beautiful forgotten dream?"

"No, I did not know that," Persephone said.

"And the souls of the dead aren't scary or disgusting. They are just people whose bodies have become less important. They still have the ability to love and laugh and cry."

Persephone took Lina's hand. "What is it that you miss most?"

Lina's eyes filled with tears. "Hades," she whispered. "You fell in love with my world, but I fell in love with the Lord of the Underworld."

"Good!" Persephone said happily, squeezing Lina's hand.

"How can that be good? I love Hades, but he loves you."

Persephone's laughter was a joyous noise that seemed to make the lights in the bakery glow brighter. "If he loves *me*, then why is he refusing to see me?"

"You've tried to see Hades?"

"Of course. I was miserable with missing your world. Then I started hearing rumors of Hades having gone mad and the spirits in the Underworld being in disarray, et cetera, et cetera, because the Queen of the Underworld had left her realm."

"Wait! Hades has gone mad?" Lina felt the color drain from her face.

"Oh, it is nothing. He is simply sulking." She made a careless gesture with her slender hands. "But the rumors made me think that perhaps I was not alone in my unhappiness. So I visited the Underworld."

"And?" Lina had the sudden urge to shake her.

"And the first thing that happened was that awful three-headed dog refused to allow me to pass." She shivered. "Edith Anne has much better manners."

"Cerberus gave you a hard time?"

"Hard time? He blocked the road, growling and slobbering. I was afraid to get near him. I actually had to call for help." Persephone shook her head in disgust.

"And Hades didn't come to you?"

The goddess frowned. "His daimon appeared instead. With that hateful black horse."

"Orion was mean to you?"

"He laid back his pointed ears and bared his teeth at me."

"I'm sorry about that. I have spoken to Orion about his attitude. He probably just thought you were me, and when he realized you weren't, well, he should have behaved better," Lina said.

"Yes, he should have. Anyway, I told the daimon that I wanted to speak with Hades. The daimon asked me if I was the Goddess of Spring, or the mortal woman, Carolina." Persephone looked annoyed.

"As if he did not already know! Even the spirits of the dead knew. The whole time I was traveling down that gloomy black road they watched me. At first they seemed happy, then when I spoke to them—simply trying to be polite—they drew away from me. I even heard them whispering things like 'Someone is masquerading as Queen of the Underworld.'" Irritably, she brushed aside a strand of hair that had escaped from her ponytail. "I can tell you, it was certainly a disturbing experience."

She paused before continuing and studied her well-manicured fingernails. Lina wanted to shake her again.

"Well, I assured the daimon that my body and my soul were the same. He disappeared, and when he returned he said that his Lord refused to see *Persephone,* and he commanded that I leave his realm and stop bothering him."

"And how does that prove that he doesn't love you? Hades is very stubborn." Lina glanced at Demeter, who was pretending to study her wine. She leaned forward and lowered her voice. "Sometimes it takes a lot of work to get him to relax and talk. Actually, he's romantic and passionate. You should try again. He will probably see you next time." Lina's stomach clenched and she hated herself as soon as she said the words. She didn't want Hades to see Persephone. She didn't want him to see anyone except her.

"I think *you* should try," Persephone said firmly.

"Me?" Lina blinked in surprise. "How can I?"

"We could exchange bodies again." Persephone gestured at Demeter. "Mother will aid us. She recognizes that her plan did not work exactly as she had expected."

Lina looked at Demeter. The goddess inclined her head in a small, regal bow. "I acknowledge the truth of my daughter's words. I was mistaken in how I handled the situation."

The awful bedroom scene flashed through Lina's memory. "I'm glad to hear you say it, but it doesn't change anything."

"Do you remember, Carolina, when you came to my oracle distraught because you had made an error in judgment?" Demeter said.

"Yes, I almost caused Eurydice a lot of pain because I made a decision without thinking it through."

"Do you remember what I told you then?"

"You told me to learn from my mistake," Lina said.

"Yes, and I have taken my own advice. I, too, did not fully consider my decision. What I have learned from my mistake is that even a goddess can be surprised by her daughters." Demeter gifted the two women with one of her rare smiles. Then she returned her full attention to Lina. "Hades was being truthful with you. He has always been different from the rest of the immortals. I believe the Lord of the Underworld did fall in love with you, Carolina."

"And I have a proposal for you," Persephone said. "You love Hades. I love your bakery and your world. Why must we live forever without our loves?"

"But Hades—" Lina began.

"Hear me out," Persephone interrupted. "As Goddess of Spring, I must be in my world for six months, then, as you would say, my 'job' is completed until the next spring. I could come here during that interlude. And while I am here, you could return to the Underworld as Queen."

Lina's head was spinning. "I would pretend to be you again?"

"No." Persephone's smile was enigmatic. "*You* would not have to pretend. Everything from the animals to the spirits knew I was not you. You will not be pretending, Carolina, you are their Queen. You will simply be housed temporarily in my body because I need yours here. I will be the one who must masquerade as another."

"No," Lina said.

"Why not?" Persephone gave a long-suffering sigh. "Oh, I give you my word that I will neatly discard any 'Scotts' before you return."

"It's not that," Lina said.

"Then what is it?"

"He doesn't want me, Persephone. He told me he loved my soul, and then when he saw the real me, he rejected me."

"Lina, he was just surprised," Persephone said.

"You didn't see his face."

"I saw his face," Demeter interjected. "And what I read there was, indeed, surprise and hurt. I did not see disdain or rejection."

"Then you saw something I didn't," Lina said.

"Perhaps you are simply making a mistake, Carolina," Demeter said.

"Maybe, but what if I'm not?" Lina felt the sick wave of pain that remembering Hades' rejection evoked. She blinked furiously. "I can't bear it if he looks at me like that again. And what if he doesn't? That might actually be worse. How would I ever know that it's not just your body he desires?"

"Can you bear to live an eternity without him?" Persephone asked softly.

Tears spilled from Lina's eyes and left shining trails down her cheeks. "What I can't bear is what it would do to my soul to have him turn away from me again—or to have him accept me only because he wanted me to be something that I'm not."

"Do not make a decision before you have pondered it properly," Demeter said.

"Yes, promise me that you will consider my proposition. Fall has just begun here. You have until the first days of spring, then I will return for your final decision."

Persephone wiped a tear from Lina's face. Then the goddess's smile became bittersweet. She reached under her sweater where a silver chain lay hidden. Without speaking, she pulled it over her head. The amethyst narcissus caught the bakery lights and sparkled.

"This belongs to you," she said, placing it carefully over Lina's head. "The chain had been broken, and then knotted. I did not have it replaced. It is just as you left it."

"Oh," Lina said with a sob. She wrapped her fingers around the bloom that had been so lovingly carved for her. "I didn't think I'd ever see this again. Thank you for returning it to me."

Anton burst from the French doors whistling a show tune from *Gypsy* and carrying a round tray which held a fragrant, steaming pizza. He glanced at Lina and came to an abrupt halt.

"Why are you crying?" His eyes flashed and he turned on Persephone. "Little Miss Cute Thing, if you made her cry, I'll—"

"No, Anton, it's nothing bad." Lina smiled through her tears, wiping her face with the back of her hand. "Persephone gave me this necklace, and it is so beautiful that it made me cry."

Anton's body relaxed. "Persephone? You mean like the goddess?"

"Exactly like the goddess," Persephone said.

"I haven't seen you here before, either. How do you know our Lina?" Anton said.

Persephone smiled. "Lina helped me grow up."

Anton looked confused.

"Persephone," Demeter called from across the room. "We should depart."

"Anton, we will need that pizza in a 'To Go' box. And could you please add a big slice of gubana, too?"

"Of course," Anton said. "Anything else I can get for Her Majesty?" He nodded his head at Demeter.

Persephone laughed. "Just the check."

"I shall pay," Demeter said. With a great sense of dignity she stood and then strode to where Anton waited at the cash register.

"With what?" Lina whispered.

Persephone shrugged her shoulders.

"Anton!" Lina said.

He looked at her.

"With these ladies we accept barter. Just be sure you drive a hard bargain."

Anton's eyes widened. "Whatever you say, boss." He faced the approaching goddess. "Well, Queen Greentree, what are you offering for pizza, gubana and wine?"

Demeter raised her haughty chin. "I prefer the title goddess. Queens have realms that are entirely too limited."

"Fine, *Goddess* Greentree. What are you offering?"

Demeter's smile was sly. "Do you have any need for a talking bird?"

"No, honey," Anton rolled his eyes. "We have way too many animals that hang around this place. Try again."

Persephone pulled on Lina's sleeve. "Leave them to their bargaining. I have one more question to ask you."

"What is it?"

"What did you do to Apollo?"

"Nothing," Lina said, surprised.

"Nothing?" Persephone asked.

"Not a thing."

"You refused the God of Light?" Persephone wasn't sure she had heard her correctly.

"Of course. I'm only interested in one god at a time," Lina said.

"Really?" Persephone tapped her perfect chin thoughtfully. "What an interesting concept."

"Sold! For one gold crown that is probably fake but I just *adore* it!" Anton squealed.

Chapter Twenty-eight

HADES brooded, and he couldn't stop staring at the sketch the little spirit had given him.

"Do you like it?" Eurydice asked.

"How did you know?" Hades' voice sounded rough and foreign to his own ears. How long had it been since he had carried on a real conversation with anyone? He couldn't remember.

"I have been thinking a lot about her. I even started dreaming of her. Only, when I see her in my dreams, she does not look like she did when she was here. But how she looks—it's hard to describe—how she looks in my dreams *feels* right. So I drew her that way. When I showed Iapis, he told me that I should bring it to you."

"I hope I did not overstep myself, Lord," Iapis said.

Hades could not take his eyes from the sketch. "No, old friend, you did not overstep yourself. You were right to show me." He made himself take his eyes from the sketch and look at Eurydice. "Thank you. May I keep it?"

"Of course, Lord. Anything I create is yours."

"No, little one," Hades said sadly. "Anything you create still belongs to her."

"Will she return to us?" Eurydice asked.

Hades looked back at the sketch of Carolina. Her mortal features were sweet and kind, her body full and womanly. He felt a stirring within him just looking at the likeness of her, and he closed his eyes, blocking her picture from his mind. He had lacked the strength to trust her, and because of that she had almost lost her soul to Tartarus. But she had battled back from the abyss only to be betrayed and wounded by his rash, thoughtless words. He did not deserve the gift of her love.

"No," Hades said. "I do not believe she will return to us."

Eurydice made a small, sad noise, and Hades opened his eyes to see Iapis taking the spirit into his arms.

"Hush, now," the daimon soothed. "Wherever she is, she has not forgotten you. She loved you."

"Please leave me," Hades rasped.

Iapis motioned for Eurydice to go, but he stayed in his Lord's chamber. His concern for the god gnawed at him. Hades did not pace back and forth in frustration. He did not work out his anger at the forge. He refused to eat and he rarely slept. He held court, passing judgment over the somber dead as if he belonged among their ranks and had been condemned to eternally wander the banks of Cocytus, the River of Lamentation.

When Persephone tried to see the god, Iapis had felt a stirring of hope at Hades' display of anger. But it was short-lived. As soon as the Goddess of Spring left the Underworld, Hades had withdrawn within himself again. The god could not continue as he was, yet Iapis saw no respite ahead. Time seemed to fester the dark god's wound instead of allowing him to heal.

"Iapis, do you know what happens when one soul mate is separated from the other?" Hades asked suddenly. He was standing in front of the window that looked out on the area of his gardens that joined the Elysia forest and eventually led to the River Lethe.

"Soul mates always find each other," Iapis said. "You know that already, Lord."

"But what happens if they cannot find each other because one of them has done something inexcusable?" Hades turned his head and looked blankly at Iapis.

"Can you not forgive her, Hades?"

Hades blinked and focused on the daimon's face. "Forgive her? Of course I have. She was only keeping her oath to Demeter. Carolina's sense of honor would not allow her to betray her word, not even for love. It is myself that I cannot forgive."

"Yourself? How, Lord?"

"Carolina Francesca Santoro is a mortal woman with the courage of a goddess, and I hurt her for the most empty of reasons, to salve my own pride. I cannot forgive that in myself. How can I expect her to?"

"Perhaps it is much like the night you insulted her," Iapis said slowly. "You have only to ask, and then be willing to remain and hear the answer."

Hades shook his head and turned back to the window. "She bared her soul to me and I betrayed her. Now she is beyond my reach."

"But if you would agree to see Persephone—"

"No!" Hades snarled. "I will not see a frivolous shell who mocks the soul that once resided within her body."

"Hades, you do not know that the goddess mocks Carolina."

"Cerberus rejected her. Orion loathed her. The dead called her a charlatan. That is knowledge enough for me," Hades said.

"She is a very young goddess," Iapis reminded him.

"She is not Carolina."

"No, she is not," the daimon said sadly.

"Leave me now, Iapis," Hades said.

"First let me draw a bath and set out fresh clothes for you." When Hades started to protest, Iapis blurted, "I cannot remember the last time you bathed or changed your clothing! You look worse than the newly dead."

Hades' powerful shoulders slumped. Without looking at the daimon he said, "If I bathe and change my clothing, will you leave me in peace?"

"For a time, Lord."

Hades almost smiled. "Then so be it, my friend."

* * *

HADES settled back into the steaming water. The black marble pool was built into the floor of his bathing room. He rested against a wide ledge that had been carved from the side of the pool. A goblet of red wine and a silver platter filled with pomegranates and cheese had been left within reach of his hand. The few candles that were lit glowed softly through the rising steam like moonlight through mist. Hades drank deeply from the goblet of wine. He had no appetite and he ignored the food, but the wine left a satisfying wooziness in his head. Perhaps, for just one night, he would drink himself into oblivion. Then he might sleep without dreaming of her. In one gulp he upended the goblet and looked around for more. Iapis had left a pitcher close enough that he did not have to leave the soothing heat of the pool to refill his cup.

"That daimon thinks of everything," he muttered.

"Not quite everything."

Hades jerked at the sound of her voice, and dropped the goblet. It clanged as it bounced against the marble floor.

Persephone blew on the steam. It parted and suddenly she was visible to Hades. She lounged on the ledge opposite him, and though she was submerged in water up to her shoulders, her naked body was as fully exposed to him as his was to her. The goddess's eyes rounded in surprise. Carolina was certainly no fool. She had had no idea the dour Lord of the Underworld was so delectable.

"Hello, Hades. I do not believe you and I have been formally introduced. I am Persephone, Goddess of Spring."

He averted his eyes from her and lurched from the pool, quickly wrapping himself in a robe. She could see his jaw clenching and when he spoke it sounded like he was forcing his words through gritted teeth.

"Leave my presence! I refused to see you."

"I know you did, but I have a problem, and you are the only god who can help me solve it, though Apollo is definitely more hospitable, and would be very willing to aid me in this particular venture." She ran her fingers playfully through the hot water. "But after talking to Lina, you appear to be my only recourse."

"Apollo!" Hades said fiercely. "What has he to do with Carolina?"

"Nothing, even though he wishes otherwise."

The rest of what she had said broke through his shock. "You have spoken to Carolina?"

"Yes, I have. Actually, I just left her bakery," Persephone said smugly.

Hades drew in a ragged breath. "She is well?"

"Her body is in excellent shape and her business is thriving."

Hades studied the drops of wine that had splattered from the goblet to the floor. "Good. I am pleased that she has—"

"I was not finished," Persephone interrupted. Flicking her fingers across the top of the pool, she rained water on him.

He glared at her. "Then finish."

"What I was going to say is that her body is good, her business is fine, but *she* is miserable."

"I . . . she . . ." Hades began and then stopped. He raked his hand through his damp hair.

"I—she—what?" Persephone prompted. "Lina told me that sometimes it was difficult to get you to relax, but if I was stubborn enough, I could get you to talk."

Hades felt his face flush. Then his gaze sharpened on hers. "She wanted you to talk with me? Why?"

"Oh, I do not believe she really wanted me to talk to you. She just said it because she thinks that you're in love with me."

Hades snorted. "That is ridiculous."

"Thank you, kind god."

"I did not mean any offense," Hades said quickly.

"Oh, I know, I know," Persephone said.

She brushed her hair back from her face and one of her breasts broke free of the surface of the pool, its taut mauve nipple pointed directly at Hades. The god cleared his throat and turned his head, focusing on the platter of fruit and cheese.

"I think it would be easier to talk with you if you joined me in the other room." He pointed to a cabinet near him. "There are robes there in which you may cover yourself."

"Wait!" Persephone said before he could leave the room. "First there is something that Lina and I need to know."

Hades looked at her, careful to keep his eyes focused on her face.

"Just stay where you are, and believe that this is very important—to all three of us."

"What is it you need to know?" Hades asked.

"This," Persephone said. She stood up.

The hot water flushed her slick skin. The nipples of her breasts were puckered and looked as if they had just been caressed. Her body was long and lean and as exquisite as Hades remembered it. He stared at her as she stepped slowly and gracefully from the pool and walked with an enticing sway toward him. When she reached him, she stopped. Lifting her arms she draped them around his shoulders. Then she pressed her naked body against him and pulled him down to meet her mouth.

Hades' lips touched hers and his arms instinctively went around her. But there was nothing there. Oh, he could certainly feel the familiarity of her body, and her mouth was warm and soft, but she did not move him. It was as if he held a malleable statue. Gently, but firmly, he pulled away from her.

Persephone stepped out of his arms.

"Then it truly is not this body that you desire."

"What I desire has not changed, nor will it. I desire only one woman. It matters little what body she inhabits."

For a moment, Hades thought he saw sadness in the goddess's eyes, but the look was fleeting and when she smiled, her air of youthful nonchalance was firmly in place.

"Well, thank you for answering that question for us."

"You are most welcome." Hades took a robe from the cabinet and Persephone slipped into it. He retrieved the goblet from the floor and picked up the pitcher of wine.

"Now all we have to do is to find a way to make Lina believe it," Persephone said.

They walked into Hades' bedchamber.

Persephone stared. "Hades, this is a beautiful room."

"Thank you," he said. "Make yourself comfortable while I find another goblet."

Persephone walked to a velvet-swathed window. She pulled aside the drape and gazed out on a fantastic view of tiered gardens filled with statuary, well-tended greenery, and thousands upon thousands of white flowers, all of which were bathed in a soft, unusual light.

"Your wine," Hades said.

Persephone turned from the window. "Lina was right—it does look like a beautiful forgotten dream."

Her words made Hades' heart ache.

"Why are you here, Persephone?"

The goddess tossed her hair back and smiled. "I have a proposition for you. . . ."

"I still do not understand what I can do! Carolina refused your proposition. You cannot force her into this exchange." Hades said as he paced across the floor in front of her.

She raised one eyebrow at him. "I cannot?"

"You will not force her." Hades' words were firm, but he felt his resolve wavering. Carolina could return! He could touch her and talk to her again. Surely he could convince her of his love. He shook himself. No! She had been through enough. He would not allow her to be forced into something she did not believe she could bear.

"The two of you are mirrors of stubbornness. You refuse to force her; she refuses to go of her own will." Persephone sighed. "Then you must find a way to convince her to return without being forced."

"How?" Hades bit the word.

"I don't know that you can," Persephone said sadly. She walked to Hades and placed a hand on his arm. "If you need me, you can call me through Mother's oracle." On impulse, she kissed his cheek.

He patted her hand and gave her an endearingly paternal smile. "Forgive my rudeness to you. Old gods sometimes have cantankerous ways."

Persephone smiled back at the god who was so obviously deeply in love with Carolina. "You are forgiven," she said and disappeared.

THE forge glowed with an otherworldly heat. Sweat flew from the god's body in time with the pounding of metal against metal. Hades was hardly aware of his surroundings.

She still loved him.

He had to find a way to repair the damage he had done so that she could allow herself to trust him again. But how?

"You remind me of a foolish old spinster, Lord of the Dead."

Hades whirled around to face the sarcastic voice, and squinted against the glaring light.

"Apollo! You and your garish sun are not needed here," Hades roared.

"Oh, yes, I tend to forget." Apollo passed his hand in front of his face and the brightness of his visage faded. "Better?"

"I do not recall inviting you within my realm."

"I simply had to come and glimpse what the other half of wasted love looks like."

Hades swelled with rage. "Do not presume—"

"And what I see here," the Sun God's voice broke through Hades' tirade, "is much less attractive than the mortal version."

"Of what mortal do you speak?" Hades demanded.

"Carolina, of course. Do you know that she actually spurned me? She was honestly more interested in my mares than she was me." Apollo chuckled. "When I thought she was Persephone, her actions confused me. When I found out she was a mortal clothed in the goddess's body, I was astounded. And then to learn that she chose you over me? Truly amazing."

Hades narrowed his eyes at Apollo. "I do not think it so amazing."

Apollo grinned. "You should. Mortal women find me irresistible."

"Carolina is more discerning than most mortal women."

"And more faithful, too. She has refused the suite of at least one man since returning to her world." Apollo looked at Hades appraisingly. "And though he is only a mortal, he is definitely younger than you."

"You have been watching her?" Hades growled.

"Is that not what I already said?"

"No!"

"I think perhaps your dreary lamentation for your lost love has affected your hearing. I distinctly remember saying—"

In two strides Hades reached Apollo. He grabbed the god by the throat and lifted him off his feet.

"Tell me how you can see her!" he snarled.

"Through Demeter's oracle," Apollo squeaked.

Hades dropped the God of Light and rushed from the forge. "Saddle Orion!" he bellowed.

Inside the forge Apollo rubbed his throat and rearranged his rumpled robes. "Good deed accomplished. You owe me, Demeter," he muttered before disappearing.

Chapter Twenty-nine

"It's February, but it feels like April." Lina sighed happily. "I love it when Oklahoma weather does this," she told Edith Anne, who trotted contentedly by her side.

Rollerblades had taken some getting used to. It wasn't that her body didn't know what to do, it was Lina's mind that kept repeating thoughts like *yes, that pavement is hard* and *slow down, we're going to fall and break something.* So, even after several months of practice, Lina still took it slow, stroking the wide cement walkway that ran along the Arkansas River with controlled, careful strides.

"On your left!" someone shouted behind her and Lina moved closer to the right side of the pavement.

"Thanks," she yelled as a racing bike streaked past.

"No problem," the rider called back.

"I really appreciate it when they do that," she said to Edith Anne, who continued to keep pace with her in the grass that was just beginning to hint about future green off the side of the walkway.

Edith snorted.

"Well, you know it scares me when someone just busts past us without any warning. That big yellow-bike guy almost knocked me over last week." Lina reached down and flipped Edith's ear. The bulldog huffed at her and licked her hand. "I guess I should pay better attention, especially when it's quiet like it is this evening, but sometimes it's just so beautiful . . ."

Lina smiled. Evening was her favorite time of the day to rollerblade. Oklahoma sunsets were glorious, and sometimes, just as the sun was falling beneath the Arkansas River, the light would glint off the water, mixing pink and orange with blue and gray—and she would be reminded of the magic of Elysia. It didn't make her sad. Time had helped her with that. She liked the remembrance, in little doses. It helped to keep the emptiness at bay.

Edith Anne stopped to sniff at a particularly interesting clump of weeds.

"Hey, keep up with me! If you get mud or thistles on you, expect to get a bath when we get home."

Edith snorted a couple of times at the weeds before galloping after Lina. Lina slowed to let her catch up. She thought she heard the clop of a horse's hooves in the distance. *Interesting,* she thought, *the weather must be nice enough for the riverside stable to have opened early.* Horseback rides along the river were big business during good weather, but the business didn't usually open until April. She wondered how she'd missed the notice in the paper. Usually she liked to post things like that in the bakery. She made a mental note to check on it the next day.

The bulldog by her side again, Lina picked up her pace. She had already gone four miles, and her breath was still coming easily. Her legs felt strong. Lina was glad she had added rollerblading as a regular part of her weekly routine. Not only did it keep her body in shape, it helped her think.

And she'd had a lot to think about since Persephone's visit.

Merda! She'd been tempted by the goddess's offer. How could she not have been? To return to the Underworld as its queen . . . she would like nothing more. No, Lina corrected herself. What she would like more was what was keeping her from taking Persephone up on her offer. She'd wrestled with it over and over in her mind during the long winter months. She'd even wished she could call her grandmother and ask her advice—without her grandmother thinking she needed to be committed.

Sometimes she thought that maybe Demeter had been right and she had just made a mistake. Then all she had to do was to remember how Hades had turned away from her when she had revealed herself to him. *"Leave my realm"* had been his response to seeing the real Carolina. Time had helped to heal her, but remembering his words still caused her soul to ache.

And it was almost spring. Persephone would return soon for an answer. Lina breathed deeply and kept a steady pace while she considered, for what must have been the thousandth time, her answer. Unconsciously, Lina's hand found the amethyst narcissus that always hung around her neck.

She couldn't return. She wanted to. She even dreamed about it. But she couldn't do it. Maybe she was a coward, but she couldn't take the chance. It had taken her so long to heal. Lina couldn't break the wound open again. She would tell Persephone no. Maybe Persephone could find another mortal to exchange places with. Dolores was active in the Society for Creative Anachronisms. She'd probably be very interested in hanging around Mount Olympus and frolicking with nymphs while Persephone baked bread. The thought made Lina laugh. She could even plan a long vacation and leave the bakery in Dolores/Persephone's capable hands. Italy was nice in the spring . . .

Lina was preoccupied with planning her Italian vacation when she noticed that the clomp of horse's hooves had gotten closer and faster. She was moving to the edge of the walkway when a joyous neigh of greeting sliced the air. Lina's heart jumped in recognition.

She spun around as a large black shape overtook her. A dark muzzle was shoved in her face. Orion alternated between nickering and snorting while he nuzzled and lipped her hair and shoulders. In shock, Lina could only cling to the horse's tack and hope that in his exuberance he didn't knock her over.

"Who dares touch the dread steed of Hades?"

His words mimicked those he had spoken to her long ago, but his tone was completely altered. His voice was filled with love and longing. Lina looked up at Orion's back. He sat in a glossy Western saddle. He had replaced his archaic clothes with a black Western-cut shirt, the sleeves of which were rolled up to expose his muscular forearms, jeans and Oklahoma cowboy boots. His hair was pulled back and his eyes were bright.

Lina stared at him without speaking. The sight of him tugged at the newly healed wound in her heart. All those dark winter months he had left her to hurt alone. All that time. All that pain. The fierce surge of anger she felt surprised her.

He tried to smile, but his lips only quivered.

"You asked who dares to touch your steed, Hades." Lina's words were clipped. "Allow me to reintroduce myself to you. I am Carolina Francesca Santoro, a middle-aged mortal woman from Tulsa, Oklahoma, who owns a bakery. And I didn't dare to touch your dread steed—he stuck his face in my hands. Again."

Hades felt her words like knives. He didn't blame her for her anger. He understood it, but he wouldn't allow it to make him give up. He kicked his leg over the saddle and dismounted. He wanted to approach her, to take her into his arms, but she was staring at him with a cold, unblinking gaze that was anything but welcoming.

"You left one title from your introduction, Carolina." His voice made her name a prayer.

"I don't think so. I know exactly who I am," she said. He hadn't come any closer to her, but she still moved a step back from him.

"You are Carolina Francesca Santoro, a middle-aged mortal woman from Tulsa, Oklahoma, who owns a bakery. You are also Queen of the Underworld," Hades said.

Lina felt a tremor pass through her and she clutched her anger, afraid if she let it go, her heart would tear into tiny pieces.

"I'm sorry, Lord. You must be confused. The Goddess Persephone is Queen of the Underworld. I was just a temporary stand-in, and I wasn't up to the job."

"Your subjects feel differently, Carolina." He looked pointedly at Orion, who had stretched out his neck so that he could nibble her shoulder while she stroked his muzzle.

"Animals like me," she said. As if to prove her words, Edith Anne butted against her legs, wriggling for attention. Orion snorted and bent to blow at the bulldog.

"He reminds me a little of Cerberus." Hades nodded at the squatty dog, trying again unsuccessfully to smile.

"He is a she. And I hear she has better manners than Cerberus has been exhibiting," Lina said, and then bit her lip. She shouldn't converse with him.

"No doubt Cerberus' manners are lacking because he is feeling the absence of his Queen, as is the rest of the Underworld."

"A dog and a horse aren't anyone's subjects. And I'm not a queen. I'm a mortal woman. I do not have any subjects."

Hades turned back to Orion's saddle and pulled out the rolled-up canvas he had lodged under the pommel. "I have something for you. Eurydice tried to give it to me, but I reminded her that her work belonged to you. She still thinks of herself as Personal Artist to the Goddess of Spring, though she misses her mistress very much."

"I'm not . . . no, I don't want . . ." Lina stammered, feeling a wave of homesickness at the thought of Eurydice. Then, Hades stepped close to her. In the months they had been apart she had forgotten about his size. He seemed to surround her. Even in modern clothes he was dark and rakishly handsome. Her Batman . . .

"The little spirit drew this from a dream she had of you. She said that it felt right."

Hades was so close to her that she could feel the heat of his body.

Wordlessly, Lina took the canvas from Hades. She unrolled it and gasped.

"It's me!"

It was her—the mortal woman, Carolina Francesca Santoro—her body, her face, her smile. Not Persephone. As she gazed at the image Eurydice had drawn from a dream, her fingers began to tingle and suddenly a current of emotion traveled through the canvas and into her soul. Within the current she could hear the unnumbered voices of the dead. They were all calling to her, begging their queen to return.

Her hands trembled and she felt the knot of anger within her begin to dissolve.

"Your subjects recognize you and call for you, Carolina," Hades said gently.

"It's too bad that their god did not recognize me," she said without looking up at him.

"There is no god here now, nor any lord." Hades' voice broke, and he had to pause before he could continue. He took Lina's chin in his hand and brought her face up so that she must look into his eyes. "Tonight I am only a man who is desperately seeking his soul mate. You see, she was separated from me because of my foolishness, and I had to forgive myself before I could find her and ask that she—"

Tears began spilling from Lina's eyes.

"Do not weep, beloved."

"You turned away from me," she whispered through broken sobs. "When you saw who I really was, you didn't want me."

"No!" He pulled her into his arms and crushed her against him. "It was never you I turned from. It was pride that goaded my words and actions."

"Because you didn't want to love a middle-aged mortal," she said into his chest.

His laugh came out as a sob. "No, because I was terrified that I had lost my soul to a woman who wanted nothing more than a dalliance with an inexperienced god about which she could brag."

Lina looked up at him. "I only told Demeter about you not being with any other goddess because I was trying to convince her that you were different."

"I know, beloved. Forgive the pride of an old, solitary god." His lips were finally able to form a smile. "And please come home."

In answer, Lina pulled him down to her.

"Carolina," Hades breathed her name against her lips. "My soul has ached for you, my eternal beloved."

Before he could kiss her again, Orion bumped him from behind. The short, stout dog was sniffing around his feet. Hades glanced down to see streams of saliva on his boots.

"Orion, stop that," Lina said, pushing the big, black head aside. "Oh, Edith Anne, don't do that. You're messing up his boots."

Hades threw back his head and laughed. He swept his queen off her feet, tossed her up onto Orion's back, and then he swung up behind her with a strength that clearly said he was no mortal man.

"Hades! What are you doing?"

"Taking you out of the reach of those beasts." He wrapped his arms around Carolina and pulled her firmly back against him.

"But, Edith Anne—"

"Do not fret. Orion will go slowly. We will not lose your dog." Holding her securely, he clucked at the stallion. Orion turned his head and snorted, but he began walking, slowly, so that the bulldog had no trouble trotting by his side. Then the god returned his attention to Carolina.

"We have a short time before spring returns to your world. Perhaps you would like to show me some of this kingdom you call Tulsa," Hades said, stroking the soft brown curls that formed at the nape of her neck. He was having a difficult time restraining himself from ravishing her right there. He thought the new body she wore was seductive and womanly. She was soft and fragrant and delectably inviting.

Lina twisted around and smiled at him. "You know about Persephone's plan?"

"Who does not?" he said good-naturedly.

"I'm beginning to think that it could work," she said.

"As am I." He bent to claim her lips.

Lina pushed back from him. "Wait, you shouldn't be here; you certainly can't stay very long. You don't have anyone taking your place in the Underworld."

"No, I do not." He smiled at his queen and his soul felt light and young. "But sometimes even Death must take a holiday."

As their lips met the sun touched the bank of the river. It paused there and shone one brief, winking beam on the lovers before falling from the sky.

Today Tulsa mourns the passing of a local matriarch, Carolina Francesca Santoro. Ms. Santoro was a restaurateur, philanthropist and renowned animal lover. Ms. Santoro is not survived by any biological children, but she will be greatly missed by many who felt they were her family. For decades her chain of Pani Del Goddess bakeries have been a vital part of many Oklahoma communities. The bakeries are best known for their specialty, ambrosia cream cheese. The recipe for this delectable cheese has been a closely guarded secret for more than half a century. But do not fear, loyal Pani Del Goddess patrons. Before her death, Ms. Santoro shared the recipe with an Italian relative, her great-niece, Persephone Libera Santoro, who will be assuming the position of major stockholder of the Pani Del Goddess Corporation. The new Miss Santoro has announced that she will be dividing her time between Oklahoma and Italy. As is only appropriate considering her name, she will spend each spring and summer with us in Tulsa. To honor the memory of her great aunt, let us give her a warm Oklahoma hello!

—*The Tulsa World*,
21 March 2055

Epilogue

LINA was feeling a little breathless and displaced, which was truly ironic. She was, after all, finally wearing her own skin.

"It probably has something to do with being one of the newly dead," she muttered, holding out her arms and looking in amazement at her glowing body. She was more substantial than the dead she was so used to seeing, and she was pleased that it appeared that her body had taken on a form that was much younger than she had been at her death. With a start, Lina realized that she had materialized within her forty-three-year-old body. She laughed. "The exact age I was when I met him," she said.

The tunnel stretched before her, black and unending, but its darkness didn't intimidate her. Lina walked forward with confidence without once looking back at the last light she would ever glimpse from the mortal world.

Suddenly, a little ball of brilliance burst into being at her shoulder, and she laughed in surprise. "What are you doing here?" The globe bobbled around, wiggling like a puppy. But she didn't really need to ask—she knew who had sent the light. "Thank you, Persephone," she called to the listening air.

She walked quickly through the cluster of beautiful ghost trees that had come to be known as Persephone's Grove. As always, she enjoyed the sparkling facets that were their leaves. Lina left the grove, and blinked in surprise. Before her, the onyx road that led to her lover's palace stretched as usual to the gates of pearl, but this time the gates had been flung wide open, and behind them were multitudes of glowing, semi-substantial shapes. At the head of the teeming mass stood Hades, flanked on one side by Orion and on the other by Eurydice and Iapis.

As the stallion caught sight of her he screamed a shrill neigh of joyous welcome. Eurydice clamped one hand against her pale mouth, and with the other she waved gaily at her mistress while tears of happiness streamed down her cheeks.

But when Hades began to move toward her, Lina's entire world narrowed to hold only him. He strode to her, his eyes dancing with emotion. When he finally stood before her, he reached out, and with a gesture that was as familiar to her as was her own heart, he caressed her cheek.

"Welcome home, beloved," he whispered.

She smiled at her soul mate.

Hades spun around to face the mob. Cloak swirling, he raised his arms victoriously over his head.

"She has come!" he thundered in the voice of a god.

A shout rose from the unnumbered dead that echoed from the Underworld up and spread throughout all of Olympus. *"Rejoice! Our queen is come and she shall leave us nevermore!"*

On her throne in Olympus, Demeter raised her goblet and touched it against Persephone's as they smiled at each other in acknowledgment of Carolina's happy ending.

"Well done, my daughters," Demeter said. "Well done."

Turn the page to read an excerpt from the next book in P. C. Cast's Goddess Summoning series

Goddess of Light

Now available from Berkley Sensation!

Prologue

"I HAVE made my decision, Bacchus. The portal will remain open."

As Zeus spoke he turned his back on the corpulent god and rested his hands against the smooth top of the marble railing that framed the balcony. He gazed down at the Great Banquet Hall of Olympus. The magnificent room was teeming with young gods and goddesses. Zeus' smile became self-satisfied. The immortals were matchless in their beauty, and when they gathered as they did on this evening, their combined allure was more resplendent than all the stars in the heavens. Then his expression sobered. No matter how perfect their exterior, he had slowly been forced to admit to himself that there was something lacking in the group below him.

They lacked the sublimely mortal touch of humanity.

The Supreme Ruler of the Gods indulged himself briefly in a particularly enticing memory. Aegina . . . she had been the most lovely of maidens. Her skin had been seductive mortal cream. He could still feel the imprint of its unique softness as she had pressed herself willingly against his feathered back when he changed himself into a mighty eagle and carried her away to make love to her. No, her body had not had the sheen of perfection that gilded a goddess's complexion, but she had responded to his touch with a naive exuberance that no goddess could ever match.

"Exuberance!" Zeus thumped his palm against the balcony railing, causing thunder to grumble across the sky in response. "That is what our young immortals are missing." He didn't turn to look at Bacchus; instead his gaze roamed restlessly across the sparkling crowd. Considering, he squinted his dark eyes. What was it that Hera had said . . . *"They take for granted the gifts of their immortal power. They need to spend time away from the ancient world. Somewhere where they are not idolized and worshipped."* He had to admit that Hera tended to be right, even though he often had reason to wish his wife's powers of observation were less accurate. He grimaced, wanting to forget the knowing look of her sharp gaze, which always seemed to see into his soul.

"They have languished too long in Olympus. It is past time that they mingle with modern mortals," Zeus said suddenly.

Bacchus tried to keep the irritation from his voice. "But I am the only one of the immortals to ever show an interest in the modern world. Why must you insist that they clutter up my realm?"

Zeus looked over his shoulder at Bacchus. "Demeter and Persephone have recently visited the modern world of mortals, and, as the Goddess of the Harvest told me, Persephone became so attached to a kingdom known as Tulsa that she has made a bargain with a mortal woman so that she may return on a regular basis."

Bacchus drew a deep breath and tried not to squirm under the Thunder God's gaze. "Then why not open the portal in the Kingdom of Tulsa?"

Zeus shook his head, turning back to his contemplation of the crowded hall. His talk with Demeter had convinced him that Tulsa was not a place where young gods and goddesses could come and go without being noticed.

"No, Bacchus. I have given this great consideration. I have searched the modern mortal world. Las Vegas provides the perfect setting with its fanciful mortal re-creation of Caesar's Palace and The Forum." Zeus chuckled, remembering the silliness he had glimpsed through the portal.

"But Las Vegas is my realm! You know how much time I have devoted to making Caesar's Palace and The Forum mine. They will be meddling in a part of the world I have chosen as my own."

Zeus' head snapped around and his eyes blazed. "You presume too much! Have you forgotten that I rule supreme amongst the gods?" Thunder rolled threateningly in the background.

Hastily, Bacchus bowed his head. "Forgive me, Lord."

"Do not forget yourself again, Bacchus. What I have given, I can also take away." He stared hard at the lesser deity before returning to his scrutiny of the crowd. "Look at them. The portal has only been opened to them for a short time, but already I feel a change. Even the nymphs have become excited." He paused, scowling as he remembered how too many of the lovely semideities had chosen to be made stars and flowers and trees because they had become so bored with their lives. "Exuberance . . . that is what Olympus has lacked. And that is what Las Vegas has breathed into us once more."

"But, Lord." Bacchus covered his growing anger and pitched his voice to a concerned, paternal tone. "You know what happens when gods and goddesses become too involved in the lives of mortals. Think of Troy. Remember Medea and Jason. Consider what became of Heracles and Achilles. Are you willing to doom the world of modern mortals to chaos and heartache?"

"I do not need to be lectured by such as you, Bacchus." Zeus' voice remained controlled, but the warning was clear. Then, changing moods as easily as a spring storm cleared from the mountains, he smiled. "But I have already considered such things. I have set into place certain . . . *restrictions*"—Zeus drew the word out carefully, his eyes gleaming—"which I intend to announce tonight. My children will simply be gracious visitors, enjoying a much-desired sojourn in the Kingdom of Las Vegas." He shifted his head so that Bacchus could see his stern, majestic profile. "This discussion is over. My will stands."

Bacchus had no choice but to bow and retreat respectfully from the balcony, but his mind seethed. Once again his needs were to be ignored as Zeus played favorites. He had made Vegas his own. They worshiped him there. At The Forum he commanded the attention of an audience of mortals every day. They cheered for him. They adored him. And now he was to share his realm with the young, beautiful darlings of Olympus?

"We shall see . . ." he whispered between clenched teeth as Zeus' voice thundered from the balcony, calling the Banquet Hall to attentive silence.

"Beloved children!" Zeus beamed at the gathering. "It pleases me greatly that you enjoy my latest gift." He stretched his arms, palms open, toward the two pillars that stood in the center of the hall, between which an opaque disc of light quivered and swirled. "This evening I announce more news—I have decided that the portal may be open to our lovely legions of nymphs, as well as the young Olympians!" Excited gasps from the minor female deities and semideities present sounded like sweet music to Zeus. "But remember, my beauties, you are entering a world unused to having gods such as us walk amongst them. You do not go to meddle with mortal affairs but rather to observe and to delight in a unique world. Lest you be tempted to forget that you are only there to visit, I have decided that the portal shall only be opened at limited times."

The glowing faces below him remained all upturned and listening. Zeus searched the crowd until he found Demeter standing regally beside her daughter. He inclined his head to her in respectful acknowledgment before continuing.

"The Goddess of the Harvest has informed me that modern mortals enjoy most of their revelry during a small cluster of days which they call a weekend. So it is during mortal weekends that our portal will be open. You have from dusk on their Friday evening to dawn on their Monday to frolic with the modern mortals."

With a small gesture of one hand, he silenced the enthusiastic whispers that his words evoked.

"And now, I give to you the Kingdom of Las Vegas!" The Thunder God clapped his hands together and the crowd cheered as the sky roared in response.

Below in the Banquet Hall Artemis laughed and shook her head fondly at Zeus before turning her attention back to her brother.

"Father is certainly pleased with himself," she said.

Apollo shrugged. "I don't understand the excitement. It is simply the modern world of the mortals, not a new Olympus."

Artemis raised one perfect, golden eyebrow at him. "Thus said by the god who spent months spying on a modern mortal in the Kingdom of Tulsa."

"I was simply performing a favor for Demeter," he answered a little too nonchalantly.

Artemis said nothing, but she studied her twin as he flirted half-heartedly with a violet-tressed nymph who had stopped to talk in excited little bursts about visiting the Kingdom of Las Vegas. There was no doubt about it. Apollo had been behaving oddly ever since the Persephone debacle.

Artemis sipped her blood-colored wine, remembering how her brother's surprise at Persephone's sudden rejection and odd infatuation with Hades had turned to outright shock when it had been discovered that the soul that had temporarily inhabited the goddess's body had been that of a mortal woman. Persephone herself had been masquerading as a mortal on modern Earth. So it was a mortal woman who had rejected Apollo and fallen in love with the God of the Underworld. Artemis' lovely lips curled in a sneer. Mortals. In her experience they either whined pathetically and needed constant care, or were so ridiculously hubris-filled that they self-destructed. All in all, they were only good for mild amusement or dalliance. Not that she would ever want to dally with one, but her brother was of a different mind. Often he had laughed and shared tales with her about his latest seduction of a hopelessly naive young maiden. Artemis took another long drink from her goblet. It was good for a mortal to be gifted with the love of a god. Mortal women should be grateful to be noticed by such a god as her twin brother.

The chattering nymph had drifted away, leaving Apollo to gaze silently at the swirling portal. Perhaps that was it. Apollo needed a diversion. Her brother had spent too much time lounging aimlessly around Olympus, brooding about the silly mortal rejection. He needed to remember that mortals were weak beings who lived the span of their frantic lives within the blink of an eye. They were easily manipulated—then easily cast aside.

A slow smile spread over her flawless face. What better place for him to be reminded of the insignificance of mortals than in a modern world teeming with the creatures?

"Come, Brother," she said with a cheery smile. "Let us visit the Kingdom of Las Vegas."

Chapter One

God, she adored airports. They always reminded her of love and excitement and the promise of new beginnings. Not for the first time Pamela thought that it had probably been her deep and romantic infatuation with airports that had fueled her relationship with Duane. One glimpse of him in his United Airlines pilot's uniform, and all rational thought had leaked out of her body along with her ridiculously girly sigh of pleasure.

What a moron she'd been.

That relationship fiasco was over. Finally. Pamela closed her eyes and ran her fingers through her chic new short haircut. She wished she'd run into Duane somewhere in the Colorado Springs Airport before she boarded the Southwest Airlines jet. She would have loved to have seen his horrified expression as he realized that she had cut off all of that thick, dark hair that used to swing around her waist. The hair that he used to take such pleasure in touching and stroking and . . . Pamela shivered in disgust at the memory. Just thinking about it made her feel suffocated. Getting rid of her long hair had been the final step she had taken to free herself from the shackles of Duane's smothering love. It had been six blissful months since she'd spoken to him. After months and months of refusing his gifts, sending back his flowers, and reminding him that their marriage had made both of them miserable, the end of their relationship had finally sunk in, much to the chagrin of her family who believed that Duane was perfect for her and that she was a fool to have left him. She could still hear her brother, her sister-in-law and her parents. *He's not that bad. He gives you anything you want. He makes great money. He adores you.*

He hadn't just adored her. He had wanted to consume her. Duane Edwards had appeared on the surface to be a successful, handsome, slightly macho, charismatic man. But under that surface, where the real Duane lived, lurked a needy, controlling, passive-aggressive boy/man.

Pamela rolled her shoulders to release the tension that thinking of Duane had begun to build. On second thought, she was glad she hadn't run into him at the airport. She hadn't cut her hair to "show him!" She'd cut it because that's what she wanted. It fit with the woman she was becoming. She rested her head against the seat back. Her lips curved up.

She liked the woman she was becoming. *Satisfied,* Pamela thought. She hadn't been so satisfied with herself in years. She didn't even care that she was mushed into the window seat next to a woman whose bony elbow kept poking her while she struggled to work the cigarette-scented crossword page of the *New York Times.*

Why would anyone obsessively work crossword puzzles? Did the woman have nothing better to do with her mind? Ms. Bony Elbows cackled and filled in another blank. Pamela guessed she didn't.

No! No negative thoughts. Self-fulfilling prophecies are powerful. Negative thoughts cause negative energy. Now she sounded like her mother, God help her. She sighed and pressed her forehead against the airplane window.

Okay, she'd mentally start over. She wouldn't let the lady sitting beside her bug her, because that was a pointless waste of time, as was dwelling on negatives in general. Hell, who was she to judge? She glanced down at the book in her lap. It had been open to the same page for the entire flight. What had *she* been doing with her mind? Instead of reading Gena Showalter's scrumptious *The Stone Prince*, she'd been wasting her time thinking about her horrid ex. She was better than that—she'd worked hard to make it so.

Purposefully, Pamela shifted her attention to the view outside her window. The desert was a bizarre mixture of harshness and beauty, and she was surprised to realize that she found it attractive—at least from several thousand feet in the air. It was so different from the lush green of her Colorado home, yet strangely compelling. Turning, the plane dipped its wing down, and Pamela's breath caught at her first glimpse of Las Vegas. There, smack in the middle of desert and sand, red dirt and canyons, was a city of glass and light and snaking highways, which she could tell even from the air were choked with rushing cars.

"It's like something out of a dream," she murmured to herself.

"Damn right! Ain't it grand," Ms. Bony Elbows rasped through a throat that had sucked down too many Virginia Slim Menthol extra-longs.

Pamela shifted her irritation. "It is unusual. Of course I knew Vegas had been built in the middle of the desert, but—"

"This your first time in Sin City?" she interrupted.

"Yes."

"Oh, girlie! You are in for the time of your life." She leaned in and lowered her gruff voice. "Remember, what happens in Vegas, stays in Vegas."

"Oh, well. I'm not here for pleasure. I'm here on business."

"A pretty young thing like you can sure find time to mix the two." She waggled her penciled-in brows knowingly.

Pamela felt her jaw setting. She really hated it when people patronized her because she just happened to be attractive. She worked her ass off to be successful. And thirty wasn't young!

"Perhaps I could if I didn't own my own business, and I didn't care if my client recommended my work to others, but I do. So I'm here for professional reasons, not to play."

Her seatmate's surprised look took in Pamela's diamond stud earrings—one carat each—and her well-tailored eggshell Fendi slack suit, the classic color of which was nicely set off by a melon and tangerine silk scarf and shell.

Pamela read the look in her eye, and she wanted to scream, *No, I did not have some damned man buy me this outfit!*

"Just what is it you do, honey?"

"I own Ruby Slipper, an interior design business."

The woman's crinkled face softened into a smile, and with a start Pamela realized that she must have once been very pretty.

"Ruby Slipper . . . I like that. Sounds real nice. I'll bet you're good at it, too. Just lookin' at you I can tell you got class. But it don't look like Vegas class. What are you doing here?"

"My newest client is an author who is building a vacation home in Vegas. I've been hired to decorate it."

"An author . . ." She fluttered long red fingernails at Pamela. "That's big stuff. Who is it? Maybe I heard of him."

"E. D. Faust. He writes fantasy." Pamela only knew that because she'd looked him up hastily on Amazon during their first phone call. The man had proclaimed himself "E. D. Faust, bestselling author." She'd had no idea who he was, but when she typed his name into Amazon's search box her screen had blazed with page after page of titles like *Pillars of the Sword, Temple of Warriors, Naked Winds, Faith of the Damned* . . . and on and on. At that moment he'd instantly had her undivided attention, even though Pamela didn't particularly care for male science fiction and fantasy authors. She read a little of everything, so she'd tried a few of the giants of the genre, but it seemed they were all too much alike. Swords, magic, spaceships, blood, testosterone . . . blah . . . blah . . . yawn. But she wasn't stupid. Far from it, and one of her primary rules was never, ever say negative things about a client. So she put on a bright smile and nodded in response to her travel partner's blank look like she thought E. D. Faust was Nora Roberts.

"His current release is *Pillars of the Sword*, but he's published more than fifty books, and most of them have appeared on all the major bestseller lists."

"Never heard of him, but then I like a good crossword puzzle more than just about anything." She cackled again. "Well, anything except a long, tall man in a cowboy hat and a cold beer."

She elbowed Pamela as she laughed, this time on purpose. Pamela was surprised to feel herself smiling back. There was something honest and real about the old woman that made her craggy face and her gruff manner strangely appealing.

"Pamela Gray," she said, holding out her hand.

"Billie Mae Johnson." She returned the handshake with a firm grip and a warm smile. "Pleased to meet ya. If you need a friendly face or a cold beer, come on by the Flamingo. I'm usually working at the bar on the main floor."

"I may just take you up on that."

The stewardess announced that they were landing, and Pamela returned her seat to the full and upright position. Billie Mae shook her head and grumbled at the squares of the crossword puzzle, most of which were still empty.

"Ya have to know that the hoity-toity *New York Times* has gone to hell when they start lettin' divorce lawyers from Texas write their puzzles." She sighed and concentrated on one of the questions before looking askance at Pamela. "Hey, the snooty clue is 'metaphoric emancipation.' The answer has seven letters. All I can think of is Budweiser, and that's nine."

"Is the attorney who wrote the puzzle a man or a woman?"

"Man."

"Try alimony," Pamela said, smiling wickedly.

Billie Mae filled in the letters with a satisfied grunt, then she winked at Pamela as the plane touched down. "You just earned yourself a free beer. Hope you're as good at decoratin' as you are at crosswords."

PAMELA approached the uniformed man who was holding a sign that spelled out PAMELA GRAY, RUBY SLIPPER in gold embossed letters. Before she could speak, the man executed an efficient little bow and asked in a clipped British accent, "Miss Gray?"

"Yes, I'm Pamela Gray."

"Very good, madam. I shall take your luggage. Please be so good as to follow me."

She did and had to hurry to keep up with his brisk pace as he whisked confidently through the crowded airport and out to the waiting limo. Pamela wanted to stand and gawk when he opened the door to a lovely vintage stretch Rolls-Royce, but she slid into the dove-colored leather seat gracefully, thanking him before he closed the door.

"Well met, Miss Gray!" A deep voice boomed at her from across the limo.

Pamela jumped. Out of the shadows a man leaned forward, extending a large, beefy hand. As she automatically grasped it, the crystal chandeliers hanging from both sides of the car blinked on.

"I am, of course, E. D. Faust. But you must call me Eddie."

Recovering her composure, she smiled smoothly and returned his firm grip. Her first impression of E. D. Faust was one of immense size. As soon as he had hired her, she had, gone immediately to the nearest bookstore and purchased several of his novels, so she was familiar with his author photo. But the pictures on the back of his books hadn't begun to capture the size of the man. He filled the space across from her, reminding her of Orson Welles or an aging Marlon Brando. And he was dark. His hair, which formed an abrupt widow's peak, was thick and black and tied back in a low ponytail. His long-sleeved silk shirt was black, as were the enormous slacks and the glistening leather boots. Though insulated by layers of fat, the strong lines of his face were still evident, and his age was indeterminate—Pamela knew he must be somewhere between thirty and fifty, but she had no clue exactly where. He watched her watching him, and his brown eyes sparkled with what might have been a mischievous glint, as if he was used to being the center of attention and he enjoyed it.

"It's nice to finally meet you, Eddie. And please, call me Pamela."

"Pamela it is then." Abruptly, he tapped the dragon-head handle of his black cane against the half-lowered panel of glass that divided the passenger area of the limo from the chauffeur. "You may carry on, Robert."

"Very good, sir."

The sleek limo pulled away from the curb.

"I trust your journey has not overly fatigued you, Pamela," he said.

"No, it was only a short flight from Colorado Springs."

"Then you would not be opposed to beginning your work immediately?"

"No, I'd be pleased to start right away. Does this mean you've made a decision about the style you'd like for your home?" Pamela asked eagerly. If this exquisite car was an example of Eddie's taste and budget . . . her head spun at the possibilities. A showcase! She would create an exquisite vacation paradise fit for the King of Fantasy Fiction.

"I most certainly have. I know exactly what I desire. I found it here in this magical city. All you need do is to replicate it." Eddie tapped the window again. "Robert, take us to Caesar's Palace."